SOFTBALL STAR

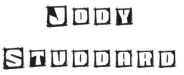

JODY STUDDARD

www.jstuddard.com

Softball Star

Cover Design: Jody Studdard
Cover Model: Molly McCall

ISBN-13: 978-1489596604
ISBN-10: 1489596607

Table of Contents

A
DIFFERENT
DIAMOND

JODY
STUDDARD

www.jstuddard.com

*For Amanda,
Lindsay, and Emily*

Chapter 1

Brooke Conrad was excited. The first game of the high school softball season was only a week away and everything was falling nicely into place. She had already won the starting shortstop position during tryouts the week before, practices were going well, and the team was starting to gel as a unit. Her school, Silver Lake High, was a traditional softball powerhouse, having won the past five Western Conference South championships in a row, and this year looked no different. They were loaded with talent at every position. Another WesCo South title, and possibly a state championship, were within reach.

It was a routine practice at first. A little stretching and light running to warm up, then various hitting drills in the team's batting cages, then some infield work. Infield work was Brooke's favorite part of practice. Like all great shortstops, she played defense with a passion. She loved fielding the ball and whipping it to first as hard and as fast as she could. Nothing made her happier than hearing the sound of the ball as it exploded in the first baseman's mitt.

But then she noticed something unusual. Silver Lake's baseball coach, Daniel West, was standing along the softball field's first base foul line, about twenty feet from the first baseman, with one of his top assistants. He was watching Brooke carefully.

Brooke glanced across the softball fields at the neighboring baseball fields. Silver Lake was a big school, and it had a series of athletic fields next to it, and the boys' baseball fields, both varsity and JV, were within eyesight of the girls' softball fields. The only thing separating them was a small parking lot. At first Brooke thought the boys must have been done for the day, since Coach West was normally with them during their practices, but the boys were still practicing. They were at various stations running drills with other coaches.

Coach West was a tall, lean man in his mid to late forties, with short, well-kept, graying hair and deep brown eyes. He wore white baseball pants and a sweatshirt with the school's mascot, a silver shark, printed on the front. He spoke softly to his assistant, but even at this distance Brooke could hear what he said.

"What do you think?" he asked. There was a hint of excitement in his voice. "I think she can do it."

The assistant hesitated, thinking about what he had been asked, then nodded.

"She looks good to me," he said. "Can she bat?"

Coach West nodded. "I watched her yesterday," he said. "She's got good power and she hits the ball consistently to all parts of the field. As far as I'm concerned, she's exactly what we need."

Brooke's softball coach, Sarah Jennings, called a break, and Brooke and the rest of the girls trotted off the field. They rounded up their water bottles and congregated in their dugout.

"What's up with that?" Faith Alexander asked, motioning toward Coach West. Like Brooke, Faith was a junior. She was their starting second baseman and leadoff hitter. She was a small, thin girl with short, cropped hair and bangs.

8

"I don't get it," Naomi Smith said. Naomi was a senior, one of the oldest and biggest girls on the team. Compared to Faith, she was a giant. She had dark skin and long, ebony hair. "He's been here all day. The boys' team must be boring him, so he came over here to watch some real talent for a change."

They laughed.

"It's something more than that," Faith said. "He's fixated on one of us in particular."

They all turned to Brooke.

Brooke didn't know what to say, but she had noticed it, too. Coach West had been watching them all, but he had been watching her by far the most. What was up with that? Why was the coach of the school's baseball team interested in her? She wasn't even certain he knew her name.

Almost on cue, Coach Jennings walked up to Coach West and they began talking. They were on the far side of the field, and Coach Jennings had her back to them, so Brooke and the other girls could only hear bits and pieces of their conversation.

"Yeah," Coach Jennings said, answering one of Coach West's questions. "She's one of my best players. I don't see why she couldn't. I'm not certain she'd want to, though. It's a pretty unusual request. What? Of course you can talk to her."

She turned and walked back to the dugout, where the girls were finishing their break and putting their water bottles back into their bags. "Everyone back on the field. Except you, Brooke. Coach West wants to talk to you."

"What's up?" Brooke asked, a bit of apprehension in her voice. There was no hiding the fact she was nervous. She had no idea what Coach West would want.

9

"I'll let him tell you," Coach Jennings said. "He has a proposition for you. It's a little unusual, but you'd be wise to give it some thought. It's a unique opportunity to say the least."

Brooke still didn't know what to think. She had known Coach Jennings since her freshman year, and she'd never known her to speak in riddles. Like most coaches, she was straightforward most of the time.

Coach West smiled warmly as she walked up. "I'm Daniel West," he said. "This is my assistant, Hugh Weller."

"It's nice to meet you," Brooke said. Like everyone at Silver Lake, she knew who Coach West was, and she had heard he was a really nice guy, but she had never met him in person.

"I don't know if you've heard or not," Coach West said, "but the shortstop for my team, Dwayne Harper, got kicked off the team."

Brooke's eyes widened. Dwayne Harper was one of the star players on the school's baseball team. He was a senior, and last year he had been selected to the WesCo South All-Conference team. He had led Silver Lake to a fifth place finish at the state championship tournament. Word had been going around school something had happened involving him, but no one knew exactly what.

"Dwayne got caught smoking marijuana," Coach West continued. "The athletic director suspended him for the season. So now I need a new shortstop."

Brooke raised an eyebrow. She still didn't know how this involved her.

"The only shortstops I have are too young. They're both freshman. They need at least a year on JV before they'll be ready to play at the varsity level. So I need you to play for me this year."

Brooke's eyes nearly popped out of her head. She couldn't believe what she was hearing.

"Me?" she asked. "I'm a girl."

"Shortstops are shortstops. I don't care if you're a girl or not. I need someone who can get the ball from short to first as quickly as possible, and as far as I'm concerned, now that Dwayne is gone you're the best shortstop this school's got. And I've been watching you the past couple of days and that's a great arm you've got. Better than most of the boys on my team."

"Are you serious?" Brooke asked. "A girl can't play on a boys' team. Can she?"

Coach West shrugged. "I don't see why not. And I think you'd like it, if you gave it a chance. But I realize this is an unusual request, so if you want some time to think about it that's fine with me. But you'd be doing me a huge favor if you did. We have a great team, with a legitimate shot at winning the state title, but we can't do it without a shortstop."

"But my team," Brooke said, "the softball team, we need a shortstop, too. I can't play on both teams."

"True," Coach West said. "I've already talked to Coach Jennings and she says you have a capable backup who can fill-in in your absence. She's not as good as you, of course, or I'd be talking to her right now, but Coach Jennings says she'll get the job done."

Brooke nodded. It was true. Her backup at short, Casey Morgan, was a year younger than Brooke, but she was a good player nonetheless. She was solid on defense and could hit the ball almost as well as Brooke did.

Coach West smiled. "Did I mention I'm willing to make it worth your while?"

Brooke raised an eyebrow.

"You girls have felt mistreated for awhile now, right? You feel like the baseball team gets all the good equipment and the nice fields. In the meantime, you get the leftovers."

Brooke nodded. Everyone knew the boys' teams at Silver Lake were treated better than the girls. That was a fact of life. It had always been like that.

"I've already talked to the athletic director and authorized him to transfer the bulk of our budget to the softball team this year. That way, you girls can get that scoreboard you've wanted."

Brooke's eyes widened. She could hardly believe what she had heard. The softball field at Silver Lake had a small, electronic scoreboard, but it was old, rusty and rarely (if ever) worked. The girls had wanted a new one for years, and they had had several car washes to raise money, but they still didn't have nearly enough.

"Really?" she asked. "We get your money for the year?"

"Only on one condition. You play for me."

Brooke didn't know what to say. Her mind was on overdrive, trying to process all the information she had been told. She wanted to help the softball team get its scoreboard, but playing for the baseball team? Could she do it? Was she good enough to play for a boys' team? And how would the boys react? Would they even want her on their team?

This was a big decision. She needed some time to think about it.

Chapter 2

"You'll be a hero," Naomi told Brooke. "You'll be known as the girl who finally got us that darn scoreboard."

They sat in the local Starbucks, just across the street from the high school's main building. Practice had ended twenty minutes ago and Brooke had told them about Coach West's proposition.

"You'll be a legend," Aubrey Nelson said. Aubrey was their starting third baseman. She was a sophomore, with a young face and long, straight bangs. A lot of people, including Brooke, thought she looked like Miley Cyrus. At least in some ways.

"What do you mean?" Brooke asked.

"How many girls have played on a boys' team before?" Aubrey asked. "You may be the first one to do it, at least at our school. You'll be making history."

"I don't care about history," Naomi said. "I just want that darn scoreboard. We've been raising money for that thing since I was a freshman. I'd like to see it before I graduate."

"Are you actually considering this?" Faith asked. Unlike the other girls, Faith wasn't excited by the idea at all.

Brooke raised an eyebrow. "A little," she said.

"You've got to be losing your mind," Faith said. "A girl can't play baseball. That's why they invented softball in the first place. We're just not strong enough. Have you seen how big a baseball field is?"

"Coach West thinks I can do it," Brooke said. "He wouldn't have asked me if he didn't. And who'd know better? He's been the baseball coach here at Silver Lake for how long?"

To be perfectly honest, no one knew. All they knew was Coach West was one of the most talented and well respected coaches at the school, and he had led the baseball team to two state titles during his tenure as head coach. There were rumors he had been offered the head coaching position at Western Washington University a few years back but had turned it down.

"I still think it's crazy," Faith said. "And what does Coach Jennings think about it?"

"I talked to her after practice for a couple of minutes," Brooke said, "just before I came over here. She didn't say much. She said she'd support whatever decision I made."

"We need you on our team," Faith said. "The boys can take care of themselves. If they need a shortstop, that's their problem."

"Speaking of boys," Aubrey said, "imagine that. You'll be teammates with eleven of the cutest boys at Silver Lake. And you'll be the only girl on the team, so you'll have their complete and undivided attention."

Brooke's eyes got big. She hadn't considered that part of the equation.

"And you'll get to play with Alex Anderson," Naomi added.

They all sighed. Alex Anderson was (arguably) the cutest boy at Silver Lake. Only Nathan O'Malley, the football team's starting quarterback, came close. Alex was a senior and was the team's star pitcher. He had been their starter since his freshman year and had already signed a letter of intent to play for the University of Washington the following spring.

"Can you imagine if he picked you up from practice in his car?" Aubrey asked.

Alex drove a silver Porsche. Next to Alex himself, it was the most gorgeous thing Brooke had ever seen.

"You three need to get serious," Faith said, snapping them back to reality. "This isn't about fancy cars or cute boys. This is about fitting in. Brooke's not going to fit in. The boys aren't going to want her on their team no matter how good she is."

"What do you mean?" Brooke asked.

"They're just not going to," Faith said. "Boys' teams are for boys. Just like girls' teams are for girls. You wait and see. If you join that team, it's going to be nothing but problems for you. I guarantee it."

Brooke didn't know what to say, so she said nothing.

"It's ridiculous," Brooke's dad said. He sat at the dining room table, finishing the last of his dinner. "Playing for a boys' team? It's the dumbest thing I've ever heard."

Brooke's dad was an attorney at a big firm in downtown Seattle. Brooke's mom claimed all attorneys were stubborn, emotional, and completely irrational ninety-nine percent of the time. He was acting the part right now.

"But dad," Brooke pleaded, "you haven't heard the details yet."

"Details?" he asked. "I don't need details. It's ridiculous. Completely ridiculous."

"Why?" Brooke asked. "Don't you think I can do it? Weren't you the one who said I was going to be the best shortstop in WesCo this year?"

"I meant the best softball shortstop," he said. He stressed the word 'softball.' "Not the best baseball shortstop."

"What's the difference?"

"They're completely different sports," he said.

"How so?"

He laughed. "There are so many differences I don't even know where to begin."

"Give it a try," Brooke said, somewhat sarcastically. If her dad wanted to be difficult, then she could be difficult, too.

"For starters," he said, "a baseball is a different size and weight than a softball. It's a lot smaller. And a baseball field is a lot bigger, the bases are further apart, there's a mound, and the players are a lot bigger and tougher. You're going to get hurt if you compete against them."

"I could get hurt playing softball," Brooke said.

"Not as easily," her dad said. "And you'll mess up your chances of getting into a good college."

"What?" Brooke asked.

"How's that going to look to college scouts? The big softball schools want softball players, not baseball players."

"You yourself said the big schools don't look at high school players anymore," Brooke said. "They just look at select players. And I'll keep playing for my select team, just like I've always done. That way I can still play in college if you want."

Her dad sighed, then took a drink from the glass in front of him. There was a long, awkward silence as he sat there, staring at her for what seemed like an eternity.

"You really want to do this?" he asked. "You've already made up your mind?"

"Not really," Brooke said. "But I'm leaning that way."

"Why?"

"A lot of reasons, I guess," she said. "But I guess it's largely because you always tell me I should try new things, and I shouldn't be afraid to go out on a limb on occasion, and well this is a really big limb."

"You can say that again," he said.

"And how many people can say they've done anything like this?" Brooke asked.

Her dad smiled. It was a begrudging smile, but a smile nonetheless. "I like your attitude," he said. "But I still think it's a terrible idea. Something bad is going to happen. I just know it."

"So I can't do it?" Brooke asked.

"I didn't say that. How old are you?"

"Sixteen."

"Sixteen? How did you get so old so fast? It seems like just yesterday you were crawling around on the floor in your diapers. Those were good days. Not the diapers, but the crawling on the floor part. Anyway, you're old enough to make your own decisions, at least some of them. But don't come running back to me when this whole thing blows up in your face. And this better not interfere with your select team in any way or there'll be big trouble. Understood?"

Brooke nodded.

"Good," he said.

He finished his dinner, stood up, and left.

Brooke hardly slept that night. The idea of playing on the baseball team was ludicrous. Even she had to admit it. She had never played baseball a day of her life. She had played softball for as long as she could remember, but her dad was right. Baseball and softball were two completely different sports, and each required its own set of skills. There was no reason to think she would excel at baseball just because she excelled at softball. If she were smart, she'd forget the whole idea, go back to her softball team and have another great season like she'd always done in the past. But for some strange reason, some reason she couldn't put in words, she just couldn't get the idea of playing baseball out of her mind no matter how hard she tried. She had always been the adventurous type, and she had always liked trying new and exciting things, no matter how difficult they were. That attitude had gotten her in trouble a few times in the past (like the time she tried a science experiment in the garage and nearly blew up her dad's car), but, like it or not, she was who she was.

And she had to admit. It didn't get much more adventurous than this.

Chapter 3

The baseball team was gathered together in a large group on one side of the infield as Coach West led Brooke up to them. Their chatter came to an abrupt end as he addressed them.

"Thanks for gathering together so quickly, guys," he said. "I'd like to introduce you to our new shortstop. Some of you may already know her from school. Her name's Brooke Conrad."

Brooke had never felt so tiny in her entire life. All of the boys, the entire team, stared at her with blank looks on their faces. No one said a word.

"Brooke was the starting shortstop for the school's softball team last year," Coach West continued. "She made the All-WesCo team. Not bad for a sophomore, if you ask me. And she also plays for one of the state's elite select teams, the Eastside Angels 18Gold team. Last year they won metros, finished second at state and seventh at nationals."

The boys remained quiet. Brooke's accolades as a softball player didn't seem to impress them much. Finally, the first baseman, a large senior named Blake Henry, spoke up.

"Coach," he said. "That's not a shortstop. That's a girl."

He said the word 'girl' as though it were dirty.

"Is this a joke?" the catcher asked. Like Blake, he was a senior, and he was the heaviest kid on the team by far. His name was Logan Sullivan, but everyone called him Skinny. "You're trying to punk us, right coach? Like last year when you said you were going to give us a day off, then made us run wind sprints the whole practice instead?"

"That was a fun day," Coach West said with a smile. "I've never seen anyone puke that much before, Skinny. But no, this is no joke. Brooke is our new shortstop. She's on loan from the softball team for a year."

"You've got to be kidding," Blake said. "I bet she can't even throw the ball all the way to first."

"Let's find out," Coach West said. "Everyone take your positions."

The boys, still somewhat mystified by what had happened, grabbed their mitts and headed to their positions in the field. Brooke hesitated for a second. She hadn't expected them to react this way. She didn't know what to do.

"Just give them a chance," Coach West said. "They'll come around. I hope."

The 'I hope' part didn't make Brooke feel much better, but not knowing what else to do, she grabbed her mitt and jogged out to short. It was at that point she actually stopped and looked around for the first time. She had never been on a baseball field before, and she had never realized how much bigger a baseball field was than a softball field. From her position at short, first base seemed a mile away. Even Blake, as big and as strong as he was, looked small all the way over there. She started to wonder if he was right. Could she throw the ball all the way to him?

The problem was actually the opposite. The bases were a long way apart, but the problem was not the distance at all. The problem was the ball. As her dad had said the night before, a baseball is a lot smaller and lighter than a softball. Brooke fielded the first ball hit to her, then dropped it in the dirt.

Lesson #1: Gripping a baseball is a lot different than gripping a softball.

Blake laughed at her.

"It's okay," Coach West said. "Try it again, Brooke."

He hit another grounder. Once again, Brooke fielded it cleanly, and this time she actually managed to transfer it to her throwing hand without bobbling it. But this time the problem was the throw. She threw it over Blake's head into the bushes at the far edge of the field.

Lesson #2: A baseball flies a lot further than a softball.

"Nice aim," Skinny said sarcastically.

"That's okay," Coach West said. "Try it again, Brooke. Nice and easy this time."

From that point forward, things got a little better, but not much. On her next attempt, she overcompensated and threw the ball too low. It hit the dirt at Blake's feet and nailed him in the shin.

"You trying to kill me?" he asked.

The next throw was a little better, but wide right, the next throw was wide left, and the next throw was too high again. Coach West tried to help her by mixing things up a little, and he hit a ball to the second baseman, a junior named Jamie Stephens.

"Turn two," Coach West called.

Jamie turned and fired the ball to second.

It would have been a great play. The only problem was Brooke was nowhere near second when the ball got there. She had miscalculated how long it would take to get there and hadn't arrived in time. The ball flew into left field.

Lesson #3: There is a lot more territory to cover on a baseball field.

Blake laughed. "What, they don't turn double plays in softball?"

"Try it again, Brooke," Coach West called. "Faster this time."

The second play went a little better than the first. Brooke got to the base in time, but once again her throw to Blake was wild. And so was the throw after that, and the one after that, and the one after that.

Brooke had never been so relieved to have a practice come to an end. She was completely frustrated and embarrassed. She had never played so poorly in her entire life. She rounded up her belongings as quickly as she could, loaded them into her softball bag, and hurried to her car in the adjoining parking lot.

She cried the whole way home.

Chapter 4

Practice the next day didn't get much better. If anything, it got worse. Brooke continued to struggle in the field, and she started doing the one thing players are taught to never do. She started aiming the ball. Any good player knew you didn't aim the ball; you just threw it. The minute you started aiming it, chaos began. And for Brooke, it was complete chaos. One throw went high, another went higher, the next even higher. And the worst thing was the harder she tried, the worse it got. Blake shook his head as an errant throw soared over his head and disappeared into the bushes.

"At this rate," he said, "we're going to be out of balls by our first game."

Brooke didn't do any better batting. She couldn't believe how much heavier a baseball bat was than a softball bat. And the helmets didn't have facemasks. That was scary. But the thing that worried her the most was the speed of the pitches. Most high school baseball pitchers threw around eighty miles per hour; most softball pitchers around sixty. She was afraid she wouldn't be able to hit the ball because it was travelling so much faster than she was used to. But it was actually the other way around. Since a baseball pitcher stands so far away from the plate, it actually negates the increase in velocity and makes the ball take longer to get there. Which was actually a bad thing for Brooke, since she was the type of hitter who liked the ball to get to her quickly. She missed the first nine pitches before she managed to foul one to the side.

"Darn," Skinny said, removing his catcher's mask. "You just cost me five bucks."

"What?" Brooke asked, turning to face him.

"I bet Jamie five bucks you wouldn't make contact all day," he said with a smile.

Brooke let out a sigh, dug her cleats into the dirt, and tried again. Unfortunately, Skinny's words had rattled her even worse than before, and she didn't do well at all. She fouled two pitches away, but that was the best she could do. As she walked to the dugout, ending her turn, she shot a quick glance at the distant fields where the softball team was practicing. She watched as Aubrey scooped up a grounder and zipped it to Naomi at first. Faith ran over and patted her on the back. It was a sweet play. All three girls were nothing but smiles.

Brooke, by contrast, had forgotten how to smile.

The ultimate humiliation, however, came after practice. As Brooke walked back to her car, someone grabbed her from behind and spun her around. It was Blake. He was even bigger and more menacing up close than he was from a distance. Skinny was at his side, as was Terrell Williams, their center fielder, and Aiden Andrews, their left fielder.

"Are you ready to quit yet?" Blake asked.

"What?" Brooke asked.

"Catch a clue," he said. "We don't want you here. A girl doesn't belong on a boys' team. Got it?"

Brooke didn't know what to say, so she said nothing.

Blake got frustrated by her lack of a response. "So be it. But if you're going to play on a boys' team, then you're going to be just like us boys. That means wearing one of these."

He held up his free hand, revealing an old, discolored jockstrap. The sight of it made Brooke recoil in fear. Unfortunately, she couldn't get far since Blake had her with his other hand.

"Hold her still," he told the other boys.

Skinny, Terrell, and Aidan grabbed her and held her in place. She tried to pull free but couldn't budge even an inch. She was by far the smallest of the group, and any one of the boys could have held her in place by himself, let alone all three at once.

The boys laughed as Blake pulled the jockstrap over her head. Brooke called out for help but nobody was near.

"You want to be one of the boys?" Blake asked. "Now you're one of the boys."

Without another word, they released her, turned, and walked away, laughing hysterically as they went. Brooke tore the jockstrap from her head, threw it to the side, and hurried to her car, locking the doors as soon as she got inside.

For the second time in as many days, she cried the whole way home.

Chapter 5

"I'm quitting the team," Brooke said.

She had arrived at practice a few minutes early so she could tell Coach West before the boys arrived. After what had happened the day before, with Blake and the jockstrap, she couldn't take it anymore. She hated to admit it, but her dad was right. A girl wasn't meant to play on a boys' team and she had learned the hard way. Now the only thing left to do was admit it and move along.

"Why?" Coach West asked. "You're doing fine."

"I can't throw. Or field. Or hit. I'm terrible."

"We all have bad days. You need to be patient. You're a great athlete. You'll get it. You just need time to adjust."

She decided to cut to the chase. To give him the real reason she was quitting the team.

"The boys don't want me here. I'm doing them a favor by leaving."

"Boys are boys, Brooke. You need to give them a chance. Give them a little time and they'll come around. They just need to see what you can do."

She was tempted to tell him about the night before, but she was too ashamed and embarrassed. In addition, she didn't want to risk upsetting the boys (especially Blake and Skinny) any more. If they found out she had ratted on them, she'd have even more issues than she already did.

"It's up to you, Brooke," Coach West said. "I'm not going to force you to do anything you don't want to. And I apologize if this has been tough on you. But please do me a favor. Give it until Friday. That's only two more days. If you're still uncomfortable by then, I understand completely."

She didn't really want to, she wanted the whole ordeal to be over immediately, but she agreed and turned to the dugout. She only got one step before Coach West's voice stopped her in her tracks.

"Brooke," he said. "I really appreciate what you've done. Regardless of how this turns out, even if you leave the team for good on Friday, you girls are still getting that scoreboard. I give you my word."

Blake, Skinny, and the other boys were amazed to see her at practice when they arrived. Clearly, they thought they had seen the last of her. And then they got worried, worried she had told Coach West about the night before, and they shot her frightening looks. When Coach West said nothing and started practice like any other day, they settled down a little. They didn't say anything to her, and they stayed pretty much to themselves, but that was fine with her. Actually, it was exactly what she wanted. She needed to focus on baseball and baseball alone, and she didn't need any distractions.

And then something unexpected happened. She found an ally.

Or at least someone who wasn't hostile.

During infield drills, Coach West hit a ball up the middle. It should have been a single, but Brooke got to it quickly, scooped it up, and made a decent throw to first.

"Nice play," Jamie said as he walked past her. He was the second baseman. He, too, had been after the ball, but Brooke had gotten to it first and made the play.

It was the first compliment Brooke had received as a baseball player. And it made all the difference in the world. After that, she could make plays again. Just like she did in softball. Well, not quite that well, since she was still getting used to the feel of the ball in her hand (it still felt so light), but now she could do it. Her throws got better and better, and as her confidence improved, she started putting some zip on them. Blake rubbed his hand as she whipped a throw to first and it hit him in the palm.

Batting practice was a similar story. She finally got her timing down, and she was able to make contact with the pitches regularly. She still didn't hit too many balls that well, but one shot got all of their attention. She sent one ball all the way to the outfield warning track. The center fielder, Terrell, caught it, but it was a nice hit anyway.

Especially for a girl.

Chapter 6

Coach West rounded them up before the beginning of Friday's practice.

"As you know," he said, "Monday is our first game, so today is our last practice before the season officially begins. So I want everyone to give a little extra today. Monday's game is against Monroe, so it's not a league game, but I want to win anyway. And we're going to need to be sharp, because Monroe is a solid team. They finished second in WesCo North last year, and word is they got a new pitcher who's pretty tough."

"He's no match for Alex," Skinny said, patting their star pitcher on the back.

It was at that point Brooke got her first chance to look at Alex Anderson. Like all of the boys, he had been at practice every day that week, but Brooke had been so preoccupied with her struggles she had hardly even noticed him. And she could hardly believe she hadn't. He was perfect in every way. Tall and lean, with slightly ruffled, dirty blond hair. His eyes were the deepest blue Brooke had ever seen. She was mesmerized just looking at them.

"That may be true," Coach West said, "but I don't want to take anything for granted. We need to get off to a good start this year. Since we're the defending South champions, everyone's going to be gunning for us, so we need to send a quick message to the rest of the league. Am I being clear?"

They all nodded.

"So let's start with some running," Coach West said.

They all groaned but took their positions on the first base foul line. One of the assistant coaches placed orange cones at various distances from the line, and they had to run from the foul line to the first one, then back to the foul line, then to the next one, then back to the foul line, and so on. They took off on Coach West's word. Brooke ran as fast as she could but was quickly left behind. Even the slowest boys on the team (Skinny and Blake) were faster than she was, and by quite a bit. She was shocked and dismayed. On her softball teams, she had always been at the front of the pack.

After running, they did infield. She struggled a bit initially and threw one ball into the dirt at Blake's feet, but then settled down and did well. After infield, they switched to batting, and again she struggled.

"You're trying too hard," Jamie said. He stood in the on-deck circle, waiting for his turn to bat. "A baseball is a lot lighter than a softball. You don't need to hit it so hard. Just focus on making contact. If you hit it square, it will rebound for a base hit."

Much to Brooke's delight, he was right. She cut down the power in her swings and instead focused exclusively on making good, solid contact. Almost instantly she got results, and they were good results. After awhile, she was even doing simple check-swings and still hitting the ball consistently through the infield.

"Thanks," she said as she ended her turn and headed back to the dugout.

"No problem," Jamie said with a smile.

As she stood in the dugout removing her batting gloves, she thought about the various boys on the team. Jamie was the only one who had been friendly to her.

Blake, Skinny, and most of the other boys were hostile. But there was one boy she had no idea about, and he was the one she was the most interested in.

Alex.

He hadn't said a word to her all week. Not a thing, good, bad, or otherwise. She wondered where he stood regarding having her on the team.

She didn't get much time to think about it. Coach West walked up and interrupted her thoughts.

"Nice hitting," he said.

"Thanks," she responded.

"So what's it going to be?" he asked.

She looked at him quizzically. She had no idea what he was talking about.

"Today is Friday," he said. "I asked you to wait until today to make your decision about quitting the team. Have you made it?"

Brooke was completely caught off guard by his question. Two days ago, she had completely, adamantly wanted off the team. But now, a mere forty-eight hours later, she wasn't so sure. She was finally starting to get the hang of this baseball thing, and the boys (even Blake and Skinny) hadn't been quite as rude toward her since the incident with the jockstrap. And one of the boys, Jamie, even seemed friendly.

"I'm not sure," she said.

"I thought you'd say that," he said. "How about if we make another deal? How about if you give it a few more days? That way you'll have a chance to play in some games. You'll really like the games."

She didn't know what to say, so she simply nodded. She had a habit of doing that. Whenever she didn't know what to do, she just went with the flow.

"Good," Coach West said. "In that case, for Monday's game, you'll be starting at short. I'm going to bat you last in the order. I know some players get offended by that, but I want you to know I'm only doing it because you're the new kid on the team. If you bat well, I'll move you up accordingly."

To be perfectly honest, Brooke wasn't offended at all. Quite to the contrary, she was relieved. Batting last in the order would cut down on her total number of at-bats, which would take a lot of pressure off of her.

And right now, she needed as little pressure as possible.

Chapter 7

The following weekend, Brooke's select softball team had a tournament in Bellevue, a city about fifteen minutes east of Seattle. Brooke played for the Eastside Angels 18Gold team, a team made up primarily of sixteen, seventeen, and eighteen-year-old girls from all over the Seattle metropolitan area. Several of Brooke's teammates from school, including Faith, Aubrey, and Naomi, were also on the team. Brooke had played for the Angels for three years. Originally, she hadn't liked it too much, since they wore white and pink uniforms that were way too 'girly' for her, but her dad had insisted she join since it was one of the most prestigious teams in the area. And after awhile she got used to the uniforms and even liked them a little, especially their logo, which was the letter "E" with a gold halo around its upper left edge.

Their first game was against a team from Redmond called the LadyCats, and it started off poorly. The LadyCats' shortstop, who was a tall, lean girl named Kiana Cruise, hit a ground ball to Brooke's left, but Brooke read it wrong and it skipped past her for a single.

It had been awhile since she had been on a softball field. She had forgotten how much smaller it was than a baseball field and how quickly a grounder could get to and past her.

"Come on, Brooke," her dad called. Like always, he sat with the other parents in the bleachers. "Adjust your angles. Read the ball better."

Unfortunately, it didn't get much better from there. In the second inning, another LadyCat batter hit a grounder to her, and she threw it into the dirt at Naomi's feet. She had forgotten how heavy a softball was and hadn't put enough power behind it. Luckily for her, Naomi made a great play and dug it out of the dirt for the final out to finish the inning.

"Don't worry about it," Naomi said as they sat in the dugout. "You'll get it back. Just be patient."

"Here's what I want to know," Aubrey said, sitting down on the bench next to Brooke. She had her batting helmet in one hand and a package of sunflower seeds in the other. "What's it like being teammates with Alex? Is he as hot as everyone says?"

Brooke smiled. "He's pretty hot."

Aubrey raised an eyebrow. "Pretty hot?"

"He's incredibly hot," Brooke said, correcting herself.

They all laughed.

"So have you spoken to him yet?" Faith asked.

Brooke hesitated. "Well, not really, but I think he looked at me once."

"He looked at you?" Aubrey asked. "Oh my God. You're the luckiest girl in the world."

Faith looked at Aubrey and shook her head in disgust. "Would you shut up for a minute?" She turned to Brooke. "Let me get this straight. You've been on the team for a week, practiced with them every day, but he hasn't said a single thing to you?"

"Boys are different than girls," Brooke said. "They don't talk too much during practice. Well, at least not to me."

"What does that mean?" Faith asked.

"Let's just say I'm still trying to fit in." Brooke didn't really know how to explain it any better than that, and to be perfectly honest she didn't really want to. And under no circumstances was she going to tell them about the incident with Blake, Skinny, and the jockstrap. She would die before she would let anyone know about that.

"But there is this one boy," she continued. "He talks to me and he's been pretty nice so far. His name is Jamie."

"Jamie Stephens?" Naomi asked. "The junior?"

"Yeah. Do you know him?"

"He's in my English class. He's really nice. A good student, too. He always does his homework and he knows most of the answers when Mr. Wilson calls on him. Which is a lot more than I can say."

They all laughed. It was common knowledge Naomi had homework issues. Let's just say the words 'Naomi' and 'homework' were rarely used in the same sentence unless the sentence was, 'Naomi didn't do her homework last night.'

"What do you know about him?" Brooke asked. Until she had joined the baseball team, she had never met Jamie before and she was curious to learn a little more about him.

"Not much, really," Naomi said. "I heard he had a girlfriend for awhile, Jessie Hines, but they broke up. Not certain why. And I think his dad is an accountant or something like that. They live on the west side of town."

"Do you like him?" Aubrey asked. "Are you going to try to hook up with him?"

Brooke laughed. "I don't know about that. I just met him, and I barely even know anything about him. I'm the one asking you for info."

She didn't get to say anything further. One of the Angels' assistant coaches interrupted from the far end of the dugout.

"Brooke," he called, a look of desperation on his face. "Where are you? You're up."

She jumped up, grabbed her bat and helmet, and darted for the batter's box.

This happened sometimes. Sometimes, the girls got so busy talking (usually about boys) they completely forgot a game was being played.

Unfortunately, her at-bat was not a good one. She was still getting used to playing softball again, and the pitches seemed like they were lightning fast. The minute they left the pitcher's hand, they exploded in the catcher's mitt. She swung and missed three straight times.

"Eyes on the ball," her dad called from the stands. From the tone of his voice, it was clear he wasn't happy.

Luckily, despite her struggles, the team did okay and won 6-2. Their next game, however, was a completely different story. They played a team from Federal Way called the Skyhawks. The Skyhawks were an impressive group with a lot of talented players, including their pitcher, who was a feisty girl named Riley Westmore, their shortstop, who was a small, thin girl named Erin Williams, and their center fielder, who was a young phenom named Melody Gold. Brooke was no match for them, not at all. She struck out once and grounded out twice. Both of her grounders were weak ones right to their second baseman. She was out by a mile each time.

The car ride home was deathly silent for the first ten minutes.

"What was that?" her dad asked.

"What do you mean?" she asked.

"What was up with your performance today? That was the worst I've seen you play in years. Hitless in six at-bats, with four strikeouts? And an error in the field? That's not like you at all."

Brooke sighed. "I had an off day. It won't happen again."

"It better not. It's this baseball thing, isn't it? It's throwing you off. Your timing, your angles. You looked like you didn't know what you were doing out there today. Like you'd never played the game before."

Brooke cringed. She couldn't believe he had figured the cause of her problems so quickly.

"I just need time to adjust," she said. "I'll get it back. You'll see."

"For your sake, I better see it soon."

Unfortunately, he didn't see it the next day. The Angels won all three of their games, but Brooke continued to struggle, both at the plate and in the field. She got one hit, a single during the final game, but that was it. In the meantime, she made two errors at short. Both were wild throws.

"See," her dad said as they drove home. "I was right. I knew this baseball thing was a bad idea."

Brooke didn't know what to say, so she remained silent the whole drive home. It was one of the most awkward, unpleasant car rides they had ever had, and it was a complete departure from the norm. Normally, the car ride home was great fun and they spent the whole time talking about how well she had done that day.

Chapter 8

Brooke was nervous. It was her first game as a baseball player, and she needed to do well to prove to the boys she belonged on the team. But she was also nervous because something unexpected happened.

Her dad showed up. Since he didn't approve of her whole 'baseball thing' she had assumed he wouldn't come. But he had. She stopped by the bleachers to say hi.

"I didn't expect to see you today," she said.

"I may not like this," he responded. "But you're still my daughter, so I'm here to give you what support I can. But do me a favor, okay? Try not to embarrass yourself too much."

The words cut right through her, right to her core. As she took her place at short to start the game, she could barely keep the tears out of her eyes.

Her dad could be such a jerk sometimes. She hated him. If it was the last thing she would do, she'd prove him wrong. She was going to make this baseball thing work just to spite him.

But things did not start well. The game was against Monroe, and the Bearcats' leadoff hitter hit the first pitch straight to her. She fielded it on a hop but rushed the throw and sent it soaring into a distant light pole.

Blake shook his head in disgust.

Jamie walked up to her as the next batter took his warm-up swings.

38

"This may make things worse," he said, "and I hate it when people say it to me, but I've got to say it anyway. You need to relax. Everything will be okay if you relax."

It wasn't easy, but she forced herself to do just that. She blocked out everything she could – Blake, Skinny, her dad, everything unpleasant, and just played ball. And amazingly, it worked. The second batter popped out to Terrell in center, the batter after that lined out to Jamie at second, and the batter after that hit a lazy grounder to her at short. She grabbed it and made a nice, easy throw to Blake to end the inning.

Despite her error, no damage had been done, and now it was their turn to bat. And they took advantage of it. Jamie led off with a single to right, Terrell sacrificed him to second, and he scored when Alex hit a single down the right field foul line. Blake followed Alex's single with a double to left, scoring Alex all the way from first.

Just like that, they were ahead 2-0.

Coach West rounded them up before the beginning of the second inning. "That was a nice start, gentlemen," he said, then caught a quick glance of Brooke and added, "and lady. Now let's keep it up. Good defense."

The score remained 2-0 until Brooke's first at-bat in the bottom of the third. Monroe's pitcher was a freshman, but he was extremely big for his age and threw really hard. Brooke had never faced anyone who threw that hard before. He struck her out with three straight fastballs.

"It's okay," Coach West said as she returned to the dugout. "You'll get it next time."

Unfortunately, she didn't. She managed to foul one pitch away, but that was the best she could do before striking out for the second time in as many tries.

But her third at-bat was another story. It was the sixth inning, and they were still leading 2-0. They had runners on second and third with two outs. Brooke knew if she could get a hit, even something as weak as a bloop single, both runs would score and the game would likely be over. Monroe had only gotten two hits off of Alex all day, and he wasn't showing any signs of letting up. The Bearcats' pitcher, however, was beginning to struggle. He was tiring, and the velocity on his fastball had dipped significantly.

This is my chance, Brooke thought as she stepped into the batter's box. She tapped her bat on the plate, measuring the distance carefully. She dug her cleats into the dirt.

The first pitch was down and away for ball one.

"Good eye," her dad called from the stands.

The second pitch was even lower. Ball two.

This was it. She knew Monroe's pitcher wouldn't want to throw her another ball. No pitcher wanted to go 3-0. As expected, he threw the next pitch straight down the middle of the plate, and she lined it back at him for a single. Silver Lake's dugout erupted in cheers as the runs came around to score. Monroe's outfielder didn't even try a throw to the plate.

As she stood on first base, she couldn't have been happier. Despite all she had gone through during the past week, she had actually done it. Somehow, she had persevered, and she had gotten her first hit as a baseball player.

They won 4-0.

Chapter 9

Their second game (against Meadowdale) was more of the same. She was nervous at first, and things were made even worse by the opposing coach. The minute she stepped into the batter's box, he called time and rushed onto the field.

"What's up with this?" he asked the umpire. "Girls can't play baseball."

"Why do you say that?" the umpire asked.

"Look at her," he said. "She's tiny. She's gonna get hurt for sure."

The umpire shrugged. "I was the field ump during her first game," he said. "She did fine."

"But there's got to be a rule against it," the coach said.

"Not that I know of," the umpire said. "So unless you've got a rulebook and can point one out, let's get back to playing ball."

Meadowdale's coach didn't know what else to say, and he didn't want to make any more of a scene than he'd already done, so he returned to his dugout and the game continued from there. Unfortunately, as was the case in the first game against Monroe, Brooke struck out quickly during her initial at-bat. Meadowdale's pitcher didn't throw as hard as Monroe's, but he had a nasty curveball that fooled her badly for strike three.

In the field, however, she played well. She made three nice plays in the first four innings and assisted on another. By the time she had her second at-bat in the fourth inning, they were leading 1-0. Their lone run came courtesy of a massive home run by Blake in the bottom of the second. Blake was a big boy, and he hit like it.

Brooke dug her cleats into the dirt and waited for the pitch. It was a fastball, and she fouled it away.

"Hands up," her dad shouted from the stands.

She did as instructed, kept her hands up nice and high, and lined the next shot down the first base foul line for a single.

She was all smiles as she stepped onto first base. Unfortunately, she didn't get to enjoy it for long. Jamie lined the next pitch all the way to the wall, advancing her to third. Then Alex hit a long fly ball to the outfield warning track. Meadowdale's center fielder caught it.

"Tag and go," Coach West shouted from his spot in the third base coach's box.

Brooke raced for home as fast as she could. The center fielder whipped the ball home, an awesome throw that reached the catcher just as Brooke got there. The ensuing collision knocked Brooke onto her back and took the wind out of her lungs. She had never felt anything like it. It was like she had run into a brick wall.

But her pain was quickly forgotten. Although the catcher had stayed on his feet, the impact had jarred him just enough to make him drop the ball.

"Safe!" the umpire yelled.

The fans cheered, and her teammates rushed out to make certain she was okay. Coach West and Jamie helped her back to the dugout. As she sat on the bench with an icepack on her neck, she overheard several of the boys talking at the far end of the dugout.

"That catcher is a monster," Terrell said. "I can't believe she took him on like that."

"I'll give her credit," Skinny said. "She may be small, but she's as brave as they get."

Brooke smiled. A compliment from Skinny? She never thought she'd see the day.

Chapter 10

Brooke's dad handed her an icepack as she sat on the couch.

"What were you thinking?" he asked, a frustrated but concerned look on his face. "You're 5'2", 125 pounds when you're soaking wet. That catcher was like 6' tall, and who knows how heavy. You could have been killed."

"It just happened so quickly," Brooke said. Her body ached everywhere, and she felt like she had been run over by a semi truck. "I didn't really mean to run into him. I was going to slide but he was blocking the plate."

"You nearly gave me a heart attack," he said as he plopped down next to her. "And I thought all those years of softball were stressful. This baseball is ten times worse. It's going to be the death of me."

He took the icepack back from her and placed it on his forehead.

Brooke chuckled. Her dad could be extremely difficult at times, but he usually came around sooner or later, if she just gave him enough time. Was this going to be one of those times?

"It was a good shot," he said. "You hit that catcher the second the ball got there. It's no wonder he dropped it. And boy were you flying down that line. That's the fastest I've seen you run in years. It reminded me of that game a few years back when you scored the winning run against the Washington Wildcats."

"That was a fun game," Brooke said.

"You can say that again," he said. "That was a nice single you had today. And yesterday. I'll be honest, I didn't think you could do it, but you did. Two hits in two days. That's not bad. Not bad at all."

They sat in silence for several minutes before he spoke again.

"Are you absolutely committed to this baseball thing?" he asked.

"I think so," she said. "It's not easy, but I think I can do it, if everyone will just give me a chance. And when I say everyone, that means you, dad."

He let out a loud, remorseful sigh. "This is the hardest part of being a parent," he said. "Sometimes you've got to let your kids do things you don't like. I'm still not happy with it, not one bit, but I'll do my best to support you from now on. And I won't make any more comments like the one at the Monroe game. That was totally unacceptable, and I regretted it the minute I said it. But my support is on one condition."

"What?" she asked.

"Stay away from 6' tall catchers from now on," he said.

Brooke laughed. "I'll do my best," she said with a smile.

Chapter 11

Brooke sat in the school cafeteria eating lunch with Naomi, Faith, and Aubrey. It had been two days since the game against Meadowdale, but she was still a little sore from her collision with Meadowdale's catcher.

"How's it going?" Naomi asked. "Things getting better with the team?"

"A little," Brooke said. "I think the players have started to warm up to me a little. Yesterday at practice, Terrell and Aiden actually said hi as I got there. And JJ said, "Nice," after I made a play. And Jamie talks to me quite a bit, but he's never been an issue."

"What's up with that?" Naomi asked.

"I'm not sure," Brooke said. "He met me after practice last night, at my car, and we spoke for awhile. Nothing serious, just small talk, but it was kind of nice. It's the first time I've talked to one of the boys off the field."

"Enough of this," Aubrey interrupted. There was clear irritation in her voice. "Jamie's nice and all, but come on. You know who we want to hear about. Alex. Any luck with him?"

Brooke smiled. "Not really. He's tough to read. He stays to himself for most of practice, and he's really focused and serious most of the time."

"That's 'cause of his dad," Aubrey said.

"What?" the girls asked in unison.

"His dad has been pretty tough on him over the years. He pushes him really hard, ever since he was little. That's probably why he's so good now. But let me get this straight. He doesn't speak to anyone?"

"Of course he does," Brooke said, "and all the other guys really like him, but he doesn't say much. And he's never said anything to me, good or bad. So I don't know if he even knows I exist."

"Most pitchers know their shortstops exist," Faith said.

"You know what I mean," Brooke said. "I don't know if he wants me on the team or not."

"You know what I heard?" Aubrey asked. "There's a rumor going around school. It's a doozie."

"What's that?" they asked in unison.

"I heard he's having issues with Alyssa."

Brooke's heart skipped a beat. Alyssa Allen was Alex's girlfriend. She was a senior and the star player on Silver Lake's volleyball team. She and Alex had been a couple since they were sophomores. This past year, as seniors, they had been homecoming king and queen.

"What kind of problems?" Brooke asked.

"Let's just say Alyssa went to a movie with someone else last week."

"Really?" they all asked. "Who?"

"I never found out," Aubrey said. "No one's sure, and as you can imagine, Alyssa isn't saying much."

Brooke could hardly believe it. Could it be true?

"Anyway," Aubrey continued, "Alex found out about it and he wasn't too happy. There's speculation they're going to break up soon."

"This could be your big chance," Naomi told Brooke.

"What do you mean?" Brooke asked.

"You're the only girl on the baseball team," Naomi said. "You spend two hours a day with him, more on game days. That's more than the rest of us get."

47

"But he doesn't even speak to me," Brooke said. "He hasn't said a single thing to me in over a week."

"That may change," Naomi said. "Especially if he and Alyssa break up."

"This is ridiculous," Faith said. "He ain't going to go for Brooke. The minute he breaks up with Alyssa, he's going to go for a cheerleader. Boys as hot as Alex always go for cheerleaders."

"But he didn't," Aubrey said. "His girlfriend is Alyssa. She's a volleyball player."

They sat there in silence for a minute, eating their lunches. No one, including Brooke, knew how to respond to that. Aubrey was right. Alex was the hottest boy in school by far. He could have had his choice of any girl at Silver Lake, including any of the mega-hot, high maintenance cheerleaders, but instead he had chosen a volleyball player. Alyssa was a pretty girl, there was no mistaking that, but she was far from being the most attractive girl in school. Maybe Alex was one of those strange, extremely rare boys who was attracted to something other than a pretty face.

Brooke could never be that lucky.

Chapter 12

As far as Brooke was concerned, Friday's practice was awesome. Well, not practice, but afterward. Jamie met her in the parking lot next to her car.

"Good job today," he said with a smile.

"Thanks," she said as she loaded her bag into the trunk.

"You seem like you're really getting the hang of this baseball thing," he said. "You did great in batting practice today. That was the best I've seen you hit so far this year."

"I'm getting more comfortable now," she said. "I don't feel so much pressure to prove myself anymore."

"The other guys are treating you okay?"

She shrugged. "They're tolerating me. Even Blake doesn't growl at me nearly as much as he used to. But I still wish someone would talk to me on occasion. Other than a quick 'Nice play' or 'Good job.'"

"I talk to you," he said.

"You're the only one," she said. "And that reminds me. I've been meaning to ask you why."

"What do you mean?"

"Your attitude toward me has been different than the other boys. Right from the start. Why?"

"What time is it?" he asked.

She checked her phone, then told him. It was 5:30 pm.

"Do you have a couple of minutes?" he asked. "If so, I'll show you."

They hopped in his car. He drove a black Camaro. It was an older model, but it was in great shape, and he had clearly put some time and money into it over the years. It had sparkling wheels and a booming stereo, with a huge subwoofer in the trunk.

"You like Green Day?" he asked as he hit a button on the dash.

Brooke nodded. Green Day was one of her favorite bands.

He drove them to a nearby softball field. A Little League team was practicing. Ten-year-old girls ran everywhere, in a somewhat random fashion, as a pair of coaches tried in vain to instill some sense of order. Brooke instantly had flashbacks of her days as a Little League player, when she played for North Seattle. Those were good days. Things were simple then.

Jamie pointed to one girl in particular, a little shortstop with a long, black ponytail. She grabbed a grounder and whipped it to first like she had done it a million times.

"That's my sister," he said. "Her name's Katherine. Everyone calls her Kat."

"You have a sister?" Brooke asked.

Jamie nodded. "She's ten. She's a shortstop like you. The minute I saw you, that day Coach West brought you to the field, I thought of her. She's not nearly as good as you of course, but give her a couple of years and she's going to be something else."

"Are you close?" Brooke asked.

"We have our moments," he said. "A few punches have been thrown over the years. And she is the baby, so my parents spoil her rotten. But overall we get along pretty well. We practice in the driveway when the

50

weather is good. She's got a great arm for a ten-year-old."

Brooke couldn't help but be touched, and a little jealous. She was an only child, and she had always wanted an older brother who would take care of her and show her the ropes. She hoped Kat realized how good she had it.

"I used to be a shortstop myself," Jamie continued. "But since the team had Dwayne, Coach West converted me to second. When Dwayne got kicked off the team, I thought he was going to move me back. Until you came along."

Brooke grew alarmed. Was Jamie upset she had taken his position?

Clearly he saw the panic in her eyes. "Don't worry," he said. "It's no big deal. I like playing second, and I really just want what's best for the team. Winning conference titles is great fun, and if this is what it takes to do it again, so be it."

Brooke was relieved. So far, Jamie was her only ally on the team. She didn't want to risk losing him.

"And I'm kind of hoping you'll do well," Jamie said. "If you can prove girls can play baseball, who knows what doors that will open up for girls like Kat in the future. Not to say there's anything wrong with playing softball, because there isn't, but it would be nice if girls could do whatever they want, right? They could play either sport, softball or baseball?"

Brooke was in shock. Most boys her age spent their time talking about sports, cars, and video games, and they were roughly as intelligent as the common chimp. Her last boyfriend, LeBron Henderson, had been one step above a monkey on the evolutionary scale. She still didn't know what she had seen in him. Jamie, on the other hand, seemed completely different. He was contemplative and caring.

"You up for some ice cream?" he asked.

Brooke was always up for ice cream, so they drove to the local Cold Stone Creamery. She got her favorite, a double scoop of chocolate ice cream in a waffle cone with caramel, sprinkles, gummy bears, and whipped cream on top. She was really hungry since she hadn't eaten since lunch and she dug right in.

"Wow," he said as he sat down at the table across from her. "You should be able to fit in with us guys no problem. You eat like a baseball player."

She looked up from her food and stopped abruptly. She had been so hungry she hadn't realized what she'd done. She'd been eating like a pig in front of a boy. How embarrassing.

"I'm just kidding," he said with a smile. "But you have something right here."

He reached forward and wiped a small splotch of whipped cream from her chin. She couldn't help but notice how soft his fingers were as they touched her skin. She started to blush.

He clearly saw her cheeks change color, because he smiled, but he didn't say anything about it. Instead, he asked her about herself, and she gave him a quick rundown of her life (boring as it was), including how she'd originally been from California (San Diego, to be more specific), but her family had moved to Seattle when her dad's law firm transferred him to its Seattle office. That was a long time ago, when she was just five. She had lived in Seattle ever since, and her main focus over the years had been softball. She had played Little League until she was eight, then switched to a select team called the Bellevue Beast. She played for the Beast for a couple of years, then switched to her current team, the Eastside Angels.

"That's pretty impressive," Jamie said. "I didn't think most girls made a Gold team until they were seniors. And you're a starter, right?"

Brooke nodded. During tryouts, she had beaten out two other girls, both older than her, for the starting position. She downplayed that fact a little, though, because she didn't want Jamie to think she was bragging.

"You don't have to be modest with me," he said. "I'm a guy, right? That's what we guys do. We go around bragging about ourselves all the time. You should hear Blake when he gets started."

Blake. Brooke cringed at the mention of his name. She hoped he and Jamie weren't too close. She hated the idea of Jamie being friends with a creep like that. And she hoped Jamie didn't know anything about the jockstrap incident.

"What's the deal with him?" she asked, trying to ferret out a little information.

"I've known him forever," Jamie said. "He's a really nice guy once you get to know him."

"Blake?" Brooke asked. "Are we talking about the same Blake? The overgrown orangutan who plays first base for our team?"

Jamie laughed. "That's a good description. But give him a chance, and you'll see. He's fiercely loyal once he warms up to you. I remember this one time when we were in middle school, these older kids were picking on me. Blake came along and beat them up. Both of them, at the same time. When I asked him about it, all he said was, 'No one treats my friend like that.'"

Brooke raised an eyebrow. She could hardly believe Blake had any redeeming qualities at all. To her, he was nothing more than a bully.

"What about the other guys?" she asked.

"They're all pretty cool," Jamie said. "Most of us have played together since Little League. We even won state one year. We didn't lose a single game all year. Skinny hit a grand slam in the championship game. I was on third at the time. It was the most exciting day of my life. At least so far."

The conversation continued from there, and it was a good one. Brooke couldn't believe how many things she and Jamie had in common. Their favorite color was green, they were both Scorpios (her birthday was October 24 and his October 28), they both loved Thai food, they both had been to France (she had gone on a family vacation when she was seven, he had gone when he was ten), and they loved rock music, the louder the better. Their only major difference was their favorite football teams.

"The Chargers?" he asked. "What's up with that?"

"I'm originally from San Diego," she said. "I've always liked them. And they have cool uniforms. I love the lightning bolts on the helmets. What about you? What's your favorite team?"

"The Seahawks."

"You've got to be kidding," she said. "I didn't think anybody liked them anymore. When was the last time they had a winning season?"

"They're in a rebuilding stage," he said.

"For how long?" she joked. "The rest of the decade?"

They laughed. Being a fan of the Seahawks was a definite character flaw, but she'd overlook it, since Jamie was so perfect in every other way.

And he was cute. She hadn't really noticed it before, but he was. He definitely wasn't a match for Alex (but then again, who was?), and he was cute in a completely different way. He was much more rugged than Alex, much less polished, with deep, black hair and auburn eyes. And his body was dreamy. He wasn't too tall, but he was muscular, with large biceps and thick, powerful shoulders.

Unfortunately, the night had to come to an end sooner or later, so he drove her back to her car at the school parking lot, and she drove herself home from there.

What a fun evening, she thought. *I wish they were all like it.*

Unfortunately, it didn't stay fun for long. Her dad was waiting for her at the door the minute she arrived.

"Where have you been all night, young lady?" he asked. "I've been worried sick."

Brooke cringed. Normally, her dad called her 'kid,' 'kiddo,' or 'Brooke.' When she was in trouble, she was referred to as 'young lady.'

"Sorry, dad," she said. "I lost track of the time."

"I've been texting you all night," he said.

She cringed again. "I left my phone in the car and forgot about it."

He raised a suspicious eyebrow. "A teenage girl forgot about her phone? For over two hours? I find that hard to believe."

Brooke's eyes widened. Had she really been with Jamie for over two hours? It seemed like fifteen minutes.

"Where were you?" he asked. "I was worried sick. I was about to call the police."

"I went with Jamie to get some ice cream. We were at Cold Stone the whole time."

"Jamie?" her dad asked. "Do I know her? Is she the new girl on your softball team? The outfielder?"

Brooke smiled. Her dad had always had trouble with names. He could never keep her teammates straight. "No," she said. "That's Danielle. Jamie is on my baseball team. He's the second baseman."

"He?"

Brooke sighed the minute he said it. A whole new can of worms had just been opened.

Her dad crossed his arms. "Have I met this boy before?" he asked.

"You haven't met any of the boys on my team," she said. "But you've seen him. At my games."

"Seen him? That's not good enough. No boy is going on a date with my daughter until I meet him first. What if he's a psycho or a loony or something?"

Brooke nearly burst out laughing. Her dad could be so ridiculous at times. "First of all," she said, "tonight wasn't a date. We just went to ice cream after practice. And he's not a psycho, or a loony, or anything like that. He's a nice kid. He even has a sister who plays Little League. She's a shortstop like me."

"Really?" her dad asked. He had a soft spot for shortstops.

Brooke nodded. Her dad seemed to soften for a second but then got all rigid and strict again.

"I don't care," he said. "If you want to go out with this Jamie again, so be it, that's your choice, but I want to meet him first."

"Whatever," Brooke said as she trudged upstairs to her bedroom. Her dad could be so stubborn and set in his ways at times. If you looked up the word 'frustrating' in the dictionary, it had a picture of him right next to it.

Chapter 13

They had two games the following week, one against Mountlake Terrace and one against Edmonds-Woodway. Brooke didn't get any hits against Mountlake Terrace (she grounded out twice and popped out once), but she made up for it against Edmonds. In the third inning, she got a nice single, and in the sixth she hit a massive shot all the way to deep left field. The ball hit the warning track and bounced over the outfield fence for a ground rule double.

Everyone cheered as she coasted into second. It was her first double as a baseball player, and also her first multi-hit day. She was all smiles.

But something unexpected happened later in the game. They were winning 5-0, and there were two outs in the final inning when Edmonds' shortstop hit a sharp grounder at Jamie at second. It was the type of play Jamie usually made with ease, but the ball took a funny hop and jumped over his mitt for an error.

"Come on, Jamie," Alex shouted from his position on the mound. "Get in front of the ball. You know better." He slapped his glove against his thigh. He wasn't happy at all.

Brooke raised not one, but both of her eyebrows. She had never seen Alex so animated before. Nor so negative. Normally, he was one of the quietest boys on the team, and when he did speak, he was always upbeat and positive. Several of the players on the team had made errors in the past (including her), and he had never once said a word about it. He would just take the ball and move on, like all good pitchers did. As such, his reaction toward Jamie was really unexpected and out of character.

But then again, everyone had bad days, and maybe this was one of them. Even the cutest boy in school was allowed to have a bad day on occasion, right?

Luckily, he struck out the next batter, ending the game, so no harm was done. Coach West rounded them up for their traditional post-game discussion in center field.

"Well done," he said. "Coaches aren't supposed to give too much praise for fear their players will let up, but I'm going to be honest with you. You look really sharp this year. We've won all four games so far, and we've done it with a combination of good pitching, solid defense, and timely hitting. I'm really impressed. If we keep working hard, I think this could be one of the best teams in the school's history."

Brooke liked the sound of that. Wouldn't that be something if the greatest team in the history of her school also just happened to be the one that had a girl on it?

Coach West dismissed them, and she rounded up her things and walked to her car in the parking lot. She hoped Jamie would be there to greet her, like he had done the Friday before, but unfortunately he and his Camaro were nowhere to be seen.

Chapter 14

Every Tuesday night, Brooke had hitting lessons. Her hitting instructor's name was Steve Johns, and he was really nice. He gave lessons in a large industrial complex in south Seattle. It was quite a drive from Brooke's house, especially in traffic, but her dad insisted on using Steve because he worked with most of the great softball and baseball players from the area. When they arrived in south Seattle, Steve was finishing up with another girl. He said goodbye to her, then came over and greeted Brooke and her dad in his customary, jovial way.

"How is everything for Miss Brooke this week?" he asked.

"Good," she said.

"Sweet. Are you ready to get started?"

Brooke nodded and they began. Her hitting lesson consisted of two different stages. The first was called vision training. Brooke stood in a batting cage, in the batter's box, as a machine shot tennis balls at her, one at a time. Each ball was marked with a number, written in one of three colors (red, green, or black). As the ball came at her, she had to hit it, and as she hit it, she had to call out the number and color on the ball. Steve started the machine at a relatively slow speed (fifty miles per hour), then gradually cranked it up to about one hundred miles per hour. At that speed, the ball was little more than a yellow blur, but Brooke had been doing this drill for long enough she could usually see the colors on the ball, and sometimes the numbers, regardless of the speed. The process helped improve her focus and concentration, and it took about half an hour.

After she finished her vision training, they moved to another batting cage, and Steve tossed balls to her from behind a protective screen. He watched her form as she hit each toss and stopped her periodically to correct little flaws in her swing. They hadn't even completed the first bucket of balls when Brooke's dad brought the drill to a premature end.

"What are you doing?" he asked. Like always, he stood outside the cage watching attentively.

"What does it look like?" Brooke asked. She had no idea what he was talking about. She was doing everything exactly the same as she always did.

"I thought you were serious about this baseball thing," he said.

"I am."

"Then show it. Get the baseballs out."

They explained to Steve that Brooke had joined the school's baseball team, and his eyes got big with excitement.

"Really?" he asked. "And you've already played four games? Well done, Miss Brooke. How are you hitting?"

"Pretty well," Brooke said. "I have four hits, one a double."

"But she could do better," her dad interrupted. "She's dropping her hands again. Work on it."

So they did. Steve exchanged the bucket of softballs for a bucket of baseballs, and they went to town. It was great fun, and they worked for at least twice as long as normal. Brooke couldn't help but notice how even the littlest change, like just changing the type of balls she was hitting, could get everyone so excited. Even her dad was smiling as she lined a pitch straight up the middle that missed Steve by less than an inch.

"Darn, Miss Brooke," Steve said. "You're dangerous as a baseball player."

"You bet I am," she said with a laugh.

Chapter 15

Their next game was against Kamiak. It was a good game, but Kamiak's pitcher was no match for Alex and Silver Lake won 3-0. Blake hit a home run, Skinny got two doubles, Jamie two singles, and Brooke one. Everyone was stellar in the field and Kamiak never got a runner past second.

But the second game that week, the one against Glacier Peak, was the one Brooke would remember forever. Alex was absolutely on fire. His fastball was nearly untouchable, as was his curveball, off-speed, and splitter. The Glacier Peak hitters were absolutely overwhelmed. By the sixth inning, Silver Lake was leading 6-0 and they were all excited. But they weren't excited about the score.

They were excited about the no-hitter.

A no-hitter is the holy grail of baseball. It is when a pitcher pitches an entire game and never gives up a hit. It is rarely done by any pitcher at any level.

So far, Alex hadn't given up a hit.

Even he was excited. Even though he had pitched all of his life, he had never thrown a no-hitter. Twice he had gotten close, but an opposing batter had always managed to break it up somehow.

The tension was intense. As they took the field to begin the seventh and final inning, Brooke could feel it. Everyone, the players, the coaches, the fans, they all wanted this no-hitter.

"You can do it, son," Alex's dad called from the stands. "Three more outs."

Alex was normally the calmest player on the field, but not today. He was sweating bullets. Brooke could see it from her position at short. As good as Alex was, he wasn't used to being in this type of position with so much at stake.

But he did his job. It took five pitches, but he struck out the first batter to start the inning. Only two more to go.

The next batter hit a grounder to JJ at third. JJ grabbed it and tossed it to first for out number two.

Only one to go.

Alex was a wreck now. He didn't say anything, but Brooke could see it in his face. His eyes were wide and his cheeks were pale. He wanted this no-hitter so bad he wasn't even breathing.

But there was one large problem. Glacier Peak's next batter was also their best batter. He was a big kid named Jessie Johnson, a power hitting lefty. Alex had gotten him out during his first two at-bats, but it hadn't been easy. Jessie's first shot had been a monster fly to center that Terrell caught at the base of the outfield wall, and his second shot had been a laser line drive that Blake snared at the last second, saving at least a double.

And the no-hitter. Had that ball gotten by Blake, Alex's beloved no-hitter would have been lost.

Brooke crouched down at short. She needed to be ready. If Jessie got a hold of one of Alex's pitches, it wasn't going to be pretty.

And then it happened. Just as she predicted, Jessie hit the first pitch, and he hit it hard, straight up the middle. At first Brooke thought she had no chance at it, it was hit too sharply, but she got a good jump and dove anyway. And it was possibly the best dive she

63

had ever made, completely outstretched as far as she could go. The ball stuck in the top of her glove, in the webbing, in what players call an 'ice cream cone.' A second later, she came crashing to the ground on her side, knocking the wind completely from her lungs. At first she thought the impact had jarred the ball free and she had dropped it (since she barely had it in the first place), but she heard the umpire's voice behind her.

"She's got it," he shouted. "It's a catch. The batter's out."

The next couple of minutes were a complete blur. She still hadn't recovered from hitting the ground so hard, and she couldn't breathe fully, but she didn't care. Alex threw his mitt into the sky and charged from his position on the mound. He scooped her off of the ground and lifted her into the air, hugging her tightly against him, spinning her around and around. He was so excited he couldn't help himself. After all the years, and after all the tries, he had finally gotten his no-hitter.

"Thank you," he said. "Thank you, thank you, thank you, thank you."

She didn't know how many times he said it, and she didn't really care. All she knew was she was being hugged by the cutest boy in the school and she liked it. A few seconds later, the rest of her teammates arrived, and they tackled the two of them right there on the spot. It was the funnest, but heaviest, pig pile Brooke had ever been in. At one point, Blake's knee was in her chest, Skinny's knee was in her back, and someone else's elbow was crammed against her cheek, and it was all quite painful, but she didn't care.

She had made the catch. Thanks to her, Alex had gotten his no-hitter.

It got even better after the game. Brooke watched as Alex's dad met him at the side of the field and gave him a bear hug. Minutes later, a small truck pulled up, and a news reporter interviewed Alex for the next day's paper. But the absolute highlight happened a few minutes later, and it involved the last person Brooke ever expected.

Blake.

He walked up to her out of nowhere, completely by himself. He had already taken his jersey off and was only wearing his Under Armour. "I never wanted you on the team," he said. "And I'm still not certain I do. But I'll be honest. That was the best catch I've ever seen. By far."

Without another word, he turned and walked away, to resume celebrating with Alex and the other boys.

Brooke was all smiles the whole way home.

Chapter 16

Brooke's softball team had a tournament the following weekend, and the girls sat in the dugout waiting for their turns to bat.

"Oh my God," Aubrey said, her eyes as big as saucers. "Let me get this straight. You were rolling around on the ground, with eleven boys, all at the same time? And Alex was one of them?"

Brooke had just finished telling them what had happened during the game against Glacier Peak. About how she had saved Alex's no-hitter with a diving catch. But the girls, especially Aubrey, weren't interested in the no-hitter. They wanted to hear about Alex hugging her after the game.

"I'd pay money to roll around with Alex on the ground," Aubrey said. "And all you had to do was make a diving catch? I'll make a diving catch. Watch me next inning."

They laughed. Aubrey was quite a riot, especially when she got excited. And she always got excited when Alex was involved.

"Here's what I want to know," Faith said. "Even that big guy, the one you say is so mean all the time, even he was impressed?"

Brooke nodded. "He said it was the best catch he'd ever seen. I couldn't believe it. I still can't. And the next day at practice, I couldn't really do much since my side was sore from when I hit the ground, so I just sat in the dugout for most of practice. All of a sudden,

Blake comes up to me and says, 'Just take it easy today, Brooke. We need you ready for Monday.'"

"What's on Monday?" Naomi asked.

"Our next game," Brooke said. "And it's a big one. It's against Alderwood."

The girls nodded. They knew Alderwood well. Alderwood and Silver Lake were arch rivals.

"Last year," Brooke said, "we beat them for the league title, but this year, the paper picked them as the favorite. The guys have been talking about it all season. Their pitcher is a senior named Christian Parkinson. They say he's as nasty as they get. He's got five different pitches, and he throws them all well. And he's really mean. He's been known to throw brushback pitches just for the fun of it."

The girls groaned. A brushback pitch is a pitch the pitcher throws high and tight, missing the batter by mere inches. It is usually done to scare the batter or to get her to move away from the plate. The girls didn't like brushback pitches at all.

"Like always," Brooke said, "we play every team twice, so the game on Monday isn't a do-or-die situation, but we want to win anyway to send a message. And it will give us a one game lead in the standings."

One of the assistant coaches called frantically from the far end of the dugout. Once again, the girls had forgotten there was a game being played. Brooke grabbed her bat and darted for the batter's box.

They were playing a team from Lake Stevens called Lake Stevens Fastpitch (LSF for short). LSF had a good pitcher, but she was nothing special. Normally, Brooke could hit her easily but she was still worried. Now that she had put so much time and effort into baseball, she wasn't certain she could hit softballs anymore.

But she could. The LSF pitcher got two quick strikes on her, but then made an error by leaving a change-up over the middle of the plate. Brooke hammered it into center field for a single. Two runs scored on the hit.

"Well done," her dad called from the stands.

Brooke could hardly believe it. Despite the terrible start to the season, despite her struggles in both baseball and softball, despite her problems with the boys and her dad, everything was finally falling into place.

Or so she thought.

Everything changed on Monday.

Chapter 17

They were all excited about the game on Monday afternoon. It was the first game of the season against their arch rivals, a nearby school named Alderwood. No one liked Alderwood because it was a new school, recently built just a few years ago, and it was filled with preppy rich kids. All of Alderwood's teams were good, but their baseball team was the best of the bunch. Everyone knew that, barring a major upset, the league champion this year would be either Alderwood or Silver Lake.

The game was at Alderwood, and as the Silver Lake bus arrived, the Eagles were warming up on the field. Brooke's eyes got large as she took a look at them for the first time. They were huge, every one of them. They looked like a football team.

"They don't scare me," Blake said as he pushed his way toward the field.

"So it's true," one of the Eagles said as Brooke unloaded her equipment in the visitor's dugout. "Mighty Silver Lake has gotten so desperate for players they've turned to the softball team for help."

Blake walked up to him and got in his face. The other boy was big, but he was no match for Blake.

"You got an issue with that?" Blake asked.

The other boy turned and left without a response. They all laughed.

Normally, Brooke would have been offended by the boy's comment, but there was something about it that made her happy.

Blake's reaction. Her greatest nemesis, the boy who had hated her from the start, had stood up for her. And she had no doubt that, had the Alderwood boy pressed the issue further, a fight would have ensued. She had only known Blake for a short time, but she had already learned one thing about him. He didn't back down. Ever.

Brooke smiled as Alderwood took the field to start the game. The pitcher, Christian Parkinson, was the boy Blake had chased away. Unfortunately, Brooke wasn't smiling for long. Christian was everything she had heard. He was awesome. He threw even harder than Alex. He struck out all three of their batters in the first inning, and one of three in the second.

Luckily, Alex was up to the challenge. He struck out two batters in the first and two in the second. When Brooke got her first at-bat in the third, there were two outs and the game was still scoreless.

Christian snickered as she stepped to the plate. He shook his head in disgust.

"How stupid is this?" he said, somewhat to himself. "A girl playing baseball. Let's see what she's got."

It was the fastest fastball Brooke had ever seen. But she got a piece of it and fouled it away.

Christian was surprised, and a little impressed. He hadn't expected her to have a chance. "Not bad," he said. "Try again."

The next pitch was even faster than the first. Brooke fouled it away.

Christian's mood changed in a heartbeat. At first he had been mildly amused. Now he was downright mad. He couldn't believe a girl had fought off two of his best pitches.

"You think you're tough?" he asked. "Let's see how tough you are."

The next pitch was a complete blur. It hit Brooke in the side of the head. It hit her so hard it blew her off of her feet and knocked her to the ground. It hurt so bad she thought she was going to die. Tears streamed down her cheeks. The last thing she remembered was the sound of the umpire above her, saying desperately, "Young lady, are you okay? Young lady? Someone call an ambulance."

Brooke awoke in a hospital bed an hour later. Her head felt like it was going to explode. A doctor, a nurse, and her dad stood over her.

"Here she comes," the doctor said.

"Thank God," her dad said.

Brooke was totally disoriented and she didn't know where she was. All she remembered was a white flash, and then she hit the ground. She sat up in the hospital bed and tried to get her bearings.

"Take it easy," her dad said. "Not too fast, kid."

"Now that she's awake," the doctor told the nurse, "I want a CAT scan pronto."

Ever so carefully, the nurse moved Brooke into a wheelchair and pushed her down the hall, to another room where they could complete the CAT scan and make certain she didn't have any internal bleeding or other damage to her brain or skull. Along the way, bits and pieces of what had happened came back to her in violent flashes, and her dad filled her in with the rest of the details.

"Man you gave us a scare," he said. "I've never seen a player hit the ground so hard. And you didn't move at all until the paramedics arrived. For a minute .

. . ." His words trailed off abruptly. He didn't want to complete the sentence.

Luckily, everything went okay with the CAT scan. Apparently, her batting helmet had done its job and the test was negative. The doctor thought she'd be fine.

"But I want a follow-up in one week," he said. "And no softball until then."

"What about baseball?" she asked.

"What?" the doctor asked. He didn't understand.

"She plays baseball," her dad responded.

"Really?" the doctor asked. "I didn't know girls played baseball. Regardless, no strenuous activity of any type until I say so. That means no sports of any type – softball or baseball."

"But I've got more games this week," Brooke said.

"And she's got a tournament this weekend," her dad said.

"Absolutely not," the doctor said. "We can't take any chances with this type of injury. Everything looks okay now, but you never know. I've seen cases where the initial scans come back okay, then everything goes bad from there. If everything looks okay after one week, I'll clear you, then you can return to play. But not until then."

Brooke and her dad were not happy, but they had no choice. The doctor knew best.

"And Brooke," he said. "Before you leave, we're going to need a urine sample."

Brooke cringed. Peeing into a cup was not one of her favorite activities. At least it was good timing. She had to go.

Something nice happened just before they left the hospital. Jamie showed up. He was still in his baseball uniform and had come straight from the game.

"Are you okay?" he asked. "I got here as fast as I could."

"I'm okay," Brooke said. "I've got a nasty headache, and the doctor says my dad has to wake me up every two hours tonight to make certain I don't slip into a coma, but other than that I'll live. How did the game go? Did we win?"

"No," Jamie said. "We lost 2-1."

Brooke sighed. Her day had just gone from bad to worse. After all she'd been through, she'd hoped to hear the team had won. At least that would have made her feel a little better.

"It got really ugly after the paramedics took you away," Jamie continued. "Blake nearly tore Christian's head off. It took all of us to hold him back."

"Blake?"

"I already told you," Jamie said. "He's fiercely loyal once you win him over. And apparently you won him over."

Brooke could hardly believe what she was hearing, but she liked it anyway.

"But then things got really out of hand," Jamie continued. "Christian was Alderwood's first batter the next inning. Alex hit him in the head with the very first pitch. It was the hardest pitch I've ever seen him throw. Christian hit the ground almost as hard as you did."

Brooke's mouth dropped open.

"They had to call an ambulance for him. The umpire threw Alex out of the game, claiming he did it on purpose. Coach West got in a huge argument with the umpire, and he got thrown out, too. But he wouldn't leave until they called the cops. In the meantime, he threw all kinds of things onto the field, just like managers do in those videos you see on YouTube. So I pitched the rest of the game, and I did the best I could, but it's been awhile since I pitched. We got one run, but they got two in the bottom of the sixth, and we couldn't come back. And it was so hard to concentrate after all that had happened."

"It's okay," Brooke said. "You did your best."

She didn't know what to say. Her mind was working overtime, trying to process all the information she'd been told, but with her headache, it wasn't easy. She couldn't believe it. Blake had nearly started a fight, Alex had gotten himself thrown out of the game, and normally calm and collected Coach West had gone crazy.

All for her.

Now she knew. Despite being a girl, they had finally accepted her. They wouldn't have acted the way they had unless they thought of her as a member of the team.

Despite the constant pounding in her head, she felt good.

Chapter 18

The ensuing week was tough for Brooke. It took two full days for her headache to go away, and even after it went away, she had trouble sleeping. She kept having nightmares of Christian standing on the mound with the ball in his hand.

"You think you're tough?" he said, a twisted smile on his face. "Let's see how tough you are."

She'd jolt awake the instant the ball hit her, and she'd be covered in sweat every time.

But her dreams weren't her only problem. Her dad got finicky again. It happened on Wednesday night, right after he got home from work. She was watching television in the living room when he plopped down on the couch next to her.

"I've been thinking about this baseball thing again," he said. "And maybe it's not a good idea after all."

"What?" Brooke asked. She couldn't believe it. "You said you'd support me."

"I know," he responded. "But that was before you got injured."

"I've been injured before," she said. "I get injured all the time. Remember that time a few years back when Naomi slid into my foot and broke my toenail off? That was bad. I could barely walk for a week. And what about the time at McCall Field when the ball hit third base and shot up into my face, and I would have lost all of my front teeth if it wasn't for my braces?"

Her dad nodded. He remembered. It wasn't a fond memory.

"And what about the time in Little League, when I slid back into third and jammed my hand so bad it turned purple?"

He smiled. "I still can't believe you finished that game."

"I had to bat with one hand," she said. "It hurt too much to use the other one. That was an adventure. And what about the time the ball hit my thumb and it swelled up so bad you had to leave work early to take me for x-rays?"

"I thought it was broken for sure," he said.

"Me, too," she said. "It doesn't matter what sport I'm playing, softball or baseball, I can still get injured, and I probably will. I always get injured. What do you call me?"

"Accident prone?"

"No, not that one. The other one."

"A ball magnet?"

"Yeah, that's it. I just have bad luck. No matter where I go, the ball finds me and hits me. It's just a matter of when."

He nodded. He couldn't deny it. It was true. But there was one distinction.

"In softball," he said, "a pitcher never threw at your head. Not intentionally."

"That Christian is a bad apple," she responded. "It doesn't mean all boys are like him. I've played in how many games so far this season, and he's the only one who's done it."

"You've still got to play them again," her dad said. "What if he does it again?"

A lump formed in Brooke's throat and her eyes got big. She hadn't thought of that, and she didn't like it at all.

"I hate those Alderwood kids," her dad said. "They're a bunch of spoiled brats. I should get someone to burn that school down. That would do us all a favor."

Brooke smiled. She liked the sound of that.

"But then again," he said, "I'd go to prison for twenty years, and I'd miss your games, and I wouldn't like that at all."

"I've been meaning to ask you about that," Brooke said. "Why did you come to my baseball games? You were so against it. I was certain you wouldn't come."

"I only have a few games left," he said. "I need to enjoy them while I can."

Brooke was puzzled by his words. "What do you mean?"

"How old are you?"

Brooke rolled her eyes. Her dad could never remember how old she was.

"Sixteen."

"Oh yeah. Well then you've only got two years left until you graduate, and then you'll be done playing, and I won't have any games left to watch. So I've got to watch as many as I can now."

"But I'm going to play in college," she said.

"I know," he said, "but you're probably going to be at some school in California, and I'll fly down there when I can, but it's not going to be the same."

Brooke smiled. Her dad was so funny. Like all guys, he liked to spend the majority of his day walking around acting tough and macho, but there was a sentimental side to him, too. And he had always been overprotective of her, but that was partially her own fault. She had always been a 'daddy's girl,' and she still remembered the time when she was three and she flipped her tricycle and scraped her arm. She ran right past her mom to get to her dad so he could make it better. Not to say she wasn't close with her mom, because she was, but in a different way. Her dad had been the one to teach her how to ride her bike, and to drive, and most importantly, to play softball.

Softball had always been their closest bond. Her dad taught her how to play as soon as she could walk. They'd be out in the back yard for hours, with a little plastic bat, hitting until the sun went down. Even in the winter months, when it got dark before her dad got home from work, they'd still practice. They went to a local hardware store and got some porch lights that lit up the majority of the yard. Brooke remembered some days it was so cold she could see her breath and barely feel her fingers, but it never stopped them, not once. They even played one day in the snow, but their practice came to a premature end when she hit the ball too hard and it flew into the neighbor's yard and the neighbor's dog, Rascal, ran off with it.

Her dad interrupted her thoughts.

"What's the name of that boy," he asked, "who came to the hospital?"

"What?" she asked.

"When you got hurt. That boy at the hospital. I saw him when I was returning from the parking lot with the car."

"That was Jamie," she said. "The second baseman. He's the boy I went to ice cream with that one night."

"I like him," her dad said.

Brooke nearly fell off of the couch. Her dad had never liked any of the boys she had introduced him to. He had that typical 'no boy is good enough for my daughter' attitude you find in a lot of dads these days.

"What do you mean?" she asked.

"That was nice of him, to come and see you and all. Since you're new on the team, he barely knows you, but he came anyway. That's the type of boy you should be dating. Not that Spyder boy. I hate that kid."

Brooke nearly burst out laughing. 'Spyder' was Bobby Sullivan, her boyfriend in the eighth grade. Everyone called him Spyder because he had a pet tarantula.

"Dad," she said, "I already told you, I didn't know he was a smoker until after I was seeing him. And as soon as I found out, I broke up with him."

"What about that Hugh kid?"

Brooke cringed. Hugh was her boyfriend in the ninth grade. He had been a total creep. She had no idea what she had seen in him.

"You have terrible taste in boys," her dad said.

"Oh my God," she said. She couldn't believe what she was hearing. Her dad was critiquing her choice of boyfriends.

"I'll pick your next boyfriend," he said.

Now she had heard everything. "Do you know how ridiculous that sounds?" she asked.

He chuckled. "You're probably right. But if I could, I'd pick that Jamie kid. He seems like a nice boy to me."

Brooke didn't say anything, but she had no choice but to agree. Jamie was definitely the nicest boy she had met since joining the baseball team.

"How are you feeling today?" her dad asked.

"Okay," she said.

"Headache any better?"

"A little," she said. Actually, it was pretty much gone, but she didn't want to tell him quite yet. She had always liked sympathy, and she wanted a little more.

"Good. Hopefully you'll get better soon. It would be nice to see you on the field again."

How inconsistent was that? Five minutes ago, he had wanted her to quit the team. Now, he wanted her to play again?

"What do you mean?" she asked.

"I actually like this baseball thing. That other night at your batting lesson with Steve, that was the most fun I've had in awhile. And that catch you made to save the no-hitter. That was spectacular. I've been bragging about it at the office all week."

Her eyes got big.

"How many dads can say they have a daughter who is so talented she can compete with boys?" he said. "Some of my partners are so impressed they're going to come and watch one of your games."

"Really?" she asked. "That's cool."

"I thought so, too," he said. "So do us a favor and get better quick."

With a smile, he hopped up and headed upstairs to change out of his suit.

Chapter 19

The games that week were agonizing for Brooke. She was what some coaches call a workhorse — the type of player who likes to play every inning of every game. She hated sitting on the bench watching. And she especially hated it now that she had finally proven herself to the boys. Now that she fit in, she wanted to be out there with them, contributing as much as possible.

But she wasn't going to be cleared until the following Monday, so she had no choice but to sit and watch.

The game on Tuesday, their second game of the season against Edmonds-Woodway, went well. Silver Lake's athletic director suspended Alex and Coach West one game each for their roles in the Alderwood game, so neither of them were allowed to be there. An assistant coach took Coach West's place and Jamie did the pitching. And he did a good job. He only gave up four hits and they won 3-1. Blake hit a two-run homer and Terrell hit a solo shot. The only down spot was Brooke's replacement, Benji Hampton. He was a freshman and the normal starter on the JV team, but they called him up to fill in for Brooke until she could return. He struck out all three at-bats and made two errors in the field. The second error was on a throw from Skinny behind the plate. Skinny's throw was great, and it would have nailed the runner by a mile, but Benji dropped it.

When the inning was over, Skinny walked up to Brooke in the dugout. She was sitting on the bench next to the bat rack.

"I hope the doctor clears you soon," he said. "I can't take much more of Benji."

On Thursday, for their game against Meadowdale, Alex and Coach West were back and they cruised to another easy victory. Jamie led the way with three singles and Blake had another home run, a massive shot to center. The highlight of the game, however, came after the fourth inning. Alex walked into the dugout, tossed his mitt to the side, and sat down next to Brooke.

"How are you?" he asked.

She nearly passed out on the spot. It was the first time he had actually spoken to her.

"Okay," she said, quickly sitting up and straightening her bangs.

"I never got a chance to thank you for that catch," he said. "I know most shortstops wouldn't have even tried for that ball. I'll never forget what you did."

She could feel her cheeks getting warm. Oh God, was she blushing? How embarrassing.

"My dad already got a stand for the ball," he continued. "With one of those fancy display bases, and he put it in my trophy room. I've been treated like royalty ever since."

He turned to face her. He was even cuter close-up than he was from afar. His deep blue eyes were radiant as he spoke.

"I owe you," he said. "If you ever need anything, anything at all, just ask and I'll make it happen."

Coach West called him, so he hopped up and got ready for his next at-bat. Brooke grabbed her phone. She had to text Aubrey and tell her what had happened.

Unfortunately, one of the assistant coaches saw what she was doing and frowned.

"I don't know about softball players," he said, "but baseball players don't have cell phones in the dugout."

She waited until he wasn't looking, then continued her message. This information was too important to wait.

"You won't believe it," she wrote. "Alex just sat down and talked to me. He said he'll never forget my catch. He says he owes me."

Aubrey's response was instant. "OMG," she wrote. "You're the luckiest girl in the world."

Chapter 20

The doctor cleared Brooke on Monday, and her first game was the next day against Mountlake Terrace. Unfortunately, returning to play wasn't as easy as she had hoped. She was jumpy. She was afraid the ball was going to hit her again, and during her first at-bat she jumped away from the plate even though the pitch wasn't anywhere near her. She struck out her first two at-bats before getting a bloop single in the bottom of the sixth. It was just over the third baseman's hands and was more luck than anything, but she'd take it anyway. In the field, she was solid, and she caught a throw from Skinny and slapped it on the runner's foot just before he touched second base.

"Out!" the umpire yelled.

"It's nice to have you back," Skinny said as they walked off the field.

They won the game easily, beating the Hawks 6-2. Jamie got two singles and a double, and Blake had a triple. As always, Alex was stellar on the mound.

Their next game was against Glacier Peak, and once again they cruised. Brooke still felt a little uneasy at the plate, but she was inspired when she looked in the stands and saw her dad and two other guys wearing suits. No doubt they were his partners from the firm. They cheered as she got a single in the second and laid down a perfect sacrifice bunt in the fourth. The loudest cheer, however, came in the fifth inning, when she,

Jamie, and Blake turned a magnificent double play to end the inning.

The highlight of the game, at least as far as Brooke was concerned, came the next inning, in the dugout, when Alex sat down next to her.

"Do you mind if I ask a question?" she asked him.

He shrugged.

"That day when Christian hit me with the pitch, did you hit him on purpose?"

He smiled.

"Why?" she asked.

"No one hits my shortstop and gets away with it. Especially if that shortstop is you."

It was his turn to bat, so he didn't get a chance to elaborate. But Brooke was happy anyway. The fact he had called her 'his shortstop' was more than enough for her. It was the best compliment she could have ever received. She sent Aubrey a text.

"OMG," Aubrey wrote back. "Then what did he say?"

"He said, 'Especially if that shortstop is you.'"

"OMG. He likes you. There's no doubt about it."

"No way."

"WAY," Aubrey responded.

That night, as Brooke climbed into her bed, she kept repeating Alex's words over and over in her head. She was obsessed with what he had said.

"No one hits my shortstop and gets away with it. Especially if that shortstop is you."

It was the second sentence that had her so fixated.

"Especially if that shortstop is you."

What did it mean? Aubrey was convinced it was Alex's way of telling Brooke, in a very subtle way, that he liked her. But even if that were true, what did it mean? Did he 'like' like her, as in how friends like one another, or 'really' like her, as in boyfriend-girlfriend type of stuff? And if it was the boyfriend-girlfriend type of stuff, how could that be, since he already had a girlfriend?

She tossed and turned all night. It was amazing how one little sentence could cost her so much sleep.

Chapter 21

The next day, life got even better. It was Friday, so like every Friday, everyone was excited for the weekend and a couple of days off. Brooke sat at a table in the school cafeteria eating lunch with Naomi, Faith, and Aubrey. Aubrey was in the middle of giving them the latest gossip when her eyes got big and she stopped mid-sentence. The color drained from her face. Brooke turned to see what she was looking at and saw Alex standing right behind her.

"Hi," he said. "I wanted to stop by and see how you're doing."

"Good," she said. "How about you?"

"Good. My parents are out of town this weekend, so I'm having a party at my house tonight, and I'm inviting all the players on the team, so you can come if you'd like. And feel free to bring anyone you want, so if you all want to come, that'd be great. I've heard a lot of good things about the softball team this year. It'd be nice to meet you all."

The minute he left, Aubrey nearly passed out. "Oh my God," she said. "Someone pinch me. I think I'm dreaming. No, wait. This dream is too good. Don't pinch me. I don't want to wake up. Ever."

"I can't believe it," Naomi said. "We're invited to a party at Alex Anderson's house. I never thought I'd see the day. It's amazing."

"No it's not," Faith said. "It's not that big a deal."

"It isn't?" Naomi asked.

"No," Faith said.

"So you don't want to go?"

"Of course I want to go. It's just not that big a deal."

They all laughed. Faith could be so ridiculous at times.

The party was all Brooke could think about the rest of the day. In math class, they had a pop quiz, and she couldn't concentrate at all, so she knew she bombed it for sure, but it didn't matter because she was going to Alex's party that night. She had a lot to do in the meantime. She had to pick out something to wear, do her hair, get some breath mints, the works. She barely managed to get ready in time. The girls picked her up at 8:30 pm and they rode together in Faith's car to Alex's house. His dad was some type of big-time real estate developer and they lived in a ritzy part of town in the biggest house Brooke had ever seen. It was more like a mansion than a house. It had a huge swimming pool in the back and a gorgeous view of the Cascade mountains.

"Thanks for coming," Alex said as he greeted them at the door. Already a lot of kids were there, mostly seniors, but some juniors and sophomores. The place was packed, and people milled about in just about every room. Most of the baseball team was there, but Brooke hardly recognized them. She had rarely seen them without their uniforms or practice gear. Terrell, Skinny, and Blake sat in the living room playing a video game on the largest flat-screen television Brooke had ever seen.

They looked up the minute the girls walked into the room. Blake motioned to Terrell.

"Show some manners, schmuck," he said. "Give Brooke your chair."

Terrell shook his head, clearly disgusted. "Let me guess. Since she's a lady, she gets my chair?"

"No," Blake said. "Since she's an infielder, she gets your chair. We infielders stick together."

Terrell shook his head, but he did as told. Somewhat hesitantly, and not knowing what else to do, Brooke took his seat.

"You any good at video games?" Blake asked.

"Not really," Brooke said. To be perfectly honest, she had never liked video games much. Except Rock Band. But she wasn't going to tell Blake that.

"This is my favorite fighting game," Blake said. "Here, I'll teach you."

He handed her a controller and showed her how to play, and she spent the next ten minutes doing her best. And it was actually pretty fun. Everyone, including Alex, cheered as her fighter punched Blake's fighter and knocked him over the edge of a balcony onto the ground below. She jumped over the balcony and finished him off.

"You're certain you've never played this game before?" Blake asked.

They were about to play again when Alex stepped in. "I'm going to steal the ladies away for a minute, Blake. I want to show them around a little."

Blake nodded, then turned to Brooke. "You come back. I want a rematch."

Alex led them into the kitchen. It was the largest, fanciest kitchen Brooke had ever seen. It had an island in the middle that was covered with chips, salsa, soda and just about every other party food you could imagine.

"Help yourself to whatever you'd like," he said. "But go easy on the Cheesy Puffs. They're really spicy. They finished Skinny off at the last party."

He led them outside, showed them the pool (it had a waterfall on one side), then led them upstairs to show them the rest of the house. Every room was immaculate. Even his bedroom. It was large but simple, with sports posters on the walls, including a large poster of Randy Johnson over his desk.

"You like Randy Johnson?" Brooke asked.

He nodded. "He's my hero. I wish he still played for the Mariners."

There was another room just down the hall from Alex's room. Alex tried to skip it, but the girls spotted it and headed inside.

Brooke was amazed. The entire room was filled with trophies. Alex's trophies. There were trophies in every shape, size, and color imaginable.

"How embarrassing," he said. "This room was my dad's idea. He's into this type of stuff."

"It's amazing," Brooke said.

"You'll recognize that one," he said, and pointed at a small podium in the exact middle of the room. Sitting on it was a dirt-stained baseball on a fancy display base. Brooke's eyes got big as she realized what it was. It was the ball she had caught to save his no-hitter.

"Every time my dad has guests over," Alex said, "he brings them up here to show them that ball. It's his pride and joy. Mine, too."

They headed downstairs and rejoined the party. A couple more people arrived, so Alex went to greet them and left the girls in the dining room to mingle with other guests. It was great fun. Brooke saw several people from her classes, and met several new ones, including some of the school's volleyball players. Apparently they were Alyssa's friends.

Remarkably, however, she didn't see Alyssa. That seemed strange. It was Alex's party, but his girlfriend wasn't here?

She mingled from room to room for several hours and even had her rematch with Blake. Remarkably, she won again. In the meantime, Naomi, Faith, and Aubrey spent the majority of the night hanging out with Blake, Terrell, JJ, and Skinny, and they all seemed to get along really well.

"You guys should come to one of our games," Naomi said. "You'll be impressed."

"I'm kind of worried," Terrell joked. "If you girls all play like Brooke, we guys are in big trouble. Before we know it, you'll take over the baseball team."

"I don't think you've got anything to worry about," Naomi said. "Brooke's the only one of us who's brave enough to try baseball."

"When you say brave," Faith asked, "do you mean crazy?"

They laughed.

The highlight of the night came an hour later, when Alex asked Brooke to step out on the patio with him. They stood near the edge of the pool, alone.

"I just wanted to thank you again for coming," he said. "It means a lot to me to have you here. I know this has been a tough season for you, dealing with the team and all, especially Blake."

"He seems to like me now," she said, trying to put a light spin on things.

"You can say that again," he said. "You should have seen him that night Christian hit you in the head. He was a wreck. He wanted to hunt Christian down and kill him on the spot. It took all of us to calm him down and keep him from doing something stupid. I'm still worried about next week's game."

Brooke's eyes widened. She had forgotten. Next week was the big rematch with Alderwood.

"It's going to be ugly," Alex continued. "I know it. We've had issues with Christian in the past. Ever since Little League. Twice we've had fights."

"Fights?" Brooke asked. "During games?"

Alex nodded. "It happens sometimes, especially when Christian is involved. One year he beaned JJ in the back. JJ charged the mound. It was ugly. And another year he hit Skinny. I had to get ten stitches in my forehead after that fight. Right above my eye. I still have the scar if you look closely."

She did, and he was right. It was barely visible, but it was there, just above his right eye. It was probably the only flaw he had.

Brooke's thoughts returned to what he had just said. She still couldn't believe it. "Boys fight during games?" she asked.

"Sometimes. Don't you girls?"

Brooke shook her head. To be honest, she had never even heard of such a thing. Girls were notorious for being catty and talking bad about one another (including their own teammates), but she had never heard of a fight during a game.

"What do you do?" she asked.

"What do you mean?" he asked.

"During a fight. What do you do?"

"Just punch anyone who comes near you. And I usually stay close to Blake or Skinny. That way, if I get in trouble, they can come to my rescue."

She nodded. Now she was really nervous about the upcoming game. When she had initially agreed to play for the baseball team, she hadn't known there would be any fights involved.

"But enough of that," Alex said. "We'll worry about that next week. We're supposed to be having fun right now. So tell me a little about you. You're my star shortstop and I hardly know anything about you."

92

They spent the next hour or so talking. She told him about her, and he told her about him. He was originally from California (Laguna Beach), but his family moved to Seattle when he was ten. He had an older brother named James who was a sophomore at UCLA.

Brooke's heart stopped. Alex was so gorgeous she could hardly imagine what an older brother would look like.

Like all teenage boys, he loved loud, obnoxious music, action movies (the Rock was his favorite actor), and cars. He took her down to the garage to show her his car.

It was a silver Porsche. She didn't know what type, and she really didn't care. To her, any Porsche was a good Porsche.

"You want to go for a spin?" he asked.

"Yeah," she said, maybe a little too enthusiastically.

It was the nicest car she had ever seen. All leather interior, rocking stereo, voice-activated ignition, the works. And it handled like a dream. They zipped around corners with ease.

"Can you drive a clutch?" he asked.

She nodded.

"Give it a try," he said, hopping out at a stop sign and switching seats with her.

She could hardly believe what was happening. She was just about to drive a Porsche. It was a small step up (to say the least) from her Volkswagen Jetta.

But then something unexpected happened. She feathered the clutch wrong, the car lurched forward violently, then died and came to an abrupt halt. They laughed as Alex's phone, which he had set on the console between them, flew into the back of the car.

"I forgot to mention," he said, "the clutch is a little touchy. Sometimes it's easier to start in second."

She tried to follow his instructions and shift the car into second, but the gearshift wouldn't budge.

"It's also a little finicky," he said. "Here, I'll show you."

He put his hand on top of hers and helped her shift into second. The minute his hand touched hers, her heart raced and the temperature in the car increased by at least ten degrees, maybe more. Brooke didn't fully recover until he removed his hand from hers.

"That should do it," he said. "Now give it a try."

And she did. The takeoff was a little rough, but fun nonetheless. The car had amazing power and cornered like a dream. She drove it around the block and headed back toward Alex's house. Aubrey greeted them the minute they pulled into the driveway.

"Tell me I did not see that," she said.

"See what?" Brooke asked.

"You driving a Porsche. With Alex in the passenger seat next to you."

Brooke smiled.

"Oh my God," Aubrey said. "You're the coolest girl in the world."

Brooke and Alex returned to the patio and continued talking for another hour, maybe two. Unfortunately, things soured a little as time went on. It had been a great night, but there was one thing Brooke had to know.

"Where's Alyssa?" she asked. "I haven't seen her all night."

Alex's eyes got big for a second, then returned to normal. "She couldn't make it," he said.

And then Brooke thought of something else. There was another person she hadn't seen all night.

"And Jamie?" she asked. "I've seen the rest of the team, but not him. It's not the same without him around."

Alex's eyes got big again, even bigger than when she had asked about Alyssa. "He couldn't make it, either," he said. "Apparently something came up. I'm going to get something to drink. Do you want anything?"

"I'm okay," she said.

He walked away, into the kitchen, and she didn't see him again that night.

Chapter 22

Coach West was about to begin his traditional pre-practice speech when Blake stepped forward with a request.

"Coach," he said. "Some of the guys and I were talking, and we were wondering, we know it's unusual to take a day off from practice, especially with a big game like Alderwood coming up soon, but well the softball team has a game today, and they invited us, and it means a lot to them because they got their new scoreboard—"

"They got their new scoreboard?" Coach West asked.

"Yeah," Blake answered. "They've had it for awhile, but it just got installed, so today is the first day they're going to use it, and it's kind of a big deal, and well we'll make up practice tomorrow if you want, and it seems appropriate since Brooke came from the softball team and—"

Alex came to his rescue. "What Blake is trying to say," he said, "is we want to go."

Coach West raised an eyebrow. "You guys have never shown any interest in the softball team before," he said. "Why now?"

They all shot glances at Brooke.

Coach West nodded. "Is it true? Do you all want to go?"

It was unanimous.

"And we're serious," Alex said. "We'll make up the practice tomorrow if you want."

Coach West smiled. "I don't think there'll be any need for that," he said. "This is something we should have done years ago. If I remember right, the girls are four-time defending WesCo South champions, right Brooke?"

"Five," Brooke said, correcting him.

"Even better," he said. "They definitely deserve the attention. Have fun."

Brooke could hardly believe it. These were the same boys who originally wanted nothing to do with her. Now, they were skipping their own practice, two days before the huge rematch with Alderwood, to support the softball team.

Coach West stopped her briefly as she was rounding up her stuff. "I told you," he said. "If you gave them a chance, they'd come around. They're a good bunch."

"You can say that again," she said with a smile.

The girls on the softball team took a break from their warm-ups as they all walked up. Brooke watched, wide-eyed, as Faith said hello to Blake.

"You made it," she said. "I hoped you'd come."

"I told you Coach West would let us. He's pretty cool. He had no problem with it at all. Oh, and I brought you this. You said you like white roses."

He handed her a single, white, long-stemmed rose.

"Blake," she said, a huge smile on her lips. "You're so sweet. Thank you. I love it. But I gotta go for now. The game's about to start."

She took the rose and headed back to the dugout. Brooke beat her there. She had to know what was going on.

"You and Blake?" she asked. She couldn't believe it.

"He's amazing," Faith said. "He called me the night after the party. I usually prefer texting, but Blake doesn't spell too well, so we talked instead, until 2:00 in the morning. We would have talked longer but my mom made me hang up. He's so sweet."

"Blake?" Brooke asked.

"Oh, I know," Faith said. "He seems all rough and gruff on the outside, but once you get to know him, he's a big teddy bear."

Brooke almost fell over. A teddy bear?

"And guess what?" she said. "He can bench press over three hundred pounds. That's like you and me combined. Plus some."

She was about to say something more when Naomi rushed up, a big smile on her face. "You guys won't believe it," she said. "Remember how I was talking with Terrell at the party? Guess what? He just asked me out. We're going out this weekend."

Brooke was in heaven. She had never seen her friends so happy. They were completely ecstatic.

She turned to Aubrey. "What about you?"

"I'm working on it," Aubrey said as she glanced at the bleachers, where all the boys were sitting, waiting anxiously for the game to begin. Almost on cue, JJ waved at her.

They would have talked more, but Coach Jennings called the girls over for a brief pregame meeting. Brooke walked over and was about to sit down with the boys when Jamie stood up and called out to Coach Jennings.

"Coach," he said. "Is Brooke still on your roster?"

"I think so," she said. "I meant to remove her, but to be honest, I forgot completely about it."

98

"Then she's still eligible to play for you if she's available, right?"

Coach Jennings nodded. She didn't know where Jamie was going with this.

"Technically," Jamie continued, "she's a baseball player now, but we'd be willing to loan her to you for a day, if you'd like. But we get her back when the game is over."

Skinny stood up next to Jamie. "And I'll vouch for her," he said. "She won't let you down."

They all laughed.

Coach Jennings looked at Brooke. "What do you think?" she asked. "We could always use an All-Star shortstop."

"Come on, Brooke," Jamie said. "You always get to see us play baseball. Now we want to see you play softball."

Brooke was hesitant. "The game's about to begin," she said. "I left all my gear in my car."

"Leave that to me," Terrell said. He was the fastest player on the team. He grabbed Brooke's keys from her, darted across the field to the parking lot, grabbed her bag, and was back in a flash.

"I guess I've got no choice," she said upon his return.

Everyone cheered.

It was the fastest change Brooke had ever made, and she was still struggling with her left cleat as she took the field to start the game. And then she noticed it.

The new scoreboard. It was in left field, in the exact same position as the old one, but it was at least twice as big, and it was one of the fanciest scoreboards she had ever seen. It had a video screen on one side where each girl's name, number, and photo appeared as she came up to bat.

"Do you like it?" Naomi asked.

"I love it," Brooke said.

The game began, and it was great fun. With all the boys there, it was the biggest crowd the softball team had ever had. And it was rowdy. The boys cheered with every pitch, and they went crazy when Brooke made a running catch in foul territory to end the third inning. Overall, she had a good game (she got a single and a sacrifice to score a run), but the night belonged to the other girls. They were determined to impress the boys, and boy did they. Aubrey had three singles, Naomi a double and a triple, and Faith launched a massive home run over the new scoreboard in left. It was the longest shot she had ever hit.

"That's my type of girl," Blake said with a smile.

It was a blowout. Silver Lake won 10-0.

Chapter 23

Brooke was nervous. The whole team was. It was the big day. The rematch with Alderwood. Brooke was still worried about what Alex had told her at the party. She didn't know what she'd do if a fight started. She'd never been in a fight before.

Coach West called Blake over to the dugout just before the game started. Brooke was at the opposite end of the dugout, watching Alderwood warm up in the infield, but she could still hear his words. "I'm going to change the batting order today," he told Blake. "You're going to bat after Brooke."

"After Brooke?" Blake asked. That was unusual. Since he was their main power hitter, he usually batted in the fourth spot, right in front of their other power hitter, Skinny.

"I want you in the on-deck circle when Brooke bats," Coach West said. "That way, if Christian throws at her again, you'll be closer to the mound."

"And?" Blake asked.

"If he throws at her, I want you to take care of things the old-fashioned way. Understood?"

Blake nodded. Apparently he knew what that meant. Brooke wasn't exactly certain, but she had a good idea, too.

"And Blake," Coach West continued, "since I'm your coach, if anyone found out I gave you those instructions, I'd get in a lot of trouble."

Blake nodded. "You never told me nothing," he said.

"You're a good boy," Coach West said.

Now Brooke was really nervous. She could hardly believe it. Alex wasn't the only one who thought something bad was going to happen today. Coach West thought so, too.

The game went okay for the first two innings. Just like the first game, it was a classic pitcher's duel between Christian and Alex. Neither boy had given up a hit when Brooke stepped into the batter's box to take her first at-bat in the bottom of the third inning.

Normally, Brooke loved batting. It was one of her favorite things in the whole world. But not today. Today, she was scared breathless. The minute she stepped into the batter's box, she started having flashes of her first at-bat against Christian. She could still hear the sound of the ball as it struck the side of her helmet. Her head started to throb just thinking about it.

And Christian didn't make her feel any better. He stood on the mound, staring down at her from above, smiling menacingly.

"Don't even think about it," Blake said from his spot in the on-deck circle.

"Look at that," Christian told Brooke. "They got you a bodyguard. How sweet."

His first pitch was an absolute fireball. Pure heat, straight down the middle. Brooke swung and missed.

She wasn't happy she had missed the pitch, but she was relieved. At least he hadn't thrown at her.

She snuck a quick peek at her dad in the stands. He looked as nervous as she felt.

The second pitch was low for ball one. The third was low as well. The fourth was straight down the middle. She turned and hit it as hard as she could, straight back at the mound. Christian lunged but missed it by an inch. It flew into center for a single.

Now he was mad. He couldn't believe he had given up a hit. To a girl.

Unfortunately, Blake struck out to end the inning, and the pitcher's duel continued from there. The game was still scoreless when Brooke batted again in the sixth.

This time, she was a little more comfortable stepping up to the plate. Christian hadn't tried to hit her the first time; maybe he wouldn't try this time, either. Maybe nothing ugly would happen today after all. Maybe it would just be a good, old-fashioned, well-played game.

But then it happened. The very first pitch came right at her, but unlike the first game, it didn't hit her square in the head this time. Instead, it just grazed the side of her helmet, but it was enough to knock her to the ground anyway. When she recovered and got back to her feet, the entire infield was complete pandemonium. Blake had charged the mound instantly, and he was on top of Christian pounding him like there was no tomorrow. In the meantime, the Eagles' catcher and first baseman were on top of him, pounding on him, and Skinny, Terrell, and JJ were on top of them. A few feet to the side was another pile of bodies, including mostly everyone else from both teams. The umpires and coaches were trying to pull them apart, but they were outnumbered and weren't making much progress.

Brooke didn't know what to do. She was still in shock, since she had narrowly avoided another trip to the emergency room, and she felt terrible, just standing there at home plate, by herself, doing nothing, while the boys were fighting to protect her. Not knowing what else to do, she wandered slowly toward the nearest pile.

She didn't know what she was going to do when she got there, but she felt she needed to go anyway.

When she got there, something unexpected happened. Christian loomed up in front of her. He had somehow managed to pull himself free from the mass of struggling bodies. Blake had clearly gotten in some good shots. Blood ran from the side of Christian's mouth and one eye was swelling shut. Regardless, he was laughing hysterically, like he was enjoying the whole terrible thing.

The sound of his laughter snapped something inside of Brooke, and she did the one thing she thought she'd never do. She waited until he turned to face her, then punched him in the face as hard as she could.

He went down in a heap.

Chapter 24

Brooke was a legend at Silver Lake High School. Word of what she had done spread through the school like wildfire. She was the girl who knocked out the infamous Christian Parkinson, the most hated rival the school's baseball team had ever had.

Unfortunately, she wasn't there to enjoy it. The school's athletic director suspended every member of the team for their roles in the fracas, and they got differing lengths of time based on their particular role. Blake got the longest suspension (a week), Brooke got three days, and everyone else (including Coach West) got a day. But it didn't matter to Brooke, because she needed some time away from school to respond to all of the text messages she received. By noon of the first day, she had received 354 messages from 152 different people, all wanting to know the details of the fight. Like all teenage girls, Brooke loved text messages, but she actually started to get frustrated because her phone was (literally) on the verge of exploding all morning long. In the time it took her to respond to one message, she'd get five more.

Her FaceBook account was no different. In one day, she got new friend requests from 120 different people. Most of them were people she had never even heard of.

And she got a nickname (not that she really wanted one). Everyone called her "Boxin' Brooke" and the members of the school's wrestling team named her an honorary (but unofficial) member of the squad.

Even her dad was impressed. He tried to do the proper grown-up thing and tell her fighting was never a solution to a problem, but he couldn't keep up the charade for long.

"Where'd you learn to punch like that?" he asked.

Brooke shrugged.

"That kid never had a chance. I bet you broke his nose. It was spectacular."

Later, she heard him in his den, speaking with one of his friends on the phone. He had his laptop computer on the desk in front of him. "Go to YouTube," he said. "What? Yeah, some kid took a video of it using his phone. It's pretty dark, but you can still see things okay. Do you see it? Watch carefully. Right at the end you'll see Brooke. Can you believe it? Man that girl can punch. Look at her form. It reminds me of Tyson back in his prime."

Brooke smiled. In a strange sort of way, it was fun being Boxin' Brooke. The only bad thing was her hand. She had punched Christian so hard she had shattered two of her nails.

That sucked.

Chapter 25

Brooke sat in the school cafeteria, eating lunch with Naomi, Aubrey, and Faith. It was her first day back at school following her suspension. Faith was in the middle of complaining about her French teacher (apparently, she had misplaced one of Faith's assignments for the third time this year), when Jamie walked by. He didn't say anything, but his appearance immediately got their attention. Faith stopped her story mid-sentence. Everyone remained silent until he was out of earshot.

"I still can't believe it," Naomi said.

"Me, neither," Faith said. "It blows my mind."

Brooke looked at them. "What?" she asked.

"You haven't heard?" Aubrey asked. "Where've you been? It's been all over school the past few days."

"I've been at home," Brooke said. "I was suspended, remember?"

"Oh yeah. Anyway, do you remember awhile back when I told you Alex got mad at Alyssa because she went to a movie with another guy? Guess what? It was Jamie."

Brooke's mouth fell open. Now it all made sense. She couldn't believe she hadn't figured it out earlier. The game against Edmonds when Alex had barked at Jamie for making an error. Now she knew why he had acted so out of character and had been so mad. It had nothing to do with the error. It was about Alyssa. He was mad because she had gone out with Jamie. And the night at Alex's party. No wonder Jamie and Alyssa weren't there. They were probably together.

As if on cue, Aubrey added, "Apparently they went out again."

"No way," Faith and Naomi said.

Brooke's mind was on overdrive. Jamie and Alyssa? She couldn't believe it.

Aubrey continued. "Apparently Alyssa told the girls on the volleyball team she really likes Jamie, and she's thinking about breaking up with Alex so she can be with him. She even went to Alex's house one night to do it, but Alex got so upset she chickened out and didn't go through with it. And now she doesn't know what to do."

She wasn't the only one. Brooke just sat there, absolutely speechless, her head spinning. She didn't say anything the remainder of the lunch break.

That night, after practice, things got ugly. Brooke was loading her bag into the trunk of her car when she heard a sound and looked up. Most of the rest of the baseball team had already left, so the parking lot was empty with the exception of two cars, a Porsche and a Camaro, parked side-by-side at the far end of the lot. Alex and Jamie stood between the cars, talking about something. Brooke knew she shouldn't eavesdrop on their conversation, but after what she had learned at school earlier in the day, she couldn't help herself. And immediately she got worried, because the conversation wasn't pleasant.

"You need to stay away from her," Alex said. His face was red, and he was clearly frustrated. "I'm not going to tell you again."

"She's not your property," Jamie responded. "She can do whatever she wants. If she wants to see me, that's her choice."

"You and I have been friends a long time," Alex said. "I've never asked you for much. But I'm asking for one thing – stay away from her. You know she's my girlfriend."

"Have you spoken to her?" Jamie asked.

"I don't need to," Alex said, growing even more frustrated. "I need to speak with you. And you need to do what I say. I'm not going to tell you again."

"Or what?" Jamie asked. Like most people, he didn't like threats.

Brooke's heart was about to break. She was watching the two nicest boys on the team, the two boys she cared about the most, threatening one another. It was going to explode.

And it did. Alex pushed Jamie with both hands, right in the chest, as hard as he could. Jamie fell back against his Camaro but was able to catch himself before he dropped to the ground. He righted himself, then turned back to face Alex. There was rage in his eyes.

The fight was on. Alex got in a couple of blows, including one that hit Jamie in the mouth and bloodied his lip. But Jamie turned the tide quickly. He wasn't as tall as Alex, but he was a lot bulkier, more muscular, and lightning quick. He punched Alex in the stomach, then in the chest, then in the stomach again. Alex fell to the ground gasping for breath. Jamie jumped on him and pummeled him repeatedly.

Brooke darted toward them as fast as she could. She had to do something. She couldn't let this continue, and she got there just in time. Jamie was about to punch Alex in the face when she grabbed him from behind.

"No!" she yelled. "Jamie, please stop."

That was all it took. The sound of her voice snapped Jamie out of his frenzy and he returned to

109

normal. He covered his eyes in shame as he looked down at Alex and realized what he had done.

"Alex," he said. "I'm sorry. I never thought this would happen."

He got up, climbed into his Camaro, and drove off. A tear ran down his cheek as he disappeared from view.

Brooke tried to help Alex, but he pushed her away. He was furious. He climbed up and got into his Porsche.

"Alex," she asked. "Are you okay?"

"I'm fine," he said, as he spit blood out of his mouth.

"Where are you going?"

"To find Alyssa," he said. "I'm going to put an end to this one way or another."

He raced off.

Chapter 26

Brooke paced from one side of her bedroom to the other for most of the night. She called Aubrey and Naomi, but they didn't know what to do either. But then she got a call from a number she didn't recognize. Usually, she didn't answer unfamiliar numbers, but this time she did, hoping it was someone who knew something, anything, about Alex. And it was. It was Blake.

"Brooke," Blake said. "I got your number from Faith. We guys are at Alex's right now. We need you to come over as fast as you can. Alex locked himself in his room and he won't come out. He says he's quitting the team."

"What happened?" she asked.

"He went over to Alyssa's and she broke up with him. He's a mess. He won't listen to anyone. We're hoping he'll listen to you."

She didn't know why he would, why he would treat her any different than any other member of the team, but at the same time she had to do something. She jumped in her car and raced to his house as fast as she could. She was amazed she didn't get a speeding ticket. When she got there, several members of the team were in the upstairs hall outside Alex's room. They looked terrible. They were worried sick.

"He won't even respond anymore," Blake said. "I don't know what to do. JJ and Terrell are worried he's going to hurt himself. They want me to kick the door in."

Brooke thought for a minute. "Where are his parents?"

"We're not certain. No one has their numbers. They go out of town a lot."

Great, Brooke thought. So much for asking for their help.

"Do you think I should kick it in?" Blake asked.

To be perfectly honest, Brooke didn't know what to do. She had never been in this type of situation before. But kicking in the door seemed so drastic. She wanted to try something else before they went to that extreme.

"Let me try something first," she said. She walked up to Alex's door and confirmed it was locked.

"Alex," she said through the door. "It's me, Brooke. Are you okay?"

There was no response.

"Alex," she said. "Please let me in."

There was no response.

She was really starting to sweat now. She was nervous, and all the boys were watching her wide-eyed, hoping she could do something, and that was making her even more nervous. Blake stood at the far end of the hall, pounding his forehead against the wall.

Then she thought of something.

"Alex," she said. "Do you remember that time, awhile back, when we were sitting in the dugout and you thanked me for saving your no-hitter? You told me if I ever needed anything, anything at all, I just needed to ask and you would make it happen. I'm asking now. I need you to open the door and let me in."

There was a painfully long silence. At first she thought it hadn't worked, her plea had fallen on deaf ears, but then it happened. The lock clicked, and the door opened just a hair, just enough for her to squeeze in and close the door behind her. Alex was on the bed, lying on his back, staring blankly at the ceiling. His eyes were bloodshot and he'd clearly been crying. A lamp was on the floor in pieces.

She didn't know what to say, so she just sat down on the bed next to him.

"You shouldn't have come," he said. "This isn't your concern."

"It is," she said. "I may be the new kid on the team, but it's still my team. And if a member of the team is in trouble, I'm in trouble."

He didn't know what to say in response, so he said nothing. Instead, he rolled onto his stomach and buried his head in his pillow.

"The guys are worried about you," Brooke said. "Just about everyone's out there. And Blake is so upset he's banging his head against the wall. I've never seen anything like it."

"He does that sometimes," Alex said.

"He told me you're quitting the team."

"I have no choice," he said. "I can't go on like this after all that's happened. I'm a wreck. I can't focus at all. There's no way I can pitch. You guys will be better off without me."

"No we won't," Brooke said. "We need you, Alex. And not just for your pitching. You're our leader. Everyone looks up to you. We respect you. And we care about you. If we didn't, why would we all be here right now? From what I've heard, things are getting pretty hot between Blake and Faith. I bet he'd rather be with her tonight, at a movie or something, but he's not. He's here with you, and he's worried out of his mind."

Alex rolled over, revealing his face. She hoped that was a good sign, a sign she was making some progress. At least a little.

"Blake," Alex sighed. "He's always been the sensitive one. Every group has one. One time, in Little League, JJ broke his leg and Blake was so worried he started crying."

Brooke's mouth nearly fell open. Blake cried?

"But don't tell him I told you," Alex said. "Or he'll beat me up for sure."

"I won't say a thing," Brooke said.

There was a long silence.

"How are you feeling?" she asked.

He gave her a funny look, as if to say, "What do you think?"

"Sorry," she said. "That was a dumb question. I'll assume things didn't go well with Alyssa."

"She broke up with me," he said. "She started crying. She said she was sorry, she didn't mean to hurt me, but she just couldn't help it. She's got feelings for Jamie."

Brooke nodded. She didn't know what to say.

"But I don't blame her," Alex said. "Jamie's a great guy. We've been friends forever. I can't believe we got into a fight. I'm sorry you had to see that."

"It's no big deal," she said. "I'm just glad neither of you got hurt." Then she remembered the blood coming from his mouth when she last saw him. "Did you?"

"I'm fine," he said. "I guess I should have seen this coming a long time ago. Alyssa and I have had issues for awhile now. At least six months, maybe more. I noticed something was different between us even before she started seeing Jamie. It was almost like the spark between us had gone away. But I wasn't willing to give up. She and I had gone out for so long, almost two years, that I thought things would get better eventually, if I just stayed patient. And one day I thought we would eventually get—"

114

His words trailed off. He didn't want to finish the sentence.

"I guess I was just being silly," he continued. "What do our parents say? Acting like a teenager?"

Brooke groaned. Her dad had used that expression many times over the years. Just thinking about it made her mad.

There was a long silence.

"I guess all things end eventually," he said. "Including relationships. Have you ever been through something like this?"

Brooke shook her head. Sadly, her longest relationship had only lasted six months. Maybe less.

"Not really," she said. "But I can still understand."

"I still remember when I first started seeing Alyssa," he said. "Back when we were sophomores. There was word around school Farrah Hemingway wanted to hook up with me. Do you know her?"

Brooke shook her head. She had never heard that name before.

"She was a senior at the time," Alex said. "She was the captain of the cheerleading team. She had just broken up with her boyfriend and was looking for a replacement. The guys said I would be a legend if I hooked up with her. Since she was an older girl and all. And I'll give her credit. She was hot. She was tall and thin, with a great—"

"I don't need all the details," Brooke interrupted. She put special emphasis on the word 'all.'

"Sorry," he said. "Anyway, the guys wanted me to hook up with her, but then I met Alyssa and she was so perfect. We got along so well, and her smile was amazing. All she had to do was look at me and it made me warm all over. I know it probably sounds stupid, but it's true."

Brooke was speechless. There was a small tear in the corner of her eye. It didn't sound stupid at all. Actually, it was one of the most touching things she had ever heard.

Alex sat up. Amazingly, he looked a little better. Not much, but a little. Maybe talking was helping him.

"I bet you never thought it would come to this," he said.

"What?" she asked.

"When you joined the team," he said. "I bet you never thought you'd end up sitting in the pitcher's bedroom trying to convince him not to quit the team."

Brooke smiled. "A lot of things have happened I didn't expect," she said. "I never expected to have such a tough time finding my place on the team. I never expected to get hit in the head by a pitch. And I definitely never expected to punch out the opposing pitcher. But that's the way it goes sometimes. Sometimes you just have to deal with what happens and move on the best you can."

"I'm not as strong as you," he said. "A girl who plays baseball? It doesn't get any stronger than that. I'm not certain I can move on."

"You can," she said. "And you're stronger than you realize, Alex. You just need to give it some time. Everything will be okay. I hope."

"I hope?" he asked.

"Well," she said, "it's not like I have a crystal ball or something. But I have faith. And you need to have faith, too."

He sighed, then nodded.

"Can we head back out now?" Brooke asked. "With the others? They're probably wondering how things are going in here. And I think I can still hear Blake hitting his head on the wall."

They listened, and she was right. There was a steady thumping coming from down the hall.

"I hope he doesn't need stitches again," Alex said.

"Stitches?" Brooke asked.

"It happened once," Alex said. "A few years back. He got really upset when he struck out to end a game. We spent a couple of hours in the ER."

They stood up, he straightened out his clothes to make them somewhat presentable, and together they walked into the hall.

Chapter 27

The next day, Brooke's softball team had a tournament in Tacoma, a city about half an hour south of Seattle. Their first game was against a team from Oregon called the Pony Express. It was a good game, and the Angels trailed most of the way, but they came back to win 3-2 in the final inning. Brooke got a single and a double and Faith hit a solo home run.

"Where's all this power coming from lately?" Brooke asked as they rounded up their stuff. They still had another game, but they had a couple of hours until it began.

"Blake's been giving me some tips," Faith said. "He knows a lot about power hitting."

Brooke smiled. She should have known better.

"So," Aubrey said, joining in from the side. "How's Alex today? Have you spoken to him?"

Brooke nodded. "He called me just before the game. He's doing fine. He still seems a little sad, but he's definitely better than yesterday."

"Good," she said. "Hopefully he'll be better soon. But I still can't believe it. Alyssa had two of the hottest boys in school fighting over her. And it was an actual fist fight. It's so romantic. She's the coolest girl in school."

"Wait a minute," Brooke said. "I thought I was the coolest girl in school?"

"That was last week," Aubrey said. "This week, it's Alyssa."

Brooke sighed. Fame was so fleeting.

"So anyway," Faith said. "What's your status?"

Brooke raised an eyebrow. She didn't know what Faith was talking about.

"With Alex? Now that he and Alyssa are a thing of the past, the door is wide open for someone new to step inside. Someone like you."

Brooke's heart missed a beat. She had been so busy lately, so preoccupied with everything that had happened, she hadn't had a chance to think about it.

"I think he likes you," Aubrey said.

"Me, too," Faith said. "I saw how he was looking at you at the party. He was just holding himself back because he was confused about his relationship with Alyssa. But now that that's over, who knows?"

Brooke was hopeful, but she didn't have much time to think about it. Something, or to be more precise, someone, caught her eye.

There was a Little League team playing a game on an adjacent field. Brooke watched as the team's shortstop, a little girl with a long, black ponytail, fielded a grounder and whipped it to first. Brooke recognized her instantly.

It was Kat. Jamie's sister.

She looked in the stands, and there he sat, watching Kat attentively.

"Way to go, sis," he said as she trotted off the field to end the inning. "Great throw."

She was all smiles as she headed into the dugout.

Brooke was so jealous. If only she had had an older brother to impress like that.

She turned to Faith and Aubrey. They were busy talking and hadn't seen Jamie yet. "I'll catch up with you guys in a couple of minutes, okay?"

They headed off. Brooke walked up to Jamie. He was watching Kat take her practice swings and didn't see Brooke until she sat down in the bleachers next to him.

"How are they doing?" she asked.

"Good," he said. He smiled at her, but he was clearly uncomfortable. She could tell it in his voice. "They're winning 4-3."

"And you?" she asked. "How are you?"

"Okay," he said. "I'm sorry about yesterday. Thank you for breaking up that fight. I don't know what I was thinking. I lost my mind for a couple of minutes."

"It's okay," she said. "Things happen. I'm just glad you and Alex are okay."

"Me, too," he said. He paused for a second as Kat walked up to the plate. "Hands up, kid," he called. "Eyes on the ball."

He turned to Brooke. "Alex called me a couple of minutes ago. I was so surprised I didn't know what to do at first. I almost didn't answer. He apologized for everything. He said it was all his fault, and he should have never acted the way he did."

He paused for a second as the pitcher whipped the ball to the plate. It was a nasty fastball. Kat swung and missed.

"That's okay," Jamie called to her. "You'll get the next one." He turned back to Brooke. "I told Alex it was all my fault. I should have never gone out with Alyssa in the first place. I knew she was his girlfriend. But I just couldn't help it. There's something about her. Something magical. Her smile is to die for."

Brooke chuckled. Where had she heard that before?

They watched as Kat swung again.

"Strike two," the umpire called.

"What did Alex say?" Brooke asked.

"He said he cared too much about Alyssa to do anything to hurt her, and he wants our relationship, his and mine, to go back to the way it was, back before this whole mess began, so he's going to do his best to move on. And he wished us well."

Brooke had never felt so relieved. Nothing made her happier than hearing Alex and Jamie were going to be friends again.

"Can I ask you something?" Jamie said. "Did you have something to do with this? Did you talk to him?"

Brooke smiled. "We may have discussed a few things," she said.

"Then I owe you," he said. "I can't thank you enough."

They watched as Kat turned on a pitch and hit it as hard as she could. Everyone cheered as the ball raced toward the outfield fence and cleared it by at least twenty feet. It was the longest home run Brooke had ever seen a ten-year-old hit.

"She's an amazing young lady," Brooke said.

"She's not the only one," Jamie said.

Chapter 28

The whole team was excited. There was nothing quite like the state playoffs. It was do-or-die time. If they won, they advanced to the next round and still had a chance at the state title. If they lost, their season was over.

Their game was in Mount Vernon. It was a long bus ride, but it gave Coach West plenty of time to brief them on the day's opponent.

"From what I hear," he said, "Mount Vernon is strong top-to-bottom, but their key player, like a lot of teams, is their pitcher, Ned O'Bannon. He doesn't throw really hard, but he's got a lot of junk pitches. His curve is supposed to be wicked. So we're going to have to be patient at the plate and wait for him to make an error."

Ned was exactly as advertised. During Brooke's first at-bat, she was completely fooled by his pitches. His first pitch was a nasty curveball, his second was a screwball, and the third was something she had never seen before. As far as she could tell, it was some type of change-curve-screw combination, if there was such a thing.

She struck out on three straight pitches.

And she wasn't the only one who was fooled. Blake really struggled. He was by far their best power hitter. He led the team in home runs and runs batted in, but he had one major flaw. He couldn't hit curveballs to save his life. Ned caught on quickly and struck him out all three times.

After Blake's final at-bat, he was so frustrated he threw his helmet against the wall in the dugout.

Luckily, Brooke fared a little better. She struck out again during her second at-bat, but during her third attempt she managed to get a piece of a breaking ball-curve-slider-changeup combo and hit in into right field for a single.

And it was really good timing, because Jamie was up after her. Jamie was their best batter by far. He didn't have as much power as Blake (no one did), but he had no real 'holes' in his swing. He led the team in almost every offensive category: hits, walks, on-base percentage, batting average, and total bases. No pitch fooled him for long, and he already had two hits earlier in the game. Ned's pitches, as strange as they were, weren't confusing him at all.

He wasted no time. He hit the first pitch all the way to the outfield wall. Brooke took off from first, knowing she could easily make it to third, but then something unexpected happened. Mount Vernon's center fielder played the rebound wrong and bobbled the ball. Coach West saw the bobble and waved Brooke on. She rounded third and headed for home as the center fielder scooped up the ball and made the throw.

Brooke wasn't the fastest player on the team, but she was fast enough. She slid under the catcher's tag for the go-ahead run.

And that was all they needed. Alex struck out all three batters in the seventh and they won 1-0.

The following rounds were more of the same. All of the games were close, but Silver Lake always found a way to win in the end. Skinny was the hero of the second game (he had two singles and the game-winning home run), Alex was the hero of the third (he pitched a two-hit shutout), Jamie was the hero of the fourth (he went 3-3, with 3 singles, including the game winner in the bottom of the seventh), and Terrell stole the show in the fifth, making a great diving catch in center that saved at least two runs.

Before they knew it, they were in the championship game.

Chapter 29

The team was excited. This was the day they had been waiting for all season long. The state's championship game. Every team in the state of Washington wanted to make it to this game, but only two teams had.

Unfortunately, the other team was Alderwood. They, too, had advanced through the playoffs.

"We meet again," Christian said as he took his warm-up tosses before the game. He wore a protective mask over his face.

"What's wrong with your face?" Skinny asked. "You get punched by a girl?"

Everyone laughed.

But Brooke didn't laugh for long. She was nervous. This was one of the biggest games she had ever played in, and she was worried about Christian. Was he going to throw at her again? If he was mad at her before, he was probably furious now.

Everyone was there, including her dad and all of the girls from the softball team. It was one of the biggest crowds she had ever played in front of.

The umpires discussed things with both teams before the game began.

"We're well aware of the history between these teams," the head umpire said, "and we'll tolerate nothing today. Anyone gets out of line, in any way, they'll be ejected instantly." He looked at Christian. "There will be no brushback pitches." He looked at

Brooke. "And no punches. Does everyone understand?"

Everyone nodded.

The game started minutes later, and, as always, it was a pitcher's duel between Christian and Alex. Every time Christian struck out a batter, Alex did the same. Neither boy had given up a hit when Brooke stepped to the plate in the third.

Christian glared at her from behind his mask. In a way, he looked even scarier than before. His first pitch was a nasty curveball for strike one. His second pitch was a fastball that she swung at and missed. She fouled away the next two pitches, but then struck out on a wicked breaking ball in the dirt.

As she walked back to the dugout, she was mad at herself for striking out, but she was also relieved. Christian hadn't thrown a single pitch anywhere near her. Hopefully it would stay that way.

The game was still scoreless when she batted again in the fifth. Once again she went down swinging.

She didn't want to, but she had to give Christian credit. If nothing else, he was a good pitcher. Next to Alex, he was the best pitcher she had ever seen.

The game was still scoreless in the bottom of the sixth. Alex was throwing a gem of a game. He had only given up one hit all day, a little blooper in the second, and he was absolutely on fire. He had struck out ten batters already and was showing no signs of letting up. Since he was a senior, this was his last game as a high school player and he was going out in style.

But disaster struck. Christian (of all people) got a hold of one of Alex's pitches and lined it straight up the middle. It was a rocket of a shot, and it hit Alex in his pitching arm, just above his elbow. He went down clutching his arm. The ball rebounded to the side, and

Brooke actually got to it and threw Christian out at first, but nobody (except the umpire) even noticed.

They were all looking at Alex. He was hurt. Coach West called time and rushed to the mound. After a couple of minutes, Alex managed to get up, but his arm was in bad shape. He could move his fingers and make a fist, but that was all. He tried to raise his arm above his head, to mimic a pitch, but he could only get it part way before the pain was too intense.

"It's going to need x-rays," Coach West said. "It's probably broken."

Brooke felt awful. In a way, she felt worse than when she had been injured. At least when she had been injured, it had been over quickly. She had blacked out seconds after the ball hit her. But now, just standing there, watching Coach West lead Alex back to the dugout, she felt so worthless. She wanted to help but there was nothing she could do.

Christian didn't make things any better. From the Eagles' dugout, he said, "Poor Alex has a boo-boo."

Brooke was tempted to punch him in the face again, but she knew she'd never get close before the umpires caught her and threw her out. And regardless, that wasn't the best way to beat him anyway. They needed to beat him by winning the game.

But it wasn't going to be easy. They were in trouble. The game was still scoreless, but they had lost their star pitcher. She wasn't sure they were a match for Alderwood without Alex.

But they had to try. Jamie took over pitching, and despite getting only a couple of minutes to warm up, he did a great job. He got the final two outs to finish the inning relatively easily.

Brooke overheard Alex as she entered the dugout. He was sitting next to his dad.

"I'll go after the game," he said. "I'm not leaving until then."

"Son," his dad said. "We need to go. Your arm could be really hurt."

"I don't care," Alex said. "I worked my entire life for this game and I'm not leaving until it's over."

His dad clearly wasn't happy, but he said nothing more. He knew his son wasn't going to budge.

As Brooke stepped into the batter's box for her next at-bat, she could tell Christian was happy. There was a huge smile on his face, and he rocked back and forth on the balls of his feet like a little kid. He had Silver Lake right where he wanted them. Without their ace, he knew they were in trouble.

And Brooke didn't help any. She went down swinging on three straight pitches. Christian seemed even better than before. Now that Alex was gone, he could smell blood and he was going for the kill.

But he had a surprise coming. Silver Lake was a good team even without Alex. Jamie was the next batter, and he refused to surrender, even for a second. He fouled off pitch after pitch after pitch after pitch. Brooke lost count after the eighth.

And then it happened. Christian got frustrated and did something he rarely did. He made a mistake. He threw a pitch straight down the middle, and Jamie turned and hammered it over the outfield fence. The ball flew a mile.

They all cheered and mobbed Jamie at home plate. Thanks to him, they had the lead 1-0. Now they just needed to hold it.

As Brooke took the field to start the bottom of the seventh, she could hardly believe it. They were three outs away from the state championship. It was so close she could taste it.

But things did not start well. The first Alderwood batter hit one of Jamie's pitches into left field for a single. The second batter walked. So did the third. Before Brooke could wink an eye, the bases were loaded and there were no outs.

Coach West called time and walked slowly to the mound. He tried to hide it, but he was nervous, too.

"Jamie," he said. "What's up?"

"I don't know," Jamie said. His face was flush and his eyes were wide.

Brooke knew. He was scared. He had never been in a situation like this before. He was a second baseman, but he was being asked to pitch to one of the best teams in the state of Washington in the biggest game of the year. Anyone would crack under the pressure.

"Son," Coach West said. "You're doing just fine. You've got to calm down. With that home run you just hit, you're the hero of the game. You don't need to do much more, and you don't need to do anything fancy. Just throw strikes. Okay?"

Jamie nodded.

Without another word, Coach West turned and walked back to the dugout.

Brooke was really sweating now. Jamie wasn't the only one who was being affected by the pressure. It was affecting her, too. Her heart was pounding in her chest.

Come on, Jamie, she thought. *Please throw a strike. Please.*

And he did.

The only problem was the batter crushed it. He hit a perfect line-drive, and he hit it so hard it would have destroyed an average shortstop.

But Brooke wasn't an average shortstop. She was ready. She caught the ball for an out, then turned instantly to second. The runner, thinking the ball was going to get past her, had left the base. By the time he realized she had it, he was only a step away.

She reached out and tagged him for the second out.

Then she glanced at first. That runner, too, had left the base. He was turning to dive back but he wasn't there yet.

She threw the ball harder than she had ever thrown it before. It sounded like an explosion as it hit Blake's mitt.

At first, she didn't realize what she had done. She just stood there in complete shock as her teammates swarmed and tackled her.

She had won the state championship by turning a game-ending triple play.

Chapter 30

The following week, there was a celebration to honor the team's accomplishment, and a 'State Champions' banner was hoisted into the rafters of the school's gymnasium. Everyone cheered as Alex, his arm in a cast, took the podium and made a speech on behalf of the team. They cheered even louder when Coach West joined him on the podium and they presented the year's 'Most Valuable Player' award to Jamie. Jamie was all smiles as he accepted his trophy.

But the highlight for Brooke was afterward. Alex invited them to his house, and everyone from both the baseball and softball teams was there. Brooke mingled for awhile, then made her way to the patio. Alex was sitting by himself in a chair next to the pool.

"What are you doing out here?" she asked, taking the seat next to him.

"Just thinking about things," he said.

"Like what?" she asked.

"It was such a crazy season," he said. "With you coming along, and the battles with Christian, and now the championship. I guess I just needed a couple of minutes to slow down and unwind a little. It's funny how quickly things move these days. The whole season is a blur to me."

"Me, too," she said.

"What was it like?" he asked.

"What?" she asked.

"When you turned that triple play. It was incredible. Do you know how rare triple plays are? They're even rarer than no-hitters."

Brooke tried to act cool, like she'd done it a million times. "I was just doing my job," she said. "That's what we shortstops do."

Alex raised an eyebrow. "I've been playing baseball my entire life," he said. "And I've never seen a shortstop turn a triple play before."

"I'm special," Brooke said.

He nodded.

They turned as a couple appeared at the far end of the patio, near the entrance to the kitchen. It was Jamie and Alyssa. Alyssa smiled.

The guys are right, Brooke thought. Alyssa did have a gorgeous smile. No wonder they were all so gaga about her.

"We're out of chips," Jamie said, "so we're going to the store to get some more. Do you guys want anything?"

"I'm good," Alex said.

"Me, too," Brooke said.

They turned and left. Alex watched silently as they disappeared from view.

"You okay with that?" Brooke asked.

"With what?" he asked

"With Jamie and Alyssa. As a couple?"

Alex shrugged. "I invited them. Like you said, we've got to move on."

Brooke felt bad for him, because he was clearly still heartbroken over the break-up, but at least he was handling it okay.

"I've been meaning to ask you," he continued. "I'm not really ready for a serious relationship yet, but if I were, would I ever have a chance with a girl like you? I mean, I'm no big-time two-sport

132

softball/baseball star like you, but I have a few redeeming qualities."

Brooke nearly fell into the pool. She tried to calm herself and stay as cool and as collected as possible.

"You might," she said. "But you'd have to treat me right."

"Of course I'd treat you right," Alex said. "Otherwise, you'd punch me in the face like you punched Christian. I'm not taking any chances with Boxin' Brooke."

They laughed.

"It's getting pretty chilly out here," Alex said. "Let's go back inside with everyone else."

He stood up, took her hand in his, and led her inside.

She had never been so happy.

FASTPITCH FEVER

JODY STUDDARD

www.jstuddard.com

For Danielle Lawrie,
Ashley Charters,
and the rest of the 2009
Washington Huskies
fastpitch team

National Champions

Trouble with Riseballs

Everyone thinks being a fourteen-year-old fastpitch softball player is nothing but fun and games. Trust me, it isn't. Take today for instance. It's the final inning, and my team, the Washington Wildcats, is losing to our arch rivals, the Bellevue Beast, 4-3. We have two outs in the final inning, and it's my turn to bat. Normally, I like batting, and I'm pretty good at it, but not today. The Beast's pitcher, Nichole Williams, is really tough, and she's already struck me out twice earlier in the game. She throws several different types of pitches, and she throws them all well, but her best by far is a nasty riseball. I've never seen anyone throw a riseball as well as her. No matter how hard I try, I just can't hit it.

As I step into the batter's box, I glance quickly at the stands. My dad is sitting with the other parents in the bleachers, and he doesn't look happy. He hates it when my team loses, and he especially hates it when I strike out. If I know what's best for me, I better hit one of these riseballs, or it's going to be a long car ride home for sure.

Nichole winds up, then throws. It's just what I was dreading. Another riseball. I swing as hard as I can, but I miss it by a mile.

"Strike one," blue shouts. In softball, we call the umpires blue, since they usually wear blue uniforms.

I shoot a glance at my dad. He doesn't say anything, but his face is turning red.

Nichole winds up again. This riseball is even nastier than the first. I miss it by two miles.

"Strike two," blue shouts.

"Come on, Rachel," my dad calls from the bleachers. "Keep your eyes on the ball. Keep your hands up."

I take a deep breath as I dig my cleats into the dirt. This is my last chance. If I don't hit the next pitch, I'm in deep.

The final riseball is so fast I barely see it. I miss it by three miles.

The Beast players cheer and congratulate Nichole. In the meantime, I walk back to our dugout, my head down in defeat. My coach, Ryan Taylor, greets me and tells me, "Good try," but I'm not concerned about him right now. I take my time rounding up my gear and putting it into my softball bag. I've learned from experience it's best to give my dad a few minutes to cool down after a bad game.

It's deathly silent in the car until we're half way home.

"What's the deal with riseballs?" he asks.

"I've never been able to hit riseballs," I respond. "You know that."

"But why?" he asks. "They're just like any other pitch."

"No, they're not. They start low, like a fastball, but then they go up. I always swing under them."

"So swing higher," he says.

"It's not that easy," I say. "I can't tell how high they're going until they get there. And then it's too late. Especially against someone like Nichole. She throws so hard."

My dad shakes his head. "It isn't that difficult, Rachel. You just need to have quick hands. Here, I'll show you."

We stop at McCall Park. McCall Park is a Little League field just a couple of blocks from our house. My dad and I practice there a lot when it isn't being used by someone else.

My dad walks to the pitching circle with a bucket of balls in one hand. We keep a bucket of balls in the trunk at all times, just for occasions like this, when he wants to teach me something. In the meantime, I take my place (somewhat hesitantly) in the batter's box.

"Hitting a riseball isn't rocket science," he says. "Just keep your eyes on the ball, as it comes in, and keep your hands up high. Don't let them drop, or you'll swing under it, just like you've been doing. Okay?"

I say okay, even though I know better. My dad and I have been through this drill hundreds of times. I've been playing softball as long as I can remember, and I've never been able to hit riseballs, no matter how hard I've tried, no matter how hard I've worked. Regardless, my dad insists he can teach me. He's extremely stubborn that way.

He throws me a riseball. I miss it by four miles.

"Rachel," he says. "Keep your eyes on the ball. Watch the ball hit the bat."

He throws me another pitch. I miss it by five miles.

He throws me another pitch. I miss it by six miles.

"Are your eyes on the ball, young lady?" he asks. He's clearly getting irritated again.

"Yes," I say as I bang my bat on the ground. He's not the only one getting irritated.

He throws me another pitch. I miss it by seven miles.

"Are you concentrating?" he asks.

"Yes," I say.

"It doesn't look like it. It looks like you're messing around. Get serious. Get ready and hit the ball. I'm not going to tell you again."

He throws another pitch. I miss it by eight miles.

"Rachel," he says as he steps out of the pitching circle. "Take that fancy bat of yours and hit the ball. Got it?"

"I'm trying," I plead.

"You're not trying hard enough. Try harder."

He throws another pitch. I miss it by nine miles.

Now he's furious. "I swear to God, Rachel, if you swing and miss once more, you're grounded for a week."

One pitch later, I'm grounded for a week.

Grounded

It's been two days since I got grounded, and it's been a complete nightmare. My dad took away my cellular phone, so I can't send text messages to my friends, and he took away my laptop computer, so I can't chat online. Life without a phone and a computer is almost unbearable. It's cruel and unusual, if you ask me.

Luckily, I probably won't have to endure the whole week. My dad gets irritated easily, but he doesn't usually stay that way for long, so in the past I've rarely had to serve my whole sentence. He usually gives my phone and computer back a few days early, and I'm hopeful he'll do the same this time, especially if I do well in today's practice game against the Redmond LadyCats. The LadyCats are a good team, and their coach is friends with Coach Ryan, so we scrimmage against them a lot. Just like us, they're a 16u select team, so all of their players are sixteen or under. I'm only fourteen, so technically I should still be on a 14u team, but my dad thought I was ready for a challenge and switched me to the Wildcats at the beginning of the season. I'm the youngest girl on the team, and that made me a little nervous at first but not anymore. My teammates don't care how old I am as long as I play well.

But all of this is irrelevant right now, at least as far as I'm concerned. The only thing that matters is playing well and getting my phone and computer back as soon as possible.

I take a deep breath as I step into the batter's box and tap my bat on the ground, measuring the distance to the plate. I feel much better than I did during the game against the Beast. The LadyCats' pitcher, Amy Smith, is good, and she throws hard, but she doesn't throw any riseballs.

"Strike one," blue shouts as I miss the first pitch.

I glance up at my dad in the bleachers. He shakes his head from side to side. He didn't like that swing at all.

The next pitch is a fastball straight down the middle of the plate. If there's one thing about softball I've always liked, it's fastballs straight down the middle of the plate. I whip my bat around and hit the ball right back at Amy. It gets past her and rolls into center field for a single. All of the fans, including my dad, cheer as I run safely to first.

My next at-bat is largely the same. Amy gets two quick strikes on me, but then makes a mistake by throwing a pitch down the middle. This one isn't a fastball, it's some type of slow changeup, but it doesn't matter. I hit it down the right field foul line for a double. My dad cheers as I slide into second.

My final at-bat is the best of them all. I hit the first pitch so hard it bounces off of the outfield wall. The LadyCats' center fielder doesn't get to it until I pass second and am cruising toward third. I don't even have to slide. It's a stand-up triple.

I look at the stands. My dad is quite happy now. The other dads are patting him on the back and whooping it up loudly.

He's not the only one who is happy. If everything goes according to plan, my phone, computer, and I should be reunited in no time.

We win the game easily, 7-3, and my dad takes me to Cold Stone Creamery on the way home. It's kind of a tradition for us. We get ice cream a lot, especially after big victories. I order one of my favorites — a double scoop of cookie dough ice cream with chocolate and caramel syrup, stuffed into an oversized waffle cone, with whipped cream on top. My dad gets his favorite, a banana split. He's all smiles as we sit at a table eating.

"That single was nice," he says between bites. "Straight up the middle. Just like I taught you."

I nod.

"And that triple was a monster shot," he adds. "For a minute there, I thought you hit it out."

"Me, too," I say.

"Another ten feet, and it was gone. Maybe not even that far."

We eat for a few minutes in silence, then he reaches into his coat pocket and pulls out my phone. It's the minute I've been waiting for. The moment of truth. I can barely contain my excitement.

"You can have this back," he says, sliding it across the table to me.

"What about my computer?" I ask.

"It's at home. I'll give it to you when we get back."

I stand up and give him a hug. After two long, painful, excruciating days, my life has finally returned to normal.

Out-of-the-park

Today is a big day for me. My team is playing Lake Stevens Fastpitch (LSF for short). They're a good team, and their pitcher, Olivia Sanchez, throws really fast, but the reason the game is so important is because my dad has an older brother, Jim, and his daughter Megan plays for LSF. I actually like Uncle Jim and Megan quite a bit, but my dad and Uncle Jim don't get along too well, so my dad always wants me to beat them whenever we play. On the drive to the game, he gives me added incentive to play well today.

"Rachel," he says, "I want you to go all-out today."

"I always go all-out," I respond.

"I want you to go completely all-out," he says.

"Completely all-out? How do I do that?"

"I don't know, but you'll find a way."

I sigh. I have no idea what he's talking about, but whatever. Sometimes, it's best to just agree with him and move along.

"Today is a good day to play money ball," he says.

"Really?" I ask. I definitely like the sound of that. 'Money ball' is a game my dad made up years ago. We do it whenever he wants me to play really well. He gives me ten dollars for a single, twenty for a double, thirty for a triple, and one hundred for a home run.

"Are you up for it?" he asks.

"Oh yeah," I say, maybe a little too enthusiastically. I've never been one to turn down a chance to play money ball. And it's really good timing, because my bankroll is a little low right now. Actually, my bankroll is always a little low, but regardless I

144

could definitely use some money. Especially since I spotted a cute pair of shoes at the mall the other day.

Unfortunately, the game starts off shaky. LSF bats first, and my cousin Megan hits a double all the way to the warning track that scores two runs. Luckily, we get the final out before they do any more damage. As I walk to the dugout, I overhear my dad reassuring one of the other dads in the bleachers.

"Don't worry," he says, nice and calm. "Rachel will get those runs back."

Then, when the other dad walks away to talk to someone else, my dad rushes over to me in the dugout. Now he's all serious and urgent.

"Rachel," he says. "Get those runs back. Now."

Our first two batters get on base, and it's my turn to bat. I definitely feel the pressure now. I need to get a hit, to make my dad happy, and I also want to win some money. After all, it's not every day we play money ball, and I want those shoes bad. I wonder what pair I should get, the black ones or the brown ones?

I never get a chance to decide. The LSF pitcher throws me a fastball, and I hit it a mile – straight up. The catcher tosses off her mask and catches the ball with ease.

"The batter's out!" blue yells.

As I walk back to the dugout, I sneak a peek at my dad. He is not impressed.

I don't bat again until the third inning. At this point, we're still trailing 2-0. I try even harder to get a hit this time, but all I manage to do is hit a weak grounder that barely gets past the pitcher. Cousin Megan scoops it up and throws it to first.

"Out!" blue yells.

My next at-bat is in the fifth inning. We're still down 2-0. I hit the ball hard to the outfield, but the right fielder catches it no problem.

145

"Out!" blue yells.

My next at-bat is in the seventh inning, and we're still losing 2-0. I'm really feeling the pressure now. This is my last chance to bat, and if we don't score some runs, we're going to lose for sure. That will make my dad really mad. And if that isn't bad enough, I haven't gotten a hit all day, so I can pretty much kiss my new shoes goodbye.

I sometimes wonder if playing money ball is a good idea. Sometimes I try too hard and don't do well at all.

All I know is right now I need to concentrate. We have two runners on base, one on second and one on third, and if I can get a hit, even something as weak as a bloop single, they'll score and that will tie the game. And if I can somehow hit a home run, we will come from behind and win.

I take a deep breath as I step into the batter's box. The first pitch is low and outside.

"Good eye," my dad says from the bleachers.

The next pitch is straight down the middle. I swing and miss.

"Strike one," blue shouts.

I want to shoot myself. That pitch was perfect. I should have hit it a mile. Now I'm starting to get frustrated.

The next pitch is high heat (a fastball above my hands). I'm not supposed to swing at high heat, because it's never a strike, but I can't control myself and swing anyway.

"Strike two," blue shouts.

Now I'm really frustrated. If I strike out, the car ride home is going to be unbearable.

Much to my surprise and delight, my agony ends in the blink of an eye. The next pitch is a little low, but straight down the middle, just where I like it. I turn and hit it as hard as I can. The ball jumps off my bat and soars straight toward the outfield. It clears the fence by at least twenty feet.

My teammates go crazy as blue shouts, "Home run!"

I round the bases and my teammates tackle me at home plate. It's a giant pig pile, with me at the bottom. Everyone is laughing and cheering, and it's great fun. The parents take pictures with their cameras and cellular phones.

As you can imagine, my dad is quite happy. Actually, that's a complete understatement. He's ecstatic. He's more excited than I've ever seen him before.

"An out-of-park home run," he says as I reach the car. "How did you do it? Girls your age never hit out-of-the-park home runs. I've never seen anything like it."

I know I'm in hog heaven now. "Don't you owe me something?" I ask.

"What?" he asks.

"One hundred dollars," I answer. "For a home run."

"Oh, yeah," he says. "I got so excited I forgot. Actually, one hundred is for a normal, in-the-park home run. An out-of-the-park home run is even better. It's worth two hundred."

I can hardly believe my ears. Two hundred dollars? I've never had that much money in my entire life, except maybe that one year at Christmas when Grandpa Frank gave me a bunch of money.

"Really?" I ask.

"We'll stop at the ATM on the way home. After we get ice cream, of course. But give me your phone. I want to call your mom."

I hand him my phone, but he can't remember how to dial it, so I do it for him.

"Babe, it's me. You won't believe it. Rachel just hit an out-of-the-park home run to win the game. It was a monster shot. It cleared the fence by at least thirty feet. What? Dinner? Yeah, we'll stop at the store and get something. I'll let Rachel pick. She earned it."

He hangs up the phone and turns back to me. "I want to call Chuck and tell him."

I dial the number for him.

"Chuck, you won't believe it, Rachel just hit an out-of-the-park home run. It was in the bottom of the seventh. It cleared the wall by at least fifty feet. What? Definitely. At least fifty, maybe more. Anyway, I'll tell you about it at work tomorrow. I gotta go."

We hop in the car and head for the ATM. Along the way, my dad calls his boss, two co-workers from his office, and Grandpa Frank. It's quite ironic, because normally he's adamant you shouldn't drive and talk on the phone at the same time. As a matter-of-fact, I think it's illegal in the state of Washington. Oh well. Apparently state laws are forgotten when out-of-the-park home runs are involved.

For the rest of the night, I'm treated like royalty. At Cold Stone, I get a triple scoop with extra fudge, at the grocery store I get to pick everything for dinner (I pick spaghetti with meatballs, my favorite), and my dad takes me to the mall so I can spend some of my home run money on that pair of shoes I wanted (I get the black pair). When we get home, my dad does my chores and helps me with my homework.

Life is good when you hit an out-of-the-park home run. I need to do it again. Hopefully soon.

Scouting Reports

I'm sitting at the dining room table with my text books spread out all around me when my dad gets home from work. He has a piece of paper in one hand and an urgent, concerned look on his face.

"Hey, Rachel," he says. "What are you doing?"

"What's it look like?" I say. "My homework."

"Put that away. I've got something to show you. Something important."

He pushes my books to the side and hands me the piece of paper. "I got this from Chuck Williams, a guy at my office. His daughter, Rebecca, plays on the Woodinville Wolves. They played Skyhawks Fastpitch last weekend."

Instantly, I recognize the name. My team plays Skyhawks Fastpitch in a tournament tomorrow.

"Is it a scouting report?" I ask.

"Oh, yeah," my dad says. "And a good one."

I look at the paper. It's a list of names, with notes next to each one. My dad and I go through it together.

"Chuck says they're really good, with talented players at every position. Their pitcher is a girl named Riley Westmore. Apparently she's a real firecracker and she throws a lot of heat. So you're going to have to have quick hands if you want to get any hits against her."

"I like heat," I say. "Does she throw any riseballs?"

"No. Not that I know of."

I breathe a sigh of relief. I hate riseballs.

My dad points at the list again, at the name on the very bottom. "We've also got to worry about this girl, Melody Gold. She's the center fielder. She's one of the youngest girls on the team, probably the youngest, but she's lightning fast and Chuck says she's one of the best outfielders he's ever seen. He says if you hit one anywhere near her, you're as good as gone. His daughter, Rebecca, hit one all of the way to the fence but Melody caught it anyway."

"Wow."

"Exactly. I've got to call your coach and give him this info. Where's his number?"

I hand my cellular phone to him. "It's in my contacts under Coach Ryan."

He takes the phone but stares at it blankly for several seconds. He's never been very good with technology. Once, a few years back, he couldn't even figure out how to turn my laptop on. It was pathetic.

I take it from him, dial Coach Ryan's number, and hand it back. He heads into the kitchen. I hear him talking as I resume my homework.

"Ryan, yeah, this is Mike Adams. How are you? Good, I'm good. Anyway, I wanted to tell you I got a scouting report for tomorrow's game. What? Yeah, it looks good. It's for the Skyhawks. I got info on all of the girls, including their backups." He pauses momentarily. "Ryan, just a second. Can you hold for a second?"

He comes back into the dining room. "Rachel, why is this darn phone beeping?"

"It's a text message. Just ignore it. I'll check it later."

He nods, then returns to the kitchen. "Ryan, are you still there? Anyway, the main girl we've got to worry about is their pitcher, Riley, and there's another girl named Melody. What? Yeah, I've got a whole list, written out. No, not here at the house, but there's a store right around the corner. We can fax it to you from there. It's no problem at all. Rachel and I will head there right now."

My dad heads into the room. "Ryan wants us to fax the scouting report over to him as soon as possible. Let's go."

"I'm doing my homework."

"That can wait. He needs this right now. And I'll get you one of those iTunes cards if you come."

I smile. I have to give my dad credit. He knows me well. Bribery gets me every time. Especially if the bribery involves an iTunes card. Or ice cream. Ice cream works, too.

The next day, with the help of my dad's scouting report, we are able to beat the Skyhawks 3-2. I get two hits, a single and a double. On the other side of the field, the Skyhawks' star players, Riley and Melody, are every bit as good as advertised. Riley pitches the entire game and strikes out nine batters, including me in the fifth. In the meantime, Melody roams the outfield like a lion roaming the Serengeti. My team's shortstop hits a ball all of the way to the warning track in the sixth inning, and against any other outfielder it would have been a double for sure, but Melody darts under it and catches it on the run.

"Wow," my dad says. "She's awesome."

"You can say that again," I say.

Road Trip

This weekend is my team's first big road trip of the season. I'm really excited because I love road trips. My dad loads the car with our suitcases and gear, and I throw a bunch of blankets and pillows in the back seat so I can kick back in style as he drives. We stop at a video store so I can get some movies to watch on my laptop along the way.

"I don't know why we're getting any movies," my dad says. "You'll be sound asleep the minute we hit the road."

"Not this time," I say. "I'm wide awake today."

Ten minutes later, I'm sound asleep.

Our tournament is in a small city called Leavenworth. It's about two hours from Seattle, but it only seems like ten minutes since I sleep most of the way. I wake up as my dad pulls into the hotel parking lot. We check in at the front desk, carry our stuff up to our rooms, and head for the most important place in the hotel — the pool. Several of my teammates have already arrived, and I waste little time joining them in the water. We goof around for about an hour, then the parents round us up and we head out as a group for dinner. Leavenworth is a pretty town, with Bavarian architecture, and we go to a nice German restaurant. The players sit at one table, and the coaches and parents (mostly dads) sit at another. We girls talk about the things important to us (school and boys), and the coaches and dads talk about the things important to them (who is going to win this year's World Series,

Super Bowl, NBA Finals, Stanley Cup, and Rose Bowl). After awhile, they mix it up and talk about electronics and cars, but before long they revert back to their one true love, sports. After dinner, we head back to the hotel, where the real fun begins. The parents stay in their rooms, on one floor, and we girls stay in our rooms, four girls per room, on another. I share a room with our shortstop, Miranda Scott, our third baseman, Grace Donovan, and our first baseman, Lauren McCoy.

"So is it true?" Grace asks Lauren. They're both sitting on one bed, watching television.

"What?" Lauren asks as she flips channels.

"You went out with Steve Smith last week?"

"Yeah. We went to a movie."

"You lucky dog," Miranda says. She's sitting on the second bed, next to me. "He's so cute."

"I know," Lauren says. "I just stared at him the whole time. I don't think I paid attention to the movie at all. What about you? I heard you went out with Logan Frank?"

"I'll never do that again," Miranda says. "He's a jerk. He's so full of himself. He hardly paid any attention to me at all. He kept texting his buddies all night. At one point he went to the restroom and didn't come back for half an hour. Don't ask me what he was doing in there."

"And they say we girls take a long time in the bathroom," Grace says.

There is a short silence before the girls turn to me. "What about you?" Miranda asks. "How come we never hear about your boyfriend?"

"I don't have one," I answer.

"How come?" Grace asks.

"My dad won't let me," I say. "He says I'm too young."

"Too young for a boyfriend?" Lauren says. "I had my first boyfriend when I was in third grade. Matt Christopher. Do you guys remember him?"

"He was so cute," Grace says. "Too bad he moved away."

"No doubt," Lauren says.

"My dad is pretty strict that way," I say. "He wants me to focus on softball and school right now. He wouldn't even let me go to the prom this year."

"It sucks to be you," Lauren says. She's about to say something more when there is a knock on the door. It's one of the moms, serving as a chaperone for the trip. The chaperone checks in on us periodically to see if we need anything.

"Enough of this chitter chatter," Grace says as the chaperone leaves. "Let's have some real fun. Let's sneak out for awhile."

"We're not supposed to leave the hotel without a parent," I say. "What if the chaperone comes back?"

"She only comes by once every couple of hours," Grace says. "We'll be back by then. Come on, it'll be fun."

I don't really want to go, but the other girls jump up and start putting their shoes on, and I don't want to be left behind. We sneak down the hall and ride the elevator to the ground floor. Our room is located in the hotel's west wing, near the back, so getting out without being seen is pretty easy. As we pass by the main lobby, I see my dad sitting in the restaurant to the side, having a drink with Lauren's dad. His back is to me, but I can hear his voice anyway.

"No one hits like Ichiro," he says.

"You can say that again," Lauren's dad says.

We hurry along. It's about 9:00 pm, so things are pretty quiet, but luckily it's a Friday night, so there is still a little activity. We head down the street that runs through the main part of town.

"Where are we going?" I ask. I'm still a little nervous.

"We need to find some action," Grace says. "Here, this looks good."

We find a putt-putt golf course that is still open. It's arguably the nicest putt-putt golf course I've ever seen, with real grass, ornately-designed miniature buildings, and a gorgeous waterfall to one side. It's outside, but it has floodlights that illuminate the entire place brightly, and there are a lot of people gathered around, mostly teenagers like us.

"You like putt-putt golf?" Lauren asks Grace.

"No," Grace answers. "Not at all. But I definitely like that."

Without another word, she runs up and greets a group of teenage boys getting clubs at the front desk. "You guys mind if we join you for a round?"

"I don't know about this," I say quietly to Lauren.

"Come on, Rachel," Lauren says. "It'll be fun. And maybe you can finally find yourself a boyfriend."

We get some clubs and join them. There are four boys total, and they're all from around town. They go to a local high school called Cascade. They play on their school baseball team, and they are quite interested when they find out we're in town for a softball tournament.

"What position do you play?" one of the boys asks me. He looks a little younger than the others, and he is definitely the quietest of the bunch. He is tall and thin, with dark hair and deep, chocolate eyes. His name is Julio Rodriguez.

"Second," I say.

"That's funny," he says. "What a coincidence."

"Excuse me?" I ask.

155

"I'm the second baseman for our team. And let me guess, you're younger than the other girls."

"Yeah," I answer. "But only by a year."

"Me, too. The other boys are sophomores. I'm a freshman. What grade are you in?"

"Eighth."

"Sweet. You'll be in high school next year."

"I can't wait."

"Oh, I know. I was the same when I was in eighth grade. High school is much better."

"Really?"

"There's a lot more to do. Dances and stuff. And some of the older guys can already drive, so they give us rides around town. To movies and stuff. And games, of course."

"Sweet."

I'm about to say something more when Lauren interrupts me. "I need to go to the bathroom," she says. "Come with me."

I don't really know why Lauren needs an escort to the bathroom, but I go with her anyway. The minute we get inside, she turns to me with an excited look on her face.

"He likes you," she says.

"Really?" I ask.

"I can tell. I can see it in his eyes. He's got that sparkle. What about you? Do you like him?"

"I just met him," I say. "I hardly know anything about him."

"He's really cute."

"Really?"

"His eyes are gorgeous. And he has perfect teeth. The two of you would make a cute couple."

"You think so?"

She nods. "Definitely. Let's get back before we miss anything."

We head back to the rest of the group. We stay for a couple of hours, and it's great fun. Grace and Miranda get in a bit of a tiff, because both of them like the same boy (the one named Alex), and they get pretty irritated with each other as the night winds on, but I don't care because I have a good time anyway. I spend the whole night talking with Julio, and I'm amazed at how much we have in common. And the more I look at him, the more I realize Lauren is right. He is really cute.

"Maybe I'll catch up with you again this weekend," he says as we girls are about to head back to our hotel room, "before you leave town."

"I don't know if we'll be able to get out again," I say.

"There's always a way," he says with a smile.

Without another word, we girls head back to our room. Along the way, Lauren can't resist teasing me a little.

"Admit it," she says. "You like him."

"He's okay," I say, trying to sound as cool and as collected as possible.

I don't get much sleep that night. No matter how hard I try, I keep thinking about Julio. And the more I think about him, the more I'm forced to admit it would be nice to have a boyfriend. If nothing else, it would help me fit in better with the older girls.

The next day, our tournament begins. It's called the Leavenworth Invite and it features teams from all over the Pacific Northwest. We have three games. The first two are back-to-back, but then we have a two hour break before the final game. I'm pretty tired, since I didn't sleep much the night before, but other than that I feel okay. The first game goes well, and we beat a

157

team called the King County Khaos 5-1. I get two singles, both straight up the middle.

The second game is a different story. We're playing a team called the British Columbia Blast. Like most Canadian teams, they're really good, but we're actually winning until something unexpected happens. Julio and the other boys show up. Julio waves to me from the bleachers as I step into the batter's box.

I can't believe he's here. I had hoped to see him again, but I didn't expect to see him at one of our games.

"Strike three," blue shouts as I swing and miss three straight times.

A couple of minutes later, Julio comes over to me at the edge of the dugout.

"What are you doing here?" I ask.

"I just wanted to see you again," he says. "You look good."

"I just struck out."

"We all strike out on occasion," he says. "Your form looked good."

"Thanks," I say, slightly embarrassed. "I'm sure my dad would feel otherwise. Speaking of which, you need to get out of here quick. My dad will freak out if he sees me talking to a boy during a game."

"That's his problem."

"No," I say, correcting him. "It's my problem."

"You wanna hook up again tonight?" Julio asks. "Can you and the other girls get out?"

"Maybe," I answer. "I'll talk to them later. But I've got to go."

I grab my mitt and head onto the field. Julio returns to the bleachers and joins the rest of his buddies. He's actually only a few feet away from my dad, but my dad is oblivious since he has no idea who Julio is. Julio smiles at me as a Blast batter hits a ball my way. It's a lazy grounder, the type I normally handle with ease, but somehow I miss it completely. It goes through my legs into right field.

"That's okay, Rachel," Coach Ryan shouts from the dugout. "You'll get the next one."

Unfortunately, I don't. The Blast runner attempts to steal second, and I forget to cover the base. The throw from our catcher, Jessica O'Malley, flies into center field. Our center fielder, Alexis Sampson, gets to it but isn't fast enough to keep the runner from advancing to third. One pitch later, the runner scores as the batter hits a shot up the middle. I shake my head. If I had gotten that grounder, or covered second on the steal attempt, that run wouldn't have scored.

Luckily, we get out of the inning without any more damage, and we do okay until my next at-bat in the fifth. Julio is still in the bleachers, and he smiles at me again. He's even cuter than I originally realized. Like Lauren said, his teeth are perfect.

"Strike three," blue shouts.

My dad comes up to me as I walk back to the dugout.

"Rachel," he says. "What's up?"

"Nothing," I say.

"You don't look like yourself today. You seem distracted."

My heart races. If he finds out about Julio, I'm in big trouble. "I'm okay, dad. I'm just not seeing the ball well. I'll get the next one."

"Are your contacts okay?" he asks. "I can go back to the car and get another pair."

"No," I say. "These ones are okay."

I grab my mitt and head back to the field. A batter hits a grounder to me, and, unbelievably, I let it go through my legs, just like the first time. Coach Ryan asks blue for a timeout.

159

"Casey," he says to a girl in our dugout. She's one of our backup players and arguably the worst player on the team. "Go take Rachel's place at second."

I spend the rest of the game, and the entire next one, sitting on the bench watching. Grace teases me near the end of the final game.

"Hey, Rachel," she says. "It looks like you got a new position. Center bench."

Everyone laughs. But no one is laughing for long. We lose to the Blast 4-2, and we lose our third game to the Portland Pioneers 3-1.

That night, just after the chaperone checks on us, we sneak out again. As we pass the lobby, I see my dad, sitting once again in the restaurant, eating an appetizer. This time, he's with Miranda's dad.

"If you ask me," he says, "there's no doubt about it. The 2001 Mariners were the greatest team of all time . . . ."

We meet the boys at a burger joint just a few blocks from the putt-putt course where we met them the night before. There is a fifth boy with them tonight, and his name is Josh. He's older than the others, and he has a car of his own. Instantly, Grace and Miranda forget about Alex and start competing for Josh's attention. He drives us to a small park on the far side of town, which actually isn't that far since Leavenworth isn't that big. Since it's past 9:00 pm, the park is pretty quiet, and we have the entire place to ourselves. As we sit in the parking lot, Josh pulls a bottle of tequila from beneath a seat, takes a swig, and passes it to the other boys. All of them, including Julio, take a drink.

"You guys want some?" Josh asks.

"I'll try some," Grace says.

"Me, too," Miranda and Lauren say. They all take a swig, then pass the bottle to me. I hesitate.

160

"Come on, Rachel," Grace says. "A little won't hurt."

I take a drink. It's absolutely nasty, possibly the nastiest thing I've ever tasted, but I don't want to look stupid so I pretend to like it.

"If you guys like that," Josh says, "you're gonna love this."

He pulls another bottle from under the seat, and this one is even bigger than the first. Everyone takes turns drinking from it, including me. In no time, it's empty.

We break up into smaller groups, with Julio and me alone at a picnic table a little ways from the car. In the distance, at another picnic table, I can see Josh and Grace kissing. Apparently, she won the competition for his attention.

Julio sees me looking at Josh and Grace. He leans forward to kiss me.

"I'm not certain that's a good idea," I say.

"Why not?" he asks.

"We just met. I still don't know very much about you."

"It's not a big deal," he says. "All I want is a kiss. It won't hurt."

"Maybe later," I say.

Julio motions to Grace. She and Josh are still kissing. "Your friend doesn't have a problem with it," he says.

"I'm not my friend," I say.

"Have some more tequila," he says. "It'll loosen you up a little."

"I've had plenty," I say. "And I don't need to be loosened up. Actually, I'm not feeling very good right now. Maybe I should be going."

"Whatever," Julio says, and without another word, he gets up and leaves.

The abruptness of his departure catches me completely by surprise. The night before, he seemed so nice and so courteous. Tonight, he's completely different, almost to the point of being rude. Not knowing what else to do, I get up and leave. I think about asking Josh for a ride back to our hotel, but he and Grace are still kissing, and I don't want to interrupt them. My stomach is starting to get a little queasy, no doubt from the alcohol, so I decide to walk back to the hotel by myself. Luckily, it isn't far, but I don't have my jacket, so it's a chilly walk. My arms are covered with goose bumps by the time I arrive.

The next day is a disaster. I wake up feeling completely miserable, and our game is at 9:00 am, so we have to be to the field by 7:30 am. Grace, Miranda, and Lauren are no better than I am, and we look and play like zombies. We only have one game, and we lose 6-0. I strike out all three times. The only good thing is my dad. He walks up to me as I'm loading my softball bag into the car.

"Are you okay?" he asks. "You look miserable today. Are you coming down with a cold or something?"

"Maybe," I lie. "I feel terrible."

"I thought that was the case. You looked listless on the field today. Not like yourself at all. But that's okay. It happens to us all on occasion. Let's stop by the drug store on the way out of town and get you some medicine. Hopefully it'll make you feel a little better."

I'm thankful. I still feel terrible, but at least my dad hasn't figured out the real reason for my misery.

Hitting Lessons

Every Tuesday night, I have hitting lessons. My hitting instructor's name is Steve Johns, and he's really nice. He gives lessons in a large industrial complex in south Seattle. It's actually quite a drive from my house in north Seattle, especially in traffic, but my dad insists on using Steve because he once worked with Ichiro. And my dad loves Ichiro. He thinks he's the greatest thing since sliced bread, and heaven help you if you say anything bad about Ichiro in my dad's presence. One time, a couple of years back, my mom said Ichiro was overrated, and for a few tense minutes I thought my dad was going to file for divorce on the spot.

Anyway, when we arrive in south Seattle, Steve is finishing up with another girl. He says goodbye to her, then comes over and greets us in his customary, jovial way.

"How is everything for Miss Rachel this week?" he asks.

As is often the case, my dad answers for me. "Let's just say someone hit her first out-of-the-park home run."

"No kidding?" Steve asks, his eyes filled with excitement.

"It was amazing," my dad says. "She hit it so hard, it must have cleared the fence by at least seventy-five feet. Maybe more."

"That's quite a rip," Steve says. "How'd it feel?"

"I didn't feel it at all," I say. "It just jumped off my bat."

"Exactly," Steve says. "When you hit a ball perfectly, that's how it feels. Did you keep it?"

"Oh, yeah," my dad says. "The umpire had two boys chase it down for me. He said it was the longest shot he's seen by a girl Rachel's age."

"I always knew you'd hit one sooner or later," Steve tells me. "You have great form and incredible bat speed. It was just a matter of when. What about this past weekend? You were in Leavenworth, right? How'd it go?"

I look away. I don't want to talk about Leavenworth. I don't even want to think about it. It's been two days since we got back but I'm still not fully recovered.

"Leavenworth didn't go too well," my dad says.

"What happened?"

"The team lost three of four games, and Rachel struggled. She wasn't feeling well."

"That's too bad," Steve says. "But I guess that happens sometimes. We can't be one hundred percent all of the time, right Miss Rachel? Was it the flu or something?"

"Something," I answer.

"How do you feel now?" he asks.

"Okay," I answer. "A little tired, though."

"Well, I'll try to take it easy on you, then. Are you ready to get started?"

My hitting lesson consists of two different stages. The first is called vision training. I stand in a batting cage, in the batter's box, as a machine shoots tennis balls at me, one at a time. Each ball is marked with a number, written in one of three colors (red, green, or black). As the ball comes to me, I have to hit it, and as I hit it, I have to call out the number and color on the ball. Steve starts the machine at a relatively slow speed (fifty miles per hour), then gradually amps it up to about one hundred miles per hour. At that speed, the ball is little more than a yellow blur, but amazingly, I've been doing this for long enough I can usually see the colors on the ball, and sometimes the numbers, regardless of the speed. The process helps me improve my focus and concentration, and it takes about half an hour.

After I finish my vision training, we move to another batting cage, and Steve tosses balls to me from behind a protective screen. He watches my form as I hit each toss and stops me periodically to correct little flaws in my swing. Some days, I do really well, and he doesn't have to correct me very often. Other days, like today, I can't do much of anything right.

I swing and miss one ball completely.

"Keep your eyes on the ball, Miss Rachel," Steve says. "Track the ball from my hand all the way to your bat. See the ball hit the bat."

I do as told, and my hitting gets a little better for a couple of minutes. Then I foul one straight back.

"Keep your hands up," Steve says. "Don't let them drop, even if it's a low pitch. Throw the knob of the bat at the ball."

I do okay for a couple of minutes, then I foul one to the side.

"Don't pull your head," Steve says. "Keep your shoulders level and your chin down, all of the time. And rotate your hips better. Your belly button should be facing me at the end of each swing."

I pound the next ball straight into the ground.

"Step into the ball," Steve says. "And drive your front foot into the ground. With authority."

Batting is so frustrating. There are so many things you have to do, so quickly, all at once.

"Get it together, Rachel," my dad says. He's standing outside the cage, watching attentively.

I swing and miss the next toss completely.

I turn to my dad, and now I'm really irritated. "See what you did?" I ask. "You frustrated me. You know I can't hit when I'm frustrated."

"Let's try it again," Steve says, trying to calm me down. "You'll get it."

And boy do I. Usually, when I get mad, I play poorly. Today is different, and it all turns around instantly. I line the next pitch straight up the middle, super hard.

"Very good," Steve says. "That's the Miss Rachel I know."

"Awesome," my dad says from outside the cage.

The next shot is even better than the first. And the shot after that is so fast it hits Steve in the side of the arm. Luckily, he isn't hurt too badly.

"Darn, Miss Rachel," he says. "You're dangerous when you get angry."

I smile.

We resume hitting, and it goes great from then on. I hit every toss straight up the middle, just like Steve and my dad like. By the time my lesson is over, everyone is happy.

"That's the way to do it," Steve says.

"Definitely," my dad says.

Food Fight

I'm sitting in the school cafeteria eating lunch with Lauren, Miranda, and Grace.

"I still don't understand," Grace says, "what happened to you Saturday night. Why'd you leave so fast? It was a real downer."

"That's not my type of place," I answer.

"Whatever," she says.

"I don't blame you at all," Lauren says. "Those guys were creeps. As soon as you left, Julio started hitting on me. When I showed no interest, he moved on to Miranda."

Nobody wants to discuss the matter further, so we change the subject. Grace is in the middle of complaining about something (complaining is her favorite pastime) when a kid screams from across the room.

"Food fight!" he shouts. He throws a sandwich at a table of students across from him.

Complete pandemonium follows. My school, Jefferson Middle, is a big school, with about fifteen hundred students divided into two lunch sessions. As such, there are about seven hundred kids in the cafeteria right now, and almost everyone joins in the fight. Within seconds, food is flying in all directions, and people are screaming, running for the doors, and flipping tables over in an attempt to get some cover.

This is one time when being a softball player really comes in handy. I grab a burrito from Lauren's tray and let it fly. It nails a kid on the other side of the cafeteria. I grab a piece of cornbread and peg another kid as he flees for a door. A second later, an apple soars my way. I catch it and throw it back at the kid that threw it. It takes his legs out from under him and he goes down in a heap.

In the meantime, Lauren and Miranda are doing equally well. Lauren grabs a hamburger and nails a girl near the buffet line. At the same time, Miranda grabs a bowl of cherries and flings them, one-at-a-time, rapid-fire, at anyone coming within range. It reminds me of those war movies my dad watches, when a soldier has a machine gun and mows down line after line of enemy troops. It's quite a sight.

Grace doesn't fare so well. A clump of mashed potatoes explodes on the wall next to her, splattering her face, neck, shoulders, and chest. I laugh as she screams and runs for cover.

The food fight continues for at least ten minutes before the teachers break it up, and it's great fun the entire time. To be perfectly honest, it's the most fun I've had at school in a long time, maybe ever. I'll remember this day for the rest of my life.

Unfortunately, like everyone involved, I get a detention slip, which means I have to go to detention for an hour tomorrow, and I have to take the slip home and have one of my parents sign it. Of course I'm not going to show it to my mom. She'll think my behavior was unacceptable and give me a scolding. But I know my dad won't care too much, and he'll probably even laugh about the whole thing.

As anticipated, he's quite amused. He has me pull up one of the local news stations on the internet, and we watch the news report together. There's even a video of the fight since one of the students (I don't know who) took a video of it using his cellular phone. The video is extremely dark, but you can still see things okay. My dad laughs as it focuses on me, Lauren, Miranda, and Grace on the far side of the cafeteria, flinging things like there's no tomorrow. My dad pauses the video at the spot where I chuck the burrito and hit the kid in the head.

"Spectacular!" he howls, slapping his knee with one hand. "Your form is perfect during that throw. Both of your arms are up, equal and opposite, just like I taught you in Little League. And look at the spin you put on that burrito. That kid never had a chance."

We watch the rest of the video, twice, and my dad laughs the whole time. He loves the part where the potatoes splatter Grace.

"Show me how to do this," he says, grabbing the keyboard. "We've got to send this video to your grandfather."

Seconds later, he's on the phone with Grandpa Frank. "Check out the part where Rachel ducks the tomato. The girl's got reflexes like a cat."

I smile. What a fun day. I wish they were all like it.

Plan B

I'm sitting at the dining room table doing my homework when my dad walks in.

"Rachel," he says. "We've got to get ready for this weekend's tournament. You need to skip school tomorrow."

"What?" my mom asks from the kitchen. She's doing dishes. She walks into the room with a half-washed pot in one hand.

"This is a big tournament," my dad says. "If we win, we automatically qualify for the state tournament in July. Rachel and I need to do some serious practicing."

"You can practice after school," my mom says. She puts special emphasis on the word 'after.'

"That doesn't give us enough time," my dad says. "And I want Rachel to get to bed early tomorrow, so she'll be well rested for Saturday."

"She's not skipping school," my mom says. "School is too important."

"Yeah, right," my dad says.

"What does that mean?"

"Education is overrated," my dad says. "Look at me. I went to college for four years after high school, and what did it get me? I work for the man, five days a week, every week. All our education system does is produce wage slaves. I want more for Rachel."

"And skipping school is going to get more for Rachel? How?"

"If she gets good enough, she could go anywhere. She might even make the Olympic team some day."

"That's unrealistic," my mom says.

"No it isn't. She can do it if she works hard."

"I don't care," my mom says. "She isn't skipping school tomorrow. And that's final."

"I already took the day off from work," my dad objects.

"I don't care. No skipping. Is that understood?"

My dad is clearly dejected. As he turns to leave the room, he shoots me a defiant glance and whispers, just loud enough so I can hear it, "Plan B."

I nearly jump for joy. Plan B is the greatest thing ever. My dad invented it a couple of years ago when he and my mom had a similar disagreement. I get up at my normal time, pack my backpack, and ride the bus to school like always. In the meantime, my dad loads my softball bag into the trunk of his car, then pretends to go to work, but instead he meets me at school just as my bus gets there. We go to the attendance office and he signs me out for the day. After that, it's off to the park we go, and trust me, I'd rather be at the park than in my classes, especially Washington state history. That class is so boring I fall asleep the minute I think about it.

We spend the first couple of hours working on fielding fundamentals. My dad is pretty old (he turns thirty-three later this year), but he's in decent shape for a guy his age, and he works me pretty hard. He even makes me do pushups, but not nearly as many as Coach Ryan. Thank goodness for that.

"Dad, are you ever going to get a new mitt?" I ask as we play toss.

"What do you mean?" he says, glancing at his mitt. It's completely disgusting. It's old and discolored, and one of its laces is broken. "This is a good mitt. It's the same one I used back in high school. I made some great plays with this mitt."

"Whatever," I say.

171

I head to second base to take some grounders. Second has always been my position, ever since I can remember. My dad says I was born to play second, and I guess it makes sense since he played second in high school, and so did Grandpa Frank before him. I guess it's a family tradition or something. Originally, I didn't care what position I played, but my dad made it clear second was my 'chosen' spot, and I've been there ever since. And that's actually okay with me, because second gets a lot of action during games, and I like action.

As my dad hits me grounders, I think about how long I've played softball. For as long as I can remember. I never remember a time when I didn't play. My dad bought my first mitt even before I was born. It was tiny compared to the one I have now, and it was bright pink with white stripes. I still have it, but I haven't seen it in years because it's buried in my closet somewhere (that reminds me, I need to clean out my closet one of these days). My dad says he taught me how to field grounders as soon as I could walk, and I joined my first Little League team when I was five. I played three years of Little League, then switched to select ball. My first two years I played for the Seattle Stars. The Stars changed their name to the Seattle Sky after the second year. I never found out why, but I didn't really care since we got cool new uniforms. They were navy and light blue, with white lightning bolts on the pants. I played three years for the Sky, then switched to the Washington Wildcats at the beginning of this season.

After doing grounders, my dad wants me to work on my base running skills, so he gets his stopwatch and times me running from home to first. I do it four times in a row.

"Well done," he says with a smile. "That last one was great. That was your best time ever."

Then we work on bunting. Unfortunately, I don't do as well at bunting as I did at running. I miss several pitches completely, and my dad gets a little impatient.

"Come on, Rachel," he says. "Concentrate."

I miss another one. "Bunting is not that hard," he says. "Here, I'll show you."

He takes the bat from me and steps into the batter's box. "Now pitch one to me."

"Dad," I say, "I don't think this is a good idea."

"Come on," he says. "I'll show you how to do it."

"Alright," I say. "But I have a bad feeling about this."

"It's no big deal. Just throw it."

So I do. And just as I thought, it was a bad idea. My dad bunts the ball, but instead of it going into the field in front of him, it goes straight up and hits him in the middle of the forehead. It hits him so hard it knocks him flat onto his back.

At first I'm scared, but then I realize he isn't hurt, and instead he's laying on the ground laughing at himself.

"Maybe," he says, "I should leave the bunting to you."

"That's probably a good idea," I say.

"I'm hungry," he says. "You want to get some lunch?"

I'm always up for lunch, so we head to the mall. After lunch, we catch a movie, then head back to the field for a little more practice, then head home for the evening.

"How was school today?" my mom asks.

"It was great," I reply. "It was the funnest day I've had in awhile."

That weekend, my team is awesome. We win all six of our games, including a 6-3 victory over the Wenatchee Wings in the championship game on Sunday afternoon. We get a shiny trophy, championship T-shirts, and an automatic berth in the state tournament in July.

The Blackberry Storm

Today is a big day for me. The Blackberry Storm cellular phone just came out. I've been waiting for it for months, and it has everything I could ever want in a phone: a high resolution touch screen, 3.2 megapixel video camera, MP3 media player, internet connectivity, GPS, Bluetooth headset, and a built-in speakerphone. It's the greatest phone ever. I want it so bad I can taste it.

Originally, I was going to buy it with my home run money, but then I went to the mall one night with my friends and spent most of it. But that's okay, because I have a backup plan. We have a big game today, and I know if I do well I can probably talk my dad into getting it for me. But the Blackberry Storm is pricey (to say the least), so I'm going to have to put on quite a show if I want my plan to succeed.

And boy do I. In the first inning, I hit a double down the third base line. In the fourth, I get a single straight up the middle. In the fifth, I get another double, this time between the center and left fielders. And I save the best for last, launching a triple all the way to the warning track in the seventh.

It's amazing how well I can do when I'm properly motivated.

On the way home, my dad is in a really good mood, and I talk him into stopping by the mall for ice cream. As we're eating, I butter him up by telling him the main reason I hit so well is because he gave me some good advice right before the game. He eats this up. As we're leaving the ice cream store and heading back to the car, we pass the cellular phone store. What a coincidence.

"Can we stop in," I ask, "just for a second?"

"Yeah, what the heck," he says. "I've been thinking about getting a cellular phone for myself. What do you think?"

"That's a great idea," I say with a smile. "In today's world, everyone should have a cellular phone, even you. And I think I know the perfect one just for you . . . ."

Twenty minutes later, my mission is complete as we walk out of the store with a matching pair of Blackberry Storms.

The Cream

My dad has to work late tonight, and my mom went to a baby shower for one of her friends, so I have the entire house to myself until they get home. This doesn't happen very often, so I'm not about to waste the opportunity. I text my friend, Darnell Williams, and have him come over for a couple of hours. I'm actually not allowed to do this, because my parents don't allow me to have friends (especially boys) over unless I ask first, but like I always say, "What they don't know won't hurt them." In addition, I really want to see Darnell tonight. We've known each other for years, but things have gotten really interesting as of late. In the past year, he has put on some weight, especially in his shoulders and arms, and to be perfectly honest, he's hot. We started flirting a couple of days ago, in math class, then started talking at lunch, and I just know something good is going to develop.

He gets a ride from his older brother, Jamal, and arrives around 6:00 pm. That's perfect, because my dad said he wouldn't be home until around 8:00 pm, and my mom said she wouldn't be home until 9:00 pm. That gives us two hours of 'alone' time. I let him in, get him something to drink, and lead him into the living room where we sit down on the couch together. We talk for awhile, mostly about little things, and I'm amazed at how much we have in common. We both love sports (Darnell plays for our school's baseball team), food (his favorite type of food is Italian, the same as mine), and traveling. His family travels a lot, and I'm amazed at all the exotic places he's been to. For an eighth grader, he's amazingly worldly.

And cute. His eyes are deep brown with auburn specks. I'm mesmerized just looking at them.

"I'm glad you invited me," he says. "Talking to you here is so much better than at school."

"Why?" I ask.

"Because here," he says, "I can do this."

He leans forward to kiss me. Our lips are inches apart when the front door opens and my dad walks in. I fly off the couch to intercept him before he sees Darnell.

"Dad," I say, trying to sound calm, "you're home."

"Yeah," he says. "My meeting got cancelled. Thank goodness. If you've been to one meeting, you've been to a hundred."

He's about to say something more when he sees Darnell sitting on the couch.

"What's up?" he asks, raising an eyebrow.

I try desperately to think of something. I know this could get ugly if it's not handled properly. "This is my friend Darnell, from school," I say.

"Nice to meet you, Darnell," my dad says. He walks past me and shakes Darnell's hand.

By this time, I'm getting pretty nervous. I don't usually sweat too much, but let's just say I'm sweating bullets now.

"You look familiar to me," my dad tells Darnell. "You're not Herschel Williams's boy, are you?"

Darnell nods, but, like me, he's clearly nervous.

"I thought so. I used to know your dad a few years back. I always liked him. I went and watched some of your Little League games with him. That was a great team you had."

Darnell nods.

"Didn't you guys win state one year?"

"Almost," Darnell says, as he starts to realize my dad isn't hostile, at least not yet. "We got to the championship game, but we lost to a team from Tacoma. They were really good."

My dad shrugs. "That happens sometimes. That's still good though, to get all the way to the championship game. Rachel's Little League teams never got close. We were lucky if we made it through districts."

"It's not easy," Darnell says.

"What are you up to these days?" my dad asks. "You still play ball?"

"Yes, sir," Darnell says. "I play for the school team."

"What position?"

"Usually short. Sometimes second."

"I played second back in my day."

"It's a fun position," Darnell says. "You get a lot of action."

"Exactly. Speaking of baseball, I bet the Mariners are on right now. You up for it?"

Darnell doesn't know what to say, so he shrugs and sits back down on the couch. My dad turns on the television and plops down next to him.

"Who's your favorite player?" my dad asks.

"Ichiro," Darnell answers.

"I like you already."

"Ichiro is the ideal player," Darnell says. "He's fast, strong, and he has a great work ethic. I wish the Mariners had more players like him."

"Me, too," my dad says. "If they did, they might actually win a few games this season. That reminds me, what's the score?"

We groan as the score appears on the screen. As is often the case, the Mariners are losing, and they're losing badly.

Amazingly, the rest of the night goes smoothly. My dad and Darnell hit it off quite well, and they talk about all kinds of things, but mostly sports. After awhile, I actually get kind of jealous, and it seems like the two of them have forgotten about me completely.

"What do you think about A-rod?" my dad asks Darnell. "They say he used steroids back in high school. What do you think?"

"It wouldn't surprise me," Darnell answers. "I've seen some of the boys at school using them."

"Really?" my dad asks. "I always wondered about that. I've heard it's a big problem these days, but I didn't know for sure."

"What about softball?" Darnell asks. "Do the girls use steroids?"

"I've never seen it," my dad says. "I think it's still pretty rare, and I hope it stays that way. But then again, I wouldn't mind getting some for Rachel. She's always been pretty scrawny. I'd like to beef her up a little."

"Oh my god," I say. I can't believe he just called me scrawny in front of Darnell.

"I'm just kidding," my dad says. "But you could use a little weight, Rachel. It would help you hit harder."

"I already hit hard enough," I say. "I don't see any other girls my age hitting out-of-the-park home runs."

"True," my dad says, "but there's always room for improvement."

Just before 8:00 pm, Jamal comes and picks Darnell up. Originally, it was our plan to get him out of here just before my dad got home from work, but so much for that. I'm half way to my room when my dad speaks, his voice stopping me in my tracks.

"That Darnell is a nice kid," he says. "I really like him. But he better not come over again, without permission, or you can kiss your phone goodbye."

The next day, I see Darnell at school during our lunch break.

"Your dad surprised me," he says with a smile. "He's kinda cool."

"Sometimes," I say. "But you know how dads are. He has his moments."

"My dad can be a real beast sometimes. He got really mad that night Grace came over."

"Grace came over?" I ask.

For a split second, Darnell's eyes get really big. "It was awhile back," he says. "Just to hang for awhile. It was no big deal." He changes the subject. "Anyway, your dad really likes softball."

"Yeah," I say. "Sometimes I think he likes it more than I do."

"He's really proud of you. He loves that trophy case of yours. Especially your home run ball."

I nod. There's a brief silence.

"Do you want to impress him?" Darnell asks.

"What do you mean?" I ask.

He hands me a small, white, unmarked tube. "Try some of this. I've been using it for about six months now. When I started, I could barely bench press a hundred pounds. Now I can do double."

"What is it?" I ask. The tube has no label at all.

"It's called the cream. It's the bomb. It's the same stuff Bonds used back in his heyday."

My eyes grow large as I realize what I'm holding.

"Your dad likes home runs," Darnell says. "You want to give him some more? Use some of that. It won't let you down."

"Where did you get it?" I ask.

181

"From one of the other guys on my team," Darnell answers. "I'm not certain where he got it. Regardless, we all use it now. Why do you think we're so good this year? Last year, we barely won half our games. This year, we're undefeated."

I don't know what to say. I'm completely in shock. I've heard plenty of stories about steroid use in school sports, both at the high school and middle school levels, but I never thought they were so close to home. And I can't believe Darnell is one of the boys involved. No wonder he's gained so much weight in the past year.

Without another word, I turn to leave.

"Where are you going?" he asks.

"I don't know," I say. "I just need to go."

"Even your dad said you should use some," Darnell says. "He wants you to get bigger."

"Not by using steroids," I say.

Darnell snickers. "I was just like you at first. I didn't want to use steroids either. I didn't think I needed them. But you'll learn otherwise. Eventually, something bad will happen and you'll need them. Just you wait and see."

I walk away. I don't want anything more to do with Darnell, at least for awhile. Now that I know he uses steroids, I don't find him nearly as attractive as I used to. I actually find him a little creepy, especially since he's now encouraging me to use them.

But for some strange, completely inexplicable reason, I keep the tube of cream, and I slip it into my pocket where it will be safe.

Erin Anderson

I've been looking forward to today for months. My dad and I have tickets to the game between the University of Washington and UCLA. The University of Washington is the home team, since it's located in Seattle, but I'm not going to see them. I'm going to see Erin Anderson, the star second baseman for UCLA. Erin is my favorite player in the whole world, and I have a poster of her on the back of my bedroom door. When she was younger, she played for my select team, and she's widely considered the best player to ever wear a Wildcat jersey. She led the Wildcats to two state championships, in back-to-back years. In one of the championship games, she hit three out-of-the-park home runs in a row.

She's amazing in every way.

"She's the greatest player the state of Washington has ever produced," my dad says as we take our seats in the stadium. "She's the female version of Ichiro. She's strong, fast, and smart. She can beat most teams by herself."

"Really?" I ask.

"No, not really," my dad says. "But she's good nonetheless."

She comes out of the dugout, and I can barely believe my eyes. She's even bigger than I thought. She's at least six feet tall, and like most college softball players, she has big shoulders and huge thighs. When she throws the ball, it explodes in the first baseman's mitt.

My dad points at the UW pitcher as she warms up.

"Think you could get a hit off of her?" he asks.

"I don't know," I say. "I doubt it."

But Erin can. She lines the first pitch to the warning track for a double. Then, in the fourth inning, she gets another double, this one deep to left field. And in the sixth, she does what I've been waiting the whole game to see – she hits an out-of-the-park home run straight up the middle, just like the one I hit a few weeks ago.

"She's incredible," I tell my dad.

"You can say that again," he says.

Grace's Dad

Sometimes, I feel sorry for Grace. Her dad Phil isn't like the rest of our dads. He rarely comes to games and when he does, he usually sleeps in his car the whole time. Today is an exception, and he actually watches for awhile. Unfortunately, it's a day when it would have been better for him to have stayed in the car. He has a metal flask in one hand, and he sips out of it frequently, and he's clearly drunk (which is really sad since it's only 9:00 am). He slurs his words badly, and I can smell alcohol on his breath from over five feet away.

He stays to himself for most of the game. He doesn't sit with the rest of the parents in the bleachers, but instead stands near the right field foul line, just beyond the first base dugout. Things are okay until Grace bats in the bottom of the fourth. She lays down a spectacular bunt. The third baseman rushes in, scoops it up, and zips it over to first, but Grace is clearly safe by a step.

"She's out," blue shouts.

"No way," Phil shouts back, throwing his flask on the ground. "She was safe by a mile."

"I said she's out," blue repeats. Like most blues, he doesn't like having his calls challenged, especially by one of the parents.

"No she wasn't," Phil yells at him. "You need to open your one good eye, ump." He tears into blue in a rage of fury, using every swear word I know, and even some I've never heard before. I'm going to jot them down for future reference; they may come in handy some day. Blue yells back, and he's about to eject Phil from the game when my dad intervenes, trying to calm them both down. In the meantime, Grace is so embarrassed she starts crying in the dugout. We girls try to make her feel better.

Across the field, my dad continues to calm Phil down.

"It was a bad call," Phil says.

"It doesn't matter," my dad tells him. "It's not that big a deal. Bad calls are a part of the game. We only have one umpire today, and he has to cover all the bases by himself. He's doing the best he can."

"It's still not fair," Phil says, finally starting to chill a little. "Grace was safe. She got robbed."

"She'll get another chance," my dad tells him. "Grace is a good player. She'll get a hit next time. But for now, you need to come with me."

Amazingly, it works. My dad leads him back to his car. Phil climbs inside and falls asleep in the back seat. My dad returns to the field and blue thanks him.

"He's just having a bad day," my dad says, trying to downplay the whole thing a little.

"From what I hear," blue says, "he has a lot of bad days."

The game resumes, and we cruise to an easy victory, but the damage is done for Grace. She can't concentrate and strikes out during her next two at-bats. Coach Ryan has no choice but to replace her with one of our backup players, Casey Franklin. When the game is over and we're packing up our stuff to head home, my dad walks into the dugout.

"Grace," he says. "Your dad is still asleep in the car, so I'll take you home today."

"Thanks, Mr. Adams," Grace says.

"It's no problem," my dad says. "These things happen on occasion."

We drop Grace off at her home in a trailer park not too far from the field, and apparently she tells her mom what happened, because I never see Phil at a game again.

Tattoo You

Today's practice is great. Well, not practice, but afterward. On the drive home, completely out of the blue, my dad says, "I feel like getting a tattoo."

"What?" I ask, somewhat surprised. I've never really pictured my dad with a tattoo.

"I've always wanted one," he says. "But I never got around to it."

"What will mom think?"

"Who cares?" he says. "I'm a big boy. I can do what I want."

My dad is so funny. He talks big when my mom isn't around. But his attitude would be completely different if she were in the car with us right now.

Regardless, we stop at a tattoo parlor called Tattoo You. It's a small, hole-in-the-wall place in a strip mall just east of town. It's pretty seedy (to say the least), but I'm excited because I've never been inside a tattoo parlor before. The main lobby is small, and it has a couch and a coffee table on one side. The coffee table is covered with books of photographs of tattoos.

"What do you think I should get?" my dad asks.

"I don't know," I say as I thumb through one of the books. I find a photo of a half naked woman with a tattoo on her lower back. A classic tramp stamp. It's actually quite detailed, with multiple colors and intricate swirls.

"Don't look at that," my dad says. "Here. Look at this one."

He hands me another book, this one a little tamer. I actually liked the first book better, but regardless, it's no big deal, and I'm still happy. After all, it's not every day I get to go to a tattoo parlor.

A man in his early twenties greets us. His arms are covered with tattoos, and he has more piercings than I've ever seen, in his ears, nose, eyebrows, lips, and tongue. I imagine he probably has more, in places I can't (and don't) want to see.

"Name's DJ," he says. "How can I help you?"

"I was thinking about getting a tattoo," my dad says. "Something simple."

"First one?" DJ asks.

"Yeah," my dad answers.

"Any idea what you'd like?"

"I think so," my dad says. He hands him one of the books and points to a photograph of a baseball. "I want this, but yellow, so it'll look like a softball, and I want the number twenty-four on it."

Twenty-four is my jersey number. I've always worn it. I picked it years ago, when I played for the Stars, and I kept it when I switched to the Wildcats. I like it because it's the same number Erin Anderson wears. It's also my birthday (October 24).

"Sweet," DJ says. "Come on back."

He leads us down a hallway into a room with a chair shaped like the ones at my orthodontist (that reminds me, I have my monthly tightening in a couple of days). DJ has my dad sit in it, then rolls up my dad's sleeve and draws an outline of the softball on his upper arm.

"You can do tattoos in color?" I ask.

"Oh yeah," DJ says. "Some colors look better than others, and some last longer than others, but it's all good."

"Sweet."

189

I pull out my phone and text Lauren. "You won't believe where I'm at right now."

"Where?" Lauren texts back.

"A tattoo parlor. With my dad. He's getting a tattoo."

"OMG," Lauren texts. "No way."

"Take a look," I type. I send a photo to her.

"Sweet." She writes back.

DJ finishes the outline and has my dad examine it in a mirror on the wall. "What do you think?"

"Looks good to me," my dad says. "What do you think, Rachel?"

"Can you make the number a little bigger?" I ask.

"Of course," DJ says. He wipes away the original and does it again, this time with my number almost as big as the softball itself.

"Much better," I say. I take a picture and send it to Lauren. She likes it, too.

DJ takes out a strange electronic device with a needle on one end and begins the actual tattoo. The sight of it makes my stomach queasy, since I've never liked needles, but it's exciting nonetheless. As he runs it over my dad's arm, he has to wipe it periodically with a cloth of some sort. At times, there are small specks of blood.

"Does it hurt?" I ask.

"No, not at all," my dad says, trying to act tough, but his eyes are glossy.

It takes about forty-five minutes for DJ to finish. When he's done, he has my dad approve it, then wipes some sort of gel all over it. After that, he wraps it in plastic wrap to keep it clean and protected. My dad pays him and we leave.

"That was fun," I say as we climb into our car.

"And long overdue," my dad says. "I can't wait to show the guys at work."

"Can I get one someday?" I ask.

"Of course," my dad says. "As soon as you turn thirty-three."

We laugh and head for home.

A New Bat

I'm sitting at the dining room table, doing my homework, when my dad calls from his den.

"Rachel," he says. "Come in here. I've got something to show you."

"Dad," I shout. "I'm in the middle of my math assignment."

"This is important."

I'm a little annoyed, because I'm trying to get my homework done, but I don't want to argue with him because it's too much hassle. As I enter his den, he's sitting at his desk, peering intently at his computer screen. As I circle around to see what he's looking at, I bump his arm right where he got his tattoo. He grimaces.

"Be careful," he says. "My arm's still sore. Anyway, check this out. It's the brand new Synergy. It just came out a few days ago. It's the hottest bat on the market right now. All the reviews give it four stars. We might have to get you one."

My mom overhears from the kitchen, where she's doing the dishes. "Rachel has plenty of bats. She doesn't need another."

"Rachel," my dad tells me, "go shut that door."

I head over and shut the door. That way, my mom can't hear us anymore.

"What do you think?" my dad asks.

I'm instantly interested, because I love new bats, but I have to admit my mom has a point. I already have four bats.

"You can never have too many bats," my dad says. "You never know, we might be on a road trip someday, and you break a bat during a game. Then what are you going to do?"

"Use one of the other three?"

"Those are old, Rachel," my dad says. "They might not be reliable anymore."

"We just got my Stealth a month ago. It's not even broken in yet."

"Really?" my dad asks. "It seems like we've had that Stealth forever. And what about your Rocketech?"

"We got it two months ago. You got a good deal on eBay, remember?"

"Oh, yeah. Boy that Rocketech has good pop. But I hear this Synergy is better."

"Mom will get mad," I warn. "She says we spend too much money on softball."

"Softball isn't that expensive."

"I have four bats. Each one cost at least two hundred dollars, even the ones you got on eBay. That's eight hundred dollars, just for bats. And what about all my other gear? My helmets, sliding pads, uniforms, cleats, bags, mitt, and training gear."

"Man, Rachel," my dad says. "You're awfully tight for someone your age. But alright. If you're not interested – "

"I didn't say I wasn't interested."

"With this new Synergy you could hit another home run."

"Really?"

"It has serious pop. Trust me. It's the bomb."

A second later, my dad has his credit card out and my new bat is on its way.

Alexis

Today is a bad day for my team. Our starting center fielder, Alexis Sampson, quit the team. It's really sad because Alexis was one of our best players and a nice girl. I'll miss her.

It all started a couple of days ago at school. Alexis was sitting in the cafeteria with the rest of us, having lunch, when she spotted her boyfriend, Devan Lane, near the main door talking to Grace.

"I hate to say anything," Miranda said, "but that's not a good sign. I wouldn't trust Grace with my boyfriend for a second."

"Devan and I have been a couple for six months now," Alexis said. "I can trust him."

"Yeah, right," Miranda said. "Go ask him where he was last night."

"What do you mean?" Alexis asked.

"Was he with you?"

"No. I was at home. Like usual on a school night."

"And where was he?"

"I don't know. It's not like I check up on him every day."

"Well, you might want to, because a little birdie told me he was somewhere he shouldn't have been."

"What do you mean?"

"He was at the mall, having dinner with a certain someone we all know and love so much."

She shot a long, hard glance at Grace across the cafeteria. Grace laughed as Devan leaned closer and whispered something in her ear.

Alexis was out of her seat like a cork out of a wine bottle. She rushed up to them. They were too far away for us to hear, but it was obvious their conversation wasn't pleasant. After a couple of minutes, Alexis and Devan stepped outside. Alexis looked really upset. In the meantime, Grace, who stayed inside, smiled triumphantly.

After that, word spread quickly around school. Devan broke up with Alexis, and he hooked up with Grace, which was quite ironic, since Grace already had a boyfriend, but she broke up with her boyfriend so she could be with Devan.

Later that week, when I get to practice, I can tell right from the start it's going to be ugly. Alexis purposefully tries to stay away from Grace, to avoid a confrontation, but Grace goes out of her way to aggravate things.

"No hard feelings, right?" she asks Alexis. "I mean, it's not like you and Devan were much of an item anyway. He said you didn't have much in common."

"That's not what he told me," Alexis says.

"He said there wasn't much of a spark between you. He said he was just passing the time until the right girl came along. And guess what? That girl is me."

That's all it takes. The fight is on, and it's a nasty one. It takes all of us, plus Coach Ryan, plus our assistant coaches, plus several of the parents, to pull them apart. Alexis emerges from the fracas with a scratch on her cheek and a nasty gouge over one eye. Coach Ryan takes her to the emergency room to get stitches.

Our team has a code of conduct and fighting with a teammate is a clear violation of that code. Normally, both players would be suspended for two weeks.

However, we have a big tournament coming up this weekend, and Coach Ryan doesn't want us to be without two of our best players, so he decides to 'overlook' the whole thing and not punish either girl as long as they promise it won't happen again. Unfortunately, the damage is done. The next day, Alexis quits the team and, despite our best efforts (Lauren, Miranda, and I send her several text messages), she refuses to come back.

It's too bad, too. Alexis is a good player with a positive attitude, and we could always count on her to play hard and do her best. With her on the team, we had a legitimate chance of winning the state championship. Now, I'm not so sure.

The Fallout

The next weekend, we have a tournament, but it isn't meant to be. On Saturday, we get rained out, which is always a bummer, because it's not like the tournament organizer just calls up and tells us it's rained out and it's over. Instead, we get up at 6:00 am, travel all the way to the field, and 'warm up' for an hour in the pouring rain. After warm-ups, we take the field and play for an inning or two before the field turns to mud. Blue finally decides to halt the game until it stops raining. We wait for an hour or two, which actually isn't too bad, since we girls cram into one of our parent's cars and talk about boys. But then, inevitably, blue decides it isn't going to stop raining any time soon, so he calls the game and we pack up and leave. Half way home, it gets sunny.

It's quite frustrating. Sometimes, I wish I lived in California, or Arizona, or just about anywhere except the Pacific Northwest. It's hard to have a good time when every third or fourth game is rained out.

Regardless, the weather gets better on Sunday, so we head back to the field to make up our games from the day before. Unfortunately, the team is completely listless. The whole team (except Grace) is still disappointed Alexis left, and we don't play like ourselves. Coach Ryan moves our left fielder, Kimi Suzuki, to center to take Alexis's spot, but it doesn't work out that well. Kimi is a good player, but she's not used to playing center, and she makes two errors in the first game. We lose to the Arlington A's 5-1, then lose to the Bellingham Beavers 6-3. The day finishes with an especially disappointing loss to the Stinger Squad 3-0. The loss to the Stinger Squad is really upsetting because they are a 14u team, and we should never lose to a bunch of younger girls. Earlier in the season we played and beat them 11-1.

But the weekend's games are just the beginning of my problems. The real misery begins Tuesday afternoon. I'm sitting in math class, with my Blackberry Storm hidden under the edge of my desk, where my teacher, Mr. D'Angelo, can't see it. I'm texting a friend when a hall monitor walks in and gives Mr. D'Angelo a note. Mr. D'Angelo reads it and says, "Mr. Walker wants to see you in his office."

Mr. Walker is one of our school counselors, and periodically he calls kids to his office to see how they're doing, so I'm not too worried at first. When I get there, however, my attitude changes quickly. Sitting in his office, side-by-side, are Grace, Miranda, and Lauren. Mr. Walker is a short, balding man in his thirties, and normally he is quite friendly, but not today.

"Take a seat, Rachel," he says.

I shoot a glance at Lauren, as if to say, "What's going on?" and she shoots a glance at me, as if to say, "Big trouble." At the very same instant, I realize Miranda is crying.

Mr. Walker shuts the door behind me. "Your friends and I were discussing your trip to Leavenworth."

My heart stops.

"It's come to my attention," he continues, "that the four of you had quite an adventure over there. You snuck out of your room, met some boys, and did a little drinking."

"Who told you that?" Lauren asks.

"Who do you think?" Grace answers with a snarl. "Alexis."

"How did she know?"

"The whole team knows. I told them."

Mr. Walker continues. "I'm sure you're aware drinking under the age of twenty-one is a crime in the state of Washington, as well as a violation of our school's code of conduct. It's grounds for immediate suspension."

My head is spinning. I can barely believe what I'm hearing. I've rarely been in trouble at school before, and I've never been suspended.

"Before I decide the length of your suspension," Mr. Walker continues, "I want to know one thing. What were you thinking when you snuck out that night?"

"I just wanted to have some fun," Grace says.

"Me, too," Miranda says.

Lauren and I have no answer. We're speechless.

"I see," Mr. Walker says. "Well, you're going to have plenty of time to have fun now, because you're all suspended for three days. I've already made calls to your parents, and they're on their way to pick you up."

For a brief second, I think I'm going to pass out right there on the spot. I can't believe I'm suspended. My parents are going to flip when they find out. I pull my Blackberry Storm from my pocket and take one long, last look. It's as good as gone.

My dad arrives an hour later. He meets with Mr. Walker for about twenty minutes in his office, as I sit alone in the hall, then comes out with some brochures in one hand. He throws the brochures into the nearest garbage can, turns to me, and says, "Come with me."

I know what it feels like to be a prisoner on death row.

The car ride home is unbearable. My dad's face is red, so I can tell he's upset, but he doesn't say anything the whole way. It's absolutely awful. After five minutes, I wish he would just yell at me and get it over with. He pulls into our driveway, turns off the car, and just sits there. At first I'm uncomfortable and I don't know what to do, but I decide I better not move until he tells me to, so I just stay there, completely motionless.

"How old are you?" he asks. Much to my relief, the redness in his face has dissipated, and he seems surprisingly calm.

"Fourteen," I answer.

"I guess this was going to happen sooner or later. I hoped it would be later."

"What do you mean?" I ask.

"Teenagers are teenagers," he says. "Part of being a teenager is making mistakes. I made a few in my time. Hopefully you understand the magnitude of your mistake."

"I do," I say. "It won't happen again. I promise."

He nods. "You're grounded for two weeks. I want you to go to your room immediately. I'll explain the whole thing to your mom the best I can. It's not going to be pretty."

And it isn't. I head upstairs, to my room, but I stay in the hallway near the top of the stairs. From there, I can't see my parents in the kitchen, but I can hear them just fine. Like always, they start off with a little small talk, but it gets serious fast.

"How was work today?" my mom asks as she makes dinner. It smells really good, and I'm actually pretty hungry, but there's no way I'm heading down there right now.

"My day was okay," my dad says. "Pretty normal, until this afternoon."

"Really?" my mom asks. "What happened?"

200

"I got a call from Rachel's counselor, Mr. Walker."

My mom sighs. "Was she texting in class again?"

"I wish," my dad says. "I mean, no, she wasn't texting in class. Actually, she probably was, but she didn't get in trouble for it. Today she got in trouble for something a little more serious."

I cringe. This is the moment of truth.

My dad hesitates for a long second. He clearly doesn't know what to say. Finally, he just comes out with it.

"Rachel got suspended from school."

"What?" my mom says. From the tone of her voice, I can tell she's about to freak.

"Do you remember that softball trip awhile back?" my dad asks. "The one to Leavenworth?"

"Yes," my mom says.

"Rachel and some of the other girls snuck out and met some boys. One of the boys had some alcohol."

"Oh my god," my mom says. "Rachel was drinking? She's only fourteen."

"I just found out myself," my dad says.

"And what did you do?"

"I grounded her for two weeks."

"Two weeks? For drinking? That's ridiculous, Michael. You grounded her for longer when she skipped practice to go to a movie."

"That was serious," my dad says. "She shouldn't skip practices."

"This is a little more serious than skipping practices, Michael. As far as I'm concerned, that girl is grounded indefinitely."

My head drops in complete defeat. In my family, being grounded indefinitely is basically the same as getting the death penalty. Actually, the death penalty isn't quite as bad. At least it's over quickly.

"And where were you when all this happened?" my mom asks.

"What?" my dad asks. From the tone of his voice, I can tell he's caught off-guard.

"Where were you when your fourteen-year-old daughter was wandering across town with a bunch of boys drinking alcohol?"

My dad is silent.

"Tell me, Michael," my mom repeats. Her voice is getting really loud now. "Where were you? No, let me guess. You were sitting in the hotel lobby, having a drink with Lauren's dad, talking about Ichiro. Weren't you?"

I hear my dad stammer a little, but I can't make out his words.

"Why don't you just let the girl play in the middle of the highway, Michael?"

"I thought the chaperones were watching her," my dad says.

"You're her father, Michael. You're in charge of watching her. Not the chaperones."

There is a long silence before my mom speaks again.

"I'm so mad I could scream. And I better not find out she's been skipping school again to practice softball."

I almost fall down the stairs. I can't believe my mom knows about Plan B.

"You didn't think I knew about that, did you, Michael?" my mom asks. "What do you think I am? An idiot?"

My dad is completely silent. It's almost like a bomb went off in the kitchen and he disintegrated on the spot.

Without another word, my mom storms outside onto the back porch. There is a crash as the door slams and a picture frame falls from the wall and shatters. I hear my dad walk slowly into the living room. I head downstairs to see how he's doing, and when I enter the room he's on the far side, looking quietly at my trophy case. Even though he's got his back to me, he hears me coming.

"It would be best if you stayed in your room tonight," he says.

I head back upstairs. Without my Blackberry Storm, there isn't much to do except my homework. I usually do it on the dining room table since it's big and there's a lot of room to spread out, but that isn't an option tonight. So I use my desk instead, but I don't get much done because I can't concentrate after all that's happened. After half an hour, I give up, climb into my bed, and pull the covers over me. My cat, Mr. Pawsington, jumps onto the bed and snuggles. Normally, I don't like it when Mr. Pawsington sleeps on the bed because he purrs so loudly it keeps me awake. Tonight, however, I'll take any friend I can get.

Angry Hens

Practice today is no fun. As soon as we get there, my dad has to have a special meeting with the coaches to decide how to deal with the fallout from the Leavenworth trip. Technically, drinking alcohol is a violation of my team's code of conduct, and Grace, Lauren, Miranda, and I should be suspended for two weeks. However, we have a big tournament coming up, so Coach Ryan says he's willing to overlook the code of conduct this one time. However, he has decided to change our team's travel policy, and we girls are no longer allowed to stay in rooms of our own. Instead, we have to stay with our parents in their rooms, and to be perfectly honest, that's fine with me. After all I've been through, I'll do just about anything to stay out of any more trouble.

Practice itself is pretty awful, and we make a lot of errors, and it drives Coach Ryan crazy because they're mostly mental errors. He breaks errors into two groups: physical and mental. Physical errors are just bad plays, like making an errant throw or dropping a catch. He says those just happen and it's no big deal. Mental errors are the ones where you do something stupid, like throw the ball to the wrong base, or get caught out of position, or make a base running mistake. Today we make a lot of mental errors, so we get to do twice as many pushups as normal.

But the absolute lowlight of the practice comes during our final water break. I'm sitting in the dugout by myself, resting, when I overhear two of the mothers talking in the bleachers. Since I'm in the dugout, they can't see me and don't know I'm there.

"I still can't believe it," one mother says.

"Me, neither," the other says. "First the whole ordeal with Grace and Alexis, and now this."

"I just can't believe what girls were involved," the first mother says. "Grace and Miranda I can understand. I never really liked them. But Lauren and Rachel? Rachel is such a sweet, young thing. I never thought she'd do anything like this."

"I know," the second mother says. "But then again, you know what they say. It's the quiet ones you've got to watch the most. Sometimes, they can be the worst of all."

"If you ask me," the first mother says, "I think Coach Ryan should get rid of them all and start over with some new girls. We don't need their type on the team. They'll just corrupt the other girls. The good ones."

"Amen," the second mother says.

Coach Ryan calls me back to the field, and I'm happy to go because I've heard more than I wanted to hear. It's funny how fickle people can be at times. At the tournament where I hit my first out-of-the-park home run, these same women told me how wonderful I was, and how the team wouldn't be the same without me. Now, they want me gone.

Fun with Windshields

I'm in my room, cleaning out my closet (I don't have anything better to do since I don't have my Blackberry Storm or my laptop computer any more), when I hear my dad downstairs. "Sweet," he says. "It's finally here. Rachel, get down here."

When I get downstairs, I find my dad standing at the front door with the delivery man. My dad is signing some paperwork as the delivery man holds a long, narrow box in one hand.

I've seen that type of box before. It's my new bat, the one my dad and I ordered a few days ago. My dad finishes the paperwork, exchanges it for the box, heads into the living room, and starts opening it.

"Isn't that supposed to be my bat?" I ask.

My dad looks up. "Oh," he says. "Here. Open it. Don't take all day."

He hands me the box and I tear into it. And boy is the new bat impressive. It's really light, and it has a super glossy finish that sparkles when I hold it in the light just right.

"Let me see it," my dad says. He can barely control himself. He's like a kid on Christmas day. I hand it to him, and he gives it a thorough examination, including a few practice swings.

"That feels good," he says. "It's perfectly balanced. It's not end-loaded at all."

He swings it again, and his backswing nails the lamp sitting on a nearby table. It crashes to the floor.

"Oh no," he says as he examines the bat closely, right at the spot where it made contact with the lamp.

After a few intense seconds, he lets out a sigh of relief. "Don't worry. It's okay. Not even a scratch."

I wish I could say the same for the lamp.

"That thing is old," my dad says. "We needed a new one anyway. Let's go and break this bat in a little."

I'm about to say we should clean up the remnants of the lamp before we leave, but my dad already has his car keys in hand and is heading for the door. So we drive to McCall Field, but unfortunately there's a Little League team using it, so we head over to Legion Park (our backup field), but it, too, is being used.

"We'll have to use the back yard," my dad says.

"The back yard isn't very big," I warn.

"Just hit it lightly," he says.

So we head back to our house and go out to the back yard. My mom is in the kitchen as we pass through. "You two be careful out there," she says. "I don't want a repeat of last time."

My dad takes a spot on one side of the yard, and I'm on the opposite side with my new bat in hand. He tosses me a pitch. I try to hit it as softly as I can, but the ball bounces off of the bat, flies straight across the yard, and nails him squarely in the leg.

"That thing is incredible," he says as he hobbles around the yard, trying to shake it off. "Did you see that pop?"

"It felt pretty good," I say. "Are you okay?"

"Oh, yeah," he says. "It's just a stinger. It'll be fine in a second."

"Rub a little dirt on it," I say.

"It's okay," he says. "Here, let's try it again."

He throws me another pitch. Once again, I try to hit it as lightly as possible, but I actually end up hitting it even harder than the first time. The ball soars completely out of the yard, clears our neighbor's house, and shatters the windshield of a minivan parked out front.

"That's amazing," my dad says. "Did you see how high that went? I've never seen a bat with pop like that before."

There is a long silence as we look at the minivan with the shattered windshield. Finally, my dad speaks. "We should probably go talk to Mr. Wilson," he says. "He's not going to be happy about this."

"Isn't this the third time we've broken his windshield?" I ask.

"Actually," my dad says, "I think it's the fourth."

More Trouble

Today we have a tournament in Tacoma. Tacoma is a city about thirty minutes south of Seattle, and it's pretty rundown in places, and unfortunately we're playing in one of those places. The neighborhood is dirty and grimy, and the field looks like it rarely, if ever, gets any attention. The infield is covered with small rocks, and the grass hasn't been mowed in weeks. Regardless, the day starts off well, and we win our first game against a team from Oregon called the Pony Express. I use my new bat, and I get two singles, both straight up the middle. Everyone is happy, and as we warm up for our second game, I hear my dad in the stands talking with Lauren's dad.

"Did you see the Mariners' game last night?" he asks. "Ichiro stole the show."

This is our first tournament since Grace, Miranda, Lauren, and I got suspended from school, and it's good to see everyone, including my dad, finally getting back to normal. In our second game, I'm hoping to play well, because I'm still grounded indefinitely, and I'm hoping if I can get back on my dad's good side, he'll talk to my mom and I'll get my Blackberry Storm back. I know it's still a ways off, but it never hurts to be hopeful.

Unfortunately, I never get the chance. In the very first inning, a girl hits a routine grounder right at me. I move forward to get it, like I always do, but it hits a small rock and shoots straight up into my face.

Here's the worst part. I'm not wearing my mouthpiece. The thing drives me crazy, so I took it out before the game when my dad and Coach Ryan weren't looking.

The parents gasp as I lean forward and spit blood from my mouth. Blue calls an emergency timeout, and Coach Ryan runs out to help me. As he walks me to the dugout, I overhear Lauren say to Grace, "I hope she's okay."

"That's what happens," Grace responds, "when you don't wear your mouthpiece."

Coach Ryan rinses out my mouth with a squirt bottle as my dad joins us in the dugout.

"It doesn't look good, Mike," he says. "You better take her to the dentist ASAP."

My dad sighs, rounds up my gear, and leads me to the car. A few minutes later, we're at the dentist's office. Luckily, Dr. Wong has weekend hours. He takes some x-rays of my mouth and jaw.

"You're going to be okay," he says as he examines the x-rays. "There's no real damage, but thank goodness you still have your braces on. Otherwise, you'd have lost several of these front teeth, as well as this canine. You said this was a softball injury?"

I nod.

"I thought softball players wore mouthpieces?" he asks.

"They usually do," my dad interjects, as he shoots me an intense glance. I've seen that glance before. Let's just say it's bad news for me.

When we get home, I stand in the upstairs hallway, with an icepack on my jaw, as my parents speak in the kitchen.

"Tell me again, Michael," my mom says. "Where were you when Rachel got hit in the mouth? Let me guess. You were in the bleachers, talking to Lauren's dad about the Mariners' game."

There's no response from my dad.

"And you were too busy yapping about Ichiro to realize your daughter didn't have her mouthpiece in? Weren't you?"

My dad has nothing to say. He's been married to my mom for long enough to know this battle was over before it began.

In many ways, I feel sorry for my dad. He's an adult, but he gets in nearly as much trouble as I do.

The Cycle

My dad takes me to the sporting goods store and buys me a Game Face, a large, clear mask that goes over my face and protects it from ground balls.

"Dad," I complain as he pushes it over the top of my head, somewhat forcibly. "I hate Game Faces. They're so uncomfortable."

"You should have thought of that last week," he says, "before you took out your mouthpiece. From now on, you're wearing a Game Face. That way I can tell if you have it on or not."

"Dad," I plead, "I'll wear my mouthpiece from now on. I swear."

"You had your chance. Come along. And bring that Game Face or else."

So now I have to wear a Game Face every day, both at practice and during games. I hate it. It's big and bulky, somewhat like a hockey goalie's mask, and even though it's made of clear plastic, I can't see very well out of it. But at least my dad is happy, because it'll save him from getting in any additional trouble with my mom.

At least for awhile. Sooner or later, something new will happen. For us, it always does.

Today I'm playing pickup for my friend Amy George's team, the Kenmore Crushers. They're a good team, but their second baseman is sick, so I agreed to play in her place. I've played pickup a lot before, for several different teams, and it's usually fun, but it's a little uncomfortable since the only girl I know is Amy. Luckily, she introduces me to everyone, and they all seem pretty nice. Our first game is against the Redmond LadyCats and we beat them easily, 6-2. I get a double and score a run. Our second game is against the Stinger Squad, and it turns out to be quite a battle, ending in a 4-4 tie. I go one for three, with a double all the way to the warning track. The third game, however, is where the real fun begins.

I start the game by hitting a double in the first inning. I follow that with a single in the third. Then I hit a triple in the fourth.

I hear mumbling in the stands. The Crusher's head coach, Coach Frank, comes up to me in the dugout. "I shouldn't tell you this," he says, "because it'll jinx you, but you're on the verge of hitting for the cycle."

Hitting for the cycle is one of the greatest, and rarest, achievements in all of softball. It's when a batter hits a single, double, triple, and home run in the same game. Erin Anderson did it once when she was in high school.

All I need is a home run. If I can hit a home run during my next at-bat, I will have done the unbelievable.

As I take my place in the on-deck circle, waiting for my final turn to bat, my dad comes up and talks to me through the backstop screen. This is somewhat unusual, because he doesn't usually talk to me too much during games.

"For this next at-bat," he says, "I want you to forget your training. Don't worry about what Steve tells you about always swinging the same. I want you to crush it as hard as you can."

"Really?" I ask.

"Grit your teeth, and heave ho it as far as you can."

"But sometimes," I object, "when I swing that hard, I miss it completely. That's why Steve doesn't like me to do it."

"I know," my dad says. "But this is a chance at glory, Rachel. Pure glory. The cycle is the holy grail of softball. It's right up there with a no-hitter. I'm not even certain if Ichiro has hit for the cycle. Go for it. If you strike out, big deal. But if you hit it out of here, we'll remember this day forever."

He heads back to the stands.

I'm feeling the pressure now. The fans in the bleachers are watching me intently, waiting to see if I can do it. In the meantime, all of the Crushers are standing on the front edge of the dugout, watching anxiously. It's a lot quieter than normal.

The first pitch is pretty high, but straight down the middle, so I go after it with everything I have. It's a classic tomahawk chop, one of the most powerful swings I've ever taken.

Unfortunately, I miss it completely.

Everyone sighs. I can tell they want this cycle as much as I do.

I step out of the batter's box for a brief second. I'm a little rattled. The pressure is really getting to me.

My second swing is no better than the first.

"Strike two," blue calls.

A bead of sweat trickles down my side.

If my hitting instructor, Steve, could see these swings, he'd be so disappointed. This is not how he taught me to bat, but then again, this is what my dad wants. As such, I'm going to do it again, at least one more time.

That's all it takes. Every muscle in my body tightens as I hit the next pitch as hard as I can. The ball soars straight toward center field. At first, I think it's just a massive fly ball, one the center fielder will catch with ease, but it's not. It continues to climb, and climb, and climb. Everyone goes crazy as the ball clears the outfield fence by at least fifty feet.

When I reach home plate, the Crushers tackle me. The last thing I see before I'm smothered by bodies is the sight of my dad in the stands, his arms up, cheering triumphantly.

The ride home is great fun. My dad is too excited to talk to me. He calls his friends first.

"You had to see it," he tells one friend. "They couldn't keep her off the bases today. Every inning – hit, hit, hit. She was a machine."

"You had to be here," he tells another friend. "Her bat was on fire. I've never seen a girl hit like that before."

"It was incredible," he tells Grandpa Frank. "It was like she was on a whole another level, all her own. She was unstoppable."

We're over half way home before he calms down and talks to me. "I don't know what to say," he says. "That was amazing. Simply amazing."

I don't know what to say either, so I just smile. Today is the best day I've had in a long time, definitely the best day since I got suspended from school. I'm trying to savor it for awhile.

But then it gets even better. My dad does something completely unexpected. He hands me his Blackberry Storm. "You earned it," he says with a smile.

"You're giving me your phone?" I ask.

"Just until your mom gives yours back. But don't tell her I gave you mine, or you know what will happen."

"Big trouble," I say.

"You can say that again," he says.

Life is good now. Life is much better when you have a phone. I'd prefer to have my own, of course, but then again, beggars can't be choosers.

The New Girl

Today is not a good day. Coach Ryan found a new girl to join the team, to take the roster spot vacated when Alexis Sampson left after the fight with Grace. Her name is Courtney King. She's sixteen, which makes her one of the oldest girls on the team, maybe even the oldest, and she's a typical tomboy – big, strong, and extremely talented. Last year, she was in the newspaper because she played so well for her old team.

Normally, I'd be pretty excited if a player as good as Courtney joined the team. But I'm not. Actually, I'm pretty upset. She's a second baseman, and that means I'm going to have some serious competition for playing time from now on. And that really makes me mad, because I'm the type of player who likes to play every inning of every game.

It also frustrates me because my team needs a new center fielder. Center field was Alexis's position, so why didn't Coach Ryan get a new center fielder? Why a second baseman?

I'm sitting with the other girls in the dugout, and we're watching Courtney take grounders. She's so good nothing gets past her. In addition, she's so strong she can whip the ball to first in an instant.

"It looks like we just got a new starter at second," Grace says.

"That's ridiculous," I say. "I've been the starter since the beginning of the season. I've done everything Coach Ryan has asked, and now this new girl comes along and gets my spot?"

"Not necessarily," Lauren says, trying to make me feel a little better. "Coach Ryan hasn't said anything yet. You never know. He may stick with you after all."

We watch as Courtney dives to the left and knocks down a grounder that should have gotten past her easily. Even I have to admit it was a great play.

"Look at her," I say. "It's hopeless. She's older than me, and she's bigger and stronger. I'm no match for her."

"You're quicker," Miranda says.

"And we haven't seen her hit yet," Lauren says. "Who knows? Maybe she can't hit at all."

Almost on cue, Coach Ryan walks to the pitching circle and has Courtney take some batting practice. She hits the first pitch off of the outfield wall.

And the next.

And the next.

And the next.

"Have fun on the bench," Grace says.

"I don't know about that," Lauren says. "You can play outfield, right Rachel? Maybe Coach Ryan will move you to center, then move Kimi back to left."

This doesn't make me feel any better. It is true I can play outfield, and I have done it on occasion in the past, but I don't like it. I like second.

"Rachel isn't the only one who should be worried," Lauren says, shooting a glance at Grace and Miranda. "If I were you two, I'd be worried too."

"What do you mean?" Grace asks, instantly getting defensive.

"You saw Courtney's arm. She's a beast. She can probably play shortstop and third, too. What if Coach Ryan decides to keep Rachel at second and moves Courtney to short? Or third?"

"A second baseman can't play third," Grace says.

218

"Some can. I bet Courtney can."

Grace doesn't like the sound of that at all.

"Or maybe," Lauren continues, "he'll leave Rachel at second and put Courtney at short. After all, middle infielders are often interchangeable."

"That's ridiculous," Miranda says. "That's my position. I worked hard for that spot. You guys remember tryouts. I beat out two other girls."

Coach Ryan claps merrily as Courtney hits another shot off of the outfield wall.

"This isn't fair," Lauren says. "The four of us are a good infield. We have good chemistry. Now Coach Ryan is going to mess everything up by bringing in this new girl."

"There wouldn't have been a need for this new girl," Miranda says, shooting a nasty glance at Grace. "If someone had stayed away from Alexis's boyfriend."

"Don't start with me," Grace warns.

"If anyone should lose her position," Miranda says, "it should be you, Grace."

"Well, it's not going to be. Coach Ryan won't replace me. I'm the star of the team."

Courtney hits another ball off of the outfield wall.

"Not anymore," Miranda says.

The next day, we have a scrimmage against the Washington Wildcats 18u team. There are actually two Washington Wildcats teams: my team, for girls sixteen and younger, and the other team, for girls eighteen and younger. We scrimmage against the 18u team quite a bit, and since they're older, they usually win, but we always try hard anyway. Today, we're all preoccupied with one thing. Where is Courtney going to play?

Much to my chagrin, I'm the odd man out. I spend the first two innings on the bench, watching Courtney make plays (my plays) at second. And then, when I finally get to come in, Coach Ryan puts me in center field. While I'm out there, two balls are hit my way, and I miss them both. Not liking that arrangement very much, Coach Ryan moves me to second (much to my relief), but then moves Courtney to short, sending Miranda to the bench. Miranda is visibly upset as she takes a seat. A play later, a ball is hit straight up the middle, and it goes right between Courtney and me for a single.

"That was your ball," Courtney says.

"No, it wasn't," I say. "It was yours."

"Whatever," Courtney says.

Not liking that arrangement, Coach Ryan moves Courtney to third and reinserts Miranda at short. As Grace walks to the dugout, she gives Coach Ryan a look that could kill.

Two innings later, the game is over, and the older Wildcats win 6-0. Coach Ryan gathers us in center field for our post-game meeting.

"I don't understand what was wrong with you ladies today," he says. "The last time we played the 18u team we won 3-2. We looked sharp in every way. But today we got killed. I didn't see any fire out there, and at times you looked completely confused. But that's okay, I guess. All teams, even the really good ones like us, have bad days on occasion, and apparently today was one of those days. We have another scrimmage tomorrow, so hopefully things will get better then."

Yeah, right. The second scrimmage is no better than the first. Today, Coach Ryan starts Courtney at shortstop, with Miranda at second and me in center. Miranda makes an error in the first inning, and I make one in the second. Coach Ryan moves me to shortstop, Courtney to second, and Miranda to center. I make an error during the next inning, so Coach Ryan switches things again, this time moving Miranda to short, Grace to center, and me to third.

This is almost too much for me to handle. If there is one position I absolutely hate, it's third. Third is called the 'hot corner' because the third baseman stands so close to home plate balls are absolutely scorched at her. You have to have ice water in your veins to play third, and apparently I don't, because playing the position scares me to death. I spend the whole time praying nothing will come my way. Luckily, my prayers are answered, but in the meantime, Miranda and Grace make errors.

The final score is 6-1. Our only run comes when Courtney hits a solo home run in the fifth inning.

Coach Ryan rounds us up. "I just don't understand what the problem is," he says. "You don't even look like the same team from a few weeks ago. What's the deal?"

We all know, but no one wants to say it out loud. Grace is the most outspoken of us all, but even she knows better than to talk back to Coach Ryan. He doesn't like having his decisions questioned by us players.

"You girls need to step it up a little," he says. "The state tournament is only a month away, and the way we're looking, we'll be lucky to survive the first round."

He dismisses us and we head for home. Unlike normal, no one says goodbye. We round up our stuff, pack it into our bags, and go.

The Batting Order

Lauren, Grace, Miranda, and I are relieved today when we look at the lineup card and see we are all back in our old positions. In the meantime, Courtney is in center field. However, we get confused when we look at the batting order. It has Miranda batting first, Lauren second, Grace third, Courtney fourth, and me fifth.

"What's up with that?" Grace says. "I'm the cleanup hitter. I'm supposed to bat fourth."

I'm upset, too. Normally, I bat third, right in front of Grace. Now, I've been moved all the way down to the fifth spot.

Regardless, there's nothing we can do. Coach Ryan makes the batting order, and he must think this new one is an improvement over the old one.

But it isn't. Batting third throws Grace for a loop, and she strikes out all three times. In the meantime, I fare little better in the fifth spot. I line out twice and pop out once.

In the meantime, Courtney gets two doubles.

For our second game, against the Edmonds Express, Coach Ryan changes things. He moves Courtney to the third spot, puts me at four, and Grace at five.

"What's the deal?" Grace says. "If he's going to move Courtney out of the cleanup spot, why not put me back?"

We have no answers. We just do our jobs the best we can. Unfortunately, we don't do very well. I get a bloop single, just over the shortstop's glove, but that's all. Grace fouls out once and lines out twice.

Courtney gets another double.

For our third game, against the Stinger Squad, Coach Ryan changes things again. This time, Courtney leads off, Miranda is second, I'm third, Grace fourth, and Lauren is fifth.

"Why am I demoted?" Lauren asks. "I have more hits than anyone today, except Courtney, and now I'm batting fifth. Screw it. I don't even know why I try. This is ridiculous."

As are the results. Everything goes haywire. Miranda gets one hit, but that's it. Everyone else, including Courtney, goes hitless. We lose 5-0.

"Ladies," Coach Ryan says during our post-game meeting. "If you're going to bat like that, we might as well call it a season."

To be perfectly honest, nothing would make me happier.

My Hitting Slump

Things don't get much better for me the following weekend. The team does well, and we win four of five games, but I'm in a weird batting funk. I only get one hit all weekend, an infield single, and in the meantime I strike out five times. And the worst part is the harder I try, the worse I get. Our final game is against our arch rivals, the Bellevue Beast, and Nichole Williams strikes me out all three times, like always using her infamous riseball. After the third strikeout, I'm so frustrated I start to cry. On the way home, my dad borrows his phone (I'm still using it since my mom hasn't given mine back yet) and calls my hitting instructor, Steve.

"There's got to be something you can do," he says. "She's in a terrible slump. And you've got to do it fast, because the state tournament is less than a month away."

Steve decides to double the length of my lesson that week. We spend the first half hour doing vision training, like normal, but then spend an hour and a half hitting. It's pretty tiring, and after about forty-five minutes I'm sweating like a pig, but I don't complain because I'm willing to do just about anything to break out of this hitting slump. Softball is no fun when you can't hit.

We're about half way through the workout when Steve stops and glances at me. I'm wearing a tank top, so my arms and shoulders are exposed.

"Goodness, Miss Rachel," he says, "you're ripped."

"What?" I ask.

"Look at those biceps. I've never seen a girl with biceps like that before."

I look down. Actually, my biceps are pretty nice. "It's from all the pushups my coach makes me do," I say.

"He makes you do pushups?" Steve asks. "How many?"

"Too many," I say. "It sucks, but I guess it's kinda nice, in a way. Yesterday, in PE class, we had to do a fitness test, and I did more pushups than anyone else. Even the boys."

"Everyone?" Steve asks.

"Well," I say, "there was one boy who beat me, but he was the only one. And he's a beast. He's a lineman on the football team."

"That's impressive," Steve says. "With arms like that, and with that great bat speed of yours, it's no wonder you have such good power. But I don't understand what's happened lately. You say you haven't been hitting the ball hard?"

I shake my head. "Most of the time, I strike out, but even when I do make contact, I just ground out weakly, or I popup."

"She can't even get the ball out of the infield," my dad adds.

"Strange," Steve says. "Turn around for a second."

I spin around so I'm facing the opposite direction, directly away from him.

"That might be the problem," Steve says as he gives me a one-over. "Mike, come here and look at this."

My dad climbs in the cage and stands next to him.

"What is it?" he asks.

"Rachel has no butt," Steve answers.

"What?" my dad and I ask in unison.

"Look," Steve says. "The girl has no butt at all. All softball players have butts. But not Rachel."

My dad looks closer. "She's got a little butt," he says. "But you're right. It's not much."

By now, I've heard more than enough. I'm getting a little self-conscious, to say the least. I'm used to being critiqued, but the focus is usually on my performance, not my physique.

"Stop looking at my butt," I say. I turn around to face them, so they can't see it any more. But now they look at my front.

"And there's another problem," Steve says. "Look at those thighs. I've seen bigger thighs on a chicken."

I can't believe what I'm hearing.

"Quit looking at my thighs," I say. I start to turn around again, so they can't see my thighs any more, but then I realize my butt will be exposed again. I'm in a real quandary.

They laugh as they see me squirming around, trying desperately to avoid their gazes. I grab my hoodie from the edge of the cage and wrap it around my midsection, including my thighs and butt. This really gets some laughs.

"All joking aside," Steve says, "there is some truth to what I'm saying. Many softball players have big butts and thighs, and it helps them a lot, because that's where they get their power. Since Rachel doesn't have either, I bet she's relying on her biceps and bat speed. How do your arms feel right now?"

"Tired," I answer.

"Exactly. I bet the majority of your problem is fatigue. Those biceps are nice, but they can't do the job themselves, not for an entire season. We need to buff you up, especially your lower body. I've got just the thing."

At that, my fate is officially sealed. He gives me one of those lower body workout tapes and tells me to do it twice per day for the next four weeks. The minute we get home, my dad pops it in the VCR and stands to the side as I do thirty minutes of squats, leg lifts, and just about every lower body exercise you can imagine. It's pure agony. At one point, I get tired and let up a little.

"Don't dog it," my dad says. "We need you ready for state."

There's no doubt about it. Being a softball player is hard work.

Batting Strategy

I do my lower body workouts every day for the rest of the week, but unfortunately, it doesn't help much the following weekend. Just like the week before, the team does well, and we win four of six games, but I continue to struggle with my bat. I get two singles, but that's it for the entire weekend. In the meantime, I strike out four times.

On the way home, my dad tells me his newest theory regarding my struggles. "I've been watching you lately," he says, "and I'm not convinced your problem is completely fatigue. I think you have another problem. I don't think you understand batting strategy."

"Batting strategy?" I ask. I've never heard that term before.

"Batting strategy is the mental part of hitting," my dad says. "Hitting is mostly a physical activity, and that's why we spend so much time working on your form, but there's a mental part, too. If you understand the mental part, it can make things a lot easier."

"What do you mean?"

"Well, there are certain scenarios, and if you remember what to do in each scenario, it can make it easier to hit. For instance, if a pitcher has two strikes on you, and no balls, should you swing at the next pitch?"

I think about it for a minute. "If it's a strike, yes, I should swing."

"No. You shouldn't. The next pitch isn't going to be a strike."

"It isn't? Why not?"

"Why would a pitcher throw you a strike when there are no balls? She's going to throw you a ball and try to sucker you into swinging at a bad pitch."

"Oh. I see. I guess."

"What if you have three balls and no strikes?" my dad asks. "Should you swing?"

"If it's a strike, yes."

"No, Rachel. Let it go. Chances are if the pitcher has already thrown you three straight balls, she's having control problems and can't throw strikes any more, even if she wants to. So it's probably going to be another ball, so let it go and walk to first."

"But what if it's a strike?"

"Big deal. You have one strike, no harm done. But then what do you do with the next pitch?"

I think about it again, but I'm not really sure.

"Let it go?"

"No, Rachel, not at all. What if it's a strike? You've got to swing if it's a strike. Unless of course your coach tells you to take a pitch, but that would be highly unusual in that scenario."

"Oh."

I'm still trying to digest all of this. It's a little confusing, to say the least. Regardless, my dad moves on.

"What pitch do you look for if the pitcher has thrown you two fastballs in a row and has two strikes on you?"

"Another fastball?"

"No, Rachel. She's setting you up for a changeup. The change of speed will catch you off guard. So look for a changeup every time."

"But what if she throws me a fastball?"

"She's not going to. She's going to throw you a changeup, every time. Take my word for it. And if she

229

throws you two changeups in a row, then what do you look for?"

"Another changeup?"

"Rachel. Sometimes I don't think you're listening at all. The pitcher's setting you up for a fastball. Fastball, fastball, change. Change, change, fastball. Those are the most popular pitching patterns. Memorize them. Say them."

"Fastball, fastball, change. Change, fastball – "

"Rachel."

"Change, change, fastball."

"Good. Now just remember those patterns, and you shouldn't have any problem. After all, softball is pretty simple, when you think about it."

"I'm thinking about it," I say, "but it doesn't seem that simple to me."

"It is. You just need to concentrate harder."

"I am concentrating hard. I always concentrate hard."

"No you don't. Sometimes, when you're at bat, I wonder if you're concentrating at all. Remember that game against the River Breeze when you struck out twice in the same inning? That should never happen."

"I was trying."

"Questionable. It looked like you were just up there hacking away at everything. You're a hitter, not a hacker."

"What's the difference?"

"A hacker just stands up there hacking away at pitches like an idiot. A hitter, by contrast, is a skilled professional. Like Ichiro. He waits patiently for the perfect pitch, even fouls off a couple of bad ones if he has to, then picks a good one and launches it over the fence."

"What were you, when you played? A hacker or a hitter?"

"A hitter, of course."

"And you never had a bad game?" I ask.

"A couple," he says. "But they were few and far between."

"If I call Grandpa Frank, is that what he's going to say?"

I pull my dad's Blackberry Storm out of my pocket and start to dial.

"Leave your grandfather out of this," he says. "And put that phone away or I'll take it back."

I'm not about to risk losing the phone, so I hang it up as quickly as I can. We drive for several minutes before my dad speaks again.

"Say your patterns."

"Fastball, fastball, change. Change, change, fastball."

"Again."

"Fastball, fastball, change. Change, change, fastball."

"Again."

"Fastball, fastball, change. Change, change, fastball."

"Again."

I'm getting tired of this, so I say nothing.

"Again," he repeats, this time a little louder than before.

"Fastball, fastball, change. Change, change, fastball."

This goes on for the rest of the drive home. It's extremely annoying. I've never been so happy to see my house appear in the distance.

I head upstairs and plop down on my bed. Normally, I take a shower as soon as I get home, but right now I'm too tired. My arms are worn out, my shoulders are tight, and my legs and butt are sore – no

231

doubt the result of my lower body workouts. I've never felt this exhausted before. I don't know how I'm going to be ready for the state tournament in two weeks. And then there's next year. Next year I'm going to be in high school, and I'll be playing for the high school team in addition to playing for the Wildcats. I can barely handle the rigors I'm facing right now, just being on one team. What am I going to do when I'm on two?

A thought occurs to me. At first I dismiss it, but then I reconsider.

I walk over to my desk. I slide the drawer open, revealing a small, white, unmarked tube. The one Darnell Williams gave me awhile back.

I can hardly believe it, but he was right. He said I would need it eventually. And now I do. I need to get bigger and stronger, and I need to do it quickly, or I'll never be able to survive next year. My dad has already started talking about high school, and he's hopeful I'll make the varsity team as a freshman even though he knows it's a long shot. Like always, I don't want to let him down.

I grab the tube and pop it open.

But then I think about all the bad things I've heard about steroids over the years. They give you intense mood swings. And high blood pressure. And liver tumors. And acne.

Ugh. I already have enough acne. I just got two pimples on my forehead this morning. And one on the back of my upper arm. I don't need any more.

And then there are the other concerns about steroids. What if someone found out I was using them? I'd be called a cheater, and I'd get suspended from school again. And since I'm still on probation for the whole drinking thing, the suspension would be a big one this time.

And, even more important, what would my parents think if they found out? My dad would be crushed; there's no doubt about that. And my mom would be furious. She'd ground me for the rest of my life, probably longer, if that's possible. I'd never see my Blackberry Storm again.

I need a solution to my problems, but there's got to be something better than steroids. I hate to admit it, but this is one of those things I'm going to have to tough out on my own, no matter how hard it is.

I close the tube of cream, throw it in the waste basket at the side of my desk, and head for the bathroom to take a shower.

I need it. I reek.

The First Round

The state tournament begins today. It's one of the largest tournaments of the year, and it pits teams from all over the state of Washington against each other. It lasts for an entire week, and there are games played at fields all over the county. The tournament is divided into numerous age brackets and skill-level divisions, and the winner of each age bracket and skill-level division advances to the western regional tournament in California. The winner of the western regional tournament advances to the national tournament in New York. The winner of the national tournament is the champion of the United States.

Or at least I think that's how it works. I'm not really certain, since none of my teams have ever made it very far.

But this year we hope to change things. This year's team has plenty of issues, but it's definitely the best team I've ever been on. And we're excited. This tournament is what we've been preparing for all year.

But there's a lot of pressure, because it's single-elimination. You only keep playing until you lose a game. Once you lose, your season is over.

Our opponent in the first round is a team from Spokane called the Diamond Devils. They are absolutely huge. Every girl on the team is taller than me, and some of them are nearly twice my weight.

Lauren's dad points at two of the Diamond Devils' players.

"Those girls are only sixteen?" he asks.

"I want to know what they feed them," my dad says. "Whatever it is, I need to get some for Rachel."

That's exactly what I was thinking. These girls are monsters. Some of them are as big as Erin Anderson. Some are bigger.

"I have only one thing to say about them," Coach Ryan says during our pre-game talk. "The bigger they are, the harder they fall. Get out there and take them down."

We're the home team, so we fly onto the field, ready to slay the giant. And we get off to a great start. Our pitcher, Madison Stevens, is on fire, and she retires the first three batters easily.

But then I get nervous. It's my turn to bat, and I'm still in my hitting slump. I try to remember what my dad told me about batting strategy. I need to remember the pitching patterns.

Fastball, fastball, change.

Change, change, fastball.

But then something unexpected happens. The first pitch is a curveball.

My dad didn't teach me any patterns with curveballs.

Now what do I do?

The next pitch is also a curveball. I swing and miss.

"Strike two," blue shouts.

Now I have two strikes and no balls. What did my dad say the pitcher would do with two strikes and no balls? All I can remember is she'll want me to go after a bad pitch. As a result, I don't swing.

The pitch is low and outside, not even close.

"Ball one," blue shouts.

"Very good, Rachel," my dad shouts from the stands. "Well done."

I'm not sure what to do after that, but I'm excited anyway, because at least I made my dad happy for a couple of minutes. The next pitch is a fastball, and I hit it straight up the middle for a single.

The fans cheer as I reach first base safely. I feel like a huge weight has been lifted off of my shoulders. I know I'm not out of my hitting slump yet, not even close, but at least I'm off to a good start.

And so is my team. Our next batter, Grace, hits a shot all the way to the wall, scoring me from first, and the batter after that, Courtney, hits a triple, scoring Grace. As a result, we're leading 2-0 by the time I get my next at-bat two innings later.

The Diamond Devils' pitcher throws me two straight curveballs, and I miss both. I let the next pitch go by for a ball. She throws me two straight fastballs, and I foul them away.

And then I remember.

Fastball, fastball, change.

The next pitch is exactly as expected. A changeup, straight down the middle. I keep my hands back and wait until the last possible second, then trigger, exploding with everything I've got. The ball bounces off of the outfield fence for a stand-up double.

Everyone cheers as I stand on second base.

"Show me the power," my dad shouts from the bleachers.

I raise my arms and flex my biceps, like I'm some kind of big-time weightlifter or something. This is a routine my dad and I used to do a lot, especially when I was in Little League. It cracks the parents up every time.

I feel a lot better now. To be perfectly honest, I still don't completely understand my dad's whole 'batting strategy' thing, but amazingly enough, it seems to be helping, at least a little.

Unfortunately, it doesn't help at all during my next at-bat, and I strike out on three straight pitches, but that's okay. Two hits in three at-bats is a good day (even for Erin Anderson), and it's a nice start toward climbing out of my batting slump. My team wins 4-0 and we move on to the next round.

Fun on the Run

Today is the second day of the state tournament. As is often the case before games, my dad and I stop at a convenience store to get some snacks to put in my softball bag. My dad likes me to have plenty of snacks during a game so I keep my energy up. I grab a basket and fill it with candy bars, soda, and dill pickle flavored sunflower seeds. I've had a lot of sunflower seeds over the years, but the dill pickle flavored ones are the best. My dad looks at my basket, shakes his head, and dumps it out. He fills it with bananas, trail mix, and a sports drink. Thankfully, he lets me keep the sunflower seeds. I toss in a second bag.

He raises an eyebrow. "Two?"

"As soon as the other girls see them," I say, "they're going to want some. Especially Grace. She's a pig."

He laughs, then we head to the checkout counter. A minute later, we're back on the road.

"Those pitching patterns helped," I say. "Teach me some more."

"I don't think there are any more," he says. "Some pitchers have tendencies to do certain things, and to throw certain pitches more often than others, but that's up to them."

"So if a pitcher throws two curveballs in a row what's the next pitch going to be?"

"It's hard to say. It's up to her. Or her coach. Whoever is calling the pitches that day."

"So how do I know what to do?"

"You don't. You've just got to figure it out on the spot. Remember, those pitching patterns can help, but they can't make you a great hitter. That you've got to do on your own."

"I see."

Actually, I don't, but I say it anyway because I don't want to look stupid.

"Just remember the patterns I taught you, and when they apply, use them. When you get in a situation where the patterns don't apply, just be yourself. Relax and have fun. Wait for a good pitch and hammer it."

I nod. I wish it were that simple.

Our game is against a team from Forks called the Vampires. We get off to a good start when Grace hits an inside-the-park home run in the top of the first. By the time I get to bat, we're already leading 2-0.

The Vampires' pitcher is a tall, skinny girl named Bella Bettencourt. She doesn't throw very hard, but she throws all kinds of junk pitches, and she's great at hitting her spots. Her first pitch is a screwball I miss by a mile. Her second pitch is low and outside, but not by much. I start to swing but pull back at the very last second.

"Good eye," my dad says from the stands.

The next pitch is a dropball that looks good at first, but dives down just as I trigger. I swing right over the top of it for strike two.

I've always hated junkball pitchers.

I definitely can't rely on my dad's pitching patterns here. They involve fastballs, and this girl hasn't thrown a fastball all day.

So I'm going to have to take his other approach, the one from earlier this morning. I'm going to have to relax, wait for a good pitch, and hammer it.

Luckily for me, the next pitch is a good pitch, at least as far as I'm concerned. It's another dropball, but it doesn't drop nearly as much as the first one. I hit it into right field for a single.

It's amazing how good I feel after getting a hit, especially to start the day. After that, everything seems a lot simpler.

And then something unexpected happens. Coach Ryan, who is standing at third base, touches the bill of his cap.

That's our steal sign. On the next pitch, I'm supposed to steal second base.

I nearly jump for joy. If there's one thing I love about softball, it's stealing bases. But at the same time, it makes me nervous, because I was watching the Vampires' catcher before the game, warming up, and she has an absolute cannon for an arm. If I want to steal second, I better be on my toes.

And I am. As soon as the pitcher releases the ball, I'm off. The catcher grabs it and whips it to second, an absolutely spectacular throw. The shortstop slaps it down, tagging me just as my foot touches the base.

"Safe," blue shouts.

I call time, then stand up and dust myself off. I hear my dad talking to Lauren's dad in the stands.

"Even Ichiro would be proud," he says.

Apparently Coach Ryan agrees, because he taps the bill of his cap again. It actually catches me a little off guard, because he rarely has us steal bases and he never has us steal third. But apparently he wants to give it a try. Maybe he's thinking he can catch the Vampires by surprise.

I'm off in a flash. This time I go into the bag headfirst. I usually don't like to slide headfirst because it hurts, but this is the state tournament so I'm going all out. The tag comes down, nailing my hand just after it hits the base.

"Safe," blue shouts.

"Well done," Coach Ryan says as he helps me up. "You were flying. That's the fastest I've seen you run all year."

"This is the state tournament," I say. "I'm here to win."

"That's what I wanted to hear. Now all we need is for Courtney to hit you in."

And she does. She hits the next pitch deep into the outfield, almost to the warning track. The Vampires' center fielder catches it, but I tag up and head for home, scoring easily. They don't even try to get me at the plate.

From there, we cruise. In my third at-bat, I get another hit, a single, and we end up winning 5-0.

Our next game is a completely different story. We're playing Missfits Fastpitch, a really good team from Everett. Their pitcher is a tall, athletic girl named Paige Parker. She is one of the best pitchers I've ever seen, and she throws super hard. Her pitches look like yellow streaks as they come at me. She strikes out ten of our first twelve batters, including me twice. The game is still scoreless when I take my third and final at-bat in the bottom of the sixth. Thankfully, and somewhat miraculously, I'm finally able to hit one of Paige's pitches. It flies into left center and bounces off of the outfield fence. By the time the Missfits' outfielder is able to retrieve it and throw it back to the infield, I'm standing on third with a two-out triple.

Coach Ryan calls time and walks over to me.

"We've got two outs," he says, "and that was the first solid hit we've had all day. I don't think we can count on another. We may need to manufacture a run the old-fashioned way."

"What are you thinking?" I ask.

"You did a good job stealing bases yesterday. How about doing it again?"

"I'm on third."

"Exactly. I want you to steal home."

I nearly pass out on the spot. Is he crazy? Has he finally lost his marbles? Stealing home is nearly impossible. Especially against a really good team like the Missfits.

"It's time," he says, "for a suicide squeeze."

A suicide squeeze is one of the riskiest plays in all of softball. The runner has to take off from third the instant the pitcher releases the ball. In the meantime, the batter has to bunt it down the first base foul line, and the runner has to slide into home plate before the catcher can get to the ball, return, and tag her. If the batter misses the pitch, or if she doesn't bunt it far enough, or if the runner doesn't get there quick enough, it's a disaster of epic proportions.

But then again, I guess that's why they call it a suicide squeeze. If you don't do it right, it's the death of you.

Coach Ryan sends the signal to the next batter, Courtney. Her eyes get big as she realizes what he's just called. I can tell she's as nervous as I am. I wonder if she's ever done a suicide squeeze before. I never have.

The instant Paige makes the next pitch, I fly down the baseline faster than I've ever run before. I'm half way to home by the time the ball gets there. Courtney squares around and bunts it nicely, but it only gets about two feet in front of her before it stops dead in the dirt. The Missfits' catcher jumps forward, grabs it, and dives desperately to her left, tagging my foot just as it

242

slides across home plate. It's so close even I don't know if I'm safe.

I never hear blue's call. All I hear is a tremendous roar as our parents jump for joy in the stands. I don't even try to get back up. I just lay there, on my back in the dirt, with my arms up in celebration. My teammates dive on top of me. It's the best pig pile ever.

We win the game 1-0. My dad borrows his phone and calls Grandpa Frank in Arizona. "You had to see Rachel during that squeeze. She was a complete blur. She was at least three quarters of the way home by the time the pitch got there. The catcher never had a chance."

The third, fourth, and fifth rounds of the tournament aren't quite as dramatic, but they're fun nonetheless. All of our games are close, but we always find a way to win in the end. Grace is the hero of the third game (she hits another in-the-park home run), Miranda is the star of the fourth (she goes 3-3, with two doubles and a triple), and Courtney wins the fifth (she hits two in-the-park home runs, one a grand slam). In the meantime, I get five more hits, including four singles and a double.

"I guess it's official," my dad says. "Your hitting slump is a thing of the past."

"Thank goodness," I say. "I won't miss it, not one little bit."

The Championship Game

Today is the day we've all been waiting for all season long. The championship game. Every softball player in the state of Washington dreams of getting to this game. It's been our main goal all year.

I'm nervous. Big time. The whole team is. Our opponent is the one team we knew we would eventually face, the one team we hate with a passion.

Our arch rivals. The Bellevue Beast.

"I can't believe it," Grace says as we're sitting in the dugout, watching the Beast warm up. "Check out their new center fielder."

I can hardly believe my eyes. Standing in the outfield, shagging fly balls, is our old center fielder, Alexis Sampson.

"Good job, Grace," Miranda says. "As if they weren't good enough before. Now they've got Alexis."

"It's not my fault," Grace says. "I didn't make her join that team."

"Yeah, but you definitely made her leave ours."

Coach Ryan overhears the conversation and brings it to a halt. "The past is the past," he says. "There's nothing we can do about it. I don't care if Alexis is out there or not. We can beat them regardless. Understood?"

We're quiet.

"Understood?" he repeats, a little louder than before.

"Understood," we say, but it's not too convincing.

"Then get out there and do it."

We're the home team, so we take the field to start the game. Everything goes well until my first at-bat in the bottom of the inning. Normally, I like hitting. But not against Nichole Williams. She's too good.

The first pitch is a nasty fastball. I foul it straight back.

The second pitch is another fastball. I foul it to the side.

The third pitch is a changeup, low and away. I watch it for ball one.

The fourth pitch is my greatest nightmare. A riseball. I miss it by a mile.

"Strike three," blue shouts as I walk back to the dugout.

The game continues from there. It's a classic pitcher's duel. Both teams get a few hits, here and there, but neither has scored a run when I bat again in the fourth inning.

The first pitch is a curve for strike one.

The second pitch is a fastball. I foul it away.

The third pitch is a ball in the dirt.

Here it comes, I think. *The dreaded riseball. The bane of my very existence.*

I miss it by two miles.

I hang my head in shame as I walk back to the dugout. It's official. It's hopeless. If Coach Ryan were wise, he'd remove me from the game and have someone else bat for me. At least my replacement would have a chance. Even the worst player on the team, Casey Franklin, could do better than me.

"Rachel," my dad says from the edge of the dugout. "Come over here."

A tear runs down my cheek as I walk over to him.

"What are you doing?" he asks.

"What do you mean?" I respond, wiping the tear away.

"You look like you've given up."

"I have."

"Don't ever say that," he says. "It's not over yet. You're going to get one more at-bat before the game is over. You need to have a little faith in yourself. I do."

I grab my glove and take my position at second. Unfortunately, the inning doesn't go as well as the earlier ones. The Beast's shortstop hits a double to start things off, the next batter moves her to third with a grounder to first, and the next batter, Alexis, hits a sacrifice fly to bring her in.

The Beast players congratulate Alexis as she returns to the dugout. Nichole gives her a hug.

They lead 1-0.

The score remains the same until my final at-bat in the bottom of the seventh. Grace and Miranda are on first and third when I step into the batter's box.

That's the good news. Here's the bad news.

There are two outs. It's all up to me. If I get a hit, Miranda will score from third and that will tie the game. If I get a big hit, like a double, triple, or home run, we'll win.

But if I strike out, it's over.

I've heard stories about how the greatest players of all time relish chances like this. A chance to shine in the spotlight, when all the pressure is on them and them alone. Erin Anderson won ten different games in her last at-bat.

I must not be the next Erin Anderson. I'm not relishing the moment at all. I'm scared out of my mind. I'm literally petrified. Everyone is looking at me. The fans, the parents, my teammates, my coaches. Even a stray dog in the parking lot is looking at me. They're all counting on me to come through in the clutch. Right here, right now.

I'm not sure I can do it.

Not against Nichole.

But I have no choice but to try. I dig my cleats into the dirt. I tap my bat on the plate. I take a deep breath.

This is it. The biggest moment of my softball career. Possibly the biggest moment of my life. The state title is on the line.

The first pitch is the fastest fastball I've ever seen. It sounds like an explosion as it hits the catcher's mitt.

Nichole realizes how big this moment is, too. She wants a state title, too.

The next pitch is a curveball. I foul it away.

"Strike two," blue shouts.

The next pitch is a ball, low and inside.

"Time," I say as I step out of the box. I need a minute to collect my thoughts and steady myself. My hands are shaking. I know what's coming next. It doesn't take a rocket scientist to figure it out.

I hear my dad in the stands. "Have faith in yourself, Rachel."

The next pitch is the nastiest riseball I have ever seen, and trust me I've seen plenty of nasty riseballs in my time. As it comes at me, something funny happens. I decide I'm going to hit it, no matter what it takes. I lock my eyes on the ball and watch it fly all the way to my bat. For a few brief, terrifying seconds, everything slows all around me. I swing with all my might.

A miracle happens. I hit it.

And I hit it hard. It flies straight toward center field, a massive shot, just like the home runs I've hit in the past. Our fans go crazy as the ball races toward the outfield fence.

For a brief second, I can hardly believe my eyes. I just hit the ball that won the state championship. I am the next Erin Anderson.

But something unexpected happens. Alexis races from her position in center field, at full speed, and catches the ball just as it clears the top of the outfield fence. She hits the fence hard, falls to the ground, then gets up, with the ball still in her mitt. She holds it up for blue to see.

"The batter's out," blue shouts. "The game's over. Bellevue wins."

The Beast players pile on top of Alexis in center field. I can barely believe what has happened. I'm in complete shock. I actually managed to do the impossible, to hit a riseball out-of-the-park, only to have it robbed by my old teammate.

A few minutes later, after I've packed up all my gear, my dad greets me at the car. I think he's going to be disappointed but he's all smiles instead.

"Well done," he says as he takes my bag and loads it in the trunk.

"We lost," I say.

"Yeah, but it was a great game. And you finally did it. You hit a riseball. And you hit it well."

"Alexis caught it."

My dad shrugs. "That happens sometimes. It's her job, right? And you've got to give her credit. It was a spectacular catch. But just because she caught it doesn't mean it wasn't a great hit. As far as I'm concerned, it was your best hit all year."

"Even better than my home runs?"

"By far," my dad says. "You didn't give up, even when you thought it was hopeless. That's the sign of a great ballplayer. It reminded me of the first time I saw Erin Anderson play, back when she was in her first Little League All-Star game. She was so nervous she had a panic attack right there on the spot. They had to stop the game for ten minutes to let her recover."

"Erin Anderson?" I ask, incredulous.

My dad nods. "She didn't let it stop her. Later in the game, she hit a double. And look at her now. She's a legend." He walks around the car and opens my door for me. "But enough of this yappin'. You up for some ice cream?"

I'm always up for ice cream.

Minutes later, we're at Cold Stone. I order a triple scoop, with chocolate, caramel, nuts, miniature marshmallows, sprinkles, and loads of whipped cream on top.

It's an awesome creation, if I say so myself.

DOG IN
THE DUGOUT

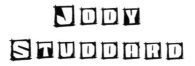

www.jstuddard.com

For Debbie and Shelby

August 25

Today was the best day of my life. I've wanted a puppy for as long as I can remember, and my dad finally agreed I could get one, but only on one condition. I had to hit a home run in today's game against the Edmonds Express.

I was excited, but I knew it wasn't going to be easy. The Express' pitcher, Amy Adams, was really good. She threw super hard, and she had a bunch of different pitches, including a nasty changeup that was nearly impossible to hit. I've never seen a girl throw a changeup as well as Amy. It was at least twenty-five miles per hour slower than her other pitches, and she used it to strike me out easily during my first two at-bats.

But that wasn't my biggest concern. My biggest concern was I had never hit a home run before. Never. In my entire life. I've played fastpitch softball for as long as I can remember, and I'm a good hitter (most days), but for some strange reason I had never hit a home run.

But then again, I had never had so much at stake. I wanted that puppy, and I wanted it bad. So I was going to hit a home run if it killed me.

I took a deep breath as I stepped into the batter's box. I dug my cleats into the dirt. I was nervous. Big time. It was the bottom of the seventh inning, so it was my last chance. I glanced at the stands and saw my dad sitting in the bleachers with the rest of the parents, watching attentively. My team, the Seattle Sky, was losing 6-5 with two outs, but the bases were loaded so everyone was hoping I'd get a hit and we'd come from behind to win.

But I didn't care about that.

I just wanted that dog.

The first pitch was a nasty fastball, high and away. I knew I shouldn't swing at it, because it wasn't a strike, but I was too excited and I swung anyway.

"Strike one," blue shouted. In softball, we call the umpires blue because they wear blue uniforms.

I looked over at the stands. The parents (especially my dad) weren't happy with that swing at all.

The next pitch was in the dirt, for a ball, as was the one after that, but the fourth was pure heat. It blew by me so fast I didn't even have a chance to swing at it.

"Strike two," blue shouted.

I stepped out of the batter's box. My coach, John Smith, sent me signals from the third base coach's box, but I wasn't paying any attention at all. I was down to my last chance. One more strike and it was over. I could kiss that puppy goodbye.

Luckily for me, one more strike never happened. Amy tried to finish me off with her patented changeup, just like she had done earlier in the game (twice), but I was ready this time. I kept my hands back until the very last second, then swung with everything I had. Every muscle in my body tightened as I hit it.

And I didn't just hit it. I crushed it. Harder than I'd ever hit a ball before. It leaped off of my bat and raced toward the outfield fence. It was a monster shot, the best I've ever hit, and it cleared the fence by at least twenty feet (maybe more).

When I got to home plate, my teammates tackled me. It was a great pig pile, and I had tears of joy in my eyes. Everyone thought I was happy because I had just won the game, but my happiness had nothing to do with that. All I cared about was my puppy. I could hardly believe it, but I had done it.

And believe it or not, I had already picked out a name.

Homer.

August 26

Homer is the greatest puppy ever. I got him from a friend of mine, Lea Levin. Lea is one of my teammates on the Sky (she's our first baseman), and her dog, Molly, just had puppies. My dad and I drove to her house in Marysville, which is about twenty minutes from my house in Seattle. When we got there, all of the puppies were in a makeshift pen Lea's dad had constructed in the garage. They were so cute. They were half chocolate Labrador and half Chow, so they pretty much look like chocolate Labradors, but they have black tongues like Chows. And they have big, floppy ears. There were ten in the litter, but two of them had already been taken by other people, so there were eight left for me to pick from. I took turns holding at least five of them, but they all seemed so gorgeous I couldn't decide which one to get.

So my dad solved the problem for me. He took an old, weathered softball from a shelf on the wall and tossed it into the pen. All of the puppies ignored it, except one. He was sleeping on the far side of the cage, on a little pile of rags, completely by himself. I didn't even notice him at first. He was by far the smallest of the group and was definitely the runt of the litter, but he was absolutely adorable. He jumped up as soon as the softball rolled past him and immediately chased after it. He tried to get it in his mouth and pick it up, but it was too big for him, and all he managed to do was lose his balance, fall over the top of it, and flip completely onto his back. But he wasn't discouraged, not in the least, not for a second. He scrambled to his feet and darted after it again, trying to get control of it once and for all. It looked like a wrestling match between a puppy and a softball, and somehow the softball was winning.

My decision was made.

"That's him," I said. "That's Homer."

Ten minutes later, we were heading for home.

August 27

Life is good when you have a puppy. Today Homer followed me everywhere, except when he got tired and needed a nap (which happened about once every twenty minutes). Everything he did was so cute. He couldn't get into our living room, because it's sunken and he's too small to get down the step leading into it from the hallway. So I teased him by going into it without him, and he howled in agony every time I did it. I think he has separation anxiety. So I grabbed him and helped him down into the living room with me, and then everything was good again.

He's loaded with toys. My dad and I went to the pet store earlier in the day, and he's totally spoiled now. He's got all kinds of stuffed animals, squeaky toys, and rawhide bones, and one of the rawhide bones is actually so big he can't even lift it, but he likes it anyway. My dad thought it was hilarious to watch him try to carry a bone that was almost as big as he was, and it was pretty funny, especially when he tried to pick it up and he ended up flipping completely onto his back in the process.

But my cat wasn't happy at all. His name is Cinnamon, and I've had him since I was eight, so he's seven now. He's big and orange, with a plump belly and a long tail that is striped like a raccoon. He's been my only pet until now, and he's used to having my complete and undivided attention, so he wasn't happy about having a dog in the house. He gave Homer a nasty look, and when Homer ran over to say hi (he just wanted to be friends), Cinnamon slapped him on the nose. And he slapped him hard. Homer yelped and jumped back so quickly he hit one of my mom's decorative plastic plants and knocked it into the fireplace. Luckily my dad got to it before it caught on fire. In the meantime, I rescued Homer. He wasn't hurt badly, but he did have a speck of blood on his nose where he got slapped.

That reminds me. I need to clip Cinnamon's claws.

Unfortunately, Homer hadn't learned his lesson. He wanted so badly to be friends with Cinnamon he wandered over to him again, about a half hour later, this time a little more cautiously than before, and tried to sniff him. Unfortunately, the result was the same as the first time. Cinnamon reached out with one paw, claws out, ready to strike. But this time I was ready, and I jumped in the middle to protect Homer from the blow.

But then I realized something. I was the one who was going to get slapped.

And he slapped me good. Right in the side of the leg. It was a nasty scratch, at least an inch long, and it hurt like a beast. I was really angry.

"That does it," I said as I grabbed Cinnamon and headed for the back door. "You're gonna spend the night outside, you bad cat. And don't come back until you have a better attitude."

I tossed him out onto the porch and returned to Homer. He wagged his tail and looked up at me with his big, droopy, brown eyes.

"Don't worry," I told him. "You have nothing to worry about. I'll protect you from that mean cat."

August 28

Homer loves to play fetch. I didn't even have to teach him. Somehow, inherently, he just knew how. We couldn't use a softball, since a softball is too big, but he had no problem with a tennis ball at all. Everything was great fun until I tossed the ball down the hall and it went down the staircase. Homer tried to follow it but he didn't realize how slick the hardwood floor in the hallway was, slipped on it, and fell down the staircase.

I nearly freaked out as I watched him bounce head-over-paws down the steps. But amazingly, once he got to the bottom, he popped up and headed after the ball, completely unfazed, like nothing had ever happened. But then he realized something. He was too small to make it back up the stairs. No matter how hard he tried, he just couldn't get his tummy up and over the steps. So he finally gave up and shot me an irresistible 'please help the poor puppy' look with his big, round eyes, and I couldn't help but run down the stairs and carry him back to the top.

Not too long after that, I gave him his first bath. I don't think he really needed it, 'cause he was already pretty clean, but what the heck. My dad and I had gotten some shampoo and a brush when we were at the pet store the day before, and I wanted to see how well they worked. My older sister, Chloe, joined in and helped me scrub him. He was so small he fit in the kitchen sink with ease. My mom wasn't too happy about us giving a dog a bath in the kitchen sink, but she got over it quickly. Which was good, because my dog was going to get pampered, whether she liked it or not.

My dad and I set up a kennel for Homer downstairs, in the family room, and I decided to sleep with him for the night. My room is upstairs, with the other bedrooms, but I didn't want to leave him alone since it was his first night away from his mother and siblings. I was afraid he'd get lonely if I left him by himself for too long. I put him in his kennel and closed the gate, but he didn't like that at all and banged on the gate with a paw, so I let him out and he slept with me in a sleeping bag on the couch.

It doesn't get any better than that. A girl and her puppy. It's a match made in heaven. I should have hit that home run years ago.

August 29

It isn't easy owning a puppy. This morning, Homer had an accident on the living room carpet.

And on the family room carpet.

And on the dining room carpet.

And on the bedroom carpet.

I don't understand what the problem was. I took him outside every twenty minutes, to take care of business, but whenever we went outside, he never had to go. He'd just spend his time sniffing around the yard and chasing after butterflies. But as soon as I brought him back inside the house, there was an accident.

My mom was furious. Apparently, the carpet is precious to her. She got our steam cleaner out of the hallway closet and made me clean the floor after each of Homer's accidents. Homer didn't like the steam cleaner at all. It was so loud it scared him, and he ran down the hall and hid in the dining room under the table until I was done.

And that wasn't the only problem. He wouldn't sleep, either. At least not by himself. Last night, I didn't mind sleeping with him downstairs, in the family room on the couch, but tonight I was pretty tired so I wanted to sleep in my room in my bed (as you can imagine, my bed is a lot more comfortable than the family room couch). But Homer would have none of it. As soon as I put him in his kennel, turned out the light, and left, he started barking.

"Don't worry about it," my dad said. "He'll stop in awhile."

He didn't. It went on for an hour straight, with him barking nonstop as loud as he could. Finally my dad got mad and shouted, "Get down there and do something about that dog."

So I went downstairs, got him, brought him up to my room, and let him sleep with me in my bed. That worked great, and he slept perfectly until 3:30 in the morning. Then, much to my chagrin, he was wide awake and ready to play. So I put him on the floor, hoping he would keep himself busy with his chew toys, and I could get some much-needed shut-eye, but then he had an accident on the carpet. So I scooped him up and took him outside. And then I stood with him outside, in the cold, for twenty minutes as he did absolutely nothing.

Ugh.

September 7

It's getting old fast. It's been almost two weeks now, and no matter what I do, Homer will not stay in his kennel downstairs, and he will never sleep all night. So I'm getting pretty tired. It's not easy getting up every day at 3:30 in the morning.

And it's ruined my social life. Not to say I ever had much of a social life, but now I never get to do anything. I mean, I can't leave Homer alone by himself, he's just too small. Maybe when he gets a little older, but for now . . . .

The final insult happened this evening. Cinnamon sat on the back of the living room couch, looking at me, as I cleaned up another of Homer's accidents. Cinnamon has always been an arrogant cat, ever since he was a kitten, and he gave me one of those smug 'I told you so' looks. He thought he was so smart.

Stupid cat. I should have gotten rid of him years ago.

September 8

My dad and I took Homer to the dog park for the first time today. It was pretty fun, but Homer surprised me. He didn't like the other dogs. He sniffed them, but other than that he didn't want anything to do with them. But he loved all of the people who were there. He made friends with everyone. They all thought he was so cute, and they were amazed how soft his fur was. They thought I gave him a bath every day, but really I don't (it's actually been several days since his last bath). His hair is just naturally soft and shiny. I wish I could say the same for mine. Especially today. Despite my best efforts, it looks like a mess.

Anyway, my dad got this brilliant idea to put Homer in the water. The dog park is located on a long, rocky beach on the east side of Puget Sound.

"He's part Labrador," my dad said. "He'll love the water. Labradors always do."

Homer hated it. A wave washed in and went right over him, completely soaking him to the bone. He climbed to shore and looked like a shivering, wet, mangy mess.

"Good idea, dad," I said as I wrapped a blanket around him and dried him off. He was freezing.

"Maybe he'll like it when he's older," my dad said with a shrug.

We took him to a pet store, but that didn't go over too well, either, because a mean poodle bullied him. I actually didn't know the words 'mean' and 'poodle' could be used in the same sentence, but trust me, they can. That poodle was fierce.

But then we found something he really liked. Softball practice.

My dad, Chloe, and I practice at least once a week at McCall Park. McCall Park is a Little League softball field not too far from my house. It's actually within walking distance, but we were too lazy to walk, so we drove instead. We took Homer with us. He sat on one side of the field and watched as my dad pitched a bucket of Wiffle balls to Chloe and me. Wiffle balls are small, about the size of a golf ball, made of plastic, and hollow, and we use a stick bat to hit them. A stick bat is a small, thin bat used by players during practice drills. Since it is thinner than a normal bat, it makes it a lot harder to hit the balls, so you really have to work on your concentration and focus. We finished a bucket of balls, and I put my stick bat down near home plate so I could help my dad and Chloe pick up the balls so we could do another round. But when I came back to get my stick bat, it was gone. I looked all over, and finally spotted Homer standing at third base with it in his mouth. He had a big, happy look on his face.

"You silly dog," I said. "Give that back."

I walked up to him and tried to take it from him, but he darted away just as I got within arm's reach. I raced after him, and he ran away again, and the chase was on. He darted to second base, then to first, then to home, and then back to third. I finally caught up to him and got my stick bat back, but when I looked up I saw my dad standing there with a stopwatch in his hand and a big smile on his face.

"I should have thought of that years ago," he said. "That's the fastest I've seen you run in years. That was one of your best times ever."

"Very funny," I said. I wasn't amused, but I had to admit, it was a good workout. I was still breathing heavily.

And unfortunately, it wasn't the last workout for the day. After we completed the next bucket of balls, I set my stick bat back down on the ground, and guess who grabbed it and ran off?

That darn dog.

September 10

Something interesting happened at school today. I met a new boy. Well, I didn't actually meet him, but I saw him. I was sitting in the school cafeteria, eating lunch with my friends, Lea Levin (I got Homer from her) and Kimi Sasaki, and like always, Kimi was complaining about her mom (her mom owns a teriyaki restaurant and she makes Kimi work at it some nights after school, and Kimi hates it because it's boring and the customers are rude to her), when a boy walked by I had never seen before. He wasn't too tall, and was actually a little on the stocky side, but he had nice, muscular shoulders, thick arms, and short, shaggy, blond hair. His eyes were deep blue and absolutely sparkled in the light. He carried a tray of food and sat down with some of the school's football players at a table in the middle of the room.

My school, Monroe High, is a big school, and being a freshman I was new there, so there were a lot of people (especially upper classmen) I didn't know, but there was something about this boy that made him stand out.

"Who's that?" I asked.

"That's Logan McCoy," Lea answered. "He's a new kid, a sophomore. He transferred here from some school in Texas. Something happened with his family, so he's living with his uncle for a year."

"What happened?"

"I'm not really certain," Lea said. "But he's supposed to be really nice, and they say he's an awesome football player. Apparently he was the starting halfback on his team in Texas last year, even though he was just a freshman. Word is he's probably going to be our starter this year."

"I thought Travis Henry was our starter," Kimi said.

"He was," Lea said. "But apparently Logan is better. And he's dreamy. Just look at him."

Lea didn't need to tell me. I already was. To be honest, I was staring at him. There was something about him that mesmerized me. I didn't know if it was just because he was new to our school, or because he was from somewhere different, or just because he was so good looking, but regardless, I couldn't focus on anything else the rest of the day.

Which was really bad, since I had a pop quiz in math class. I haven't gotten the scores back yet, but I bombed it for sure.

September 11

I need a bigger bed. Mine is too small, because both Homer and Cinnamon sleep with me every night. Cinnamon sleeps on one side of me, Homer sleeps on the other, and I'm squeezed in between. And Cinnamon takes up a lot of room, because he can't sleep like a normal cat, and instead he has to sleep on his back with his legs stretched out as far as they will go, and he's a big cat when he's stretched out like that. And Homer isn't much better, because he's grown a lot since I got him and he takes up nearly as much room as Cinnamon.

Both animals are ridiculous at times. They are super competitive with each other and get jealous whenever I give any attention to the other. Homer doesn't bark too much, but he gets mad and barks at Cinnamon if I pet Cinnamon for too long. And Cinnamon doesn't like to be barked at, so he hisses back. But both seem to be tolerating each other, because Homer still wants to be friends with Cinnamon, and Cinnamon seems to be getting used to having Homer around, albeit grudgingly. And, as I mentioned before, Homer has grown a lot in the past few weeks, and he's actually a little bit bigger than Cinnamon now, but he still knows to keep his distance, because whether he's bigger or not, Cinnamon will smack him on the nose if he gets upset.

September 12

Homer learned a new trick today. My dad, Chloe, and I went to McCall Park to practice, and, like the first time we took him, he sat patiently on one side of the infield as my dad pitched a bucket of Wiffle balls to us. But about half way through the bucket, Homer trotted onto the field, picked up one of the Wiffle balls in his mouth, carried it over to the bucket, and dropped it inside.

"Did you see that?" my dad asked. There was an amazed look on his face. "Did you teach him that?"

I shook my head. I was as amazed as he was.

"Get another one, Homer," my dad said.

So he did. He trotted over to another ball, one I had hit down the first base foul line, grabbed it, brought it back, and plopped it into the bucket.

"That's incredible," my dad said.

Practice went on from there, and it was great. With Homer picking up the balls for us, as Chloe and I hit them, it sped things up a lot and made it a much better workout. Normally during a practice we do ten buckets total, and it takes us about half an hour. But today, with Homer's help, it only took fifteen minutes. So then we had more time to work on other drills like throwing and fielding.

"That's an amazing dog," my dad said as we headed for home.

Homer barked. That was his way of saying he agreed.

September 13

Today I went to the football game. I'd like to say I went because I love football, or to show my school spirit, but to be honest, I really just went to see Logan. I've been fascinated with him ever since I saw him that first day in the cafeteria, and I've been hearing around school how good he is, so I wanted to see for myself.

I wasn't disappointed. Like all of the games, it was really festive, with the cheerleaders jumping around and waving their pompoms in the air, and the band playing music (really loud), but the real excitement began when the teams took the field and the game began. As predicted, and despite being only a sophomore, Logan had won the starting halfback position, so he took the field to start the game. I don't really know too much about football, so I didn't really know what was going on, but apparently things started well. Our quarterback, Caleb Smith (Chloe's boyfriend), handed Logan the ball, and he ran through a small opening in the line of players up front (the really big, heavy ones), darted to the left, then ran twenty yards before the defenders dragged him down from behind. Everyone in the stands went crazy, and the cheerleaders jumped around. One girl did a back flip. The next play was more of the same. Caleb took the ball and dropped back to make a pass, but he couldn't find any receivers to throw the ball to, so he turned and flipped it to Logan. Logan caught it and darted forward, dodging two defenders before finally being forced out of bounds. It wasn't quite as long a run as the first one, but it was good nonetheless. Everyone cheered again, and the players patted Logan on the back.

I sat there in complete awe. Logan made one great play after another. In no time, we were winning 14-0. Logan scored both of the touchdowns.

But the highlight of the game, by far, happened in the fourth quarter. At that point, we were way ahead (28-0, I think). Logan had just scored another touchdown, and as he headed to the sideline to get a drink and take a break, he looked up into the stands, right where I was standing. For a brief second, our eyes met, and he smiled at me, and my heart raced like never before.

At that point, I knew what needed to be done. I needed to meet him. And I needed to do it soon.

September 14

Today I found something Homer likes even more than practicing with my dad, Chloe, and me at McCall Park. He likes practicing with my team. I play for the Seattle Sky, a 16u select team made up of girls from all over the Seattle metropolitan area. We took Homer to practice today, and the girls on the team swarmed around him the minute he hopped out of the car. And of course he loved the attention.

"He's grown so much," Lea said. She hadn't seen him since the day we got him from her house. "He's adorable."

"He's the cutest dog I've ever seen," Kimi said.

The girls led him into our dugout and he seemed right at home. He sniffed around for a couple of minutes, took a quick look at our bats hanging in the bat rack and our bags hanging on the wall, and then rushed back to the girls to get more attention. Our second baseman, Haley Jones, took a bandana out of her softball bag and wrapped it around his neck. It had our team colors (blue and gray) and our logo (the word Sky shaped like a lightning bolt) on it.

"There," she said. "Now he's our official mascot."

Even our coaches liked him. They started laughing when they sent us to do our warm-up laps and he followed us. But he didn't follow for long. Homer loves to run, and he has limitless energy, so after the first lap he darted to the front of the group and led us from there. He'd even slow up on occasion so he could look back and make certain we were all keeping up.

After our warm-up laps, we did our stretching and other beginning-of-practice drills, including pushups and sit-ups. The coaches laughed as Homer strolled down our lines and barked at any girl who wasn't doing a good job.

"He's great," Coach Smith said. "He's a little drill sergeant."

After that, we did numerous other drills, sometimes as a large group and sometimes at different stations in groups of two or three. Homer roamed the field like he owned the place, and he helped everywhere he could. When I was batting, I hit a ball foul and it went over the fence and into a nearby parking lot. Homer darted after it, grabbed it (he's now big enough he can pick up softballs), and brought it back.

The only bad part of practice happened a few minutes later. Our third baseman, Casey Morgan, has a strong arm, but she has control problems on occasion. Some of the girls call her 'Wild Arm' behind her back. Anyway, she threw one ball too high and it flew across the field and nailed Homer right in the side. He wasn't hurt, but boy did it anger Coach Smith.

"Casey!" he shouted. "Did you hit our new mascot?"

Casey didn't know what to say, so she just stood there with a stupid look on her face.

"We have a new rule," Coach Smith announced. "Anyone who hits the team mascot owes me a lap. Get moving, Casey."

Then he turned to Homer and said, "Homer, you lead her. And make certain she doesn't dog it."

Everyone (except Casey) laughed at the pun.

Off they went. Casey did her lap around the field, and Homer led her the whole way. And normally Casey would have been mad (after all, no one likes to do a punishment lap), but since she had Homer with her, it didn't seem too bad. And Homer wasn't mad, even though Casey had hit him with the ball, because that's just how he is. He doesn't get mad easily, and he never holds a grudge. And everything was settled for good at the end of the lap when Casey apologized to Homer and gave him a big kiss on the top of the head.

September 16

This weekend, my team had a tournament in Tacoma, a city about thirty minutes south of Seattle. Our first game was against a team from Redmond called the LadyCats. We were really excited because this was our first game with an 'official' mascot. Homer sat in our dugout and watched attentively, with his team bandana wrapped around his neck. His eyes were bright, and I could tell he loved every minute of it.

During my first at-bat, I fouled a pitch away, and the ball cleared the fence and went into a flower bed. Homer darted from the dugout, grabbed it, and ran back toward the field.

Blue saw him and turned to me with a puzzled look on his face. "What's he doing?" he asked.

"He's getting the ball for you," I said. "He likes to help."

Homer ran up to blue and dropped the ball at his feet.

"I'll be darned," blue said. "I should have thought of that years ago. Thank you, fella."

"His name's Homer," I said.

"Thank you, Homer," blue said. He reached down and patted Homer on the head.

Homer returned to our dugout, and the game continued from there, with Homer retrieving foul balls whenever we hit them. And blue loved it, because it sped up the game and made things a lot easier for him. Normally, he had to find someone to go and get the ball for him, and there would be frequent delays.

And it was a great game. The LadyCats are a really good team, and they led for most of the game, but we came back and won it in the final inning when Casey hit a double off of the outfield wall that scored Lea all the way from first. I played the whole game in my normal position (shortstop), and I got two hits, a double and a triple.

Our second game was almost as noteworthy. It was against a team from Wenatchee called the Wings, and it went well until the fifth inning. Our starting pitcher is a girl named Laura King, and our backup is her identical twin sister Hannah. They both play catcher, too, so when one girl is pitching, the other catches. Laura started to struggle, and she gave up two hits in a row, so Coach Smith decided to take her out and replace her with Hannah. Unfortunately, Laura didn't want to come out (she thought she was doing fine), and Hannah didn't want to go in (she didn't feel like pitching today). So the girls did what they always do when presented with the same situation. They went into the dugout, waited until Coach Smith wasn't watching, and switched jerseys. They had been doing this for years, and all the other girls knew about it, but remarkably Coach Smith had never figured it out. He cheered as Laura walked to the circle and, now pitching as Hannah, struck out the next batter easily.

"That's exactly why I made the change," he said. "Laura did a great job today, but she was out of gas. I doubt she would have lasted another batter or two."

But she did. Laura pitched the rest of the game, and she didn't give up another hit the whole way, and we won 7-6. I got two doubles and a sacrifice, and I stole two bases (I love stealing bases — it's so exciting).

But our third game was a disappointment. It got rained out. Looking back, I guess I should have seen it coming. It had been getting cloudier and cloudier as the day progressed, so I guess it was just a matter of time. I don't know why they call Washington the Evergreen state. I guess it's because of all the evergreen trees that grow here, but to be honest if I were in charge, I'd rename it the Evergray state. Everything in Washington is gray. The buildings are gray, the streets are gray, even the sky is gray (most of the time). And even my team is gray. We're called the Seattle Sky, but we wear gray uniforms. If that doesn't tell you something, I don't know what does.

September 18

Today was a great day. I was at school, and I was standing at my locker with Lea, when I saw Logan at his locker down the hall. For a brief second, our eyes met. Just like at the football game, my heart raced the second he looked my way.

"I want to meet him so bad," I told Lea.

"So does everyone," Lea said. "He's dreamy. Why don't you go and say hi? It can't do any harm."

"Just walk up to him?" I asked, somewhat incredulous. "I don't know. I'm not usually that outright. Especially with boys."

"Just use the old book drop trick," Lea said. "It works every time."

"Book drop?" I asked. "What do you mean?" I had never heard that term before.

"Just pretend you're walking past him," Lea explained, "and accidentally drop your books at his feet. He'll help you pick them up, and hopefully say something, and things will flow from there."

I was skeptical at first. "I don't know," I said. "That sounds pretty corny to me."

"Trust me," Lea said. "It works every time. That's how I hooked up with Tom Ottweiler."

"Tom Ottweiler was a jerk," I said. "You broke up with him a week later."

Lea shrugged. "True. But at least I got to meet him. How will you ever find out anything about Logan if you just stand over here on the opposite side of the hallway staring at him all day? Go over there and give it a try."

I didn't really want to, I still had serious misgivings about Lea's book drop plan, but I had to admit she had a point. If I ever wanted to meet Logan, and I definitely did, I needed to do something. I grabbed a stack of text books from my locker, arranged them just right, so I could drop them without damaging them, and headed in his direction. But I was really nervous, and I started to have second thoughts the minute I got near him, and, not even realizing what I was doing, I just stopped and stood there, frozen in place for several really long seconds. And while I stood there, trying to decide if I was actually going to go through with it or not, another girl, Hailey Wetmore, a sophomore in my math class, stepped in front of me, walked up to Logan, and dropped her books at his feet.

"Oh," she said, a surprised look on her face. "How clumsy of me."

Reflexively, Logan bent down and helped her pick up her books.

I stood there in complete shock. Hailey had beaten me to the punch. And she had used the exact same book drop plan I was going to use. If I had had a gun, I would have shot myself right there on the spot.

"Here," Logan said, with his deep, southern accent. It wasn't as thick as some southern accents I've heard, but it was unmistakable nonetheless. And exotic, at least to me. "Let me help you with that," he said. He grabbed Hailey's books off of the floor, organized them neatly into a stack for her, and handed them back.

"You're so kind, Logan," she said, fluttering her eyelashes at him. Up until then, I had never noticed how long Hailey's eyelashes were. They were the longest (and nicest) eyelashes I had ever seen. "It is Logan, right?"

"Yeah," he said. "You're Bailey, right? You're one of the cheerleaders?"

She smiled, somewhat awkwardly. "Actually," she said. "It's Hailey."

"Oh," Logan said. "Sorry. Anyway, I saw you at the game Friday night. You guys did a great job. It really helps fire us up. I saw you do a back flip. That was great."

"Thanks," she said.

There was a brief, awkward silence, as they both stood there, looking at one another. Clearly, neither of them knew what to do next. I didn't know what to do, either. I just stood there, less than five feet away, watching them with a stupid look on my face.

Finally, Hailey broke the silence.

"So anyway," she said. "I just like, well, broke up with my boyfriend, and so I was wondering, since you're new in town and it doesn't seem like you have a girlfriend yet, maybe you'd like to grab some dinner. Maybe tonight?"

Logan smiled. "I'm flattered," he said. "But unfortunately, tonight isn't good for me. I have practice after school, and then I promised my uncle I'd help him with some things around the house. Chores and stuff. It's kinda silly but you know how it is. With family."

"Really?" Hailey asked, a look of complete disbelief on her face. Like most cheerleaders, she is mega-hot, so she's not used to being turned down very often. To be honest, it's probably never happened before. She was completely speechless, and she had no clue what to do. After a couple of long, awkward seconds, and without saying anything more, she turned and hurried away.

After hearing that, I was completely disheartened. If Logan had turned down Hailey Wetmore, one of the most popular, attractive girls at our school, I knew I had no chance at all. I turned to head in the opposite direction when his voice stopped me in my tracks.

"Can you believe that?" he asked. "She used the old book drop trick on me. How lame. Like I haven't seen that before."

I gulped. I didn't know what to do. Or say.

But then my eyes got big as I realized something. He was talking to me. Logan McCoy, one of the best players on the football team, and one of the hottest boys at school, was talking to me.

"I wish girls wouldn't be like that," he said. "I know I'm new here, so it's not my place to be criticizing people, but I just wish they'd be more honest. If a girl wanted to meet me, I wish she'd just walk up and say hi."

I didn't know what else to say.

"Hi," I said.

"That's more like it," he said. "You're Angel, right? Angel Williams?"

I couldn't believe it. He knew my name.

"Yeah," I said.

"I saw you at the game last week," he said. "I asked around, and people told me who you were. They say you're a great softball player. They say you'll probably make the varsity team this year even though you're just a freshman."

"Really?" I asked. I wanted to learn more, especially who had said it, but softball had to wait. For now, I needed to focus on Logan and Logan alone. This was my big chance. I was actually talking to him, and I needed to make the most of the opportunity.

But unfortunately, I couldn't think of anything to say. I just stood there, completely silent, like a complete dork. After a few seconds, I could feel my cheeks getting warm. I was clearly blushing.

"I should be going," Logan said. "Class is about to begin, and since I'm new here, I don't want to be late. Need to make a good impression on the teachers, right? But anyway, I was wondering. I hope you don't think this is too forward, since we just met, but I've been wanting to ask you for awhile now, ever since I saw you at the game, if you wanted to go and do something. Like maybe grab some dinner. Or coffee. Maybe tonight."

My heart missed a beat. Had he actually asked me out? I knew I was dreaming. After all, nothing this good ever happened to me in real life.

But then I remembered something.

"I thought you had to help your uncle tonight?" I asked. "With chores."

Logan smiled. "I just made that up," he said. "To be honest, I didn't want to go out with Bailey. I mean Hailey. But I'd definitely like to go out with you. If you're interested. Can you get free? It doesn't have to be anything fancy. Just coffee if you'd like. I hear Starbucks is really popular here in the Northwest. We could grab a mocha or something."

At that point, I was too happy to even speak, and too in shock to realize what was happening. My only response was an excited nod.

"Ok, good," Logan said. "I have practice right after school. Can I meet you after practice at the Starbucks right across from the football field?"

I nodded.

"Sweet," he said. "I'll see you then."

He rushed off to class. The minute he left, I nearly passed out right there on the spot. My head was completely spinning.

I couldn't believe it. I had a date with Logan McCoy. I was in complete heaven.

So I met him after practice, at Starbucks. I was nervous at first, but it was amazing how quickly I settled down and felt at ease with him. Logan was really nice, and soft spoken and gentle. And courteous. He ordered a pumpkin spice latte (I love pumpkin) for me, and he got a white chocolate mocha for himself, and we grabbed a couple of chairs in a corner and lounged around for hours. I told him about my life (boring as it was), and he told me about him, how he was from a small town about an hour west of Dallas called Huckstin.

"I've never heard of Huckstin," I said.

"No one has," he said. "It's a small place. Too small. But it's nice, in some ways. My dad is a mechanic, and he has an auto shop, and he does really good business, especially in the spring and summer when the weather is good. I work at the shop with him on occasion, when he needs extra help. I'm actually pretty good at fixing cars, at least simple things, so if you ever need anything, just give me the word."

I liked what I had heard. Logan was cute, charming, good at football, and handy. It didn't get any better than that.

He went on to tell me about his family, how his parents had divorced when he was young, and how his dad had been awarded custody of him, and how his dad had remarried a few years later, and how he now had two younger half-brothers named Hank and Billy Bob. Then we talked about what we liked, and what we didn't, and I couldn't believe how much we had in common. We both loved Italian food (especially lasagna, with extra cheese), our favorite color was blue, our favorite band was Green Day, and our birthdays were both in October (his birthday was on October 1 and mine was on October 24).

The more we talked, the more I liked him. And when I say like, I mean like like, like how a girlfriend likes her boyfriend. Not like how a brother likes his little sister. But there was one thing I was still curious about.

"Do you mind if I ask?" I said. "Why did you move to Seattle? And why by yourself, without your family? That seems a little unusual."

For a brief second, Logan's eyes got large. This was clearly a subject he didn't like to discuss. His voice was quiet as he gave me an explanation.

"I had an argument with my stepmother," he said.

I raised an eyebrow.

"Actually," he continued. "I had several arguments with my stepmother."

"What do you mean?" I asked.

"She means well," he explained, "but she just doesn't treat me the same as her sons (my half-brothers). She tries, but it just wasn't meant to be. And it really upsets me sometimes. One night, right at the end of summer, we had a big argument, and I got mad and called her a witch. So then my dad got really mad. Which is pretty unusual for him, since he's really easy-going most of the time. So he told me to apologize, but I wouldn't."

"So he sent you to Seattle?" I asked.

Logan laughed. "Of course not," he said. "Moving to Seattle was my idea. My dad was completely against it at first. He was mad, don't get me wrong, especially since I wouldn't apologize, but he would never send me away because of it. He's not like that at all."

"It was your idea to come here?" I asked.

"Yeah," Logan said. "I've always liked my uncle, and one time a few years back he floated the idea of me coming to stay with him for awhile, so I finally thought, *What the heck?* And I thought it would be good because it would give my stepmother and me some time to cool down. And I felt really bad for my dad."

"What do you mean?" I asked.

"My dad is in a bad situation," he said. "He has me, from his first marriage, and he has his other sons (my half-brothers) from his current marriage. Hank is five and Billy Bob is four. They're good kids most of the time, and we get along pretty well. But my dad is always caught in the middle. My stepmother always wants him to spend his time with Hank and Billy Bob, since they're her sons, and she gets really upset if he spends too much time with me. So he tries his best to balance his time between the three of us, but it isn't easy, and sometimes I don't make things any easier on him, either, especially since I want him to spend the majority of his time with me. A few years back, I got really mad because he went to one of Hank's games instead of mine, and I demanded he divorce her, so he could spend more time with me, but of course he wouldn't, and now looking back I think it was pretty stupid I did that, because that wouldn't have been fair to him or my younger brothers. It's just really complex. Anyway, my dad finally agreed to let me come up here and live with my uncle, but only for a year. And I have to call him at least once a day. But don't tell the guys on the football team that part or they'll think I'm a wuss since I have to call my daddy every day."

I smiled. I didn't care what anyone else thought about Logan. All I cared about was what I thought.

I liked him. I liked him a lot.

September 22

I discovered the most annoying, obnoxious person on the planet today. It's my older sister, Chloe. She's seventeen, so she's two years older than me. She thinks she's so cool since she's a junior (and I'm just a freshman) and since she has a driver's license (and I don't). In addition, her boyfriend, Caleb Davies, is a senior and the star quarterback on our school's football team, so she's really popular, and she reminds me of it daily.

"Is your boyfriend the star quarterback on the football team?" she asked. "Oh wait, I forgot. You don't have a boyfriend, do you?"

Chloe and I have always been competitive. She plays fastpitch, too, for an 18u team called the Washington Wildcats. Since she's older than me, she's bigger, stronger, faster, and more experienced, but of course I'm still better. Chloe's okay, but she's nothing special.

Anyway, my team had a big tournament this weekend in Everett, a city about fifteen minutes north of Seattle. It was an 18u tournament, so it was for older teams, but my team entered it anyway since we've been doing well lately and Coach Smith wanted to challenge us by putting us up against the older girls. Despite being the only 16u team in the tournament, we started the weekend well and beat a team from Puyallup called the Pressure 4-0. We then beat a team from Arlington called the A's 5-4. But then the real action began.

We got to play Chloe's team.

Chloe made fun of me before the game began. "We'll try not to embarrass you little girls too much," she said. She put special emphasis on the word 'little.'

She and her teammates laughed as they headed to their dugout. Chloe's teammates are almost as obnoxious as she is.

I hate to admit it, but I was a little apprehensive. Chloe's team is really good, and they win almost all of their games. And Chloe is their star pitcher, so it was going to be me against her, head-to-head, sooner or later.

We had never faced one another before. Not in a game. Being sisters, we've practiced together forever, at McCall Park and in the back yard, but we had never had a game against one another until today.

"I heard your sister is really good," Lea said as we warmed up. I could see a look of concern (and fear) in her eyes. "They say she throws really hard. And they say her changeup is nasty."

"She's okay," I said. "But we can handle her."

Maybe not. Chloe was on fire to start the game, and she struck out our first six batters easily, including me. I went down swinging on three straight fastballs. The pitches sounded like explosions as they hit the catcher's mitt.

"Better luck next time," Chloe said as I walked back to the dugout.

Luckily, our pitcher, Laura, was almost as impressive, and the game remained scoreless until I got my second at-bat in the fourth inning. This time, I did a little better, and I fouled the first two pitches away.

"Look at that," Chloe said from the pitching circle. "Someone finally showed up to play. Let's see how you can handle an inside pitch."

The next pitch was pure heat, and it nailed me in the forearm. It hit me so hard my arm went numb for several minutes. I couldn't even feel my fingers.

"Shake it off," Chloe said. "It's not that bad. It barely grazed you."

"BS," I shouted at her. I was really mad. It hurt bad. "You did that on purpose. You hit me intentionally." I was about to say something more but blue intervened and sent me to first base.

Unfortunately, Chloe struck out the next batter to end the inning, so we had to take the field.

"Are you certain you're okay?" Coach Smith asked as I grabbed my glove and headed to short. "I can put in a sub if you want."

"I'm okay," I said. "I'll be fine."

As far as I was concerned, I had some unfinished business to attend to. Someone needed some payback. And she needed it soon.

It didn't take long for me to get my chance. Chloe was the first batter that inning and she hit a shot off of the outfield wall. Our center fielder, Kimi, grabbed the ball and whipped it to me at second, but Chloe got there first. It wasn't even close, but it didn't matter. I slapped the tag down anyway, as hard as I could, right in Chloe's face.

"Knock it off," she shouted, pushing my glove away.

"You knock it off," I responded, and I pushed her back.

Things were about to escalate and get really ugly, but Homer darted from the dugout, got between us, and broke it up. He wasn't happy to see us fighting, and he growled at us to let us know exactly what he thought of our behavior.

And he wasn't the only one who was upset. Blue called our coaches over for a meeting at home plate.

"That behavior is unacceptable when I'm in charge," he said. "I should eject both of them right now."

Chloe and I took a deep breath and glanced at our dad sitting in the stands. He didn't say anything, but his face was turning red. We knew we were in deep trouble if we got ejected.

Luckily, we didn't. Blue gave us a warning and the game continued from there. The Wildcats got a run that inning, and another the next, and they were leading 2-0 when I got my final at-bat in the top of the seventh.

"We meet again," Chloe said as I took my place in the batter's box. She had a big smile on her face, and she rocked back and forth on her heels like a little kid. She knew she had the lead, and she only needed three more outs to beat us.

I dug my cleats into the dirt, tapped my bat on the plate, and took a deep breath. This was my last chance to prove myself. I needed to grit my teeth and get a hit.

But it wasn't easy. The first pitch was a nasty riseball, and I missed it by a mile. The second was a curveball, down and away. The third, fourth, and fifth were fastballs, and I fouled them all away. I barely got a piece of the last one. For a second I thought I was a goner, but I nicked it somehow and managed to stay alive.

Then Chloe threw me a changeup, probably hoping to fool me with the change of speed. And it was a nasty changeup at that, at least twenty miles per hour slower than her fastball, but I was ready, and it didn't fool me at all. I kept my hands back as long as I could, then swung with everything I had. I hit it hard, straight up the middle, and it nailed Chloe and ricocheted to the side.

That'll teach her, I thought as I ran to first. *She won't make fun of me again.*

But then something unexpected happened. Out of the corner of my eye, I saw Homer dart from our dugout and run to the pitching circle. That was strange, because even though Homer was new to the softball world, he knew to stay off of the field until a play was over.

But then I realized what had happened. Chloe was hurt. And she was hurt bad.

She was lying on the ground, in the middle of the pitcher's circle, flat on her back. Her face was covered with blood and she wasn't moving. I hadn't realized it at first, but the ball had hit her straight in the face.

I nearly freaked out as I realized what I had done.

I had killed my sister.

Luckily, she wasn't actually dead. She started moving again as soon as Homer got to her, and she sat up as her coach and my dad ran onto the field to help her. She had a nasty gouge on her cheek and forehead, where the ball had hit her, and my dad wrapped it up the best he could to stop the bleeding. But it was a complete mess, and he didn't have enough wrap, so he turned to Homer.

"Sorry, fella," he said. "I need to borrow this."

He took Homer's bandana from around his neck and wrapped it around Chloe's forehead. In no time, it was soaked with blood. In the meantime, Chloe's coach asked her how she was, but she was crying too hard to give a coherent answer.

By this time, I was a complete wreck. I was almost as bad as her. Tears ran down my cheeks. I never meant to hurt her so bad. I wouldn't have minded hurting her a little, by hitting her in the shoulder, or the leg or arm, but I didn't mean to hit her in the face. Coach Smith saw me and ran over to comfort me.

"She'll be okay," he said, putting a hand on my shoulder. "Hang in there. It's not your fault. These things happen on occasion. You know what they say. There's nothing soft about softball."

I appreciated the effort but it didn't make me feel any better. An ambulance arrived a few minutes later, and the paramedics lifted Chloe onto a stretcher and carried her off of the field. My dad and I followed them and climbed inside the ambulance to ride with her to the hospital. One of the paramedics was about to close the door when we heard a bark and Homer jumped inside.

"We don't usually allow dogs in the ambulance," the paramedic said.

"He's a special dog," I told him. "He goes where we go."

Not knowing what else to do, the paramedic shrugged, closed the door, and we were off. I turned to Chloe and could barely control myself.

"I'm sorry," I said. "I didn't mean to do it. I was just trying so hard. I thought it was a good hit."

"It was," Chloe said. Her face was wrapped in bandages and Homer's bandana and she had a huge icepack on her forehead. She looked like a mess, but luckily she had calmed down a lot and was only crying a little now. "It was a great hit," she said. "One of your best."

"Really?" I asked.

"That's what dad taught us, right?" she said. "Hit the ball up the middle. You did your job. And you did it well. I thought I had you with that changeup, but you weren't fooled. Well done."

I didn't know what to say. I appreciated the compliment, especially from her, but I was too worried to know what to think. Much to my relief, we arrived at the hospital a few minutes later, and they wheeled Chloe into another room for a formal examination and a CAT scan. Luckily, everything came out okay, and the

CAT scan revealed no internal damage or bleeding of any type. The doctor stitched up her forehead (it took twenty stitches) and gave us some instructions to follow after we headed home.

"I want to see you for a check-up in a couple of days," he told Chloe. "And no softball or anything physical until then. Okay? Other than that you should be fine."

"I have a terrible headache," Chloe said. "It feels like a bomb exploded in my head."

"I'll give you something for that," the doctor said. "It should go away in a day or two. After that, you'll be fine."

I let out a huge sigh. I've never felt so relieved in my entire life. Chloe can be a real witch at times (actually, she's a witch most of the time), but regardless, I wanted her to get better as soon as possible. When we got home, I made her a bowl of soup (clam chowder, it's her favorite), and Homer and I climbed into bed with her and we all surfed the internet together using her laptop computer. After an hour, Cinnamon saw us in her bedroom, and he didn't want Homer to get all of the attention, so he joined us too, and it was pretty crowded in that bed, but it was actually pretty nice, and it was the most time Chloe and I have spent together in a long time.

I guess it's true what they say. Sometimes bad things can be good things, in a strange sort of way, because they bring you closer together. This incident brought Chloe and me closer together, at least for a couple of hours.

September 23

My dad is a professor. He teaches history at the University of Washington, and he's taught there for quite awhile now, as long as I can remember. But he's not a normal professor, at least as far as I can tell. He doesn't come home and read history books, or magazine articles, or anything intellectual like that at all. Instead, he spends most of his time playing Rock Band. And he's pretty good at it, especially when he plays guitar or drums (but he sucks at keyboard). Chloe and I join in on occasion, and I play bass (or guitar when my dad is playing drums). Chloe likes to sing, so she's our front man. She has a pretty voice, especially on songs with a lot of melody. Homer is our manager, and Cinnamon is our fan club president. We formed our own imaginary band called *Crazy Crew*. Today, since Chloe is still recovering from her concussion and can't do much, we spent quite awhile playing, and it was really fun. But the only bad thing was we spent a lot of time arguing over what songs to play. My dad loves the hard stuff, especially death, thrash, and speed metal. Ugh. His favorite bands are Five Finger Death Punch (ouch), Godsmack (good lord), and Korn (I've never understood why a band would want to be called Korn, let alone why they would spell their name with a K). It hurts my ears to even think about it. Chloe, Homer, Cinnamon, and I, by contrast, like 'normal' music, and our favorite artists are Green Day, Katy Perry, and Snoop Dogg. Homer loves Snoop. He bobs his head to the thumping bass.

And luckily, since there are more of us than my dad, we usually outvote him, so we only have to listen to his devil worshipping music on occasion.

September 24

Just my luck. Coach Smith got fired today. Our dads finally got sick of him and got rid of him for good. I guess I should have seen it coming. After all, the dads always think they can do a better job than the coach, no matter how hard the coach tries and no matter how well he does. But that wasn't the real problem. Our dads were still upset about how last season ended, and for good reason. Coach Smith, like all coaches, always says softball is all about the girls, but everyone knows it isn't. It's about the coaches. And all they really care about are their own daughters (how much playing time they get) and winning. A perfect example of that happened last year when my team flew to Los Angeles to play in a big tournament (it was our big 'out-of-state' tournament for the year). My teammate, Olivia Sanchez, was in a batting slump, so Coach Smith hardly played her during the trip, so her parents spent all that money to fly to California, and they rented a hotel room and a car, basically for nothing. Olivia was so upset she started crying in the hotel lobby. We girls tried to make her feel better, but Coach Smith didn't really care, and he spent the rest of the night sitting in the hotel bar, drinking beer and talking about how his brilliant decisions had led us to a big victory earlier in the day.

But the final straw happened at the final tournament of the season in Wenatchee. Another of my teammates, Kristin King, broke her arm diving to make a catch during a game. It was a spectacular catch, one of the best I've ever seen, and it won the game for us. Of course Coach Smith was happy about that. He even called the emergency room as they were doing Kristin's x-rays to see how she was doing. But since it was the last tournament of the year, Kristin had to do tryouts in order to make the team for this season, but of course she couldn't do tryouts since her arm was in a cast (and as you can imagine it's kind of hard to play softball in a cast), so Coach Smith cut her from the team. And then she was really screwed, because since her arm was broken she couldn't do tryouts for any other team, and so last I heard she hadn't made any team at all, even though her arm was finally better.

So I'm not really too upset about Coach Smith being fired. In many ways, he was a jerk. One time, he yelled at me when I messed up a play, but that wasn't really a big deal, I guess, and I probably shouldn't have messed up the play in the first place. But here's what I'm upset about. His replacement is my greatest nightmare. It's my dad. The other dads decided my dad was the best choice to be the new coach, so he's it. And now he doesn't want the other dads to think he's favoring me in any way, so he's being twice as hard on me as he is the other girls. Today, at practice, Kimi let a ground ball go through her legs and he called out, "That's okay, Kimi. You'll get the next one." A few minutes later, I let one get past me and he yelled out, "Keep your mitt in the dirt, Angel. You know better than that. I'm not gonna tell you again."

As if that wasn't bad enough, when we girls were sitting in the dugout, taking a water break, Kimi had the nerve to say, "I'm so glad your dad is the new coach, Angel. He's the best coach, ever. You're so lucky to have a dad like him."

298

"What?" I said. "You've got to be kidding. My dad is a pain in the neck."

"No way," Kimi said. "Your dad is so cool. He's not like my dad at all. My dad is a beast. He's in a bad mood all the time."

"That's nothing," Lea said. "My dad is the worst of all. He yells at me all the time, and he never listens to me at all."

I don't care what they say. I've met both of their dads. Kimi's dad's name is Craig, and Lea's dad's name is Dale, and they're both really nice guys. But my dad, he can be a real jerk at times, especially the time when I was eight and I spilled paint on the kitchen floor. I realize he told me to be careful and make certain the lid on the can was on tightly, but he still didn't need to be such a beast about it. So now that he's the new coach, this could be a frustrating year for me. But at least one good thing came of the coaching change. On the drive home from practice, I asked my dad about Kristin, and he said to call her and get her back on the team. He didn't care that we already had a full roster of twelve girls, and he said we would play the rest of the season with thirteen. So I did, and now Kristin is officially my teammate again, and that makes me really happy. Kristin is a nice girl, and it was completely unfair what happened to her, so it's good to see things finally made right.

September 27

Today I went to the football game, to see Logan (of course), and just like last week, he was amazing. Our game was against Snohomish, and it was a road game, so Lea's mom gave us a ride. There were three of us total, Kimi, Lea, and me. We cheered as the game started, and our team wasted little time getting on the scoreboard. Our quarterback, Caleb Davies (Chloe's boyfriend), threw a pass to one of our receivers, a senior named Kellen Allen, and he ran eighty yards for the score. It was a great play, and quite exciting, but nothing like what Logan did a few plays later. Logan took a handoff, rushed through the line, sidestepped a would-be tackler, and dragged three more tacklers into the end zone for a touchdown. All three tacklers were bigger and heavier than Logan, by a lot, but he would not be denied.

There's no doubt about it. He's perfect. In every way.

September 29

Until this year, I had never played for the same team for more than a season. Every year, something always happened. My first year, when I played for the King County Khaos, my dad got in an argument with the coach, so we decided to move on to another team (which was actually okay, because the team I moved on to, the Eastside Angels, was much better than the Khaos). The Angels seemed really good at first (like they always do), but it was kind of strange, since my name is Angel and I played for the Angels. That got a few laughs. Unfortunately, things soured by the end of the season (my coach got a divorce, then started spending a lot of time with his new girlfriend, then started showing up late to games, then started skipping practices). You can imagine how that went over with my dad. So I moved on to the Seattle Softball Club, and that was a really good team, but it disbanded after a year when most of the girls, for various reasons, decided they wanted to play for other teams. So I moved on to my current team, the Seattle Sky, which still seems pretty good, despite the recent coaching change, but I'm not getting my hopes up, because I know how it works. Sooner or later the girls will start arguing amongst one another, or the dads will get upset with something, and on I'll go from there. I don't really like it, but what can I do? It is what it is.

Today was a stressful day. One of our games was against my old team, the Eastside Angels. Most of my former teammates are still on the Angels, and several of them are still my friends. It was good to see them again, but at the same time I needed to do well against them. After all, who wants to play poorly against her old team?

The Angels' pitcher is a girl I've known forever. Her name is Ashley Martinez, and she goes to my school. We're pretty good friends, but we're both really competitive, and we've had some heated arguments in the past year over who is the better player. As such, I knew I better not strike out against her, or I'd hear about it for sure on Monday morning.

Unfortunately, the game didn't start well. Ashley got two quick strikes on me, then finished me off with a nasty riseball.

"Good try," she said with a smirk.

She was being nice on the outside, but I knew what she was thinking. She thought she was better than me.

As I sat in the dugout, I was furious at myself. Ashley wasn't even that good. How in the world had she struck me out?

My next at-bat came in the third inning. This time I did a little better, but not much. I hit the first pitch really hard, but straight at the Angels' shortstop, Brooke Conrad (another friend of mine). Brooke caught it with ease.

"Better luck next time," Ashley said with a smile.

At that point, she was really getting on my nerves. I needed to get a hit during my final at-bat. Unfortunately, it wasn't meant to be. I fouled two pitches straight back, then struck out swinging at a fastball. In the dugout, Homer shook his head in disgust. Even he was disappointed with my pitiful performance.

Ashley sent me a text message after the game. It read, "Don't worry about today's game. We all have bad games on occasion. Some of us more often than others."

I deleted her message without responding. I'll get her back the next time we play. Just you wait and see.

October 2

I was sitting in my bedroom, at my desk, working on my math homework (did I ever mention I hate math?), when I got this feeling someone was looking at me. I looked up and there was Chloe, standing in the doorway to my room, staring at me with an astonished look on her face.

"Is it true?" she asked.

I had no idea what she was talking about.

"Is it true you're seeing Logan McCoy?"

My heart raced the minute she said Logan's name.

"We're not really seeing each other," I said. "But we did go out. Once. It was nothing fancy. But it was nice. And he did say he wanted to go out again."

"Don't be so modest, Angel," Chloe said with a smile. "You've got that boy eating out of the palm of your hand. He's totally gaga over you."

My heart raced. Did Chloe know something I didn't? Something about Logan?

"Caleb and Logan have been hanging out a lot lately," Chloe said. "I know it's kind of unusual, since Caleb is a senior and Logan is a sophomore, but I guess that's how football players are. They don't care what grade you're in as long as you're good. Anyway, we all went out to dinner the other night, after practice, and Caleb invited Logan, and we're all sitting around talking, and Logan said something about this girl he went out with, a freshman who is a softball player and is really hot. And he said he really liked her. And then he asked if any of us knew her. And Caleb said, 'What's her name?'"

"Really?" I asked. I couldn't believe what I was hearing. It was too good to be true. "And he said me?"

"Of course he said you," Chloe said. "And then he got really embarrassed, because the other guys started laughing, since they know who you are, and they know you're my sister, but Logan didn't know."

"They didn't give him a hard time, did they?" I asked. I hated the thought of them making fun of Logan.

"Of course not," Chloe said. "They really like him. And that's amazing, since he just moved here, but they all say he's a great player, and he's really nice as well. I decided I better spend a little time with him myself, to find out what he's like and all. After all, I can't have some weirdo hanging out with my little sister."

My heart froze. Chloe had talked to Logan? About me?

"It was a little awkward at first," she said. "He was pretty embarrassed. He says we don't look much alike."

It's true. Chloe and I are both tall and thin, but our similarities end there. She has blue eyes, whereas mine are deep brown (chocolate, to be more precise), and her hair is much longer and lighter than mine. I'm a lot prettier but don't tell her that. It'll just make her mad.

"But things got much better as time went on," she said. "He's really nice. And his accent is adorable. It's mesmerizing just listening to him. And let's just say he's crazy about you."

"Really?" I asked. "What'd he say?"

Chloe smiled. "He wouldn't say much once he found out you were my sister. He knew I'd tell you.

But let's just say I could tell. He had that look in his eyes."

"That look?" I asked.

"Yeah, you know. Every time I mentioned your name, his eyes sparkled. And he wanted to know everything about you. What softball team you played for, how long you've played, blah, blah, blah. I don't know what you did, but you got him. Hook, line, and sinker."

I sat there, completely speechless. I couldn't believe what I was hearing, but I knew one thing for certain. I wanted to hear more.

"The other guys think it's hilarious," Chloe said.

"What?" I asked.

"Caleb and Logan, the two star players on the football team, are dating sisters. They think it's cosmic or something."

"Cosmic?"

"Meant to be," she said. "And I have to agree. It is pretty funny. It caught me completely off guard. I always knew you had potential, Angel. And this Logan, as far as I can tell, he's a good guy. I think you found a winner there."

She turned to leave, but then stopped briefly to say one last thing.

"It's hard to believe," she said. "One day, my little sister could be almost as popular as me."

With a chuckle, she turned and left.

I was in seventh heaven the rest of the night. My head was spinning, and I just couldn't sit still. I never did finish my homework. I couldn't believe it, but it was actually true.

Logan liked me.

October 3

My dad is a beast. He's still giving me a hard time at practice, and he's definitely being harder on me than the rest of the girls. He made me run an extra lap today because I missed a fly ball. It's true I was daydreaming about Logan at the time, and that's the reason I missed the fly ball, but still, that's no reason to get all fussy and single me out like that. The other girls (especially Lea) miss fly balls all the time, and he doesn't make them run extra laps. On the way home, I was about to yell at him and give him an earful, but then I decided to bite my lip and let it go. He was in a good mood (to him it had been a productive practice), and I didn't want to ruin the moment with an argument. And besides, if there is one thing I learned a long time ago, dealing with parents is extremely tough, and I have to choose my battles wisely. I only have so much energy, and I can't go wasting it on little things. And my dad is new to this coaching thing, so hopefully things will eventually change and he'll start treating me more fairly.

October 4

Angel Williams

I've never really liked my name. The Angel part is okay, but Williams is so plain. So common. I might as well be named Angel Smith, or Angel Jones, or Angel Davis.

Angel Dell Williams

Ugh. I've never liked my middle name at all. It's too old-fashioned. Forget I even mentioned it.

Angel McCoy

That sounds a lot better. It's exotic, and catchy, and it has a definite flair to it. I like how it looks. I like how McCoy has a little c right before the big C.

Logan and Angel McCoy

That sounds really good. It's definitely meant to be.

October 5

Today my team had a tournament in Mount Vernon, a city about an hour north of Seattle. It was an older tournament, for 18u teams, but it started well. Our first game was against a team from Oregon called the Portland Pioneers and we won 4-3. I went two for three with two singles, and I made a couple of nice plays in the field, including a running catch to end the third inning. Our second game was against a team from Yakima called the Yellow Jackets. They wear these awful, yellow uniforms with black stripes. They are the brightest uniforms I've ever seen, and I had to put my sunglasses on just to look at them. But anyway, the game went well and we won 5-4. I went one for three with a double.

But that was the end of the fun. Our third and final game was against a team called Stanwood Fastpitch (SFP for short), and their pitcher, Kaitlyn Kingsbury, is really mean. She likes to throw brushback pitches just for the fun of it. In case you don't know, a brushback pitch is a pitch the pitcher intentionally throws high and tight, missing the batter's head by inches. Brushback pitches are thrown to scare and intimidate the batter, and it was working. Kaitlyn's pitches were scaring the you-know-what out of us. We hadn't gotten a single hit through the first four innings, and I struck out badly during my first at bat. My dad got so frustrated he called a timeout and challenged blue.

"She's throwing at my batters," he complained.

"There's nothing I can do," blue responded. "Brushback pitches are legal, as long as she doesn't hit the batter."

Begrudgingly, my dad returned to the dugout, and the game continued from there. Before we knew it, we were losing 2-0.

But then everything changed. Kaitlyn made a huge mistake. Between innings, she walked over to the stands and spoke to my sister, Chloe. Chloe's team, the Wildcats, had the day off, so she was watching from the bleachers (actually, she was spending most of her time texting her friends, but she'd look up on occasion, especially when it was my turn to bat).

"I haven't seen you in awhile," Kaitlyn said. "How's it going?"

Chloe and Kaitlyn used to be good friends, back when they were younger. Kaitlyn used to come over to our house quite a bit, sometimes to spend the night. But things soured a year ago when they had a huge fight over Caleb. Caleb had originally been Kaitlyn's boyfriend, but he broke up with her so he could go out with Chloe.

"Good," Chloe responded. "How about you?"

"Not bad," Kaitlyn said. "You still playing for the Wildcats?"

Chloe nodded. They were both being cordial, but there was obvious bad blood between them. I could feel the tension ten feet away.

"And how are the mighty Wildcats doing this season?" Kaitlyn asked.

"Not too bad. And you?"

Kaitlyn shrugged. "Same old, same old. You see how it is. They got us playing these younger teams a lot lately. It's a complete waste of time, if you ask me. I'll be lucky if I even break a sweat today. All these

310

young teams suck. Especially this one. That dog they've got for a mascot is cute, but the rest of the team is completely worthless. There's not a good player in the bunch."

"Really?" Chloe asked, raising an eyebrow. "What about the shortstop?"

Kaitlyn shrugged. "She sucks, too."

Chloe smiled. "I see. Well, it was good seeing you, Kaitlyn, but I gotta go. I've got something to take care of. Some unfinished business."

Chloe got up, headed back to our car in the adjoining parking lot, unloaded her softball bag (since she wasn't playing today, I'm not certain why she brought it, but I'm grateful anyway), and carried it into our dugout. She plopped it down on the bench and turned to my dad.

"Do you have a spare jersey?" she asked.

"Yeah," he said. "A couple. They're in the equipment bag. Why?"

"I need to teach Kaitlyn a lesson," she said, "so I'm pitching from now on. Where's the ball?"

Every head in the dugout turned as one.

"You're playing for us?" I asked. I couldn't believe it. Chloe had never played for us before. Technically, most of the time she couldn't, since she was older, but today she could since we were playing in an 18u tournament.

"Only on one condition," she said, and she turned to address us all. "Every girl on this team goes all-out from here on. Understood? I'm sick of Kaitlyn and her prissy attitude. And I'm especially sick of those brushback pitches. Are you with me?"

We cheered. Homer barked. And then we charged onto the field like a team reborn. We weren't afraid of Kaitlyn anymore. Now that we had Chloe pitching for us, we knew the tables had been turned, and now we had a chance to win.

Chloe did not disappoint. She was still changing into her uniform as she headed onto the field (she was having a hard time getting her left cleat on), but once the inning started, she was all business. She was absolutely on fire. Being her sister, I've known her forever, but I've never seen her throw that hard before. Her pitches were exploding in our catcher's mitt. The SFP batters were completely overwhelmed. All three of them struck out the first inning, and two of three the second.

In the meantime, we scored three runs. Kaitlyn was clearly rattled (she couldn't believe Chloe was pitching for us), and the velocity of her pitches dipped significantly. Lea started things with a single, Laura walked, I hit a single to load the bases, and Chloe hit a massive triple off of the outfield wall to score all three of us. Chloe hit it so hard at first I thought it was going to be a grand slam, but not quite. Regardless, it gave us the lead, 3-2, and we held it until the final out of the final inning.

And then the real showdown began.

The grudge match of the century.

It was Kaitlyn's turn to bat.

Chloe versus Kaitlyn. Head-to-head.

Chloe's first pitch was so fast I could barely see it. From my position at short, it was a nothing but a yellow blur. And it missed Kaitlyn's head by an inch. Maybe less. It was so close Kaitlyn's knees buckled and she fell to the ground in an attempt to get away from it.

"Hey," she yelled at Chloe. "You did that on purpose."

Chloe smiled. "It's not so fun," she said, "when they come at you. Is it?"

Kaitlyn got up, dusted herself off, and the battle continued. The next pitch was straight down the middle, and the second was pure heat for strike two. Chloe tried to finish her off with a nasty changeup, but Kaitlyn fouled it away. Chloe went back to the heat, but Kaitlyn fouled it away, and the next, and the next, and the next.

It was a battle of epic proportions. Chloe and Kaitlyn had hated one another for a long time, and neither girl was going to back down, not for a second. And I had to give Kaitlyn credit (even though I didn't want to), she was a good batter. Chloe's pitches were so nasty they would have destroyed a normal batter, but somehow Kaitlyn managed to stay alive, and she was really making Chloe work. I could see a layer of sweat on Chloe's brow as she threw pitch after pitch after pitch.

And then it happened. Kaitlyn finally got a hold of one of Chloe's pitches. She didn't hit it well, it was really nothing more than a weak blooper, but it was big trouble for us because it was hit over our third baseman's head but way too shallow for our left fielder to catch.

So it was up to me. I took the best angle I could, and I came charging from my position at short as fast as I could, and I dove as far as I could. It was probably the best dive I've ever made, completely outstretched as far as I could go, and I hit the ground so hard I didn't even feel the ball go into my mitt. At first I didn't even know I had it, but as I lay there on the ground, face down on my stomach, I heard my teammates cheering (and Homer barking) triumphantly in the background.

Chloe helped me up and clapped me on the back as we walked back to the dugout.

"Thanks," she said. "I really wanted that one."

"You helped us," I said. "I thought I'd return the favor."

"We make a good team," Chloe said.

"You bet we do," I said.

From the dugout, my dad smiled. Like all dads, he loved it when his girls got along.

We won 3-2.

October 6

Today was a scary day. Logan had another game, so of course I went. It was against a high school called Mariner, and everything was going smoothly at first. We jumped to a big lead when Caleb completed two touchdown passes to the receivers, and then Logan added to the lead by scoring a touchdown of his own. And, like normal, it was a sweet play. Caleb handed him the ball, but he was in big trouble right from the start because a defender slipped through the front line and barreled down on him. Somehow, miraculously, he slipped away and darted to the side, and then it was off to the races. He turned the corner and rambled along the sideline for fifty yards. The defenders finally caught up to him and dragged him down from behind, but not until he had crossed the goal line. Everyone in the stands went crazy, and the cheerleaders (except Hailey Wetmore) did their jumps and back flips.

But the fun (especially for me) ended in the fourth quarter. At that point, we were leading 24-0, and it was clear we were going to cruise to another easy victory. And if that wasn't good enough, we were threatening to score again. We had the ball and it was first down on Mariner's fifteen yard line. Caleb tossed the ball to Logan, and Logan raced through the line, but a defender grabbed him by an arm, and another grabbed him by the waist, and two more piled on top of him. They went down in a heap at the five yard line. At first I didn't think much of it, and I even cheered because it was close to a first down, but then I noticed something was wrong. The audience had gone deathly silent, and the cheerleaders had dropped to one knee. One of the players wasn't getting up, and much to my chagrin he was wearing an orange jersey.

My heart stopped. It was Logan. He was lying there, on the field where he had fallen. He was moving, a little, but he was clearly in a lot of pain, and he was holding his left knee with both hands. The referees blew their whistles and waved their arms to indicate an injury timeout, and our trainers and coaches ran onto the field to help him.

It only lasted a few minutes, but it seemed like an eternity. At one point, I looked over, and I saw Chloe in the stands a few rows down, with her friends like usual. She looked up at me with a comforting look on her face.

"He'll be okay," she said.

Luckily, he was. A few minutes later, the trainers helped him up, and he was able to walk off the field by himself, without any help. Apparently, he had twisted his knee badly, but not bad enough to cause any serious damage. But our coaches had seen enough, and they weren't going to take any more chances with their star running back, so they took him out and he didn't play any more for the rest of the game.

Which was fine with me. After all, I like this football thing, and having a boyfriend who is a football player is nice, but why does the darn sport have to be so rough? If I were in charge, I'd make it so only one player could tackle Logan at a time.

But then again, if I did, they'd never have a chance.

October 7

Logan came to my game today. He still had a limp, from his injury, but all-in-all he was okay, and he told me to not worry about him.

"I've been injured before," he said. "It's no big deal. I'll be back to full speed in no time. Just you wait and see."

Logan always has such a good attitude, and he's always so easy-going and upbeat. I could learn a lot from him. Like today. I was happy, because he was there to watch me, but I was nervous, too. Big time. I was used to being the one doing the watching, as Logan played, and I wasn't used to being the one being watched. But now that he was here, I wanted to impress him, and I wanted to impress him big. I wanted to show him how good I was. He was the star football player. I was the star softball player.

But it didn't start well. The first batter hit a grounder right at me, and I let it go through my legs for an error.

Wonderful, I thought. Whenever I went and watched Logan play, he always did so well and put on such a big show for me. But now that he had come to watch me, what did I do? I stank up the place. I was so embarrassed I couldn't even look at him in the stands.

"It's okay," he said. "You'll get the next one."

Luckily, I did. It took a couple of batters, but sure enough, I got a much needed chance at redemption. A batter hit a ball to my right, and she hit it really hard. I normally prefer to move over and get in front of the ball, but it was moving much too quickly and I didn't have enough time to position myself properly. So I reached over and grabbed the ball with my backhand, which has never been one of my strengths, then turned and fired it to first for an out.

"Sweet play," Logan said, and he had a big smile on his face.

His smile got even bigger in the bottom half of the inning. It was my turn to bat, and I was nervous again, because I didn't want to strike out with him watching. But I had nothing to worry about. The pitcher threw a fastball straight down the middle of the plate, and I turned and lined it past her for a single. Everyone, especially Logan, cheered as I made it to first base.

But the highlight of the game came in the sixth inning. At that point, I was two for two, with two singles, so I was having a solid game and I was feeling really good. As the game had progressed, my confidence had improved, and Logan seemed really impressed, so I was happy, but not completely. In my mind, Logan deserved a lot more than just singles. He deserved a big hit. Something with some power.

It was time for some fireworks.

So I went up to the plate with a mission, with one thing, and only one thing, on my mind. I was going to give the ball a one-way ticket to the outfield fence. And boy did I. It took three pitches, but I hit the ball so hard it flew all the way to the deepest part of the field. The centerfielder made a running stab at it, but she missed it, and before she could recover and throw it back to the infield, I was standing at third base with a stand-up triple.

Logan was all smiles.

And so was I.

October 9

Today was one of the greatest days ever. Logan came over for dinner, and I was pretty nervous at first, since this was the first time I've ever had a boy over for dinner, and my dad always worries me when it comes to boys (you never know how he's going to act), but it went really well. My dad liked Logan right from the start, and he loved the fact Logan was a running back, just like he had been when he played at Monroe, way back in the old days. To be honest, I didn't even know they had football back in those days, and it must have been when they wore those strange, leather helmets. Well, maybe not. Anyway, my dad's actually pretty old, almost forty-five, but he still has a good memory for a guy his age, and he can remember every detail of every game just like it was yesterday. Which is quite ironic because he can never remember my mom's birthday or their anniversary, and he got in a lot of trouble this past year because of it, but that's a story for another day. Anyway, he and Logan exchanged stories all night, and my dad was really fascinated with the fact Logan played football in Texas.

"What's it like in Texas?" he asked as he started dinner. "I heard school ball is huge in Texas."

Logan nodded. "It is. In some of the smaller towns, like Huckstin, the entire town shuts down on Friday night. Everyone goes to the game. And when I say everyone, I don't just mean the students and their parents, like up here in the Northwest. I mean

319

everyone. Little kids, grandparents, shop owners, the mayor, everyone."

"Amazing," my dad said. "No wonder there are so many great players from Texas. And no wonder the Longhorns are so good every year."

I wasn't certain who the Longhorns were, but to be honest, I didn't really care. As long as my dad liked Logan, that was all that mattered to me.

"Do you ever go to the games, Mister Williams?" Logan asked.

"You can call me Dan," my dad said.

Chloe, my mom, and I all shot glances at one another. That was a good sign. My dad would only let a boy call him by first name if he was really impressed. Even Chloe's boyfriend, Caleb, wasn't allowed to call him Dan.

"I used to go," my dad said. "But I stopped a ways back. I got so busy with other things. Family, softball, and all. But it would be nice. I miss those old games."

"You should come," Logan said. "We have a big game this week against a school called Arlington. I don't know much about them, but they're supposed to be really good."

My dad's eyes got big. "I hate Arlington," he said. "They were our rivals back when I played. We lost to them the first two years, but finally beat them the third year. Do me a favor and beat them, Logan."

"Yes, sir," Logan said. "I mean, Dan."

"You're a good kid, Logan," my dad said with a smile. "And maybe you're right. Maybe I should come and watch that game on Friday. I wouldn't mind seeing my old Bearcats kick some Eagle butt."

Dinner was fine, but the highlight of the night, by far, was afterward, when Homer and I walked Logan out to his car in the driveway. It was actually his uncle's car, but his uncle let him borrow it for the night.

"Your family is really nice," he said. "I really like your dad. He's a nice guy. He reminds me of my dad."

"He has his moments," I said. "But trust me. You don't want to be around him on a bad day."

Logan smiled. There was a brief, somewhat awkward silence. Logan opened the door to his car, and I could tell he was excited about something, and he clearly wanted to say something, but he wasn't sure how to say it.

"There's something I wanted to ask you," he said. "It's a little unusual, and I completely understand if you say no, but well, since we've been going out for awhile now, and since I've officially been introduced to your family, and I think it went okay, I was wondering if you would consider wearing my jacket. I know it's not a Monroe jacket, since I'm new at Monroe and I haven't lettered here yet, but it's still a jacket. And it's mine. From last year, at my school in Texas."

He reached into the car and pulled out a fancy letterman's jacket. It was maroon and navy, with a huge letter H on the front, Logan's last name (McCoy) on the back, and a silver star on the left sleeve.

He held it up for me to see. "I think it would look good," he said. "Maroon looks really nice with your hair."

I snatched it from him so fast I didn't even realize what I had done. I don't know why he had been so nervous. Of course I wanted to wear it, and I wasted no time slipping it on. It was really heavy, and way too big for me, especially around the waist, but I didn't care, not one single bit.

I had a letterman's jacket.

Logan's letterman's jacket.

I was on top of the world.

October 10

I was the talk of school all week. Everyone noticed the minute I showed up wearing Logan's letterman's jacket. And I loved every minute of it. Most of my classmates were happy to see me in it (you should have seen Lea's eyes), but I could tell some of them (including Hailey Wetmore) weren't. They were jealous. They wanted to be the girlfriend of the school's star running back.

Too bad for them.

And I didn't mind the fact it wasn't a Monroe jacket at all. If anything, I liked it. It made me unique. The other girls had black and orange jackets that pretty much looked the same. Mine, however, was completely different. It was maroon and navy, and Logan was right. It went perfectly with my hair. And I should know, since I spent over an hour last night standing in front of the mirror admiring it.

The highlight of the week happened today. I went to the game, to watch Logan, and guess who showed up? My dad. He came over and stood next to me in the bleachers.

"What are you doing here?" I asked. I never expected to see him at a game.

"I kept thinking about what Logan said," he responded. "He's right. I've been away for too long. I need to see another game, if nothing else just for posterity's sake."

The game started minutes later, and we cheered as Monroe took the field, with Caleb and Logan at the front of the squad, and we booed as Arlington came out. There was the coin toss, and the kickoff, and Arlington got the ball first, but I didn't really care about that, and to be honest I really only watch when Logan is on the field. As soon as we got the ball, I got excited and turned to my dad.

"Get ready," I said. "It's show time."

And indeed it was. On the first play, Caleb made a nice pass to one of the receivers, then did a handoff to the fullback on the next. But the real fireworks began on the third play.

Caleb handed the ball to Logan. Logan rumbled eight yards for a first down. It took three defenders to take him down.

"Not bad," my dad said. "Not bad at all."

The next play was more of the same. Logan went around the left side of the line for a five yard gain, then on the next play he rushed for five more. But then something amazing happened. Caleb pitched Logan the ball, and he ran to the right side of the field.

"Sweep right," my dad said as he watched. But then his eyes got big. "There's nothing there," he said. "Cut back against the grain, Logan."

The line of blockers in front of Logan collapsed, and there was nowhere for him to go. So he slammed on the brakes and did exactly what my dad had said. He cut back to the left and raced into the open field.

"Pick up the receiver's block," my dad said as a defender moved in on him.

Logan angled to the left, just enough to get behind one of his teammates, who knocked the incoming defender for a loop.

And then it was a sprint to pay dirt. Sixty yards later, Logan was standing in the end zone celebrating.

"That's my boy," my dad called, and our bleachers went crazy. The band played an especially lively version of *Tequila*.

"That's how you do it, Angel," my dad said as soon as the music died down. "You see how Logan felt out his blockers, and how he was aware of his surroundings, even when the play didn't develop as designed? That's great field recognition. Great awareness. And great improvisation on his part. You can't teach that kind of stuff. That's really well done. Go Bearcats!"

To be honest, I didn't really have a clue what my dad was saying (I had no idea what field recognition was), but I didn't really care. As long as he was happy, I was happy.

And boy was he happy. Logan scored two more touchdowns, and we won the game easily, beating the hated Eagles 28-3. The three of us celebrated by going to the mall and getting ice cream.

October 14

Today was the first day of my team's big 'out-of-state' trip for the fall season, and it was in Las Vegas. I was actually a little sad, because I knew I wouldn't be able to see Logan for three whole days, and I knew I would miss him terribly, but he made me feel a little better just before we left for the airport.

"Don't worry," he said. "Just like always, I'll send you texts all the time, and I'll even throw in a few goofy photos to keep your spirits up. Sound okay?"

"I guess so," I said, but really it didn't. To be honest, I didn't want to be away from him even for a minute.

"But it's on one condition," he said.

I raised an eyebrow.

"Have you ever hit a home run in Vegas before?"

I shook my head. This was my first tournament in Las Vegas, so I'd never gotten any hits, of any type, in Vegas before.

"Then you need to hit a home run for me," he said.

Instantly I grew apprehensive. "I don't know," I said. "I don't hit too many home runs. It's pretty rare. Actually, it's very rare."

"You can do it," he said. "I know you can. That's how you got Homer, right?"

I was about to say something when he interrupted.

"Have faith," he said. "And send me word as soon as it happens."

Off to Vegas I went. And unfortunately, getting there turned out to be quite a chore. Lea's parents didn't come, so Lea flew with my dad, Homer, and me (Homer had to ride in a doggy carryon cage — it had plenty of room, but he didn't like it too much), and we had a layover in Oakland. Oakland is a small airport, but a nice one, and we actually had a good time, and we had dinner at California Pizza Kitchen, but just as we finished our dinner we heard an announcement our flight was delayed for two hours. So Lea and I spent most of the time playing cards, with Homer in his carryon case (he's a lot heavier than I originally realized), and my dad read the newspaper. Finally our plane was ready, and we departed, but once we got to Las Vegas, it was already 10:00 pm, so we were pretty tired, and then we had to stand in a line for a rental car for almost forty-five minutes. And it was pretty ridiculous, since my dad was the next person in line, but it still took forever to get to him. The rental car companies need to make some improvements when it comes to customer service. Anyway, we finally got a car, but then it was another thirty minutes until we got to our hotel in a suburb in northern Las Vegas. I was getting pretty grumpy at that point (I tend to do that when I get tired), but my attitude changed completely the minute I saw our hotel.

It wasn't a hotel. At least not like I picture hotels. It was the hotel I've always dreamed of. It was huge, with multiple wings, and in many ways it resembled a resort more than a hotel. My dad went to check us in at the front desk, and Lea, Homer, and I darted around, taking a look at everything we could. There was a small mall, with numerous fancy shops, right inside the main lobby, a huge fitness/workout center, with a million treadmills, and a pool with a gorgeous waterfall. I thought I had died and gone to heaven. A few minutes before, I had been almost asleep in the car. Now, I was wide awake and full of energy. I wanted to get my swimming suit and jump in the pool right at that very moment. But of course it was way too late for that, so we headed up to our room, and my mouth fell open the minute I opened the door and looked inside. It was huge, with two of the biggest beds I have ever seen, a walk-in wardrobe/closet, and a bathroom that was bigger than my bedroom at home.

"We need to play in Vegas more often," I said.

Lea and my dad nodded. Homer barked.

October 15

Unfortunately, the excitement of arriving in Las Vegas was dampened this morning when the drama began. My team is a great team, and I really like it, but there is one thing I always hate.

Picking our uniforms for the day. It's always an ordeal. It all started when Laura sent a text message to the rest of us saying we should wear black pants, jerseys, and socks. But then Casey sent a text saying, "Are you crazy? We're in Vegas. It's gonna be 100°. We'll die in solid black. Let's wear gray jerseys, pants, and socks." But then I responded by saying, "I hate solid gray. It's so blah. Let's wear gray jerseys, black pants, and gray socks." But then Olivia responded, "OMG. You can't wear gray socks with black pants. That's so 90s. Let's wear gray jerseys, black pants, and black socks." And then Kristin responded, "Gross. I wouldn't be caught dead in that combo. Let's go for black jerseys, gray pants, and gray socks."

"What do you think?" I asked Lea.

"I don't know," she said. So we got out my uniform, spread it out on the bed in front of us, and what do you know? Kristin's combo actually looked okay. So I texted back to her, "Sounds good to me." So Lea and I got dressed, and did our hair (because you can't play softball unless your hair looks good), then we went down to the lobby to meet the other girls for breakfast, but when we got down there we saw the other girls were wearing one gray sock and one black sock.

"Didn't you get the last text?" Kristin asked. "We decided to mix up the socks a bit."

So Lea and I trudged back upstairs and changed our socks to match everyone else.

"Why can't you girls be like boys?" my dad asked. "Boys don't care about their uniforms. They wear whatever uniform they find lying on the floor. And it doesn't even have to be clean."

"That's gross," I said, and we headed back downstairs for breakfast.

Despite the uniform fiasco, the day went well. We had three games, and it was really hot (almost 100° by noon), but we had fun. Our first game was against a team from Nevada called the Gold Rush. We won 3-2. I got one hit, a single that scored Hannah and Casey. Our second game was against a team from California called the Bat Busters, and they killed us. I'd list the highlights, but there were none. But we made up for it in the final game, beating another team from California (the Breeze) 5-4. I got a single and a double, but Kristin was the real hero. She won the game by hitting a massive home run in the bottom half of the final inning.

And then I remembered something. I had promised Logan I would hit a home run for him. I needed to get to it as soon as possible.

But unfortunately, it was the final game of the day, so Logan's home run would have to wait. We went back to the hotel, played in the pool for awhile (the waterfall was gorgeous), then went to the Strip for awhile. The dads and coaches went to a restaurant for steak dinner (it's a tradition of theirs) while we girls roamed around the Strip. I had never been to Las Vegas before, so I was pretty amazed. The lights were so bright, and the place was so busy and lively. We went on a roller coaster at a casino, then grabbed dinner at Subway (I think it's funny that of all the restaurants in Las Vegas, many of which are very fancy, we chose Subway), but it was good nonetheless. I ordered my favorite, a 6" sweet onion chicken teriyaki on wheat bread, with extra olives. After that we headed back to the hotel. I didn't like the idea of leaving Homer in the hotel room too long by himself. After all, he gets lonely easy. And I didn't want to risk any 'accidents' on the carpet.

Right before I went to bed, I got a text from Logan. "Any luck with my home run?" he asked.

"Not yet," I said.

"You'll get it soon," he said. "I know you will."

I hoped he was right. I didn't want to let him down.

October 16

I can't believe it, but Logan was right. Our first game today was against a team from northern Nevada called the Lone Wolves. That name seemed strange (and highly contradictory) to me. How can you be lone, and yet be wolves? Shouldn't it be Lone Wolf? Anyway, the Lone Wolves were leading 3-1 when I got my second at-bat in the bottom of the fifth inning (I popped out during my first at-bat). We had two runners (Haley and Casey) on base and two outs. The Lone Wolves' pitcher was a tall, thin girl with straight, blond hair, and she threw really hard, but she didn't have great control of her pitches and sometimes left them over the middle of the plate. I waited patiently for the right pitch, then swung with everything I had.

This one's for Logan, I thought as I hit it.

And I didn't just hit it. I killed it. I knew it the minute it left my bat. It was a three-run home run, and it went even further than the first home run I had hit, the one that had won me Homer. Everyone cheered as I rounded the bases and stepped on home plate. My dad patted me on the back, and Homer licked my face.

But the best compliment, by far, came from Logan.

"I knew you could do it," he texted. "After all, you're the best player I've ever seen."

He's a good boyfriend. I think I'll keep him for awhile.

We had two more games later in the day, and we won one of them. I got two hits (a pair of doubles) in the first game and one hit (a triple) in the second. All-in-all, it was a fun day.

October 23

Logan had a game today, and it was a big one. It was the first round of the state football playoffs. My dad came, and like always he was really excited.

"This game is a big deal," he said. "The playoffs always are. It'll be great if they win. All three years I played at Monroe, we won the league championship each year, but we never won a playoff game. All three years we lost in the first round. One game was close, but the other two were complete blowouts. It kills me to even think about it. So if they win today, they'll have done something I never managed to do."

"Sweet," I said. "Do you think they have a chance?"

My dad nodded. "They're a great team," he said. "They haven't lost a single game all year. And if anyone can do it, it's Logan. The kid is great."

The game started minutes later, and it was a spectacular battle. I was so nervous I could barely hold still. The other team was a high school from Tacoma called Stadium, and they were really good. They knew Logan was one of our best players, and everywhere he went, they followed (en masse), and they swarmed him every time he got the ball. But he didn't give up, and on a handoff in the third quarter he finally broke free, into the clear, and rambled twenty yards to the three yard line. It took three defenders to take him down. On the next play, he went straight through the middle and punched it in for the touchdown.

That was all we needed. We won 7-0.

October 25

I saw one of the dumbest things ever today. We had a game against a team from Bellevue called the Beast, and all of their players got really excited when their starting pitcher showed up. Their dugout was a flurry of activity as she arrived, and she had something in her arms. It was wrapped in blankets, and she put it on the bench.

"What is it?" I asked Lea. She sat to my right, watching all the commotion with me.

"Apparently," she said, "they heard how popular Homer is, so they got a mascot of their own. He's making his debut today. His name is Beast."

I looked over, and what did I see, but a tiny dog sitting on the bench. I didn't know exactly what type of dog it was, and I didn't really care, but it was one of those designer dogs girls carry around in their purses. It was so small my cat, Cinnamon, could have had it for breakfast.

"That's a mascot?" Kristin asked.

"Its name is Beast?" Olivia asked.

"That's ridiculous," Casey said.

And it was. Beast didn't do anything the whole game. He just sat there, shivering in the cold. He didn't lead his team during their warm-up exercises, and he didn't chase after foul balls for blue.

Speaking of blue, we had the same blue who umpired the first game I brought Homer too, the same one who was so amazed (and thankful) when Homer chased after foul balls for him. He looked at Beast and shook his head in disgust.

"That's no Homer," he said.

"You can say that again," I said.

October 27

Today was a strange day. It started off really bad. Chloe got in a fight with my dad. Chloe's seventeen, and she wants a car, but my dad doesn't want to get her one. It's been an issue for awhile now (basically since the day Chloe got her driver's license), and it boils over periodically, including today.

"I don't understand," Chloe pleaded. "It's not like a car is that expensive."

My dad raised an eyebrow. "Not that expensive?" he asked. "Have you looked at car prices lately?"

"I just did," Chloe said. "Online. There's a great VW Jetta at a dealership in the U district. It's only $18,000."

"Only $18,000?" my dad said, laughing. "And where are you going to get $18,000? Do you think $18,000 grows on trees?"

"Don't you have some money saved up?" Chloe asked. "I thought most people saved money."

"*Some* people save money," my dad said, putting special emphasis on the word 'some.' "And yes, I have some money saved up. But it's not for something silly like a car. It's for something important."

"Like what?" Chloe asked.

"Like an emergency," my dad said. "Or your college education."

"I don't need any money for college," Chloe said. "I'm going to get a softball scholarship."

"That's great if you do," my dad said, "but we can't count on it, Chloe. Scholarships are hard to get,

335

and you just never know. You may get turned down, or hurt, or whatever. I want to have money just in case."

Chloe stomped her foot. "If I don't get a scholarship," she said, "I'm not going."

"What do you mean?" my dad asked.

"If a college doesn't give me a scholarship, then screw them. I'm not going."

"That's a terrible attitude," my dad said. "Don't ever say things like that. That kind of attitude will get you nowhere in life."

"I don't care," Chloe said. "I want a car. Think about how nice it would be for everyone. You wouldn't have to drive me around all the time."

"I don't mind driving you around, Chloe. That's what parents do."

Chloe sighed. She turned to me, as though she wanted me to help her out. I was sitting on the couch, in the living room with them, with my computer on my lap, but there was no way I was getting involved in this one. Homer sat next to me. He had his head on the couch and a sad look on his face. He hated it when Chloe and my dad fought over things.

"Why can't I have a car?" Chloe asked. "I'll find a cheap one. A used one. Something, anything, please dad."

"I just don't think it's a good idea," my dad said. "You haven't been driving for that long, and you're not that experienced. You need more time before you get a car of your own. I don't want any accidents."

"I'm a good driver," Chloe said. "You said so yourself. Just the other day. Remember?"

"Yes," my dad said. "You're an excellent driver when I'm with you. But I'm not sure how you'll do on your own. You're going to be racing all over town, with your friends in the car, not paying attention, and you'll probably be texting while you're driving."

"No way," Chloe said.

My dad stared at her. "You're a teenage girl. What is the longest you've ever gone without sending a text?"

"That's ridiculous," Chloe said. "I can't believe you said that."

"The truth hurts," my dad said.

"All my friends have cars," Chloe said. "It's embarrassing."

"I'm not getting you a car to enhance your social standing," my dad said.

"It's not fair," Chloe said. "Amy's dad got her a car, and she barely had to ask for it. And it's super nice. It's a Mustang."

Chloe was talking about her teammate on the Wildcats, Amy Ferguson. Amy's dad bought her a Ford Mustang. It was a used one, but it had low miles and was in great shape. I saw it at school and was impressed.

"I spoke to Amy's dad about that," my dad said. "Amy earned it."

"What?" Chloe asked.

"Her dad said he wasn't going to get it for her, but she's been working so hard he couldn't resist."

"What do you mean?"

"He said she's been practicing at least two hours every day for the past two months, and he doesn't even have to ask her any more. She just goes out and does it. And she's been doing really well as a result. Her batting average is over .400."

I nodded. The last time I watched one of Chloe's games, Amy was spectacular. She had two singles and a double. And she made a great play on defense.

"Whatever," Chloe said. "She's still not as good as me."

"I don't care if she's as good as you or not," my dad said. "All I care about is how hard you work. Amy's been working really hard, so she earned her car. How hard have you been working lately?"

Chloe was quiet.

"How many times have you practiced this week, other than your team practices?"

Chloe didn't say a thing. She hadn't practiced at all on her own this week. Or last week. Or the week before that.

"So I don't know why we're even having this conversation," my dad said. "You're old enough to know how the world works. If you want something from someone, you need to do what they want. I want you to practice more."

"Fine," Chloe said, and she stomped out of the room as loud as she could. I could hear her footsteps all the way upstairs.

My dad turned to me. "If you ever act like that," he said, "you're grounded for a week."

I sighed. I hated it when he did that. I hadn't even done anything wrong, but I was in trouble anyway.

A few seconds later, Chloe was back, with a big frown on her face. She tossed my mitt into my lap.

"Come on," she said. "Apparently I need to practice, and I can't do it without a catcher."

"I'm busy," I said. Really I wasn't, I was just playing *Tetris*, but I didn't feel like practicing.

"Get moving," my dad said. "You could use the practice, too."

I sighed. Leave it to Chloe to get me involved in her problems.

So we went to McCall Park, and we worked on Chloe's pitching. I wore my old catcher's gear and caught for her. I could tell she was really mad at my dad, because she throws really hard when she's mad, and in no time my hand was stinging. I had to take a small break to let it recover. Homer licked it to make it feel better.

"Sorry," Chloe said. "Dad just makes me so mad sometimes. He doesn't understand."

She was about to say something more when a car pulled up. It was Caleb and Logan. Apparently, they had been driving by and they saw us, so they stopped to say hi.

"What are you two doing?" Caleb asked.

"What's it look like?" Chloe asked. "Apparently, if I practice for two hours every day for the next two months, I might get a car. But I'm not getting my hopes up."

Caleb and Logan nodded. They didn't know what Chloe was talking about, but they both knew the best way to deal with a high-maintenance chick like her, especially when she was in a bad mood, was to nod and play along.

"Mind if we join in?" Caleb asked. "I want to bat."

"That's stupid," Chloe said. "You can't bat."

He laughed. "I'm the star quarterback for the football team, Chloe. I can do anything."

"Really?" she asked. "Like what?"

"Like hit a stupid softball," he said. "After all, it's a girl's game."

I cringed. Caleb shouldn't have said that. Chloe was already in a bad mood, and making a questionable comment like that in front of her was a huge mistake.

"A girl's game?" she asked. She had one hand on her hip and an eyebrow raised.

I've seen that look before. It meant big trouble for Caleb.

"Not that there's anything wrong with that," Caleb said. "But come on. If you girls can do it, then we football players can. Throw me a pitch. I'll show you."

Chloe shook her head in disgust. "Don't start crying when you get hurt," she said, and took her spot in the pitching circle. Caleb grabbed a bat from her bag, and I took my place (somewhat hesitantly) behind the plate. Logan and Homer sat in the bleachers. Homer wouldn't watch. By now, he was an experienced softball mascot. He knew this was going to get ugly and he didn't want to see it.

The first pitch was so fast Caleb didn't even react. He just stood there as the ball exploded in my mitt.

"You just gonna stand there all day?" Chloe asked. "You can't hit the ball unless you swing at it."

Caleb had a stupid look on his face and no response whatsoever. He had had no idea the pitch was going to be that fast.

The next pitch was just as nasty. This time, he actually managed to swing at it, but way too late. Chloe laughed.

"I thought football players could do anything," she said. "After all, this is a girl's game, right?"

Caleb got really serious. He was a star athlete, and he was going to prove it to Chloe.

But Chloe fooled him completely. She threw a changeup. And it was a dandy. It was at least twenty miles per hour slower than her previous pitch. Caleb was so caught off guard he couldn't adjust in time. He had already completed his swing, and had the bat on his opposite shoulder, before the pitch was half way to him.

Logan fell over in the stands laughing.

"You think you can do any better?" Caleb asked. He was mad. He wasn't used to being embarrassed, especially by a girl.

Logan shook his head. "No way," he said. "I know better. These softball girls are the real deal. Don't mess with them. We had one girl, back at my school in Texas, the baseball players were making fun of her, so she had them all line up, and she struck them out one-by-one. Every one of them. Without even breaking a sweat. It was the craziest thing I've ever seen. They never made fun of her again. And some of them started asking her for advice."

Caleb smiled. He handed the bat back to Chloe. "Maybe you're right," he said. "Maybe we football players should stick with football, and let you softball players take care of softball."

"That's a good idea," Chloe said. "And it's a good thing you learned your lesson on that pitch."

"Why?" he asked.

"Because the next pitch was going to be a brushback," she said.

"What's a brushback?" Caleb asked.

"Trust me," I said. "You don't want to know."

October 30

Today was the second round of the state football playoffs, but it didn't go well. Our game was against a school from the Eastside called Skyline, the defending state champions. I knew we were in trouble right from the start. They were huge. Every boy on the team was over six feet tall, and most of them were over 250 pounds. They made Logan, Caleb, and the rest of our team look small by comparison. Skyline hadn't lost a game all year, and most of them had been blowouts.

But we made a game of it. Logan and Caleb are great players, and they battled to the end. Skyline jumped to a quick lead, 14-0, but we battled back and tied it by halftime (Logan scored one touchdown and Caleb the other). We kicked a field goal to take the lead in the third quarter, but Skyline came back with a field goal of their own, and then another. They led 20-17 with just thirty seconds to play. We marched down the field, and Logan made one last, gallant dive toward the end zone, but the defenders (at least six of them) swarmed him and knocked him to the ground. The final whistle sounded as he was lying on the ground, with the ball in his hands, at the one yard line.

Normally after games, Logan meets me briefly before he goes to the locker room to change. But today he didn't. Instead, I found him sitting on the player's bench, at the side of the field, with one of the assistant coaches.

"You're a great player, Logan," the coach said as he picked up a water bottle and walked away. "Keep your chin up."

I waited until the coach had walked away, then sat down next to Logan on the bench. The minute I saw his face, I became concerned. He had tears in his eyes.

At first I didn't know what to do. I knew football meant a lot to him, but I didn't know it meant this much.

"Are you okay?" I asked.

"I can't believe it," he said. "One yard. One measly yard. That's all I needed."

His helmet was lying on the ground at his feet. He kicked it to the side.

"You did your best," I said.

"I wanted to win," Logan said.

"It's just a game," I said.

"I know," he responded. "But winning means a lot to this school. And this school has been really good to me, ever since I got here. You've all treated me so well. I wanted to give you something — a state title — in return."

"Last week," I said. "You gave us a playoff victory. My dad said Monroe had never won a playoff game before you came here. Even back when he played. So you gave us that. And that was a big deal to him. And he's pretty hard to impress most of the time. So I think you've already given us a lot, Logan. You just need to realize that. And there's always next year."

"Not for me," he said. "I won't be here, remember? I have to return to Texas."

I nodded. I had forgotten about that. It was something I didn't like to think about.

"Still," I said, "you did a lot. This was the first game we lost all year. And to Skyline. They're the champs. Those guys are huge."

It took a minute, but he finally smiled. "You can say that again," he said. "Especially that inside linebacker. Wow. I haven't seen a kid like that in a

343

long time. It's funny. They say everything is so big in Texas, including the football players. But you've got some big players here in Washington, too, especially on that team. What do they feed them?"

"Venti white chocolate mochas," I said, "with a shot of steroids. Two on game days. With whipped cream on top."

My comment was completely ridiculous, but apparently it worked. Logan couldn't help but chuckle.

"How are you feeling?" I asked.

He shrugged. He looked a little better, but not much.

"Maybe this will help," I said.

I leaned forward and kissed him on the lips.

To be honest, I still can't believe I did it. I'm not normally that aggressive, and I had never kissed a boy on the lips before, but it just seemed like the right thing to do. And, to be completely honest, I had wanted to do it since the first day we met.

"Now how do you feel?" I asked.

His eyes were big. I had caught him completely by surprise.

"A little better," he said.

"Just a little?" I asked. "Then maybe you need another."

I kissed him again. By the time our second kiss was done, his mood had changed completely, and he had pretty much forgotten about football entirely.

"Some of the guys," he said, "are going out to dinner. I guess it's an end-of-the-year tradition or something. Do you want to go?"

"Of course," I said. "It sounds like fun."

We hopped up, and, hand-in-hand, walked off the field.

November 25

Thanksgiving Day. I'm so stuffed I'm going to die. My mom made garlic mashed potatoes, and I love them. I had three servings. Even Homer is stuffed. He got a special plate of food. I made it for him myself. I don't usually let him have 'people' food, but since it's a holiday, I thought I'd make an exception. I gave him a little bit of everything, and he gobbled it up.

December 10

Today was a grand and glorious day. It snowed last night, at least eight inches, so they cancelled school. And thank goodness, since I didn't do my English homework last night. I meant to, but I got too busy watching *The Cake Boss* (I love that show), and by the time it was over I was too tired. Since it only snows once or twice a year in Seattle, it's a big deal, so Chloe and I slipped on our boots and headed outside to play in it. And it was really fun, since it was Homer's first time in the snow. At first, he didn't know what to do. It was pretty deep, nearly up to his tummy, so he just stood there and looked at me like, "You gotta be kidding me." But as soon as Chloe and I darted out into it, he followed, because he never likes to be left behind. We started a snowball fight, but it quickly turned into just Chloe and me throwing snowballs at Homer, and he loved catching them. He didn't actually catch any, they just exploded the second they hit his mouth, but he loved it anyway. After about half an hour, he disappeared for a few seconds, and when we looked over to see where he'd gone, what did we see?

Yellow snow.

December 25

It's Christmas Day, and, like most Christmas Days, it was great fun. Everyone got a load of loot, including Homer. He got three new chew toys (he tore up one of them immediately), plus a tug-of-war rope and a fancy new serving dish (one of those elevated ones that are good for a dog's back because they don't have to bend down to eat their food). In the meantime, I got a bunch of things. My mom got me some new jeans, because my old ones were getting pretty tight, and I don't care what the scale in the bathroom says I have not gained five pounds (but I decided to go easy on dinner anyway, just to be safe). But I did have an extra serving of my mom's garlic mashed potatoes, 'cause those potatoes are to die for. Chloe got me a purse, a really cute one with a matching wallet inside. My dad got me a new bat, this year's version of the Stealth, because it's supposed to be the hottest bat on the market.

"With that bat," he said, "you'll hit a lot of home runs this year. I hear it has serious pop."

It was all great, but the best present I got, by far, was from Logan. It was a necklace, with a gold pendant shaped like a heart hanging from it, and when you opened the pendant it had a photo inside. And the photo was the best one he could have ever picked. I don't remember who took it, or when, or where, but it had me on the right, Logan on the left (with his arm around me), and Homer in the middle. Like always, Homer had his tongue hanging out of his mouth.

Chloe took a look at it, and even she was impressed.

"You know," she said. "As far as boyfriends go, that Logan's not bad. Not bad at all."

I stood in front of the mirror, in the bathroom, staring at my new necklace for the rest of the night.

January 15

I don't know how she did it, but Chloe finally pulled it off. She talked my dad into getting her a car. They went shopping, and they came home with it a few hours later. And it's really cute. It's a silver Volkswagen Jetta. It's a few years old, but it's in great shape, with low mileage and no dents or scrapes at all. Chloe was as happy as a clam. She took a photo of it and texted it to all of her friends. She took me and Homer out for a drive around the block so she could show it off to us. We stopped at Cold Stone Creamery on the way home. It was great fun. Chloe and I, like most sisters, have a strange relationship. Some days we get along fine, and other days we don't get along at all (especially on days when she stays in the bathroom all morning doing her makeup and I need to use it). Today we got along great, and I enjoyed every minute of it.

And it's good news for me, too. Next year, when I get my driver's license, I'm going to want a car, too. And now that my dad got one for Chloe, he'll have no choice but to get one for me, too. That would only be fair, right?

Sweet.

February 14

Today was Valentine's Day, and it was the best Valentine's Day ever. Logan took me out to dinner, to a fancy, Italian restaurant in downtown Seattle, and it was fun because we dressed up. Logan looks stunning in a suit, especially the one he wore, which was dark gray with narrow, vertical stripes. His tie was navy blue, and it went perfectly with his suit. I wore a tight, pink dress Chloe helped me pick out at the mall last week. My dad wasn't too happy about it (he felt it showed too much skin), but luckily he didn't make too much of a fuss. Logan liked it and said it was, "Hot." He gave me a bouquet of white roses (my favorite), a big box of chocolates (heart-shaped, of course), and a teddy bear he made at the store in the mall where you can make your own stuffed animals. He dressed it in a softball uniform, and it even had a miniature bat and ball. And tiny cleats on its feet. It was absolutely adorable.

Dinner was spectacular. I ordered lasagna, and it was delicious. Logan got seafood fettuccine, and he let me have a few bites to see how it was. It was as good as my lasagna, if not better. After dinner, we went to a movie, then he dropped me off at home (Chloe and I have a 10:00 pm curfew, but my dad extended it to 11:00 pm since it was Valentine's Day). Chloe was waiting for me at the door. She, too, had gone out for dinner, with Caleb, and she had arrived home just a few minutes before I did.

She had a big smile on her face. "What'd you think of the softball bear?" she asked.

My eyes got big. "You know about the bear?"

She nodded. "Logan showed it to me the other day. It's so cute. He said it took him an hour just to pick out the jersey. He got the gray one because it was the one that looked the most like your Sky jersey."

I was nothing but smiles the rest of the night. I took my softball bear upstairs and set it on my bed, right in the middle of the bed, right on top of my pillow. Homer's eyes got big as he saw it. He likes to chew on things (my white sandals will never be the same), and to him my softball bear was nothing more than a big chew toy.

"Don't even think about it," I told him.

He hopped down and, with a dejected look on his face, headed down the hall.

March 16

Logan is the best boyfriend ever. I don't know how he did it, but before school this morning, when I wasn't looking, he slipped little notes into my belongings. I found the first one a couple of hours later when I was in math class and my teacher, Mr. McEnroe, told us to open our books to page 127. The minute I grabbed my book, I saw something sticking out of the top of it, and at first I thought it was a bookmark of some sort. Upon closer examination, however, I saw it was a small note, not much bigger than a business card, in a miniature envelope (later, Logan told me he had made the envelopes himself). It read, "I miss you." Of course that brought a smile to my lips. But it got even better than that. An hour later, in history class, I opened my history book, and there was another note. This one read, "I miss you really bad." An hour later, in English class, I opened my book and found another note. This one read, "Do you miss me?" At that point, I started wondering how many notes he had hidden, and I tore through the rest of my books as fast as I could. Ms. Ferguson, my English teacher, shot me a curious glance as she saw me sitting at my desk, digging frantically through my belongings, but she didn't say anything and probably thought I was just searching for my homework from the night before. Anyway, I found three more notes, including one in the front pocket of my backpack. They all had cute little messages on them, and each was sillier than the last. One of them was a drawing of three stick figures. The tallest stick figure wore a football helmet, the second stick figure wore a softball mitt, and the third stick figure was Homer. I showed all of my notes, including the drawing of the stick figures, to Lea.

"You're the luckiest girl in the world," she said. "Why can't I have a boyfriend like that?"

So I decided I needed to do something for him. As soon as school ended for the day, I went to the bookstore and got some fancy paper (the type usually used for making certificates) and a package of foil seals, and I made him a 'Boyfriend of the Year' award. I made it on my computer, and printed it on my dad's laser printer, and with the fancy paper and foil seal, it looked really official. A couple of hours later, I met him for dessert at Cold Stone Creamery and gave it to him, and his eyes lit up the minute he saw it. We both laughed. It was a great day.

May 15

I'm going to shoot myself. Today, my team had a tournament in Kent, a city about fifteen minutes southeast of Seattle. Unlike most tournaments, which last the whole weekend, this one was only for a day, but it started well. Our first game was against a Canadian team called the Leafs. Like most Canadian teams, they were really good, but we jumped to a quick lead and held on to win 4-3. Our second game was against the Redmond LadyCats, and we cruised to an easy victory, winning 10-1. I used my new bat, the one my dad got me for Christmas, and I got two hits in the first game and three in the second.

But that was the end of my fun. Our final game was against my old team, the Eastside Angels, and my arch rival, Ashley Martinez. It was the first time I had faced Ashley since the game back in the fall when she completely embarrassed me. As such, I was really determined to do well today, and I really wanted to get back at her. But things didn't start well. Ashley's first pitch was a riseball, and I hit the bottom of it and launched it a mile — straight up. The Angels' catcher caught it for an easy out.

"Can't get 'em all," Ashley said in her typical, arrogant way.

My next at-bat came in the fourth inning and it didn't go any better. Ashley got two quick strikes on me, and then finished me off with a fastball. I hit it, but weakly, and it went straight to the second baseman. I was out by a mile.

My final at-bat came in the sixth inning. I dug my cleats into the dirt and tapped my bat on the plate, and I was really determined to get a hit this time. But once again, my hopes were short lived. I hit the first pitch straight at the shortstop. She didn't even have to move to make the catch.

"Softball isn't easy," Ashley said as I walked back to the dugout.

I hate her. If it's the last thing I do, I'm going to get her. And I'm going to get her good.

Someday.

May 22

I'm starting to get worried. It's less than a month until Logan has to move back to Texas. I may never see him again. And even if I do, I won't get to see him very often, at most once or twice a year, and even that much is probably a long shot. I don't know what I'm going to do. My eyes get misty whenever I think about it. This year has been so wonderful, first when I got Homer, and then when I met Logan, I never want it to end.

Logan and I sat at Starbucks talking about it.

"There's no way you can stay another year?" I pleaded. "You said you liked it here."

"I do," Logan said. "But I already asked my uncle. He's been really generous, but he can't afford to support me for another year. And it doesn't matter anyway, even if he could, because my dad wouldn't allow it. My dad didn't want me to come here in the first place, remember? It was my idea. I was the one who convinced him. There's no way I can convince him to let me stay for another year. I already tried."

"What about the summer?" I asked. "At least you could stay until the end of summer."

Logan shook his head. "My mom gets custody of me during the summer. And my dad says if I don't go, he'll be in contempt of court and he'll get in trouble with the judge. Something to do with a parenting plan or something. I don't really know what that means, but I don't want to get him in any trouble. He has enough to worry about with my stepmother and my two younger brothers."

So that was that. Like it or not, Logan was moving back to Texas on the last day of the school year.

As such, I better enjoy these last few weeks. They're all I've got.

June 1

Homer is a hero. He saved us all. Well, four of us. It all started on Friday. This weekend my team had a big tournament in Los Angeles. We flew to LA on Friday afternoon and arrived around 4:00 pm. We went into Long Beach, because my dad hates LAX (he says its way too big, and the last time we went there it took us over an hour to take the shuttle from the main terminal to the rental cars). Long Beach, by contrast, is nice and small, and it cracks me up because you depart the plane right onto the tarmac, then walk straight to baggage claim, which is also outside. I wish all airports were like it. My dad rented a Camaro, and it was really sweet. It was jet black, with a sun roof, leather interior, nice stereo, and power everything. I couldn't wait until the other girls saw me in it. I knew they were going to die. Anyway, after we got our car, we headed for our hotel in Irvine, but we were hungry so we stopped along the way for dinner. We went to a restaurant on Newport Beach, right on the end of the pier, and we sat outside on the deck so Homer could be with us (I don't think dogs are allowed out there, even though it's outside, but the restaurant wasn't too busy and the waitress thought Homer was adorable so she allowed it). We got sushi, and it took awhile for it to come, but once it did it was well worth the wait. We got several different types, and it was all good, but the baked lobster was to die for. I've always liked sushi (especially nigiri), but I've never had sushi that tasted like that before. I ate every piece and instantly wanted more, so we ordered a second batch.

As we walked back to our car, we stopped at a booth and got some sunglasses, since I forgot mine (every trip, no matter how hard I try, I always forget something). I even got Homer a pair, since they have doggy sunglasses in LA (LA is so cool, they have everything). After that, we headed to our hotel and checked in, and it was a nice hotel, but nothing like the one we had stayed at in Las Vegas in the fall.

The next morning, we had three games, and they went relatively well. We won two of them, and everyone played well, and even the third game (the one we lost), was close. After that we went to Huntington Beach for awhile, and we got boogie boards, and we even put Homer on one for awhile. He actually went about ten feet before a wave hit him and blew him over, and we all laughed as he doggy-paddled back to shore. After that, he was content to stay on the beach and watch from there, and he even chased away a seagull that was trying to get near our blankets.

"Darn it," Kimi said. "I wish Homer had chased that seagull away a little sooner."

"Why?" I asked.

She held up her blanket. Right in the middle of it was a big, white splotch.

But the real drama happened later that night, when we returned to our hotel. We were goofing around by the pool, and some of us (Lea, Kimi, Kristin, and I) decided we wanted some candy, so we walked across the street to the convenience store on the corner. It wasn't actually that far, and our hotel was still in sight. Homer came with us, on his leash. We took about ten minutes, and we got our goodies (I got coconut M&Ms,

my favorite), and we were heading back to our hotel when two men walked up and blocked our path down the sidewalk. One man was tall and thin, and the other was short and heavy, and they both wore old leather jackets that looked really dirty. Neither man looked like he had shaved in a week. The shorter man had a tattoo of a dragon on the side of his neck and a thick bullring in his nose.

"What do we have here?" the taller man asked, looking us over. The tone of his voice was really creepy (to say the least), and he slurred his words like he had been drinking.

"Some young ladies out on the town," the shorter man said. "Looking for a good time, I'd guess."

We were completely caught off guard, since none of us had seen them coming, and I instantly felt apprehensive and said nothing. Lea took the initiative and addressed them.

"We're just trying to go back to our hotel," she said.

"Why do you want to do that?" the taller man asked. "A hotel is so boring. Why don't you come with us tonight? Leo and I will show you a good time."

At first, we didn't know what to say, so everyone was quiet. But finally Lea (she's the bravest of us all) mustered an answer.

"No thanks," she said. "We just want to go back to our hotel. Please step aside."

The taller man was instantly offended. "I'm just trying to be friendly, missy," he said with a scowl. "I just want you to come with me for awhile. I won't hurt you. Well, not too much."

He reached out and grabbed Lea by the wrist.

That was all it took. The minute he touched Lea, Homer tore from my grip, his teeth bared, growling louder than he's ever growled before. He hit the man squarely in the chest and blew him back onto the ground. The man was so surprised he didn't know what to do, and Homer grabbed him by an arm and shook him something fierce. The second man, the shorter one, tried to come to his rescue, and he kicked Homer in the side, but Homer turned and fought him off, too, and he bit him on the arm. Before we could do anything, both men had decided they had had enough, and they turned and tried to run away, but it was already too late because a passing police officer had spotted the confrontation and cut them off with his squad car. Within seconds, he had pulled out his gun, arrested both of them, and loaded them into the back of his car.

"Are you ladies okay?" he asked us.

We were still pretty shaken (especially Lea, she was crying), but we were okay, and we were more concerned about Homer than anything. We wanted to make certain he was okay. Although the altercation had only lasted a few seconds, it had been extremely violent, and Homer had been kicked in the side really hard. Luckily, he was okay, and he was already calmed down and acting like normal, like nothing had ever happened.

"That's one heck of a dog you've got there," the police officer said. "He's as brave as they get. What's his name?"

"Homer," I said.

The police officer took us back to our hotel, and the minute our dads and the other girls saw us walking up with him, they got worried and came running, and we told them what had happened.

"I got there as soon as I could," the officer said. "But I'll be honest. I may not have gotten there in time, if it wasn't for that dog. He saved the day. There's no doubt about it."

Homer has always been treated well by the team, since he is our beloved mascot, but from that point forward (and especially for the rest of the night), he was treated like royalty. All thirteen girls gathered around him and started petting him at once, and we all gave him big hugs. He didn't seem like he was injured, but we put an icepack on his side just to be sure. And of course he loved every minute of it. He's always liked attention, so he was in complete heaven. But the funniest thing of all was he acted like he hadn't done anything extraordinary at all. And to him he hadn't. After all, to him, we are his girls, and no one is going to mess with his girls when he is around.

June 6

I had a really bad dream last night. I dreamed the school year had ended, and Logan had moved back to Texas, and he forgot about me completely. The minute he stepped off the plane in Texas, he forgot my name, and he forgot about all the wonderful things we had done during the past year. And then he got a new girlfriend, a high-maintenance cheerleader with a thick, southern accent. They went to one of his football games, back at his old high school in Huckstin, and she cheered and tossed her pompoms in the air as he scored a touchdown. After the touchdown, he ran off the field, swept her up in his arms, and kissed her on the lips.

I awoke with a start, and I was covered in sweat.

June 7

I was sitting in the living room, with Homer at my side, watching television with my dad, when his cell phone rang. He glanced at the phone's screen and looked over at me with a puzzled look on his face.

"That's funny," he said. "It's Chloe. Normally she only sends me texts."

I nodded. Like most teenage girls (including me), Chloe prefers texting, and she rarely makes phone calls. Except to her boyfriend Caleb, but that's because he doesn't like to text very much. Like a lot of teenage boys (especially football players), Caleb can't spell very well.

My dad shrugged and answered the phone. "Hey Chloe, what's up?" The expression on his face changed in a heartbeat. His smile disappeared and was instantly replaced with a look of grave concern. "Chloe, you need to calm down. I can't understand a word you're saying." He paused. "What? Are you okay? I don't care about your car. Are you okay?"

My mom was in the kitchen, making dinner, but she overheard the conversation and rushed into the room. She had a knife in one hand and a cucumber in the other. There was a look of complete panic on her face.

"Thank goodness," my dad said. "Tell me where you are. I'll come get you. Okay, okay. No, it's okay. What? Yeah, I know where it is. I'll be right there. It'll just take a minute."

I could barely wait until he hung up. But my mom beat me to the punch.

"What happened?" she asked.

My dad was already up and putting his coat on. "Chloe was in an accident. I need to go get her."

"Can I come?" I asked.

"Whatever," my dad said, but I could tell he was too worried to have even heard my question.

My mom and Homer came with us. We arrived at the accident a few minutes later. It was on a small highway not too far from our house. My heart stopped the minute I saw Chloe's car. It was upside down in the ditch, and it was completely smashed. The windshield was shattered and the entire top was caved in. A police car and an ambulance were parked next to it, both with their lights on. Two paramedics were treating Chloe. She had a small cut on her forehead, and she looked totally distraught, but other than that she was unharmed.

My dad pushed his way through the paramedics and gave her a hug.

"Thank goodness you're okay," he said.

"My car," Chloe said. Tears dripped from her cheeks. "It's destroyed. I wrecked it."

"It's okay," my dad said. "We'll get you another one. I'll call the insurance company tomorrow morning and we'll take care of it. All that matters is you're okay."

She gave him another hug, then turned and gave my mom one, then me and Homer. Her face was red and covered in tears.

I couldn't help but ask what had happened.

"It was raining," she said. "I couldn't see very well, and I didn't see the exit until it was too late, but I tried to make it anyway. And the car flipped. Twice. I was so scared I thought I was going to die."

I didn't know what to say. I've never been in an accident like that, so I couldn't really relate, but at the same time I could imagine how scary it must have been. I would have freaked out if I had been in the car with her.

My dad was listening carefully, and his face was as white as a ghost, but I'll give him credit, he stayed completely calm. Since he had never wanted Chloe to have a car in the first place, I thought he was going to say something like, "I knew this was going to happen," or "I told you so," but he never did. Instead, he said, "Accidents happen. I'm just glad you're okay." Then he went and talked to the police officer and the paramedics, and he made arrangements to get Chloe's car towed to a wrecking yard, and then we went home. It was a sad night, and Chloe was really upset about the loss of her car, and she cried herself to sleep, but we were still thankful. At least she was okay.

June 10

Today was one of the best days ever. My school has two end-of-the-year dances. The first is called senior prom, and it's for seniors and their dates. The second is called summer prom, and it's for everyone else. Senior prom is the more prestigious of the two (you know what they say, it's all about the seniors), but summer prom is fun anyway, and since I'm a freshman, it was my first time to go, and I was pretty excited. Lea and Kimi were excited, too. Two players on the school's baseball team had asked them to go, and both boys were really cute.

Like always, it took me a long time to get ready. I wanted everything to be perfect. Chloe had helped me pick out a dress a few days before (she's really good at that type of thing), and it was really cute, if I do say so myself. It was fancy, but not too fancy, and it was solid black and shiny, and it made me look really slim. Of course my dad didn't like it, because he felt it was too tight, but I didn't care what he thought. I wore a matching pair of heels (they weren't really that high, but I had a beast of a time getting used to them anyway), and my necklace, the one Logan had given me for Christmas.

"Stunning," Chloe said as she walked into the bathroom to help me with my final preparations. Normally, she would have been getting ready, too, but she and Caleb were going to senior prom the following night, since Caleb was a senior. "I'm impressed."

Logan picked me up about twenty minutes later, wearing a black tuxedo, and he looked spectacular, even better than when he had worn the fancy suit to take me out on Valentine's Day. My parents took photos of us in the living room, and then we went to dinner, then met everyone at the dance. It was in the school gymnasium, and I must give the dance's organizers credit, they did a wonderful job. The entire gym was decorated with banners, and lights, and streamers, and it looked sensational. The music was loud, but not overly so. Lea and Kimi looked stunning, especially Lea. She's usually kind of tomboyish, so to see her wearing an elegant dress with her hair down, it was really special. We all waited until a slow song began, then headed onto the dance floor. I wrapped my arms around Logan's neck as he placed his hands on my hips. I've always been so amazed. Logan has such big hands, but he is always so gentle when he touches me. We swayed slowly to the music, and I glanced around as we danced, and in the corner of the room I saw Hailey Wetmore standing quietly with her date (one of the backup players on the football team). She was looking right at me, and she had an irritated, jealous look on her face. I don't think she's ever gotten over the fact Logan turned her down, nor the fact he chose to go steady with me instead. I smiled at her, then leaned forward and kissed Logan on the lips.

"What was that for?" he asked.

"For being you," I said.

Just for curiosity's sake, I looked back over, toward where Hailey had been standing, but she was nowhere to be found.

June 15

Today was the last day of school. Normally, I love the last day of school. Everyone is so excited, and I can finally start sleeping in every day, and there is no more homework to do and no teachers to put up with for three whole months. But despite all of that, I didn't like today at all. If I could have had it my way, I would have postponed today forever.

Today was the day Logan was leaving.

He picked me up for our final date around 6:00 pm. He had to be at the airport at 8:00 pm for his flight to Dallas, so it didn't give us much time, just over an hour, but it actually turned out to be more than enough. I had always pictured our last date would be something grand, and elegant, and romantic, something I would remember and cherish for the rest of my life, but it wasn't. I could tell right from the start it wasn't meant to be. Logan wasn't himself. I could see it in his eyes. He's normally so upbeat and lively. But tonight he was sad and lifeless, and he was literally a shell of himself. He tried his best, but his smiles were forced, and they were nothing more than an act, a final, desperate attempt to have some fun with me one final time.

We went to dinner, but we didn't say much (I guess there wasn't much to say), and I guess we were just putting in our time, waiting for it to be over. Twice I almost started to cry, but somehow I managed to stay strong, even when he dropped me off at my door. He had a note in his hand.

"I knew I was going to have a tough time tonight," he said. "And I didn't want to risk blowing my chance to tell you how I feel, so I wrote it all down. But please do me a favor and wait until after I leave before you read it. Okay?"

I nodded. I was in no mood to disagree with him about anything.

"Have a safe flight," I said. "I'll miss you."

"Thanks," he said. "I'll miss you, too."

I gave him a final kiss, and he left.

I rushed upstairs to my bedroom the minute he pulled out of the driveway. I didn't even stop to say hi to Homer in the hallway like I normally do. I jumped on my bed and tore the envelope open. It read,

Angel,

I always thought you had the most appropriate name. You've always been an angel to me. I knew you were special the minute I saw you in the stands that first night at my game. I'm not certain if I will ever see you again, but I promise I will never forget you. I will stay in touch and I will hopefully get to come back to Seattle soon. I love you. I've loved you from the moment I saw you. And I always will.

Logan

I sat there in complete shock as I read the letter. I was frozen in place, staring at the words on the paper, and it was at that point I first realized what love was. It was the most wonderful thing I had ever felt, but also the most awful. I was so happy to learn how Logan felt about me, but also so upset he was leaving and I might never see him again. I felt like my heart was going to burst in my chest.

A lone teardrop fell from my cheek and landed on Logan's letter, right on the word 'love.'

I sat there for what seemed like an eternity, completely paralyzed by my feelings, completely unable to move. Homer, who had jumped onto the bed next to me, could tell something was wrong, and he nudged my arm with his nose but I didn't respond. Not knowing what else to do, he hopped from the bed and ran down the hall to get Chloe, who was fixing her hair in the bathroom. He pulled her by one pant leg down the hall toward my room.

"Homer," she said, somewhat annoyed. "What in the world has gotten into you? Angel, what's up with your—"

Her words trailed off as Homer pulled her around the corner and she saw me sitting on my bed, Logan's note still in my hand, my eyes filled with tears.

"Angel," she said. "What's wrong?"

I handed her the note. Her eyes got misty as she read it. "That's so beautiful," she said. "I've never seen anything like it."

And then she did the only thing possible to make me feel any better. She sat down and gave me a hug.

June 17

It hasn't been easy the past couple of days. Chloe is still recovering from her car accident, and I'm still recovering from Logan moving back to Texas. I've kept pretty much to myself, and I've spent a lot of time in my room with just Homer and Cinnamon. I sent a couple of text messages to Logan, and I found out he made it back to Huckstin safely, and it seems like everyone is really happy to have him back (especially his dad). They had a big party for him, and apparently everyone was there, including several of his cousins he hasn't seen for years. He said even his stepmother was happy to see him, and she gave him a hug and apologized for everything that had happened between them in the past. I told him I was happy for him, and I wished him well.

I had softball practice today. It was my first practice since Logan left, and it was actually pretty surprising. Well, not practice, but afterward. I had just gotten out of the shower, and I was sitting in my bed, petting Homer and Cinnamon, when my dad knocked on my bedroom door. He had a cup of hot chocolate in one hand and a saucer with a blueberry muffin in the other.

"Can I come in?" he asked.

"Sure," I said.

"I thought you might like a little snack," he said. "I know I worked you guys pretty hard today, so you must be hungry."

"A little," I said. Actually, I wasn't (I haven't had much of an appetite since Logan left), but since my dad went to the trouble of bringing it to me, I thought I'd at least be polite and take it. And it was actually pretty good, especially the hot chocolate. My dad isn't much of a chef, but he is pretty good when it comes to using a microwave.

He sat down on the edge of my bed. I could tell he wanted to say something, but he wasn't exactly sure how to say it. "I wanted to ask you something," he said. "I noticed at practice today you seemed pretty listless. Your effort was good, you definitely were trying, but you just weren't your normal self. Your throws didn't have much zip on them, and you didn't have any zest in your step at all. Your sprint times were your worst in years."

I sighed. I knew what was coming. I was in trouble.

"You're heartbroken," my dad said. "Aren't you?"

My eyes got big. I couldn't believe what I had just heard. My dad, arguably the most insensitive person on the planet, had figured out what was wrong with me? I was in complete shock.

"You haven't been the same since Logan left," he said. "I can see it. It doesn't take a rocket scientist to figure it out. And I want you to know it's okay. I understand."

I couldn't believe it. My dad had never acted like this before, at least as long as I could remember. Who was this strange person sitting on the edge of my bed, and what had he done with my dad?

"I've been there myself," he said.

"What?" I asked. I had no idea what he was talking about.

"I'll show you," he said.

He got up, went down the hall, and climbed into the attic. We have one of those attics you can enter through an opening in the ceiling in the hallway. It has a door that covers the opening, and an extendable ladder that descends from the door. Technically, Chloe and I aren't allowed to go up there (my dad says it's dangerous), but we used to do it all the time when we were younger and my parents would leave us alone in the house for awhile. We keep all kinds of stuff up there, like our fake Christmas tree and miscellaneous other holiday decorations. My dad disappeared for quite awhile, and I could hear him digging through things, clearly looking for something in particular. And then I heard him grimace.

"What happened?" I called.

"I just stepped in a cobweb," he said.

I cringed. I hate cobwebs. Oh well. Better him than me.

A few minutes later, he came back down with something in his hand. It was an old shoebox, and it was tattered and worn, and it looked like it was at least a hundred years old. Maybe older. He sat down next to me on the bed and opened it, revealing a bunch of crinkled photos and newspaper clippings.

"What's this?" I asked.

"A bunch of old junk," he said. "I should have thrown it out years ago, but I didn't. Sometimes memories are hard to get rid of. But anyway, this is what I wanted to show you."

He dug through the shoebox and pulled out an old photo. It was pretty faded, and it looked like it had been taken a long time ago. But it was still nice, and it was of a very attractive girl (approximately eighteen) who had long, brown hair and sparkling eyes.

"That's Jennifer Snow," my dad said. "She was my girlfriend in high school."

"Really?" I asked. "You had a girlfriend before mom?"

"Of course I had a girlfriend before your mom," he said. "Several. I mean, well, a few. Anyway, Jennifer and I were a couple from the beginning of our junior year until we graduated."

Wow. I was really surprised. I never knew much about my dad's life before my birth. He never really talked about it much, and I guess it was just kind of hard for me to picture that my dad was more than just my dad, and he was a real person, and he had actually been a kid once, just like me, and he had gone to high school, and even had a girlfriend.

"What was she like?" I asked.

"Wonderful," my dad said. "In every way. She was the prettiest girl I've ever met. But don't tell your mom I said that. And she was smart, and kind, and we got along really well. She loved history just like I do. Some days we would just sit around and talk about how cool it would have been to have lived in ancient times, back in China, or Rome, or the wild, wild west, or whenever. It was really nice."

Sitting around talking about the ancient past wasn't my cup of tea, but if that's what turned my dad on, so be it.

"She was the first girl I ever loved," he said. "I went and saw her every chance I got."

"What happened to her?" I asked.

"Same thing that happens to most high school couples," he said. "Once we graduated, she went to a college back east, and I stayed here and went to Washington. Like all couples, we exchanged letters for awhile, but then eventually she met someone new, and eventually I met someone new, and we moved on. But that isn't relevant. What I wanted to tell you was those first few weeks, after she moved back east, that was the hardest time of my life. I was so lonely I thought I was going to die. I didn't see how I could go on without her."

"What did you do?" I asked.

"Not much, really," he said. "There wasn't much I could do. I just gave it some time, and slowly I started to heal. And that's what you need to do now. Don't rush things, and don't try to recover too quickly. Just give yourself some time. And if you need some time off from softball, that's okay, too. I know how stressful softball can be at times. And, after all, it's just softball. It's not the end of the world or something."

I was in complete shock. My dad had never been so understanding in his entire life, at least not with me, and he had never let me skip practices before (except the one time a few years back when I had a fever and my temperature was 102°).

"Thanks," I said. "But I don't understand. Why didn't you show me this photo before?"

"This was a tough time for me," he said. "The toughest time in my life. Sometimes I try to forget it completely. Even now, after all these years, when I think about it, it still hurts."

I was completely amazed. This was a side of my dad I had never seen before.

Then something caught my eye. The shoebox was full of other stuff, including a bunch of newspaper clippings. "What's this?" I asked.

"My articles," he said. "From when I played ball."

I grabbed one of the articles and read it. Its headline read, "MONROE BEATS LAKE STEVENS 21-6." Below it was a photo of my dad, in a football uniform, celebrating in the end zone with his teammates.

"That was a fun game," he said. "It was my junior year. I scored two touchdowns."

I grabbed another article. This one read, "WILLIAMS LEADS MONROE TO VICTORY." Below it was another photo of my dad, again in the end zone, with a big smile on his face.

I was impressed. I had always known my dad played football in high school, but I never knew he was a star.

"But they're not all good articles," my dad said. "Look at this one."

He handed me an article with another photo. In this photo, he was lying on the ground on his back, near the sideline, with a glazed look in his eyes. The trainers were treating him. The headline read, "WILLIAMS SUFFERS CONCUSSION IN LOSS TO EDMONDS."

"What happened?" I asked.

"I was stupid," he said. "It was my senior year. We ran a sweep right, and I already had the first down, so I could have stepped out of bounds and avoided any contact, but I got cocky and tried to cut back for a few more yards. The linebacker put his head down and hit me helmet to helmet. Nowadays that's a penalty, but not back then. He hit me so hard it knocked me completely out of bounds. I was so stunned when I finally started to recover, I realized everyone in the stands was completely quiet, and the cheerleaders were down on one knee, so I knew someone was injured. I looked around to see who it was, and then realized everyone was looking at me."

"Did they take you out of the game?" I asked.

"No," he said. "Back in those days, they didn't take you out just because you got a concussion. They didn't know much about concussions back then, how dangerous they can be. They just gave me a small break, had me sniff some smelling salts, then sent me back out. But I wasn't the same after that, and I didn't play well. We got killed."

He looked kind of somber for a minute, but then his mood changed in a heartbeat when he saw another article. "Here's a funny one," he said as he handed it to me. It had a photo of him catching a pass with a defender right behind him. "In this game, a guy hit me so hard in the stomach I walked over to the sideline and threw up right there on the spot. I didn't even have time to take my helmet off, so the vomit went right through my facemask."

"Gross," I said.

"When I got done," my dad said, "I looked up, and my coach was standing over me, with one hand on my shoulder, and do you know what he said?"

"What?" I asked.

"He said, 'Are you done yet?' And when I said yes, he said, 'Good. Get back out there on the field. Sweep left on three.' I headed out and finished the game. And I actually did pretty well. I scored two touchdowns."

I laughed. "That reminds me," I said, "of the time a few years back, at Chloe's game. I think they were playing the Wolverines. Do you remember how she said she had an upset stomach, but Coach Jenkins made her play anyway, and she hit a single, but as soon as she got to first base she kept running and went straight off the field and got sick behind the Wolverines' dugout?"

My dad laughed. "That was pretty funny. I've never seen anyone run straight off the field before. Even blue was laughing. But poor Chloe. She was miserable."

We looked through the articles for a couple more minutes. I couldn't believe how many there were. And then I noticed something.

378

"Your uniforms," I said. "They were black. And your helmets. Now we wear orange."

"They must have changed them after I graduated," he said. "And thank goodness. There's no way I'd be caught dead in those bright orange uniforms you kids wear nowadays."

I laughed. My dad was so traditional. Of course he'd prefer old-school black over our modern orange ones.

"Did you notice something else," my dad said, "about my uniform? Look at my number."

I looked at one of the photos and saw my dad's jersey number. He wore number 24. The same number Logan wore.

"Apparently," he said, "it's a Monroe tradition or something. The great running backs always wear number 24."

I didn't really know what to say. Thinking of Logan made me sad again, but I had to admit, I felt a lot better. I couldn't believe it, but my dad had actually cheered me up a little.

"I should be going," he said. "But feel free to keep the articles if you'd like."

"I'll do that," I said. "I'd like to read a few more, if it's okay."

"Of course it is," he said. "And hang in there, kid. Things will be okay. You wait and see."

He got up, turned, and left.

To be honest, food hadn't tasted very good to me since Logan left, but I grabbed my hot chocolate and blueberry muffin and finished it, and I have to admit, it was actually quite good.

July 14

Today was the first day of Washington's annual championship tournament. It's a huge tournament, lasting several days, featuring the best select softball teams from all over the state. It is really fun, but extremely stressful. It's a single elimination tournament, so you keep playing until you lose a game. Once you lose, you're out of the tournament and your season is over.

Our first game was against a team from Spokane called the Tomahawks. They were really good, but Laura pitched a gem of a game and we won 2-1. Olivia won it for us with a double in the fifth inning that scored Haley and Kimi. I got two singles.

Our second game was against a team from Puyallup called the Pressure. Once again, we played well, and we won 6-4. I didn't get any hits, but I made several nice plays in the field. One of them was a running backhanded catch that saved at least one run, maybe two. Everyone patted me on the back, and Homer gave me a lick on the face, as I headed into the dugout at the end of the inning.

But the best game by far was the final one of the day. It was against a team called the Avalanche. I had never heard of them before, and I had no idea where they were from, but boy were they good. They jumped to a quick lead and held on from there. The score was 2-0 going into the final inning. But then, thankfully, we made a breakthrough. Casey and Kimi got singles, and Lea walked to load the bases, and Kristin hit a bases-clearing triple to win it for us. We swarmed her at third base and tackled her right there on the spot, and it was one of the greatest pig piles ever. Everyone joined in, including Homer, and he got flipped onto his back and buried beneath a pile of bodies as we rolled around, but he didn't care, and he even liked it, because to him it was all fun and games.

July 15

Today was the next-to-last day of the state tournament, and we were all excited. Our game was against a team called the Everett Extreme, and we knew if we won, we'd be in the championship game tomorrow, and we couldn't wait. And the game went well right from the start. Hannah was our starting pitcher, and she didn't give up a single hit until the fifth inning. In the meantime, our bats were on fire, and we jumped to an early lead when Lea and Laura got back-to-back singles, and I hit them in with a double. In no time, we were up 2-0. Everyone was in a good mood and completely fired up. Even blue was in a good mood, and it was the same blue who umpires a lot of our games, the same one who likes Homer so much. Anyway, we cruised from there, and we were leading 7-0 in the final inning with only one out to go. Victory was so close I could taste it. The state championship game, the biggest game of the year, was only one out away.

But then disaster struck. The one thing I never imagined possible. My greatest nightmare. I was standing at my position at short, and the batter was a girl named Mandy McCormick. Mandy is a good batter, but nothing special, so I knew we had a good chance to get her out, but I was making certain I was ready, just in case she hit one my way. Mandy hit a foul ball over the backstop into the nearby parking lot, and like always Homer darted after it. In the meantime, the game continued, since blue had a second ball, and the next pitch was a strike.

Only one strike to go, I thought. *One more strike and we're in the state championship.*

I could barely contain my excitement.

But then I heard a loud screech from the parking lot, like someone had slammed on his brakes and slid his tires, and it was followed by a dull thud and a painful yelp. When I looked over to see what had happened, I saw a large truck, and a man climbing out of the driver's seat with a frantic, scared look on his face. And when I looked in front of the truck, I saw Homer, lying on the pavement, with a softball on the ground next to him.

He wasn't moving.

My heart stopped. I didn't even wait for blue to call a timeout. I threw my mitt down and ran as fast as I could. And I wasn't the only one. Every girl on my team, even the girls in the dugout, ran for the parking lot. When we got there, Homer was finally moving, but barely. He was hurt bad. The truck had hit him really hard. Tears streamed down my cheeks as I saw him lying there. He was trying to get up, but he couldn't. He was so disoriented he could barely move. Finally he just gave up and collapsed on the ground.

"I'm so sorry," the driver said. "I didn't see him until the last second. I tried to stop."

"We need to get him to a vet," my dad said. He, too, had rushed to the parking lot with us.

A car raced up. It was blue. "Come with me," he said. "I know the closest animal hospital."

"What about the game?" my dad asked. "It's not over."

"Screw the game," blue said. "That dog helped me all year. Now it's my turn to help him."

383

My dad scooped Homer up, and we climbed in the car with blue, and we raced down the street. Luckily, the animal hospital wasn't far away, and we ran inside, and the veterinarian was waiting the minute we got there since my dad called ahead using his cell phone and told him we were coming. He took Homer in back and immediately started an examination and treatment. In the meantime, I stayed in the waiting room with blue, my dad, and several of the other girls.

And then I lost it. Completely. I was already crying, even before we got to the hospital, but now I was a complete wreck. It was a complete, uncontrollable flood of emotion. In my mind, I had already lost Logan (possibly for good), and I couldn't bear the thought of losing Homer, too. I collapsed in a chair and balled my eyes out. My dad, blue, and the other girls tried to comfort me.

"Now, now," blue said. "Hang in there, young lady. Everything is going to be okay. Homer's a tough dog. He'll be fine. Just you wait and see."

Luckily, blue was right. The vet came out about twenty minutes later (it seemed like an eternity), and he said Homer was still in shock, and he had three broken ribs and a fractured front leg, but he was going to be okay. I've never felt so relieved in my entire life.

"But I need to keep monitoring him," the vet said, "just to be safe. Just to make certain there's no internal bleeding or other damage. So I'm going to keep him overnight here at the hospital."

I objected. "He's never been away from me for a night," I said. "I can't leave him. I'll stay here with him."

The vet smiled. "Unfortunately," he said. "I can't allow that. It's against the hospital's policy. But don't worry. We'll take good care of him, and you can come get him tomorrow afternoon. I should know by then whether he's completely okay."

"Tomorrow afternoon?" I said. "We have our championship game first thing in the morning. He's our mascot. He's never missed a game before. We can't play without him."

"I'm sorry," the vet said. "He's just not going to be ready by then. You girls will have to play without him."

I didn't know what to say. I was relieved, because I knew he was going to be okay, but I was heartbroken, since he couldn't come home with me, and I was disappointed because he had to miss the championship game.

"I know you're upset," my dad said. "But always remember the big picture. He'll be back with us tomorrow night. And that's all that really matters, right?"

I didn't want to admit it, but he was right. Things could have been a lot worse. He could have died.

So we went back to the field, where everyone (including the other team) was still waiting. They were all relieved to hear Homer was going to be okay, but completely bummed when they learned he couldn't come to the championship game tomorrow.

But then I remembered something. Technically, we weren't in the championship game yet. We still had one strike to go. Were they going to make us finish the game? After all that had happened, I was so stressed I didn't feel like playing any more.

Luckily, we didn't have to. Blue met with the coaches, and the Extreme's coach put the whole issue to rest.

"I don't think it's fair," he said, "to make the Sky girls come out and play again, just for one batter.

They've been through so much already, losing their mascot. We concede."

"Thank you," my dad said, with a huge sigh of relief.

"And good luck tomorrow," the Extreme's coach said. "You guys are a great team. I hope Homer gets better soon. He may not be our mascot, but we like him anyway."

How nice, I thought. Over the years, I had seen a lot of opposing coaches, and many of them were complete idiots. All they cared about was their own team, and they would do anything to win. But not this guy. Clearly all he cared about was what was fair.

At that point, we went home. It wasn't that far a drive, but it seemed like it took forever. All I could think about was Homer. I called Logan in Texas and told him what had happened, and he tried to make me feel better, and it helped a little, but not much. I moped around the house for most of the night, and when I finally went to bed, I couldn't get to sleep. I was so used to having Homer sleeping on the bed next to me I couldn't get used to him not being there. Even grumpy old Cinnamon seemed affected. He looked around the room, then shot me a questioning glance, as if to say, "Where is he?"

He'll be back soon, I thought.

The sooner, the better.

July 16

The championship game did not start well. It was against my old team, the Eastside Angels, and my arch rival, Ashley Martinez. We knew it was going to be a tough game, but to be honest, Ashley and the Angels weren't the problem at all.

The problem was us. Without Homer, we weren't ourselves. Not at all. We were completely flat. Completely uninspired. We were so used to him being there, leading us during our warm-up jog, and barking whenever we made a great play, we just didn't know what to do without him. The entire dugout was quiet. There were no cheers at all. You could hear a pin drop.

And we got off to a bad start. We all struggled, including Laura. She just couldn't get fired up, and she couldn't throw strikes, at least not consistently. She walked the first two batters, then gave up a single to load the bases.

"She's got to hit her spots," my dad said, a look of urgency and grave concern on his face. "Or we're in big trouble."

And we were. She didn't hit her spots, and instead left a pitch over the middle of the plate, and the Angels' shortstop, Brooke Conrad, lined it down the first base foul line for a double. Two runs scored on the play.

Just like that, they were ahead 2-0.

The second inning didn't get any better. Laura continued to struggle, and the Angels scored two more runs.

"I've got no choice," my dad said. "I've got to switch pitchers."

So then Laura and Hannah came in the dugout, and my dad went out to talk to blue, and like always we girls waited to see if the twins were going to do their normal routine and switch jerseys so Laura could keep pitching.

"I don't want to switch jerseys," Laura said. "I don't want to pitch anymore."

"I don't want to pitch, either," Hannah said.

I knew we were in trouble. We only had two pitchers, and neither of them wanted to pitch.

But Hannah didn't really have a choice, since my dad had already reported the switch to blue, so she took over, but she didn't do any better than Laura. She didn't walk any batters, but she gave up two more runs, and by the end of the third inning, we were losing 6-0.

And we didn't help any with our bats. We were terrible. We didn't get any hits at all, and I struck out twice. Ashley wasn't throwing that well, but we just couldn't get motivated.

Chloe had come to watch, and she saw what was happening from the bleachers. She came into the dugout and tried to fire us up, but it didn't do much good. And, unfortunately, she couldn't help us by pitching for us, since this was a 16u tournament and she was too old to play.

So we had to win this one on our own. Without her and without Homer.

But it wasn't going to happen. We all knew it. We were just putting in our time, trying to get it over with as quickly and as painlessly as possible.

But then something unexpected happened. From the parking lot, I heard a bark. I looked over, and my eyes got big as I saw the vet from the animal hospital, climbing out of a small, white van with Homer in his arms. Homer had a splint on his front leg, and his body was wrapped in a bandage of some type, but other than that he looked okay, and he looked really excited. There was a sparkle in his eyes.

"It's Homer!" Lea said. "He's here."

"What happened?" I asked as the vet carried him into our dugout. "I thought you said he couldn't come."

"I had no choice," the vet said. "He went crazy. He wouldn't stop barking all morning. It was like he knew you had a game."

"Of course he knew," I said. "He always knows when we have a game. I'm not sure how, but he does."

It was true. On game days, Homer was always the first one up.

We swarmed him. Every girl on the team gave him a hug and kiss, and a pat on the head, and he gave us licks in return.

And that was all it took. When we returned to the field, we were a completely different team. It was almost like someone had gotten rid of all of us and replaced us with good players. We had a spring in our step, and we were excited and motivated again.

"Win this game for Homer," Chloe called from the dugout.

"For Homer!" we shouted from the field.

And we poured it on. All of a sudden, Hannah could pitch again. She threw nothing but strikes, as hard as she could, and the Angels' batters were completely overwhelmed. In the meantime, our bats came alive. Lea hit a double, Kimi a single, Haley a triple, and I got a double. Boy it felt good to finally get a hit off of Ashley. I heard her grimace as I stood at second base dusting my pants off.

In no time, we were back in it. By the final inning, we had gotten three of the runs back, and we were only losing 6-3. And we quickly loaded the bases to start the bottom of the seventh.

And here's the best part. It was my turn to bat. As I stepped into the batter's box, I dug my cleats into the dirt. I was a completely different batter than I had been at the start of the game. At the start, I had been timid and weak. But now I was confident and strong. Homer was here, and with him here, I was unstoppable.

And then I remembered what Logan had told me, right before I had gone on the trip to Vegas in the fall.

"Have faith in yourself," he had said.

And I did. With one massive swing, I knew I could win the state championship.

And I did. Amy's first pitch was a wicked fastball, one of her best. I knew I shouldn't swing at it, since it was a little low and a little outside, but I went after it anyway, with everything I had. My fingers dug into my bat as I whipped it around faster than ever before. I hit the ball so hard it flew a mile. It didn't even start to come down until after it had cleared the outfield fence.

July 25

Today was my team's 'end of the season' party. Like every end of the season party, it was kind of sad, because since it's the end of the season some of the girls will be moving on to other teams, and we won't be teammates again next year, but overall it was a good time anyway. It was at Lea's house, and the weather was nice, so we got to wander back and forth inside and out. Some people played horseshoes in the back yard, while others played Rock Band inside. There was a load of food, since it was a buffet and everyone's parents brought something, and like always I stuffed myself. After eating, we watched a funny video my dad had made that was a collection of photos he had rounded up over the course of the season. It brought back some fond memories and made me realize how quickly time had flown by. One of the photos really caught my eye. It was a shot of me batting, and sitting in the background, watching attentively in the stands, was Logan.

After the video, my dad gave the traditional head coach end of the season speech, and he actually did pretty well considering it was the first time he had given a head coach end of the season speech. What he said was pretty generic, and it was the same stuff you hear every year, but still it was fun. And then he handed out the team awards, and that was great. Laura won the most valuable pitcher award, Kristin won the comeback player of the year award, Olivia won the most improved award, Lea won the gold glove award (for the best defensive player), and I won the silver slugger award (for the best hitter). I got a trophy shaped like a bat that was covered in sparkling, black chrome.

But the best award of all, the most prestigious by far, was the final one presented by my dad, and it was the one Homer won. It was the team's MVP award.

Most Valuable Pooch.

It was really nothing more than a large cookie, shaped like a softball with bright, yellow icing, but Homer loved it, and everyone cheered as he gobbled it up.

About the Author

Jody Studdard is the author of several children's novels, including *A Different Diamond*, *Fastpitch Fever*, *Escape from Dinosaur Planet*, and *The Sheriff of Sundown City*. He is a graduate of Monroe High School (1989), the University of Washington (1993), and California Western School of Law (1995). In addition to writing, he is a practicing attorney with an office in Everett, Washington. He is a fan of the Seahawks, Storm, and Sounders FC.

Visit Jody at:

www.jstuddard.com

E-mail Jody at:

jodystuddard@jodystuddard.com

SOFTBALL STAR
Books By
Jody Studdard

A Different Diamond

Fastpitch Fever

Dog in the Dugout

Missfits Fastpitch

Silence in Center

Coming Soon!

Fastpitch U

KIANA CRUISE
Books By
Jody Studdard

Apocalypse

Coming Soon!

Multiplicity

Made in the USA
Middletown, DE
27 June 2015